MW01641298

# The Mark of Janus

# THE MARK OF JANUS

PATRICK DAVID DALEY

**THE MARK OF JANUS**



*iUniverse books may be ordered through booksellers or by contacting:*

*iUniverse*
*1663 Liberty Drive*
*Bloomington, IN 47403*
*www.iuniverse.com*
*1-800-Authors (1-800-288-4677)*



*ISBN: 978-1-4917-4694-3 (sc)*
*ISBN: 978-1-4917-4695-0 (hc)*
*ISBN: 978-1-4917-4696-7 (e)*

*Library of Congress Control Number: 2014916697*

*Printed in the United States of America.*

*iUniverse rev. date: 10/08/2014*

*For Wendy, whose constant encouragement and guidance contributed so much to the writing of this story. Your love, patience, and understanding make my life richer with each passing day.*

# Acknowledgment

To my brothers, Robert and Peter, and to the Brouitt family, with deep appreciation for their ongoing support. A special thanks to Dorothy and Stephen, for your assistance and sound advice. You were there when needed. And to John, who always knew when it was time to go beyond the golden doors.

# JANUS

In Roman mythology, Janus is the god of gates, doors, doorways, and all beginnings. The month of January is named for him. Depicted as having two faces on opposite sides of his head, Janus is able to gaze into the past with one, while the other allows him to look to the future.

In *The Mark of Janus* the island's eponymous name reflects the ancestors' belief that all those who followed should always remember the past and use it to shape the present and the future.

# Chapter 1

He was born to be orphaned before his first birthday.

The bloody, wailing, seven-pound baby boy was immediately placed on his mother's stomach by the birthing-room doctor. Nora had wanted the birth to be natural. After eleven hours of labor, it had been a vaginal delivery. The nurse gently dried the baby and suctioned out his mouth and nose. She covered the infant with a blanket and placed a woolen cap on his head. The doctor clamped the umbilical cord in two places. He then snipped it between the two clamps. After waiting a couple of minutes, he collected a tube of blood from the severed cord, so the baby's blood type could be verified.

An Apgar assessment was done to evaluate the baby's heart rate, breathing, muscle tone, reflex response, and color. Everything was excellent.

Lucas Kilgore had been in the room during the delivery. It was the couple's first child, and he'd wanted to experience every moment of his son's birth. He knew it was something he'd remember for the rest of his life. Feelings of ecstasy, pride, and love flooded over him. He was amazed at how quickly the event had transformed his world. A mantle of responsibility, of having walked through the door to manhood seemed to settle easily on his shoulders.

Everything about Lucas, from the intensity of his dark brown eyes set in an angular face topped by well-coiffed dirty blond hair to his gym-maintained, lean, muscular body spoke of a man who strived for perfection. And now he had produced a son and heir who would one day follow him as a partner in his law firm. Lucas already had his son's life planned for him. But that would come later. Today was for enjoying his accomplishment.

The nurse had swaddled the baby in a blanket. She gently handed him to Nora, whose blonde hair was damp from sweat; dark circles rested under sapphire blue eyes. The new mother cradled the child in her arms.

"He's beautiful," she said, looking up at Lucas, who was leaning over the bed.

"Welcome to the world, Sean Jason Kilgore," he said, his cheeks glistening with tears.

The nurse left the room, giving the family some time alone.

"Our baby has the birthmark," Nora whispered. "It was one of the first things I checked after they handed him to me and said everything was perfect. It's on his left thigh and in the shape of a triangle. It looks exactly like the one you have."

"I know," agreed Lucas. "I saw it during the delivery. And so once again, it passes from father to son."

"When he gets older, he's going to ask what it means," said Nora.

"And I'll tell him what my father told me." Lucas sighed. "Still, there's plenty of time for that. We have a few years before he has to be burdened with something that seems impossible when all the implications are considered."

"The meaning behind the triangle didn't impact you the way it's supposed to guide Sean," said Nora. "I really didn't believe your father until I saw the birthmark on our baby's leg."

According to Lucas's father, their little boy belonged to the world and not just to his parents.

"When Sean asks," Nora added, "you'll have to be honest with him."

"Of course I will," said a slightly exasperated Lucas.

"Has that private investigator you hired found out anything?" she asked.

"We talked a few days ago, and so far, he's got little more than what my father told me. And we both know that's not much."

Lucas often wondered if his father hadn't gone senile when he talked about the birthmark. After being told Nora was pregnant, he was adamant it would be a boy and that he'd be the chosen one.

"My father said it would be our eldest son's duty to follow the path where it led, whatever that means. With Dad's death it's hard to make sense of it all."

"But it's such a distinctive birthmark," offered Nora. "It must represent something."

"All we know is that it goes back to my great-grandfather, Joshua Kilgore," Lucas reminded her. "It's carried by the eldest son and has been passed from generation to generation. But even that's a mystery."

"Was the investigator able to find anything about your family's history?"

“According to him, there’s no record of our family past my great-grandfather.”

“But that’s impossible.”

“Not really,” concluded Lucas. “We don’t know when he arrived in this country, where he was from, or even if his original name was Kilgore. He could have changed it for all we know. I’ll give the investigator another couple of weeks, but if we don’t find anything else, that’ll be the end of it.”

“I hope we find something,” she said. “It’s important to know your family’s past.”

Lucas wondered why Nora was choosing this moment to focus on his father’s words. She’d just delivered their first child, and there was so much more the moment should hold. Did it have something to do with the mystery of giving birth? Or perhaps it was because she’d been put up for adoption at birth and had spent all of her early years in a foster home. Nora had been searching for her natural mother for years, without success.

Whatever the reason, Lucas wasn’t going to have the conversation continue. His wife was tired. Her face was drawn and pale from the loss of blood.

The baby was getting restless. The nurse had returned and said it was time for feeding. Lucas slipped out of the room. He wanted to phone the office with the news.

# Chapter 2

Lucas was a partner in the Toronto law firm, Brennan, Dolan, & Kilgore (BDK). Ten years after graduating with honors from the University of Toronto's Faculty of Law, the three—Tom Brennan, Brian Dolan, and Lucas—had built a law firm that was ranked twentieth in the country. The goal was to be among the top ten within the next decade.

All three were married. Dolan's wife had given birth a month before to their first child, a girl they'd named Hilary. Brennan and his wife had been trying to start a family for several years. Frustrated at the lack of results, Tom had undergone a variety of tests only to discover that he couldn't father a child. Undaunted, the couple had decided to adopt.

It was August, and despite the joy a new baby brought them, neither Lucas nor Nora was prepared to let Sean interrupt their work lives.

Taking time away from the office wasn't in Lucas's makeup. He was back at his desk the day after Sean's birth. Nora, a marketing executive for a large bank, was at her desk three weeks later. A nanny was hired. As the year moved into the fall and early winter, work demands steadily increased for both parents. Lucas was navigating a difficult takeover deal for one of the firm's largest clients. Nora was deeply involved in the introduction of a new customer-retention initiative.

Along with December's cold winds, the weather that year brought snow to much of eastern Canada.

Nora's foster mother was anxious to see the baby. Alzheimer's disease was quickly stealing her mind; she was to be confined to a nursing home in January. She lived in Montreal, and it was decided a perfect time to visit her would be over Christmas. It would only be for a couple of days. Both parents were busy, and Lucas, in particular, was on an early January deadline.

The plan was to fly, but at the last minute, Sean came down with a light cold. The doctor had advised against taking him on a plane, where the changing air pressure would cause problems for his ears. The train was fully booked, so their only choice was to drive. Lucas, as he did with everything, put a bright spin on the change and said it would give them a more relaxing time with the baby.

#########

A cloudy, cold morning greeted their departure from Toronto, heading east toward Montreal on Highway 401. The highway was predominately a four-lane roadway separated into two lanes running east and west divided by a large center median. When they left, the weather was ideal for driving. However, as so often happens in that part of the country, the conditions soon changed. Two hours from the city, heavy snow, driven by a strong wind, began to fall, making driving difficult.

Just before Kingston, the freezing rain arrived as an unwelcome guest to the party. The roadway was slippery and getting more hazardous with each mile traveled. Lucas saw several cars up ahead, back ends fishtailing as their drivers applied brakes. Traffic was starting to bunch up, forming two conga lines of weaving metal, glass, and gas. Lucas's Cadillac was at the back of one line, hemmed in by a Greyhound bus in the other lane. The windshield wipers were beating a steady tattoo.

As the storm worsened, they entered a part of the highway that had been cut through a rocky outcropping. The Cadillac was boxed in by a wall of rock to its right, the Greyhound on its left, and a slow-moving Pontiac Le Mans in front.

Lucas looked in the rearview mirror. Everything was blocked by the front grill, headlights, and cab of a long-haul truck bearing down on them. Lucas realized instinctively that the truck was moving too fast to slow down. Acid churned in the pit of his stomach. Fear roared through his body. He swung the steering wheel hard to the right, hoping to lessen the impact.

The truck slammed into the Cadillac, crushing the car's passenger side and rupturing its gas tank. The car went airborne. Its trajectory took the already twisted hulk nose first into the rock face, driving the front end, including the engine, into the passenger compartment. The sound of anguished metal screaming as it twisted into shapes never intended was lost amid the unfolding chaos taking place on the highway. Sliding to the ground, the wreck came to rest on what was left of its four wheels. Gas leaked from the torn gas tank, staining the cold, windswept ground.

After ramming the Cadillac, the truck jackknifed. Its cab plowed forward into the Le Mans. The trailer, filled with twelve tons of steel cable, broke free. It gored the bus's side, peeling back metal and glass. The Greyhound careened off the road and into the ditch, disgorging several passengers as it rolled on its side. Like a pile driver, the truck cab kept going forward, hurling the Le Mans into the next car in line. A chain reaction ensued, spilling fifteen broken and bent cars along the highway. Blood, glass shards, and pieces of sheared metal were everywhere.

A lone Ontario Provincial Police officer was the first person to arrive at the scene. Before leaving his car, he radioed dispatch, asking for all emergency responders. Angling his car sideways across the highway, he got out and lit flares. All oncoming cars were stopped from entering the zone of chaos. The officer then went to help the bus passengers. He'd decided, correctly, that was where he could offer the most assistance.

A newspaper article the next day reported that, along with the nine injured bus travelers, two people had died at the scene.

The coroner later estimated that Nora was killed immediately upon the first impact. It was a year before the introduction of air bags, and Lucas died when the steering wheel was driven into his chest by the impact of the car hitting the rock wall. His chest cavity had been crushed, rupturing his heart and ripping apart his lungs.

Sean was found still secured in his car seat. Somehow he'd escaped the carnage. He was covered in broken glass and bits of ripped metal. The emergency team marveled that he wasn't crying. Sean soon fell asleep in the ambulance attendant's arms.

At less than five months old, Sean was an orphan with no place to go. Lucas had no siblings, and his parents were dead. Nora had never known a father, and her foster mother was incapable of caring for a baby. Sean was placed in foster care. The plan was to put him up for adoption in the new year.

The law firm was in disarray. One of its founding partners was gone, and in an instant, the death knell was sounding for the practice. As other legal firms prepared to sweep in and poach clients from what they believed was a mortally wounded partnership, Brennan and Dolan pulled all of the firm's employees together and asked for a concerted effort to save the floundering company. And they did. Everyone from the senior partners, to the junior associates, to the paralegals, to the law clerks, to the executive assistants pitched in to save the firm and keep its client base.

It was also agreed between Brennan and Dolan that the firm's name wouldn't change. The three had known each other since the first year of law school and had been in business together for more than a decade. Lucas Kilgore was a founding partner, and his name would remain.

The hours were long and difficult. During the first months, there were some defeats but many more victories. It would take at least a year for the firm to get back on solid footing, but the early results were encouraging. Dolan was out prospecting for new clients while Brennan ensured the firm retained the ones it had.

However, other changes were about to take place in Tom Brennan's life. He and his wife, Margaret, had spent hours researching adoption agencies and protocols, but now they focused their attention on adopting Sean.

One night in early March, Tom arrived home, as usual, just before midnight. He was weary and needed sleep. In his late thirties, he had a combination of graying black hair, soft brown eyes, and firm chin that radiated calm assurance, which his clients appreciated as much as his legal stewardship.

But Margaret, a tall, willowy redhead, had news for him that gave rise to laughter and happiness his coworkers would have been surprised to see. Despite his schedule, Tom had traveled with Margaret for meetings with social workers and the adoption agency. They'd participated in the adoption training classes and completed the home study program set by the province's Children's Aid Society. All they were waiting for was approval to have Sean join their lives and make them a true family.

And on this night, Margaret told her husband they could pick up Sean the next day. Papers needed to be signed, but it was merely a formality. For the couple, it was a life-altering moment, and they fed off each other's excitement. Neither slept, but it didn't matter. During his morning shave, Tom reveled in the knowledge that he was going to be a father. He felt better than he had since the accident had almost crippled the firm.

Later that day, with the flourish of a pen, Sean Jason Kilgore became Sean Jason Brennan. Sean was nine months old when Tom and Margaret brought him home.

# CHAPTER 3

Sean had just turned fourteen years old when Tom decided it was time to tell his son he was adopted. He and Margaret shared this important news with their teenage boy. The conversation took place in Sean's bedroom—a place where Tom believed his son would feel safe and comfortable. Margaret sat on the side of the bed with Sean, while Tom took the room's only chair.

And there, amid the hockey posters, the autographed picture of Muhammad Ali, and his school books, Sean was told he was adopted. When Sean asked what had happened to his real parents, Margaret felt a tinge of sadness at his use of the word *real*. Tom explained about the accident. He told Sean as much as he remembered about Lucas and Nora. There was talk of a small inheritance that would be his when he turned eighteen. Throughout the session, Sean was told how much he was loved by Margaret and Tom.

Soon there wasn't anything more to say.

As he sat there absorbing everything he'd been told, Sean experienced a strange feeling of loss. To learn he was adopted didn't lessen his love for Tom and Margaret, but it did leave him with a sense that the life he was living wasn't his own.

Sean wanted to know about the mark on his left leg. He'd never asked because it hadn't seemed important. It was a part of his body just like his hands and feet. But now there was a need. He didn't understand why, but he wanted an explanation.

"It's a birthmark," explained Tom. "And while it's unusual, you don't have to worry that it's something bad. When you were younger, we had it examined by a doctor. He told us not to be concerned."

But Sean knew instinctively that the triangular mark represented something important. From somewhere deep inside his soul, he felt a stirring. If asked, he'd have found it impossible to describe the sensation. Within moments, the birthmark was pulsating and aching. That had never happened before. He sensed a connection to something outside himself. But what? Did it have anything to do with his real parents?

He placed his hand over it and could feel the heat though his jeans. Sean didn't tell Margaret and Tom what he was experiencing. In a world suddenly thrown into chaos, he wanted to hang onto something that was his alone.

Sean sat, not saying a word, trying to digest everything he'd learned. He looked around his room, trying to find comfort in the things that were familiar. The silence stretched until Margaret moved, gently rocking the bed.

"Do you have any questions?" she asked. "You haven't said much about what we've told you."

"Not really," he responded.

What more was there to ask? He was adopted. The people who were sitting in his bedroom weren't his real parents. The people who'd actually given him life had been killed when he was five months old. He'd survived. He could ask why but was old enough to realize that there wasn't an answer.

"If there's ever anything you want to talk about, we're here to listen," offered Tom.

"Right now, I just want to be left alone."

Margaret went to kiss the boy she'd loved as her own for the past fourteen years, but he pulled back. His mother didn't react. She got up from the bed and, along with Tom, left the room. They closed the door behind them.

Left alone with his thoughts, Sean's first reaction was rage. He'd been lied to all these years. Getting up, he paced the room. Tears came to his eyes. His anger quickly turned to self-pity. The revelation had left him feeling tired and empty.

For several months, Sean's life was filled with self-doubt and turmoil. Tom and Margaret had always treated him as their son, yet he wasn't. There were days when he felt angry that his real parents had deserted him. Withdrawn and moody, he was having difficulty accepting that he was adopted. For reasons Sean didn't understand, it made him feel less worthy than his classmates.

He turned to Hilary, Brian Dolan's daughter. She was the only person he believed would understand. They'd been friends since just after his third birthday. She was a month older and always took the lead in everything they did. He had a memory of her teaching him to tie shoelaces. Their houses were only four blocks apart in the private and wealthy enclave of Forest Hill. The two were inseparable. They were best friends before either of them knew what the term meant.

"My life has changed," he said one day while they were in her parent's library studying for midterm exams.

"What's that supposed to mean?" asked Hilary, looking up from a book on Russian history.

And then it all poured out. He told her everything, including the confusion and insecurities he now felt.

It was a lot for two fourteen-year-olds to handle. Hilary got up and walked over to where Sean was sitting. Without a word, she took his hand and pulled him up. She hugged him. Sean began to weep. Large, wracking sobs tore at his body. He held on to Hilary. She was a shelter against the storm of emotion and upheaval that had torn at his life. Neither said a word for several minutes.

When the tears had stopped, he felt neither shame nor embarrassment. Instead, there was an overall sense of relief. All the feelings he'd kept as prisoners in his mind had finally been freed. He backed out of Hilary's embrace and sat down. She plunked herself on the floor.

"So now you know," he said.

"It doesn't change anything between us," Hilary stated. "You're the same person you've always been. And your parents are still your parents. They love you. Those are the things that count."

*Trust Hilary to remind me of what's important,* thought Sean.

No longer present was the feeling of helpless rage. The weight of insecurity that had plagued him for the past months was gone. For the first time since Tom and Margaret had sat down with him, he laughed.

"You're right," he said. "Being adopted isn't such a big deal. It doesn't make me different from anyone else. You've made me see that."

"We're special friends," said Hilary, staring directly into his eyes. "And I'll always be here for you."

Sean returned her look, and for the first time in all the years he'd known Hilary, he felt a connection that he couldn't explain, but knew instinctively their relationship was becoming more than friendship.

# Chapter 4

Sean and Hilary dated through the rest of high school and college. Everyone they knew, including their parents, assumed they'd attend law school, be called to the bar, marry, and follow their fathers into BDK.

It was an expectation shared by Sean and Hilary. Neither had ever given a thought to being anything other than lawyers. Each was seeking the genuine approval of their respective parents, although they'd never admit it, even to each other. Sean wanted to show Tom and Margaret that they'd made the right decision in adopting him. Hilary sought the approval of Dolan, her strong and demanding father, who often told her that one day she and Sean would head the firm as managing partners.

The summer before law school, the young couple got a small apartment, financed by their parents. It was close to the subway line, which brought them within walking distance of their classes at the University of Toronto.

Law school was an unrelenting trek of study and hard work. The couple seldom went out, and if they did, it was infrequent visits to their parents or to a Second Cup that was just below their apartment. Their lives were wrapped up in each other, law school, and summer internships at BDK.

Both were driven to succeed. Unfortunately, the expectations they'd placed on themselves were creating two different paths for the couple.

Sean knew Hilary had a genuine love of the law. It fascinated and intrigued her. The more time she spent studying and learning about it, the more she realized this had to be her life. Hilary, unlike so many people, had found her calling.

Sean, however, was beginning to question his commitment. At twenty-three, he was no longer certain he wanted to be a lawyer.

And yet there was Hilary. He longed to tell her what he was experiencing. They were a couple, and he believed this newfound doubt was something that should be shared. But he kept putting it off. How could he disappoint her and his parents?

Sean was searching for something but didn't know what. He felt like a stranger in his own life. A siren's call was beckoning him into the unknown. A restlessness prowled within him like a caged tiger.

Buried deep within the core of his soul was the need to be something other than a successful lawyer. The more he experienced the heat and aches from the birthmark, the greater his certainty that if it wasn't for Hilary he'd be casting about to do something else with his life.

It was in his second year of law school that Sean began to seriously wonder about his birthmark. It had become raised and the triangle shape more pronounced. He could discern no pattern as to why it was sometimes hot to the touch and throbbed.

Hilary was also concerned and agreed he should see a skin specialist.

After a series of test that focused on his thigh, groin, and heart, the consensus was that, while it was unusual, the birthmark wasn't threatening his health. The results satisfied Hilary, but Sean still had questions. He wondered if the answers could lie with his birth parents.

With money from the small inheritance he'd received after turning eighteen, Sean hired a private investigator used by BDK. He told no one and swore the investigator to secrecy. Sean experienced feelings of guilt about not informing his parents or Hilary of what he was doing. He felt as though he was betraying their trust. But, he reasoned, if nothing was found, no harm had been committed. And if something was discovered, he wanted the opportunity to decide on his own what should be done with the information.

He told the investigator about his relationship to the Kilgore family. Unsure of what he was looking for, his instructions to her were simple. "Find out everything you can." He gave the woman enough money for two month's work.

After a month, the investigator came back to him. The PI and a very anxious Sean met in a restaurant several blocks away from the campus. It was evening, and only two tables were occupied. They chose a spot at the rear and ordered coffee. She placed a thin file on the table and handed Sean a check for the remaining month.

"This is the best I can do," she said. "There's no record of the family past your great-great-grandfather, Joshua Kilgore. I discovered that he wasn't born in this country. Yet there's no account of how he arrived, where he came from, or what he did when he was here. The only evidence he even existed is that he's listed as the father on your great-grandfather's birth certificate.

“And the family disappears with the death of your father. I’ve never seen anything like it. It’s as though everyone wanted to stay invisible.”

“Did you find anything about a hereditary birthmark?”

The investigator gave him a strange sideways look.

“It’s funny you ask,” she said, opening the file. “There’s a notation from a doctor who examined your father when he was six months old. He was extremely thorough and lists all the baby’s features, along with the normal length and weight. The doctor noted a birthmark in the shape of a triangle on the inside of the left thigh.”

The investigator handed the open file to Sean and asked, “How did you know about that?”

Suddenly excited, Sean ignored the question and asked if something similar had been recorded for his grandfather.

“I couldn’t find a reference to your grandfather having a birthmark. But what I did discover,” she said, searching through the thin sheaf of papers, “was a letter your grandfather wrote to your grandmother shortly after your father was born.

“Ah here it is,” she said, holding up a photocopy of two sheets of writing paper. “I guess he wasn’t there for the birth. He asks right here,” she pointed to an almost illegible scrawl, “‘whether the child has the birthmark.’ Unfortunately I couldn’t find a reply from your grandmother.”

“Where did you get this letter?” he asked.

“It seems as though your birth father, Lucas Kilgore, had a similar investigation done a few months before he was killed. I was shown the letter by the private detective who’d worked on the case. The investigator completed the assignment as best he could and handed everything over to Lucas. But the detective kept the file open because he found it interesting."

"How did the two of you connect?"

"The private detective community in Toronto is small. Once I started putting out feelers for information, it wasn't long before he heard what I was doing. He reached out to me and we met."

"Did he know anything?"

"Nothing that would add to what I've already told you," the investigator said.

Sean thought about what she'd told him. He'd learned a few things, but these new bits of information had only opened more doors into a mysterious past.

"Can I persuade you to stay on the case a bit longer?" he asked.

"There's nothing more to find out," she replied. "I'd be stealing your money. There just isn't enough information out there to build on."

She got up and said, "I'm sorry I couldn't find out anything more."

Deep in thought, Sean nodded. When he looked up, she was gone. Picking up the envelope and the file, he paid for the coffees and left.

Swiftly walking toward the subway station, Sean's well-toned body was tense; at a couple of inches over six feet, he cut through the crowd. Toffee brown hair floated over the tops of his ears and down the back of his neck in loose, unrepentant curls. Dark brown eyes, set in an angular face, gazed at the world with unabashed interest. Strong cheekbones, a straight nose that flared defiantly at the end, and generous lips further complemented the look of open curiosity. To his professors and among classmates, he was viewed as bright, intelligent, and articulate—someone, they thought, who would make a good lawyer.

He found a seat at the back of one of the subway cars and opened the thin file from the investigator. It didn't contain much. There were copies of his grandfather's and father's birth certificates, his father's will, a transcript of the conversation the investigator had with the other detective, the copy he'd already seen of the letter from his grandfather, notes on the research done on his great-great-grandfather and grandfather, and an accounting of her hours. Sean absently noted that she'd worked hard for what he'd paid her.

Changing trains at Bloor, he hurried up the stairs, and caught the subway that would take him home. He arrived at the apartment just after ten and went straight to the bedroom, where he tucked the file in his bureau's bottom drawer.

He'd shred the papers when Hilary left for school in the morning. There was no reason to keep the file. It contained nothing that brought him closer to discovering the birthmark's meaning, if there even was one. He'd reached a dead end. Time to let it go.

He was tired and hungry. Hilary was working at her desk in the living room. Giving him a distracted kiss, she told him there was some Kraft Dinner in the fridge that could be warmed up in the microwave. A green salad was on the counter. For desert, there were store-bought cookies and a full pot of coffee she'd just made.

Sean prepared his dinner, put everything on a tray, and took it into the living room. There'd be no conversation between them. That was one of the rules they'd established when first moving in together. When either was at his or her desk, he or she wasn't to be disturbed.

As he sat on the couch quietly eating, Sean stared thoughtfully at the woman he was going to marry. Hilary was tall, coming to just above his shoulders. Straight blond hair fell gently to the middle of her back. Pale skin, highlighted by deep blue eyes, clung to pronounced cheekbones and a delicate nose. Rosebud lips, usually pursed in thought, emphasized a strong chin. She was wearing a white T-shirt that fit snugly across firm, full breasts. A slender waist flared out to long, curvaceous legs.

Hilary generally wore a minimum of makeup, preferring only a light red lipstick and some blush on her cheeks.

She must have known he was studying her. Hilary looked up for a moment and smiled and then returned her attention to the document on the desk. In that moment, Sean was struck by a blinding and illuminating insight.

Nothing could diminish his love. They shared a bond that he'd never break. He never tired of the time they spent together. Hilary was his shield against a world where the darkness of broken promises and false hope prevailed. Sean couldn't imagine a life without her.

And yet, he would have to face the overriding issue of the law not being for him. But what would he do? Everything in his life had been focused on getting into law school, passing the bar exam, and working at BDK. And Hilary was committed to the two of them taking over their fathers' firm.

Finishing his dinner, he washed the dishes and went to bed. Lying on his back, with hands clasped behind his head, Sean stared at the ceiling. He retrieved his thoughts from earlier in the evening. Perhaps he could make it all work. Hopefully in time, he'd come to feel the same passion for the law that powered Hilary.

Sean finally drifted off to an agitated sleep, knowing that his hope was a remote possibility at best. He didn't awaken when Hilary finally made it into bed, just as the sun was beginning to creep over the horizon.

And so, despite his growing restlessness, Sean never mentioned a word to Hilary. His last year of law school was a nightmare of too many assignments, not enough sleep, copious quantities of self-doubt, and the struggle to keep up. Hilary, on the other hand, thrived in the environment.

It was no surprise that, when they graduated, she captured just about every achievement award. Hilary was the class rock star. Although she hadn't yet passed the bar exam, offers were pouring in from law firms across the country. Hilary declined them all, letting everyone know her intention was to work at BDK.

While his placement wasn't as high, Sean's dogged determination had led to grades that placed him in the top ten percentile of graduates. He'd received several offers, but it would have meant moving from Toronto. It was a nonstarter. He wasn't prepared to leave Hilary.

There was still the process of articling, writing the bar exam, and then the call to the bar before they could practice law. Their parents viewed the couple's eventual takeover of BDK as a foregone conclusion and, along with Hilary, were already planning the wedding. Sean had thoughts of putting off the marriage until he was more certain about his future. But once again, he was trapped by the expectations of others. It was what Hilary wanted.

He could handle the parents' objections but not Hilary's. How could he disappoint the woman he truly loved?

It was a proud day for both fathers when Sean and Hilary joined the firm. They spent a year articling, wrote the bar exam together, and were enshrined by the bar as lawyers on the same day. Six months later, they were married in a lavish ceremony that made all the Toronto papers.

As a wedding gift from the parents, the couple was given a three-week Mediterranean cruise and a mortgage-free furnished house on the Bridle Path, containing Toronto's most exclusive addresses. For Sean, it was another step along a road that didn't seem to have any forks. He desperately wanted off the treadmill, but knew he wouldn't be able to take Hilary with him. And if that was the case, what was the point? If working at something he didn't enjoy was the price for keeping Hilary, then it was one he was willing to pay.

Arriving back in Toronto from the cruise, Sean was tanned and fully prepared to begin work at BDK.

Sean realized that, if he was to keep Hilary in his life, he'd have to put his head down, keep working, and be satisfied with the life he'd chosen. The question, though, was how long before it became apparent to Hilary and their fathers that he had no desire to one day copartner the firm with his wife. He could only hope that, when that day came, the fallout was something he could control.

# Chapter 5

After dressing in a gray pinstriped suit, white shirt, maroon tie, and black shoes, Larry Blaine headed downstairs to fix his usual breakfast of cereal, two pieces of buttered toast, and coffee. He was an exact man whose morning routine seldom varied.

At just under six feet, Larry was a trim 165 pounds. He worked out three times a week at a health club in lower Manhattan. A quickly receding hairline had recently persuaded him to shave his head. Below the bald pate, a pair of dark gray eyes carefully screened the world around him. With ears cropped close to his head and a thin gaunt face, he had the look of a well-bred greyhound.

Larry lived by himself in a solid-looking brownstone on New York's east side. A short walk outside his front door was Central Park. In the other direction was the subway station he used to begin the journey to his office.

Attached to the Canadian delegation at the United Nations in New York, he had done well in the eight years since graduating from the University of Toronto's Law School. He'd studied international law, which, combined with his natural intelligence, management style, and gift for languages, had allowed him to quickly rise through the mission's ranks.

In his present position, he oversaw the placement and managed the Canadian support personnel assigned to the UN's missions throughout south and central Asia, including Afghanistan and Pakistan. It was a difficult job, filled with the stress of knowing that many of the people he oversaw worked in some of the world's most unstable and dangerous regions. While they operated under the auspices of the UN, that didn't always guarantee their safety.

As the early spring sun filtered through his front windows, Larry finished his breakfast. Looking at his watch, he saw it was time to leave. The head of Pakistan's UN delegation had scheduled an early morning meeting, and Larry didn't want to be late.

He was walking down the hallway to the front door when his cell phone rang. Larry's pulse rate quickened. The only reason someone would be calling him at this hour was if one of his people had landed in trouble. He didn't recognize the number, but that didn't mean anything. Thumbing the phone on, he placed the instrument to his ear.

"Hello, Larry. This is Elijah. I hope I'm not disturbing you."

The voice was low and calm, with just the hint of an accent that Larry knew originated from an island well north of Scotland. This was a call that had nothing to do with his work at the UN. To say he was shocked would be a major understatement. He had never spoken to Elijah—knowing of him only through stories told by his parents.

"Not at all." The reverential tone was obvious in Larry's voice. "Where are you?"

"I'm at our computer headquarters in Inverness."

Although the voice had introduced himself as Elijah, the caller was also known as the Prophet by those who followed the teachings of peace laid down more than two thousand years ago. Larry retreated to the living room and sat primly on the sofa. Forgotten for the moment was his meeting.

"How can I help you?" he asked.

"I have an important request," responded Elijah. "Do you remember Sean Brennan from law school?"

Larry went through his mind's contact list and, after a brief mental search, was able to put a face to the name.

"I remember him. We worked on some projects together. He's a bright guy and was always willing to go the extra mile to make sure we handed in first-rate assignments. He had all the makings of an excellent corporate lawyer. Why do you ask?"

"We know from our sources that he's not happy practicing law."

"But from what I understood, he was going to work at his father's law firm. It's one of the largest in Canada, and he was in line to be a named partner one day. That's a nice position to be in. Why wouldn't he be happy?"

"It's not really important," the Prophet responded softly. "The fact is I understand things could be changing, and Sean may soon be ready for a move."

Larry didn't have to ask how Elijah knew that Brennan wasn't finding the law a perfect fit. Just as Larry was part of Elijah's vast global network, he knew there were people in Toronto that would keep the Prophet up to date on whatever he wanted to know.

"What does this have to do with me?"

"I want you to contact Brennan and let him know that, if he decides to leave the law firm, there's a position waiting for him with the UN."

Larry was staggered. Did Elijah know what he was asking? Larry wielded a fair amount of influence, but he couldn't just blindly offer someone a job. He was prepared to do anything the Prophet asked, but there were certain realities to the world in which Larry operated that Elijah obviously didn't understand.

"That will be difficult. We don't have many openings in the delegation. And I'm not sure there's really anything available for a lawyer."

"I realize there isn't anything available in New York. But I think something could be found for him in a place like Afghanistan or Pakistan. In fact, I'd prefer if it was somewhere far away from North America."

The conversation was getting stranger by the minute.

"Why is this so critical?" asked Larry.

"Brennan is very important to us," said Elijah. "While we have many resources, they're not infinite. I don't want to lose contact with him if he leaves the law firm. I also want him to have some experiences that go beyond what he's been doing with his life."

"Are you sure he's going to leave? Won't his father step in and offer him whatever he wants to keep Brennan in the firm?"

"It's much more complicated than that," responded Elijah. "There's a lot happening in Brennan's life at the moment. He may not leave the firm, but all my reports indicate that, if he does, it could happen within the next few months."

"So you want me to get on this as soon as possible," responded Larry.

"That's right. All you have to do is make the phone call. If he does leave his father's firm, I'll contact you. At that point, I'd like you to connect with Brennan and offer him the job."

"But suppose there isn't anything available."

"Why don't you let me worry about that," said Elijah. "There'll be room for Brennan. All you have to do is let him know that a job is waiting for him that's completely different than anything he's previously experienced. I'm sure he'll jump at the opportunity."

"So, for now, all I have to do is contact Brennan and let him know that, if he ever gets tired of the law, there's a job waiting for him with the UN."

"That's correct."

Larry knew forces were at play that went well beyond his understanding. What he also knew was that the Prophet had ways of getting things done that would astound the world if it knew. He didn't need to think about his response.

"I'll do it today," he said.

"Thank you. It's good to know we can count on you."

"Is there anything else?" asked Larry.

But the connection had already been cut. Larry sat for a few minutes, contemplating the call. The Prophet was legendary, and to be asked to carry out an assignment by him was a privilege. He checked his watch and saw that, if he took a cab, he'd just make his meeting with the head of the Pakistan delegation. He hurried out the door intent on calling Brennan the moment his meeting ended.

# Chapter 6

Sean walked hurriedly from the University Avenue Court House to the firm's offices a few blocks away on Queen Street. The heat was unbearable. It wrapped him in a cocoon-like coat of suffocating, sweat-inducing, rancid air. He took off his jacket and threw it over his shoulder.

Finally reaching the massive steel and glass monolith that housed the firm on its top three floors, Sean went through the revolving doors into another world. The air-conditioning enveloped him. For a brief moment, he felt chilled as his body adapted to the temperature change. The impressive marble, steel, and glass lobby was wonderfully quiet. He said hello to Mickey, the concierge, and made his way to the express elevator that sped him to his floor.

Walking into his office, he saw a note on his desk pad. It was from Hilary. She wanted to see him the moment he got back.

That was the way they communicated these days—by notes. They'd been separated for eight months. The separation was amicable. No one knew, not even their parents. Hilary had called it a trial separation when she'd first talked about it. Sean wasn't surprised. In fact, he'd wondered what had taken her so long. It was obvious she wasn't happy. Sean couldn't blame her.

Over the seven years they'd been married, he'd gradually become more restless. The feeling that he should be somewhere else had begun to take on a life of its own. It was with him at the office, when he talked to Hilary, and when he went to bed. The birthmark would throb, and he'd know he was in for another night filled with an ache in both his body and his heart.

She was still living in the house on the Bridal Path. He'd taken his clothes and moved into a furnished apartment on King Street. It was within walking distance of the office. The furniture was mostly from IKEA, but the bed was comfortable and the place was cleaned once a week. He was eating most of his meals in a restaurant on Wellington.

There was only one problem with the arrangement. Sean still deeply loved Hilary. He'd gone along with the separation because it was what Hilary wanted. She'd said Sean needed time on his own to decide what he was going to do with his life. He'd tried to explain the restlessness that plagued him, the feeling he should be somewhere else.

"I know you love me," she'd said. "But we need more than love to keep our marriage alive."

"And what exactly does that mean?" he'd asked wearily, already knowing the answer.

"My commitment is to the firm," Hilary replied. "It was founded by our fathers. Surely that must mean something to you. One day, I want to take it over. And it would be wonderful to have you there with me. But I don't believe you share the same dream. You act as though it's a major hardship just being there."

"That's true," he admitted. "If it wasn't for you, I'd have a tough time even thinking about going in most days. But doesn't the fact I love you count for anything?"

"Of course it does," said Hilary, clearly struggling with her emotions. "It just isn't good enough anymore."

Sean understood. They had talked for a while longer, but Hilary had been adamant about the separation.

That night, Sean had slept on one of the living room couches. In the morning, he'd collected his clothes and was gone just as he heard her getting into the shower. And now, their communication was through pink message slips. Apart from a couple of quick telephone calls, he hadn't had a conversation with Hilary since they'd separated. He was curious to find out what she wanted.

Thankfully, they worked on different floors, so there wasn't the awkwardness of always running into each other. He'd seen Hilary only about four or five times since their separation.

When he got to her office, Hilary didn't get up from her desk. She kept it like a barrier between them and asked him to close the door. He shut it and took one of the guest chairs directly across from her.

"What is it you wanted to talk about?" he asked.

Hilary took a deep breath and let the air slowly escape her lungs. She placed both hands on the desk, palms down. He noticed she was still wearing her wedding and engagement rings. They'd agreed to keep the separation secret, so perhaps it meant all wasn't lost.

"I met with our fathers earlier this morning," she began. "They're concerned about you. You're not measuring up. It's not a question of whether you're working hard. I've seen most of your work, and it's good. But that's not enough for someone who's supposed to take over the firm with me.

"I also told them we're separated and explained why it happened."

"What did they say?" Sean demanded.

Here Hilary paused for a moment. She looked uncomfortable and not at all like the self-assured lawyer who had gained the reputation of a brilliant adversary in court.

Sean waited, wondering what sort of draconian decision the three had made.

"That we should give you a good severance package and let you get on with your life."

Stunned, Sean could only stare at Hilary. She met his gaze with unflinching blue eyes. He felt as though he'd been kicked in the stomach. A searing pain ran up through his chest cavity. His heart was on fire and pounding like a massive trip-hammer. He was having difficulty breathing.

The noise from outside the office intruded on the room's silence. The sounds of telephones ringing, people talking, and printers spewing out reams of paper invaded the space between them. Sean heard it all as if from a long distance away. It was a surreal experience. He was being let go from the firm by his wife.

"How did you get to become the messenger?" Sean asked.

"They thought it would be easier coming from me. The papers will be on your desk when you get back to your office. All you have to do is sign them and you'll be able to do whatever it is you want with your life. It's already been arranged that the files you're working on will be reassigned."

Sean didn't say a word. His mind was gradually processing the news. And he realized it was what he wanted.

Mistaking his silence for anger, Hilary said, "Look, Sean, we both know this is the right thing for you. I know you're upset, but once it all settles out, you'll see it's for the best."

"You've all done me a great favor," he answered quietly. "We both know I wasn't cut out to be a lawyer. I only did it for you."

"I know," she whispered.

Hilary's eyes had lost their intensity. Having delivered the news, she seemed unsure of what to say next.

"What are we going to do about us?" asked Sean. "Nothing will ever change how I feel about you. I hope you're not thinking of following this up with asking me for a divorce. It's not what I want, and you'll have a fight on your hands if you try for one. I love you and want a chance to prove what I can do away from the firm. We can still build a life together."

"I wasn't planning on going the divorce route," Hilary replied. "But I don't think we should see each other until you get settled into something new. Once that's done, we can decide about our future."

Sean thought about it for a few moments. It seemed like a fair compromise. Nodding his head, he said, "Fine. That's how we'll leave it for now."

He couldn't help but think how civilized it had all been.

"Have you any idea what you're going to do?" asked Hilary.

"Remember Larry Blaine? He graduated with us from law school."

She nodded.

"Well he called me a few weeks back. Larry's working for the United Nations in New York. Told me if I was ever in the city to visit him. He said the UN is always looking for good people."

"That doesn't sound even close to promising. It's not what I'd call a good job prospect."

"Well it's the best I've got at the moment. I'll get in touch with Larry, over the next few months. I'm in no hurry to find something new and won't be making any quick decisions. For the first time in my life, I've got the opportunity to sit back and decide what I want to do."

"I hope you find what you're looking for," responded Hilary. "It would make whatever decisions we're going to make about our futures a lot easier."

"I love you and want you back in my life. I'll do whatever it takes."

"Find something that makes you happy, and then we'll talk."

That was about as far as Hilary was willing to commit.

"What's the story going to be about my leaving?"

"A notice will go out tomorrow saying that you've left to pursue other opportunities."

"Well, that's the truth."

Once again, silence stalked the room, leaving Sean feeling awkward. There was nothing more to say except good-bye. He stood; Hilary remained seated. Her face was a mask. It was her courtroom look—no expression, only intense eyes that burned into him.

He walked to the door, opened it, and turned.

"Whatever happens, I'll always love you," he said.

She didn't respond.

With that, he strode out of the room, closing the door behind him. He felt like a snake shedding its skin. His old life was over. What the new one held, he didn't know. But he was looking forward to exploring the possibilities.

# Chapter 7

It was one of those days he dreaded. Crises were piling up faster than Larry could handle them. He was working the phones, trying to get a handle on what was happening in three countries. Two suicide bombings and a targeted assassination had put a number of UN personnel in danger. Larry was trying to assess the damage and determine what his next moves should be.

It was just after three in the afternoon. He was eating a late lunch that consisted of a very dry, machine-dispensed tuna sandwich. It was being washed down with strong black coffee. His stomach was objecting to one or both; he wasn't sure which. The phone rang. Larry picked it up, expecting a progress report from one of his field agents.

"Hello, Larry." The soft voice of Elijah flowed through the line.

If it had been anyone else, Larry would have put them off. But this was the Prophet. Besides his parents, there was no one more important in his life. The crises would have to take care of themselves for a few minutes.

"How can I help?" he asked.

"Sean Brennan has left the law firm. He's been out of work for a couple of months. I believe now would be a good time to get in touch and offer him a job."

Larry smiled at the Prophet's ignorance of how things worked in the world. In these days of austerity and financial cutbacks, jobs were hard to find. The UN was no different. But his department was in the midst of planning a new initiative to be implemented in Afghanistan. Although Sean didn't fit the job profile—no experience with the UN for one thing—it was the only avenue Larry might have available. If the program did get funding approval, he'd have to call in a number of favors for Sean to get the posting.

"I'll do what I can," he told Elijah.

"That's all I can ask," responded the Prophet.

Larry wasn't being ordered to find Sean a job. He was being asked to provide a helping hand. That was the Prophet's way. He was caring, considerate and possessed a deep understanding of human nature. There would be no recriminations if Larry failed.

But because Elijah was the Prophet, Larry would do whatever the man asked. He naturally wondered what interest Elijah had in Sean. He'd have asked, but an explanation would have to wait for another time. Regardless of Elijah's importance, Larry had those crises that needed his immediate attention.

"Is there anything else?" he inquired.

"No, just that. As always, this stays between us."

"Of course," responded Larry.

The line went dead. In less than a couple of seconds, the phone began to ring. As Larry picked up the instrument, the acid burning in his stomach told him he'd made a mistake with the tuna sandwich.

# Chapter 8

Sean's severance package was generous, and he could afford to be out of work for at least six to eight months if he watched his spending. He hadn't called Larry or anyone else. For the first time in his life, he had nothing to do and was enjoying the feeling. He promised himself he'd call sometime over the next month.

He'd just come in from a jog when the phone began to ring. The only calls Sean had received since being out of work were from his mother and a few friends wondering how he was doing. Out of habit, he checked the number and saw that it was a New York area code. Intrigued, he answered. It was Larry.

They exchanged pleasantries for a few minutes. Sean then explained he was out of work and asked if Larry's offer of visiting New York was still on the table.

"That's why I'm calling," said Larry. "I'd heard you were no longer at BDK and thought you might be interested in a project we're putting together."

For a brief moment, Sean wondered how Larry knew he'd left the law firm. But his curiosity at Larry's proposal quickly pushed the thought from his mind.

"Listen, I'm calling to offer you a job with the UN. We need someone in Afghanistan. It's a three-year contract, and I think you'd be a perfect fit. Unless you have something already lined up, why don't you come to New York and we can talk about it.

"It won't cost you anything. We'll pay for your flights, meals, and a hotel. If it doesn't work out, at least you've had a few days in New York."

"What would I be doing?"

"You'd be going throughout the countryside talking to village elders. We've initiated a program in conjunction with the Afghani government to register voters and hold elections. It's one way that we're trying to break the Taliban's hold on the country. If sound governance can be brought to Afghanistan, we can hopefully end the cycle of wars and counterinsurgency movements that have plagued the country for years."

"You're aware I'm a lawyer, right."

"Of course I am. We graduated together. But the last time we talked, you were fed up with the law. I telephoned your office, and they told me you're no longer with BDK."

It wasn't the truth of course, but Larry knew he couldn't tell Sean about Elijah. For Sean, the mystery of how Larry knew he was unemployed was answered.

"Anyway the fact you're home in the middle of the day tells me you haven't found anything. Are you looking for another job in legal or is that phase of your life over?"

"I'm through with the law," responded Sean.

"That's what I thought. And what I'm offering isn't the law. But I do think your legal background could come in handy.

Remember those courses on constitutional law we took? It gives you a sound base to go in and talk to these people."

Sean's first inclination was to decline the offer. He knew little about Afghanistan, except for what he read in the newspapers or saw on TV. It was a country wracked by war, and now that the United States, along with its allies including Canada, had gone in, the fighting had intensified.

But Larry was right. He hadn't lined up anything. And there was the enticement of a trip to New York. His passport was up-to-date, so there wasn't anything holding him back. Also, he was intrigued by the offer. It was about as far away from practicing law at BDK that he could get. And it was a job that could perhaps give him some measure of satisfaction. Was this what he'd been looking for? Helping a country find peace seemed nobler than the day-to-day drudgery of putting in hours at BDK.

"Are you still there?" asked Larry.

"Sorry," responded Sean. "I was just considering your proposal."

"And what do you think?"

Sean paused for another brief moment. "When do you want me in New York?"

After that, events had moved rapidly. Sean had his meeting with Larry and was impressed with what he heard. He signed a three-year contract and spent a month in New York on an orientation course. He then flew to Toronto, cancelled his apartment lease, packed his clothes in a duffel bag, and was soon on his way to Afghanistan via New York and Karachi, Pakistan. He'd tried to phone Hilary but, after several minutes on hold, had been told she was in a meeting. Sean knew Hilary had refused to take the call once she found out it was him.

# Chapter 9

The cold had a raw feel to it, and the wind that swept across the international compound in Kabul, Afghanistan, was freezing, even by the country's standards. The wind whipped the snow, creating little storm trenches where tiny particles of dirt-filled ice pellets rose up to sting his eyes and pick at his face.

The United Nations Assistance Mission in Afghanistan (UNAMA) to which Sean had been assigned was located in Compound B, Building 5-Annex. The structure was situated in what was referred to as the green zone; a heavily fortified district that was also home to various embassies and international organizations.

As he hurried toward the UN complex, Sean reflected that the conversation he'd had with Larry in New York seemed to have taken place a lifetime ago. In reality, it was two months shy of three years since he'd deplaned at Kabul's international airport. But time hung heavy in this country and seemed to move at a glacial pace. Kabul and what Sean had seen of the desolate, war-torn Afghanistan countryside were far removed from anything he'd experienced. It made him feel cut off from everything he'd known.

Sean's role was to coordinate the country's organization of future elections by serving as a liaison between the UNAMA and the Afghanistan government. This meant not only meeting with both groups on a regular basis but also involved working with UNAMA's regional office personnel throughout Afghanistan.

He'd thought a large part of his job would be working in the field and had looked forward to meeting with the Afghani population. However, his trips into the Afghan countryside were limited to about one per week. He found that, on most days, it was no different from being at BDK. There were endless meetings, conference calls, and stacks of reports to process.

A particularly fierce gust of wind shook him out of his reverie.

"This wind is brutal," said Sean to his close friend and UN translator, the Afghan born Ahmad Qazi.

Since shortly after Sean's arrival in Afghanistan he and Ahmad had established an early morning routine. Ahmad would stop by Sean's living unit and the two would cross the compound to the UN building. Once inside, they'd head to the cafeteria for breakfast before starting their day. It was an easygoing relationship that allowed Sean an insight into the country's many complexities.

Similar to most Afghan males, Ahmad was average height by North American standards; he was thin and slightly stooped. His *pakol*, or woolen hat, covered most but not all of Ahmad's short, curly hair that, along with a full beard, was prematurely gray. Etched upon his forehead were deep lines, and his face had the brown, leathery look brought on by many years in the sun and the wind. He looked older than his forty-one years.

Ahmad viewed the world through hooded and tired-looking, deep brown eyes. A prominent nose drifted to the right, giving his face a slightly lopsided look. His lips were thin and, when parted, revealed yellow and cracked teeth—the result of too many cigarettes, too much vodka, and too little care.

The translator lived with his wife and three young sons about a ninety minute walk from the compound. Although they'd been friends for three years, Sean had never met Ahmad's family.

"I can't bring a foreigner home," he'd explained. "It's too dangerous. There are spies for the Taliban everywhere. No one knows I work for the UN. I must keep it that way or my life wouldn't be worth much."

As Sean and Ahmad entered the building, its warmth enveloped them in a comforting bubble. Sean looked at his watch. He and Ahmad were slated to visit a number of villages in the Nangarhar province that day.

The type of coordination required for the times when Sean did venture into the countryside rivaled any military mission. Like all workers with the UN who wanted to journey outside the Kabul city perimeter, he had to travel in a two-car convoy of blast-resistant and heavily armored 4x4s. The vehicles carried troops provided by a private military contractor. They were accompanied by Afghani police on motorcycles, who served as outriders.

"Our ride will be here in about an hour," he told the translator. "I'm going to skip breakfast. I've got a report from New York to go through. What's on your agenda?"

"Nothing until we go out," replied the Afghani. "I'll have coffee and something to eat. Why don't I come by and pick you up once they get here."

Sean nodded in agreement and headed toward his office. Once there, he dropped his coat on a chair, switched on the computer, and waited for it to power up.

He thought back to his days at BDK and the frustration he'd felt at practicing law. Was this proving to be much different? Sometime soon, he'd have to give thought to whether working with the UN in a far-flung place like Afghanistan provided the answers he was seeking.

In the beginning, he'd hoped for so much more. When Larry first told him about the job, Sean had believed he would have a vital role to play in changing the lives of the Afghani population. He'd been filled with enthusiasm for establishing voting procedures that were Afghani led and involved everyone throughout the country. He'd set as a personal goal involving more women and young people in the process.

However, after almost three years, his idealism had run headlong into the brick wall of reality. The possibility of holding free and open elections that expressed the peoples' will was remote. Many factors conspired to render transparent and fair elections impossible.

The Taliban, warlords, and private militias controlled much of the countryside. Through intimidation, these groups would force entire villages not to cast a vote or to elect a man of their choosing.

Corruption was rampant among government officials, which would lead to rigged vote counting. And major drug traffickers supported candidates who would not impede the flow of their product to lucrative international markets. More than 90 percent of the world's non-pharmaceutical grade opiates originated in Afghanistan. It was a lucrative international industry that no one, including government officials, was willing to see put at risk.

Sean sat there for a few more minutes and let his mind wander to Hilary. Whenever he thought of her, it was with a profound sense of loss. He hadn't spoken to her since their last conversation at BDK, where she'd fired him. Three years without having her in his life hadn't dimmed his feelings. He still loved her deeply.

In the time they'd been apart, he hadn't seen anyone. Although there were some unattached and attractive women who worked and lived in the compound, Sean hadn't considered asking any of them out. He still believed in his marriage. If someone had asked him why, he would have been hard-pressed for an answer. It was a feeling he had that everything would work itself out. For now, that belief and his love for Hilary was all he needed.

The computer screen came alive with his desktop page. Seeing the change out of the corner of his eye brought Sean back to the present. He worked the mouse, bringing up the report. Pouring through the information, filled with graphs and pie charts and outlining the objectives and achievements of his mission compiled by Larry's office in New York, Sean could see the results were trending upward.

The program was meeting with success, but not to the degree Sean wanted.

It was going to take time to build an infrastructure capable of ensuring fair and open elections. Everything moved much more slowly in Afghanistan than it did in the West. And with no national communication system, the concept of staging elections would have to be brought to one village at a time. The country was about the size of Texas, with 24 million people and thousands of villages, each with one hundred houses or less. Most settlements had no schools; no stores; and, the primary reason for his mandate, no government representative. The only way the inhabitants would learn about the push for free elections was through his outreach program.

A knock on his door diverted his attention. It was Ahmad.

"Our plans have changed," the translator said. "The convoy that was going to take us out has been reassigned. Apparently there's some Taliban activity to the north and the troops have been put on standby in case they're needed."

Sean experienced a strong sense of disappointment. *Just another day in unpredictable Afghanistan*, he thought. Still, not being able to go out as planned was frustrating. How was he supposed to spread the UN election message if he couldn't visit the villages?

A rumbling stomach told him he'd skipped breakfast.

"Look I haven't had anything to eat this morning," he reminded Ahmad. "Why not join me while I grab some breakfast."

"I'd like to, but since I'm not going out, I've been asked to sit in on a meeting your tech op people are having with some Afghani government bureaucrats. What about getting together for coffee later this afternoon, after I've finished?"

"Sounds great," responded Sean. "I've got enough to keep me busy for the rest of the day. I'll meet you here."

# Chapter 10

It was late afternoon when Ahmad returned to Sean's office. Darkness was already pulling a veil over the compound. The cafeteria was almost empty. Soon the evening mealtime rush would begin. Preparation of the dinner menu was underway, and the clatter of dishes, pots, and pans mixed with the enticing aroma of food being readied.

The men had picked up coffees and were seated at one of the tables. As usual, the conversation focused on Sean's efforts to spearhead the movement toward unrestricted elections.

"The reports tell me we're succeeding," he said. "All of my representatives believe they're making headway in convincing the villagers that what we're trying to achieve is possible. The people are beginning to believe that only by voting will there be any hope of change."

"I can sense a difference when we go into the villages," advised Ahmad. "When you first began three years ago, the elders would listen, but I know they didn't believe change was possible. It's different now. They understand what you're trying to do, and there's much more interest in what you have to say.

"There's a growing commitment to voting and having elections decide who should govern the country. You and your UN representatives are making a difference."

"Why the change?" asked Sean.

"The people are tired of the constant warfare," responded the translator. "They need to believe in something. Everybody yearns for freedom—if not for themselves then for their children. This is my country. My family's history, like so many in Afghanistan, goes back more than two thousand years. For so much of that time, the country has been trapped in a never-ending cycle of tribal warfare, bitter religious disputes, destructive internecine feuds, and foreign invasions. We have had revolutions, been ruled by repressive regimes, and been conquered by despots.

"We have fallen behind so much of the world. Everyone wants to believe that, with a stable government, there can be peace. And once there is peace, we can have progress. With progress comes hope for a better future. It's a simple equation my Western friend."

The cafeteria was beginning to fill with people. Ahmad looked at his watch. It was time for him to leave. Sean offered to walk him as far as the security gate.

"A bit of fresh air will do me good," he said.

Walking across the compound's frozen pavement, Sean and Ahmad were lashed by a driving wind along with sharp snow pellets. It was bitterly cold, and while Sean could retreat inside for a hot meal, Ahmad wasn't so fortunate.

The thought of the long trek Ahmad had in front of him bothered Sean. The man worked hard for the UN and deserved a warm ride home.

"Why don't you wait and I'll have a driver take you into the city."

The translator's body immediately stiffened. He put a hand on Sean's arm.

"Thank you, but I can't arrive in a car with a driver," he said, followed by a mirthless laugh. "That would tell everybody I work for either NATO or the UN. Somebody would see me. They'd tell someone else, who'd inform the Taliban. I don't want to die on the streets of Kabul. My death would be used as a lesson to anybody who dares to coexist with the infidels."

Sean understood the dangers but persisted.

"You could be dropped off a few streets from where you live," he offered.

His words were almost ripped into the oncoming night by the wind's increasing intensity. Even in his wool-lined coat, he could feel the cold plunging into every part of his body.

"I know you mean well, my friend," said Ahmad. "But I'm used to this weather. And it's far safer to arrive at my house the way I always do."

"Why do you work for the UN if it's so dangerous?"

Ahmad stared into the distance for several seconds. Finally he spoke. "There's only one reason to take the risk. It's the money. Soon I'll have enough so that I can take my family and leave this country. I won't be here much longer. Maybe a year at the most. I'll have what I need to live in England and buy a small travel agency. That's my dream.

"My family is the most precious thing in the world to me. There's no future for my sons here. In England, they can get a proper education and my wife can be free to do what she wants. She could even get a job or go to school. None of that's possible here.

“I’m living for that day and will do everything I can to protect my family.”

Ahmad extended his right arm and they shook hands. Sean stood watching as the translator was passed through the security gate by the armed soldiers on guard duty. He soon lost sight of Ahmad, as the blowing snow quickly obscured his view.

Sean turned and began walking across the compound. The wind chased him all the way into his unit.

# Chapter 11

That night as Sean lay in bed, he pondered his future. The reports from New York, along with the words of his representatives and Ahmad told him progress, albeit slow, was being made. Still, much work remained to be done.

The question was, did he want to stay in Afghanistan on another three-year contract? The work was giving him a measure of satisfaction. But was it enough?

The simple answer was no. Just as he had when he was practicing law, he was filled with a growing belief that, like BDK, the UN wasn't where he should be spending his life. The feeling was eating away at him. It was a sense that he should be somewhere else, that there was something waiting for him. It was frustrating because he had no idea what he was looking for.

But he was determined to keep searching. He knew that more time in Afghanistan wouldn't bring him closer to answering the question plaguing him.

Sean hadn't taken any time away from the compound since his arrival in the country. There didn't seem to be any point. The only place he wanted to be was with Hilary, and that wasn't going to happen. So he'd stayed and built up a bank of three month's paid leave. He'd decided to work through to the end of his contract and then accept a compensation package that would pay him for the time he hadn't taken for R&R. That left him with another sixty days in Afghanistan.

He fell asleep satisfied that, despite the uncertainty of his future plans, he was making the right decision by venturing into the unknown.

The next day was busy. There were myriad reports to file, several conference calls with various bureaus in New York, and progress reviews with his regional representatives. It wasn't until late afternoon that he'd been able to telephone Larry.

The conversation went reasonably well, considering Sean told Larry he was leaving at the end of his contract. The initial response had been several seconds of silence. Larry then praised the work Sean was doing and offered him a new three-year contract with a considerable salary increase.

"We need you in Afghanistan," he'd said. "Your program is becoming one of our major success stories."

"I appreciate what you're saying," Sean responded, "but I'm not coming back. I've also filed papers to take my accumulated leave. There's three months due me. I'll take it when my contract ends. It's all in a confirmation letter that I'll be sending you in the morning."

"Have you got another job?" asked Larry. "I understand that, if a better opportunity has presented itself, then you have to take it."

"I don't have anything. I just believe there's something else waiting for me. I've learned a lot over the past three years. And I appreciate the opportunity you gave me."

Sean could feel his birthmark beginning to throb. The pain was radiating down his leg. He shifted in his seat, trying to ease the discomfort. It didn't help.

"You're not leaving for a couple of months," said Larry. "Why not give it two more weeks before making a final decision? Perhaps I can come up with something that will really interest you."

In the past few minutes, Sean had come to appreciate Larry far more than he had in the past three years. The man hadn't mentioned anything about giving Sean the job when he was unemployed. Larry had helped Sean out when he needed someone to believe in him. For that, he'd always be grateful.

The UN was Larry's life. But it wasn't for Sean. He'd given it all he had for three years. It was time to move on. "My mind's made up. I'm going. Thanks for everything and for making it so difficult to leave."

"I'll be in touch over the next couple of weeks," replied Larry. "All I'm asking is that you keep an open mind."

The conversation ended with Sean agreeing to hold back the letter confirming his departure for two weeks.

Placing the phone in its cradle, Sean noticed the pain in his leg was subsiding. He wondered briefly why his birthmark had flared up but didn't give it too much thought. The important thing was, now that he'd told Larry, he wanted to let Ahmad know before the news of his departure was all over the compound. He'd tell his friend in the morning when they met for breakfast.

Sean shut down his computer, switched off the desk lamp, and made his way to the cafeteria.

Later, after a meal of roast beef, potatoes, and peas, along with a desert of tapioca pudding, he ventured outdoors and walked quickly to his unit. Opening the door, he hurried in and felt the welcoming warmth. Later, as he lay in bed, his thoughts naturally found their way to Hilary. He fell asleep wondering if they'd ever speak again.

# Chapter 12

Hilary had first noticed a lack of energy about six months ago. Used to working fourteen to fifteen hour days, she was finding it increasingly difficult to summon the energy needed to maintain that pace. She had stopped going to the gym for her customary workouts because the regimen was proving too difficult. Although her eating habits hadn't changed, she was losing weight.

She needed to see her doctor. It took a week to land an appointment. After that, there'd been some preliminary tests. Once the results had come back, Hilary's doctor had immediately sent her to a carousel of cancer specialists. And now she was in an office at Princess Margaret Hospital waiting for the final diagnosis.

The hospital is one of Canada's premier cancer research, diagnostic, and care facilities. Hilary was under no illusions. She was prepared for the worst which meant some form of cancer had been diagnosed. It would mean treatment and might even include several rounds of chemotherapy, radiation therapy, or even surgery.

She would have to make adjustments to her life and office schedule, but she'd get through it the same way she conquered everything in her path—with equal parts determination, a positive attitude, and by facing the problem straight on.

The door opened, and in walked the doctor. Holding out her hand, she introduced herself as Dr. Beverly Hudson, an oncologist. Hilary took the proffered hand and then watched as the doctor settled at her desk.

A petite woman, Dr. Hudson had raven black hair worn in a tight bun. Soft brown eyes lay sheltered behind rimless glasses. Her finely chiseled face, with high cheekbones and a thin nose, gave no sign of what news she was about to impart. The doctor was wearing a crisp, white medical coat over a light blue pantsuit with matching blouse. Hilary guessed she was in her mid-forties.

"Before we begin, is there anyone waiting for you?" asked Dr. Hudson. "They can come and sit with you while we discuss the diagnosis."

Hilary shook her head. "It's just me."

The doctor frowned. "I have some difficult news for you," she said. Her eyes were warm, caring, and filled with regret.

Hilary nodded. She wished the doctor would get on with telling her the situation's seriousness. She'd scheduled a client meeting for later that afternoon and needed a couple of hours back at the office to prepare.

The doctor paused. In that moment, Hilary had a premonition the news was far worse than she'd expected.

"You have an advanced stage of pancreatic cancer. There are also cancerous tumors in your lungs and liver."

The words hit like a blow to the stomach. Hilary was having difficulty breathing. Sweat was breaking out on her forehead. For the first time in her life, she felt real and all-consuming fear. It tore through her body, ripping away at every ounce of composure she possessed. She wanted to cry, yet the tears wouldn't come. Clasping her hands, she bent over double in the chair and began to rock back and forth. Dr. Hudson got up and rounded the desk, putting a hand on Hilary's back.

The doctor asked if there was someone she could contact to come for her. Hilary shook her head. She'd told no one, not even her parents, about the tests. She'd been waiting for the results. There was always the possibility it wasn't cancer, or that it was benign. She prided herself on being independent. And what was the use of worrying her parents if it turned out there was nothing to be concerned about?

*This can't be happening to me*, she thought.

Hilary had been prepared for bad news, but the doctor's diagnosis was devastating.

"How long do I have?" she managed to ask.

"I'm not looking at it that way," replied Dr. Hudson. "We're going to treat your cancer aggressively with chemotherapy and radiation. I'm also looking at the possibility of surgery."

The oncologist began saying something about having a positive attitude. But Hilary didn't hear the words. All that kept revolving through her mind was pancreatic cancer. Her research had told her it was one of the worst forms of the frightful disease. The survival rates were tragically low.

The doctor was still talking. Hilary began to focus on the words.

"We're going to immediately begin treatment. I've booked a room for you, and I want to see you in this office at eight tomorrow morning. There'll be a nurse here who'll register you. After that, we'll get you taken up to your room and get you settled."

This was all moving too quickly. She was worried about her caseload. Checking in tomorrow was impossible. Time was needed to review everything with her father. Hilary felt devastated that she was letting him down. She knew it was an irrational thought, but that was all she could think about.

The doctor pulled up a chair and sat beside Hilary. "You have a long road ahead of you," she said. "And I'll be with you for every step."

"Can I beat this thing, Dr. Hudson?"

The doctor looked directly at her. Warmth and compassion radiated from her eyes. "It's going to be a tough struggle," she said. "There will be good days and some very bad days. It's my job to make sure you have all the care you need. Together, we'll fight this thing."

Hilary knew that was all she was going to get. The doctor wasn't going to make a promise when it involved a monster like cancer.

"I'll need a few days to clear things up at my office," said Hilary. "It's impossible for me to be here tomorrow morning. What about the beginning of next week?"

Dr. Hudson frowned; her eyes turned flinty. "This is far more serious than anything you might have at your office," the doctor said forcefully. "I want you in here tomorrow, and I'm not prepared to accept any reasons why that can't be done. We have tests and treatments already scheduled."

Hilary's composure almost cracked. She felt weak and disoriented. The situation's gravity had been brought home with the doctor's words. This was really happening to her. She was again feeling cold; yet there was a fine film of sweat on her forehead and upper lip. Her mind was raging. This was so unfair.

But then the Hilary who'd stared down and beaten nearly every top lawyer in Canada, who'd successfully navigated the legal labyrinth of every case she'd taken on, and who'd lived up to her father's incredible expectations began to assert herself. She'd put her responsibilities at BDK aside for the time it took to defeat this snake that was chewing up her insides.

This was a battle she was determined to win. Her total focus and every grain of energy she possessed would be devoted to one thing—defeating the enemy within.

"I'll be here tomorrow morning," Hilary said in firm and determined voice.

# Chapter 13

It was unusual. For one of the few mornings since they'd started working together, Ahmad hadn't knocked on Sean's door ready to accompany him across the compound. *He must be on an assignment with another group*, thought Sean. Still, it was strange that Ahmad hadn't mentioned anything about it. Breakfast would be a solitary affair.

Closing the door to his unit, he savored the morning's relative warmth. Kabul and the surrounding region were enjoying a rarity in an Afghanistan winter, temperatures well above the freezing point.

*The day won't be filled with snow*, he thought.

It was a good sign. This was his last day in the country. He was flying out the following morning. As long as this weather held, there'd be no problem with his flight. After three years, he didn't want anything to interfere with his departure.

He thought back to his conversation with Larry. The man was as good as his word. He'd phoned two weeks after their initial talk. Sean had remained firm about leaving, and nothing Larry said had convinced him to change his mind. The call had ended with the two remaining on good terms. Sean had promised to contact Larry before committing to another job. His resignation letter had been delivered to Larry several days later.

Walking slowly across the compound, Sean noted the soldiers at the checkpoints and along the barricades seemed more tense than usual. There were also more of them, and all were holding their AK-47s at the ready. It was an unnerving sight. Security being this tight around the green zone meant that, during the night, the Taliban had struck somewhere in Kabul.

Entering the UN complex, he turned left and walked down the hallway to the cafeteria. Although it was still early, he was met by the rattling of dishes, the smell of just cooked food, the captivating aroma of coffee, and a dozen conversations taking place at tables spread throughout the room. It was familiar and comfortable. While getting his plate filled with eggs, ham, and toast, he asked if anyone had seen Ahmad. The Afghani staff members behind the counter shook their heads and indicated surprise the translator wasn't with Sean.

Once he'd filled his cup with coffee, Sean looked around for a table to join. He saw one at the back of the room where several engineers who were involved in the water irrigation project were eating. They were always good company. He began to navigate through the tables and chairs, heading their way. He'd just reached the table when he felt a hand on his arm.

It was Karen, the executive assistant to the secretary general's special representative, Denis Gauthier. She looked somber, and her eyes were red rimmed.

"Mr. Gauthier wants to see you," she said.

"Can it wait for just a bit?" Sean asked. "I've just picked up my breakfast. It won't take me long. I'll be there in about ten minutes."

Karen tightened her lips. *Not a good sign*, thought Sean.

"He wants to see you now."

Something in the tone of her voice told Sean this was no ordinary summons.

"It's serious, isn't it?" he said.

Karen just nodded, her eyes filling with tears.

An uneasy feeling began to wriggle its way through Sean's stomach and into his chest. He put the tray down on an empty table and followed her out of the cafeteria and along a long hallway that led to Gauthier's office. The office door was shut, but Karen didn't bother to knock. She quickly opened it and ushered Sean in. The door closed behind him.

Gauthier was a diminutive, pear-shaped man, with thick, square glasses and a luxurious mustache. He carried himself with the studied air and mannerisms of an old and fussy French professor. His office uniform was always three-piece suits, and Sean had never seen him with his jacket off or the vest undone. French was his native tongue, and he spoke English with the precision of one who has laboriously studied the language. His desk was a messy collection of books, reports, loose pages, and several pen holders.

He was seated behind the desk and waved Sean over to one of the guest chairs. As Sean sat, Gauthier offered a quiet bonjour. He tapped his fingers on the edge of his chair and then shuffled some papers from one side of the desk to the other.

"I have some sad and terrible news," he began.

Sean's first thought was that something had happened to Hilary or to one of his parents. He was suddenly filled with regret and deep sadness that he hadn't once spoken to Hilary and only infrequently to his mother and father during the past three years.

"There's been a killing in Kabul."

Without being told, Sean knew what was coming next. His stomach muscles tightened, and he felt a chill run up his back.

"I wish there was an easier way to tell you this," said Gauthier, who seemed to have shrunk in his chair. "Ahmad was assassinated last night. The loss is devastating to all of us, but I know the two of you had become close friends. I'm so sorry for having to give you this news."

"How did it happen?"

"From what we can determine, he was walking home after leaving here yesterday evening. A motorcycle with a rider pulled up behind him. He was shot three times in the back. The Taliban have claimed responsibility."

Gauthier continued to talk, Sean wasn't listening. Ahmad was dead. Killed by the Taliban. A weary sadness overcame him as he grieved for his friend, shot dead on a Kabul street.

"Have you been in contact with his family?" Sean whispered.

Gauthier appeared confused.

"I didn't know he had a family. I checked our records this morning, and there's no mention of a wife or children."

"His family is here in Kabul," responded Sean. "Ahmad thought it was too dangerous to let anyone know he was married and had kids."

"I suppose that's a reality for the Afghanis who work for us," Gauthier said. "We'll liaise with the local militia to have them track down his address. After that, we'll see what can be done to assist the family."

Sean nodded but said nothing. His feelings were still numb from the news.

Gauthier gave him a sympathetic look. “Perhaps you should get out of here for a few hours,” he suggested, his voice filled with compassion. “This isn’t a good place for you to be right now. Too many memories.”

“Thanks. That’s a good idea,” said Sean. “If anyone needs me, I’ll be in my unit.”

Leaving the office, he walked slowly down the hallway. Some people had heard about Ahmad, and they stopped Sean to offer their condolences. He finally made it to the door and out into the compound. He stood for several minutes, trying to comprehend the death of a man who had done nothing wrong. Sean tried to make sense of it, but the rationale wouldn’t come. There was no justification. And as with all murders, that was the true tragedy.

# Chapter 14

Sean lay back on his bed and ran a shaky hand over his face. He was leaving in the morning. It wasn't supposed to end this way. He thought of a wife and children he didn't know. What would they do without a husband and father? He was angry and wanted to lash out. But at whom or, just as important, at what? The feeling of impotence only made the tragedy harder to bear. The killers would never be found. And who would even try to bring them to justice?

Getting up, he grabbed the most recent copy of *The New York Times* and climbed back onto the bed, intent on reading for a few hours. Instead, he promptly fell asleep.

From somewhere, there was a loud noise. He came awake slowly, realizing that it was the telephone. He'd been in a deep sleep, dreaming about trying to warn Ahmad. He was yelling at his friend, but the man just kept walking away. Then had come the shots. Too many to count. Bathed in sweat, Sean lay in bed, hoping that whoever was calling would hang up. But it didn't stop. Picking up the receiver, he heard Karen's voice asking if everything was okay.

In a voice thick with sleep, he told her things were as good as they could be and that he'd be back in the office to say his final farewells to the few who knew he was leaving.

"We're having a small memorial in the cafeteria for Ahmad around four," Karen told him. "I was hoping you'd say a few words."

"I'll be glad to. It's the least I can do in his memory."

After hanging up, Sean looked at his watch and saw it was just past three. Enough time for a shower and to give some thought to what he was going to say.

He arrived at the reception a few minutes after four. People were standing in small groups, each with a drink in one hand and most with a cigarette in the other. There was an open bar, and one of the engineers was pouring drinks. The mood was subdued and the conversations muted. Ahmad's killing was a stark reminder to everyone that they lived and worked in a war zone. The enemy existed just beyond the thin defensive line of soldiers, razor wire, and barricades.

Although Sean didn't feel like drinking, he picked up a Heineken from the bar. For the next hour, he joined various groups and did a lot of listening while speaking very little. He made sure to search out those who knew he was going the next day. He'd been well liked and, as is usual with good-byes, there were pledges to stay in touch. It would never happen, but the basic human need to wish that someone who has entered one's life and is leaving as a friend will stay a part of it, regardless of how tenuous the thread is strong.

It was about five-thirty when Karen came up to him. She explained that Gauthier was going to say a few words and then hand the microphone to Sean.

Just as she finished speaking, Gauthier picked up the handheld mike and strode to one corner of the room. He offered some kind remarks about Ahmad's commitment and dedication to the UN. He then passed the mike to Sean and faded into the crowd.

Standing quietly for a moment, Sean collected his thoughts. Although Ahmad had been with the UN for almost a decade, he wasn't well-known throughout the complex. Sean wanted to change that and hoped that, at the end of his words, his friend would be remembered as more than a translator.

"For those of you who are wondering what Ahmad was like," he began, "I can tell you that intellectually he was a curious, thought-provoking, and extremely intelligent man. He was forty-one and married with three children.

"Ahmad was one of those people who do their job efficiently and quietly.

"But he was more than an Afghani worker at the UN. To all of the villages he and I visited, Ahmad was the face of the United Nations in Afghanistan. He spoke both native languages, Afghan Persian and Dari, and he explained to all the village elders the many programs the UN had in place to try to make Afghanistan a better place to live; to raise a family; and for many, to farm.

"He talked about the UN's dedication to peace and the betterment of countries. He didn't always believe in the methods the UN used in its foreign offices, but he was committed to the overall concept of assisting people to better themselves.

"Ahmad was killed because he chose to work with the United Nations rather than follow the dictates of the Taliban.

"Ahmad did a dangerous job extremely well, and it cost him his life. He died for a way of life that all of us here live and, I hope, believe in. Ahmad had only the belief part to hold onto, and in the end, that wasn't enough. We became good friends, and I'll miss him."

Sean switched off the mike and placed it on top of a speaker. A number of people came up to him and said how much they were going to miss Ahmad. When the last person drifted away, Sean looked up to see that the cafeteria was empty.

He shrugged his coat on and proceeded outside, where he began to walk across the compound. Sean garnered little attention from the guards as he passed alongside the fortified perimeter and headed toward his unit. The wind, blowing in from the north, was cold and dry, telling Sean that snow would not be a problem for his flight.

The darkness enveloped him as he hurried along. The cold pierced his coat. He started to shiver.

The UN plane was leaving for Karachi at ten the following morning. From there, he'd fly to Paris and spend some time touring around Europe.

Entering his room, he switched on the portable heater and stood in front of it for a few minutes, trying to get some warmth into his body. He took off his coat, threw it on the bed, and sat in the room's one comfortable chair.

Once again, he was at a point in his life where the future appeared uncertain. It was frustrating because he didn't know what he was looking for. His only hope was that he'd recognize it when the time came.

But the years were passing. He was in his mid-thirties and still looking for a purpose to his life. That search had cost him the woman he loved and sent him from a job with a perfect future to one of earth's most desolate places. And he had nothing to show for it. Still, he had no choice. Something was driving him, and he had to see where it would lead.

He looked around the room that had been his home for three years. The only personal item, besides his clothes, was the framed photograph of Hilary taken on their honeymoon. It sat beside the phone and the UN-issued alarm clock.

The birthmark on his thigh began to throb. He stretched out the leg, trying to relieve the pain. It worked to some extent but was still uncomfortable. Getting up, he prowled the small room for a few minutes, which seemed to help. Looking at the clock, Sean saw it was getting late. He pulled his duffel bag off the closet's top shelf and began packing.

Almost everything that comprised his meager wardrobe was in the bag when the phone rang. He picked up the instrument and heard his father's voice for the first time in two months. The relationship between father and son had been strained since Sean had left BDK. Sean hadn't told Tom this would be his last day in Afghanistan. He was about to tell his father that he was heading to Paris the following day and would be out of touch for a few months, when Tom cut him off.

When Sean heard the words Hilary and cancer, his heart started to race. Tom's words betrayed an urgency that Sean had seldom heard.

"Why am I just finding out about this now?" asked Sean, the anger rippling through his voice.

"Hilary was very specific," responded Tom. "The only people who knew how ill she was were her parents and your mother and me. She was determined to beat this thing and swore us to complete secrecy. Hilary was adamant that we not tell you. She felt that with all the things you had to face in Afghanistan you didn't need the worry of her illness distracting you."

"And that was more important than telling me my wife had cancer?"

"Listen son," pleaded Tom. "I'm truly sorry you're just finding out about this. But when we last spoke she'd just started her treatment. None of us ever believed she wouldn't get better. We were wrong. The cancer spread so rapidly and it's only been in the last few days that everything has become extremely serious."

"I'll be there as soon as I can catch a flight," said Sean. "But you should have told me. I'm still her husband, or did everyone forget?"

"You're right," responded Tom. "But that's in the past. Just get here as quickly as you can."

After hanging up, Sean fell back on the bed in a daze. It all seemed impossible, but Hilary was dying. He'd fly to Karachi in the morning. Once there he'd book a flight to New York and from there to Toronto. After three years, he was going home to see Hilary. He didn't notice that his thigh was no longer giving him pain.

# Chapter 15

Sean was amazed at how small Hilary looked. There was hardly any shape to the sheet and blanket that covered her. She was curled up on her side, asleep. Her head was covered with a knitted cap. He suspected that she'd lost her hair with the chemotherapy and radiation treatments. A breathing mask covered her nose and mouth. Hilary's cheeks were so hollowed out that her face had the appearance of a death mask. Everywhere he looked there were tubes hooked up to her. He knew that one of them was a self-controlled morphine drip for use when the pain became too severe.

While he'd expected Hilary to be in bad condition, what he saw was agonizing. The vibrant, beautiful woman who he was still in love with was no longer there.

Mixed with his sadness was anger at whatever universal force had conspired to have Ahmad killed and Hilary brought to the doorway of death. A tightness clutched at his chest as he thought of the unfairness.

Why take two people in the prime of their lives? Where was the justice, the rationale?

He knew Hilary wasn't going to win this battle. The phone call from his father had indicated as much.

For a few moments, Sean wanted to leave. The travel and changing time zones had been tough. He hadn't showered or changed clothes since leaving Afghanistan. He'd booked himself into the downtown Sheraton while at the airport. Checking in, grabbing a few hours of sleep, and then getting cleaned up seemed like a good idea—anything to avoid the fact that the woman he loved was dying. But that wasn't an option.

The bed covers moved and the body under them slowly turned in his direction. Hilary was awake and staring at him. The first thing he noticed was her eyes. No longer were they the radiant and piercing ice blue that he remembered. Instead, they'd lost most of their color. They looked dull and listless.

She shifted her right hand, the one that didn't have an electronic pulse monitor attached to its index finger and tubes coming out the top of it. She beckoned him over while moving the mask down to her chest. Sean sat on a chair by the bed and clasped her hand. He could feel the bones through skin that felt like tissue paper. Her lips were dry and cracked. He asked if she wanted some water. Hilary slowly shook her head.

"You're supposed to be in Afghanistan," she whispered. "What are you doing here?"

"My father phoned saying you were in hospital. I came as fast as I could."

"It's good to see you," Hilary murmured. "You probably got here just in time."

Sean was stunned. Hilary had always met life head-on, but he hadn't expected such candor. It took him a few moments to think of something to say.

"We made some good memories," he said. "Why don't we talk about a couple of them? It'll take your mind off how you're feeling. Let's start with those early days in the apartment."

Hilary held his hand tighter.

"Don't let's pretend everything is going to be fine," she said. "This is a time for truth. I'm dying."

She stopped, and Sean could see it was a struggle for her to speak.

"Why don't you rest," he said. "We don't have to talk. I'm just happy to be with you."

Hilary swallowed and grimaced in pain. She raised her head slightly. For just a moment, her eyes cleared and there was a clarity in her look that reminded Sean of the way Hilary had been.

"Promise me one thing," she rasped, increasing the grip on his hand.

"Anything," he responded.

"Don't forget me."

"I'll never do that," he pledged. "You'll always be a part of my life."

She gave him a weak smile and her head dropped back on the pillow.

"I'm really tired," she mumbled. "Think I'll get some sleep."

Her voice was faint and hoarse. He could barely hear the words. She was drifting in and out of consciousness. Sean knew instinctively that her time was growing short.

Hilary let go of his hand. Sean bent over and gave her a gentle kiss on the forehead. The skin felt dry and brittle.

He was fighting to hold back tears, but it was no use. Twin rivulets ran down his cheeks. Sean brought a hand up and wiped them away. He heard the room door open but didn't take his eyes off Hilary. He felt a hand on his shoulder. Looking up, he saw it was his father. Tom's gaze went from Hilary to his son. If sadness and despair could be measured in grains of sand, his look would have emptied a desert.

"Let's go out to the hall," said Tom.

Sean nodded and followed his father out of the room. The door closed and they walked a few steps into the corridor. A nurse passed behind them and went into the room. The sight of Hilary had wiped all the resentment at not being told sooner from Sean. How could he be angry with anyone, especially his father, when the woman he loved was dying?

Sean reached over and brought Tom in close with a deep hug. The father wound his arms around his son. They stood, silently trying to gain strength from each other.

As Sean backed a couple of steps away he asked, "How long does she have? From the little I could tell, she doesn't look good."

"As I told you on the phone, there isn't much time left," Tom said.

"What exactly does that mean?"

"We're talking days at the most. That's why I was so insistent that you come back right away."

The reality hit Sean hard. He felt lightheaded, and his legs went weak. All the weariness and stress of the past twenty-four hours was drowning him. He was having difficulty breathing, struggling to catch his breath. He leaned against the wall.

Tom watched, his face a mask of concern.

"You need some rest. I'm going back to the office. Why not walk out with me and take a cab to the house. You'll be staying with us, of course."

Sean slowly shook his head.

"I'll be there tomorrow. I've already booked myself into the Sheraton. I need some time alone to process what's happening with Hilary. I'll stay here for another few hours and then walk over to the hotel. It's just a lot easier."

"Your mother will be disappointed. She was looking forward to seeing you this evening. But we've waited three years. So if you need some time alone, by all means take it."

Sean was grateful for the understanding. Hilary was slipping away from him. All the dreams he'd had about getting back together would never happen. The end was coming, and he wasn't ready to let her go.

"If anything happens during the night, I'll call you," Tom said.

He gave his son a long hug and proceeded down the corridor. Sean went back into the room. The nurse had put Hilary's breathing mask back on. She stayed a few minutes longer and then left. For three hours, he sat beside the bed. Hilary didn't move or come awake. Various nurses and doctors came and went, checking the machines, tubes, and read-outs. Little was said. Sean didn't ask how Hilary was doing, and no one volunteered any information.

The machines and gauges continued to give their readings, oblivious to the dwindling life they were measuring. Fluids flowed down tubes in an effort to make these last few hours as pain-free as possible.

Sean looked at his watch. It was just past nine. He'd been awake for more than thirty hours. He needed sleep. Getting up slowly, he leaned over and kissed Hilary on the cheek. He picked up his duffel bag and left the hospital.

The night air was cold and crisp. It cleared his head but not his mind. Images of Hilary chased themselves through his thoughts as Sean walked over to the Sheraton.

He checked in, rode the elevator up to his assigned floor, walked the hallway until he was in front of the right number, swiped the key card, and let himself into the room. Throwing his duffel bag on the bed, he lifted the phone and dialed room service. He ordered coffee, a club sandwich, and apple pie for desert. He left the bar fridge alone. Sean wanted a clear head in case his father called.

Later that evening after the dinner dishes had been left in the hallway for pickup, he sat on the bed letting the sorrow and anguish wash over him. Hilary was dying. And there was nothing he could do about it.

The phone rang. It was just past 3:00 a.m. Sean was awake. He was still on Afghanistan time, and despite his weariness, sleep wouldn't come. Without picking up the phone, Sean knew what his father was going to tell him.

# Chapter 16

The pews of St. Michael's Cathedral on Toronto's Church Street were full. It was a gathering of the city's elite. From lawyers, politicians, and business titans to former classmates, coworkers, and friends, they'd all come to honor Hilary. The media was there to record the closing chapter in a legal story that had carried such promise, only to end in an untimely death.

Floral wreaths dominated the altar. The speakers talked about how much Hilary would be missed and paid tribute to her tenacity and brilliant legal mind.

Sean wouldn't remember much about the service or the burial. He was one of the pallbearers and performed his duty in a fog of remorse. It seemed impossible to believe that he'd never see Hilary again. And yet that was how his life would unfold.

The reception was hosted by Hilary's parents at their house in Forest Hill. Massive chandeliers provided a range of dappled lighting across the guests as they wandered through the three heavily carpeted rooms set up for the event. In his brief opening remarks, Brian had told everyone to enjoy themselves, for the reception was a time to admire and pay tribute to what Hilary had accomplished in her life. And the attendees took his words to heart. People flowed from room to room in a desperate need to believe that death could be thwarted by sharing a laugh and a drink with the living.

In case guests found it difficult to wend their way to one of three bars, waiters and waitresses in black pants, gold lamé shirts, and black waistcoats deftly made their way through the crowd while serving glasses of red or white wine along with canapés.

The networking was intense, and the conversations animated. The smiles, handshakes, and cheek kisses rolled continuously through the room. As the hours flowed from daylight to dusk, the decibel level increased accordingly.

Sean spoke briefly to Hilary's parents. The conversation was largely one-sided as Brian focused on how much the firm would miss Hilary. Sean and Laura remained silent. Brian seemed intent on ignoring that he'd lost a daughter. Sean was relieved when a provincial judge shouldered his way into the group wanting advice from Brian on a paper he was writing. Sean said his farewells and slipped quietly away.

And now he was wedged in beside one of the bars, sipping on a Molson Canadian. Looking around the room, he couldn't help but think that two people important to his life had been taken in just a few days. He thought of the difference in the receptions, but it all amounted to the same thing. Somehow, in coming together, those who remained had used the occasions to either consciously or subconsciously push back the dark curtain of death. For a few brief moments in time, there was the realization of life's fragility and the precious gift that each new day brings to the living.

It made Sean think of his quest to do something that satisfied the deep desire driving him to find a meaning to his life. And then he laughed to himself. His quest for self-fulfillment wasn't taking him very far into the future.

Sean planned to spend some time with his parents and then catch a flight to Paris. That was about as far as his planning had gone. He was ready to leave the reception. Memories of Hilary weren't here. They rested securely in his mind, his heart, and his soul.

Sean left the house and walked down the street to his rented car. He turned the key in the ignition and slowly drove away from his past. What the future held he didn't know, but it would certainly be lonely, with only memories of Hilary to keep him company.

# Chapter 17

Larry was in a quandary. It had been a month since he'd telephoned Elijah in Inverness to let him know that Sean was leaving the UN. So far, there'd been no return call. He knew the Prophet's visits to the Scottish port city were irregular. That still didn't ease his concern. He'd been asked to inform Elijah if something happened with Sean's status at the UN. The fact he'd left and was wandering around Europe constituted a big change.

Larry needed to know what the Prophet expected. He wondered if the message had been passed along but knew his unease was foolish. Elijah was surrounded by the Guardians, an extremely capable group of men and women. He decided to wait another week. If he heard nothing from Elijah, he'd phone again.

Several days later, as he hung up from a call, the phone rang. Elijah's calm and relaxed voice immediately put Larry at ease, as it always did. It had been three years since they'd spoken. Yet the Prophet had the rare ability of making it seem as though no time had passed since their last conversation. They talked about Larry's parents, his work at the UN, and Elijah's long-standing invitation to visit him.

After about ten minutes, the Prophet easily steered the conversation to Sean. Larry told him that Sean was no longer with the UN and how much he'd be missed in Afghanistan.

"He's touring around Europe for a few months before deciding what to do next. But he promised to contact me before committing to anything specific."

And then Elijah said something that once again reminded Larry of the Prophet's vast network.

"Sean didn't make it to Europe. We heard from our people in Toronto that he's in the city."

Elijah paused for several seconds.

"His wife died from cancer two weeks ago," the Prophet said quietly. "He went back to Toronto so he could be with her."

"Hilary's dead? That's terrible news. It must be really tough for Sean, especially after what happened in Kabul just before he left."

Larry couldn't keep the emotion out of his voice as he told Elijah about Ahmad's death. "How's Sean holding up?"

"As you can imagine, he's having a difficult time," answered Elijah. "But he'll get through it. Sean's a tough-minded person."

"What do you want me to do?" asked Larry. "Is Sean still a high priority?"

"I can't stress enough how important he is to all of us," replied Elijah.

"Does he know anything about Janus?" asked Larry.

"There's no way he could," responded Elijah. "What's critical, though, is that he's destined to play an integral role in the island's future. But he's not ready for that just yet. We need to give him time to get over Hilary's death. And there are things I have to do here to prepare the islanders for his visit. Given our history, that's going to take at least a couple of years."

Larry was again reminded of how slowly everything moved on Janus.

"In the meantime, Sean's going to be looking around for work that'll interest him," continued the Prophet. "It's important we find something that uses his skills as a lawyer and the experience he gained in Afghanistan.

"There's a newspaper publisher in London who's part of our diaspora. I've already talked to him, and there's a job waiting for Sean when he's ready to start working. I believe it's something that would interest him."

"He'd have a hard time turning down the chance to work and live in a city like London," noted Larry.

"And this is where I'm going to need your help, Larry."

"Whatever I can do."

"I'd like you to call Sean and let him know that, once he's ready to start working, you have something that might suit him. He'll not be ready to talk about his future, so don't push him. We have to be considerate of his feelings. That's the most important thing right now. Appreciate what he's been through and let him take his time. Once he's finished grieving, Sean will get in touch."

"What if he doesn't call back?"

"You told me that, during your last conversation with him, he promised to call you before taking on anything new. He'll call, even if it's just out of curiosity to find out what you have that could interest him."

"Why is Sean so important?" asked Larry.

Elijah paused for several seconds. "He has the Mark of Janus."

"The raised triangle on his left thigh," Larry exclaimed. "Does Sean know what it means?"

"We're sure he doesn't," responded Elijah. "Sean made an effort to find out when he was younger. A private investigator was hired. But we managed to keep the information hidden from him. The time wasn't right for Sean to know, and it still isn't."

A stab of confusion pierced Larry's thoughts. "There's something I don't understand," he said. "My parents told me the Mark of Janus was no longer a part of the island's succession. It was supposed to have ended years ago with the death of Lucas Kilgore in the car crash. The family died out."

Elijah explained how Sean was the Kilgore's son and that he'd been adopted by the Brennan's.

Larry was staggered. Sean's future was directly linked to the island and to Elijah. He was being asked to ensure Sean made it to London. Larry was determined not to disappoint the Prophet.

"You'll hear from me, the moment I have an answer from Sean about the newspaper."

“Good. But remember, don’t push him. For this to work, Sean must believe he’s continuing to control his destiny. That’s the most important part of this plan.”

“I understand.”

Larry was about to thank Elijah for involving him when he realized the Prophet was no longer on the line. He hung up the phone and looked up the number for BDK. He knew Sean wouldn’t be there, but it was the only place he knew where to begin.

# Chapter 18

The Heathrow control tower brought the Air Canada Boeing 767-ER flying from Toronto to London in on Runway 09L/27R, the airport's northern airstrip. As the craft touched down, it used almost 5,700 feet of the approximately 13,000-foot runway in landing and slowly lumbered to Terminal Three. Sean checked his watch and saw the flight was on time, arriving just before 8:30 pm.

The aircraft pulled up to the gate, and one of the flight attendants opened the cabin door. Sean took his travel bag from the overhead bin, left the plane, strode down a long corridor, cleared customs, picked up his duffel bag from the baggage carousel, walked outside, took a deep breath of air filled with the smell of aviation fuel, and settled into a taxi. The driver put his bags in the trunk.

Sean gave the address, and soon the cab was lurching through London's congested streets. The nighttime traffic was heavy. Thankfully, the driver wasn't a talker.

Sean settled back and let his thoughts wander through the back roads of his mind.

Following Hilary's funeral, Sean had spent time at his parent's house. He hadn't done much of anything, and they'd been wise enough to leave him alone. Afghanistan and Hilary's death had left him feeling lethargic and lacking any drive to get his life back on track.

Larry had called to offer his condolences and said that, when Sean was ready to work again, he might have something for him. Still reeling from Hilary's death, Sean hadn't given the prospect much thought.

But after a couple of months, boredom had set in. Paris and Europe no longer seemed all that interesting. He wanted to work and thought of what Larry had told him. He called New York and learned that Larry knew of a London newspaper publisher who was looking to hire someone with legal and international experience to produce stories with a global perspective.

It was a rare combination, and the publisher was having difficulty filling the position. The job seemed perfect for Sean. Was he interested? Sean reminded Larry that he had no journalism skills. That didn't seem to matter. There were editors to rework his copy. What the publisher wanted was the viewpoint.

After thinking about it for a couple of days, Sean had called Larry back and asked if the job was still open. Following several transatlantic conference calls between the publisher, Brian Elder; Larry; and Sean, the deal was in place. Sean was hired as a reporter for the *London Advocate*. He didn't give any thought to the convenient timing or that, once again, Larry had injected himself into his life. All Sean knew was that London and a newspaper job were different from anything he'd done.

Would the job fill the gaping hole that was driving him to do something meaningful with his life? Could it calm the burning and aching birthmark that continued to trouble him? Only time would provide the answer, but he felt compelled to continue the search.

Through a British rental agency, he was able to find a fully furnished, one-bedroom flat close to the paper's office. The rent, though expensive, was by the month. He'd signed a six-month lease. Sean wasn't prepared to think any farther ahead. He'd received the keys in the mail only days before leaving.

Sean didn't know what to expect at the paper. He felt, though, it would be less anxiety inducing than practicing law and far safer than Afghanistan. He was again reminded that two people who he'd been close to were dead. He thought of Ahmad and the trips they'd made throughout the Afghan countryside trying to make the Afghani farmers realize the value of a free and open government—Ahmad patiently translating and never once complaining about how the villagers viewed him as a traitor for working with the foreigners.

In the end, his commitment to bettering his country had gotten him killed by the Taliban. And Sean's belief in a just and fair God had withered. It had died along with Hilary. He wasn't angry about his loss. He was still alive. Rather it was the pain Ahmad's family had to bear and the suffering Hilary had endured that angered him.

Neither of them had deserved to die, let alone in the manner they'd been taken. Where was God's mercy? It seemed in short supply. Rather than try to rationalize why God would let things like that happen in his world, Sean found the "why" didn't matter. His withdrawal from such philosophical contemplation wasn't so much a conscious decision as it was an arrival at a destination.

Sean didn't view himself as an atheist or an agnostic. In either case, a person had to have some form of belief. For an atheist, there had to be the thought that a deity didn't exist. Being an agnostic meant committing to not forming a belief about whether or not God existed. Sean had given up on the thought of God. He was indifferent. The arguments had no relevance in his life. It was simply that the existence or nonexistence of some form of deity no longer interested him.

Arriving at the apartment, the cabbie helped with his bags as far as the ground floor landing. It was a thoughtful gesture, and Sean tipped him well.

The building looked old and weary. It was small, red-bricked, three-storied, and faced directly onto the sidewalk. There was a central staircase, with two flats on each floor. Sean carried his bags up one flight of stairs and guided the key into the lock of number 2A. Switching on the light, he found himself in a small flat.

It took him all of three steps to cross what passed for a living room and into a bedroom with barely enough space for a double bed and a small chest of drawers. He placed his bags on the floor. The time was a few minutes short of midnight. His body was still on Toronto time, where it was early evening. However, bone weary from the flight, he pulled the bed covers back. The sheets were clean and crisp.

The kitchen was an alcove that faced onto the living room. And the bathroom, like the rest of the apartment, was small, with barely enough room to turn around in. The place would do just fine, and for the next six months at least, it was home.

Stripping down, he climbed into a fresh pair of boxers and a T-shirt from his duffel bag.

As he settled into bed, he wondered how Hilary would have reacted to what he was doing. The only light in the room was from an overhead bulb with the switch at the door. He was about to get up and put it off, when he decided to close his eyes for just a couple of seconds. Sleep quickly found him, along with dreams of Hilary.

# Chapter 19

Larry looked at his watch. It was just past seven o'clock on a Friday evening. He pushed back from his desk. It had been a relatively calm week. No crisis had emerged to throw his schedule out of line. He'd managed to catch up on several outstanding reports and put in place a planned initiative involving a water filtration plant for just outside Kabul. He got up and was walking over to the clothes cupboard to get his coat when the phone rang, shattering his relaxed mood.

Out of habit, Larry immediately factored in the time difference between New York and the world regions that were his responsibility. It would be close to four in the morning. His stomach muscles began to involuntarily tighten. A ringing phone at this time could only mean one thing—trouble.

He walked back behind his desk and picked up the instrument. There was a pause on the other end, and Larry prepared for the worst.

"Hello, Larry," came the unmistakable voice of Elijah. "It's rather late to be calling, but I wanted to get in touch before you started your weekend."

Larry almost laughed in relief. Still, it was just past midnight in Inverness where he assumed the Prophet was calling from.

What was so urgent that he couldn't have called him tomorrow at home?

"We're sailing for Janus early in the morning," explained Elijah, thus answering Larry's unasked question.

"What can I do for you?" he queried, fully prepared to undertake whatever task the Prophet needed him to complete.

"That's not why I'm calling," responded Elijah. "I wanted you to know that Sean has settled in at *The Advocate*, and from what the publisher tells me, he's doing well. You've done excellent work in handling everything I've asked regarding Sean. I still don't know how things are going to work out with him, but your efforts are much appreciated. Thank you for all that you've done."

They spoke for several more minutes before the call ended. But Larry didn't remember that part of the conversation. What he took with him as he began the journey home was the Prophet's gratitude for a job well done. It left him feeling elated and satisfied, which in Larry's world didn't often happen. He was going to enjoy the sensation for as long as he could. There was a French restaurant in the village Larry frequented regularly enough that he could get a table without a reservation, even on a Friday night. He hailed a cab. It was time to celebrate with a good meal and an excellent bottle of wine.

# CHAPTER 20

Sean was writing a story about neighborhood crime statistics when he noticed the date. In the hectic carousel of writing, editing, and printing deadlines it had almost slipped past him. He'd been in London for two years.

He thought back to his first day. Elder had been the initial person to meet him. Short and thin, the publisher's body was covered by a well-cut, dark suit, complemented with a white silk shirt and blue tie. He had a narrow, friendly face, marked by a hairline that looked to be retreating faster than the Brazilian rain forest.

The editor, Eddie Pitt, was a tall, overweight, bow tie-wearing, ruddy-faced, flamboyant Irishman who knew how to chase a story the way a dog goes after meat. Once he seized on something he thought was newsworthy, Pitt would quickly assign one of his nine reporters. If the story warranted it, a photographer was also dispatched. Unlike many of London's newspapers, *The Advocate* was not a splashy, sensationalism driven journal.

Pitt believed in what he called hard news. He preached that all stories should be based on fact and permitted no anonymous sources. Every quote and piece of information had to be attributable.

Sean's first year had been harrowing, with enough deadline pressure to set his pulse racing several times a week. He'd been assigned the crime beat more because there was a vacancy than his corporate legal background. He learned how to develop and maintain a list of contacts, how to chase down a story, and how to write quickly and efficiently.

Pitt ruled the newsroom like a benevolent dictator. A hard taskmaster, he was fair and honest. He was quick to chastise a poor effort but was equally generous in praise of solid reporting. Sean was a quick learner. The one thing that truly made Pitt's day was if *The Advocate* could break a story before any of the other London dailies. Sean had scooped the competition a number of times during the past two years.

He was a regular front-page contributor and often had the paper's headline story. His hard work and diligence were noticed by Elder. Several weeks previously, Sean had been promoted to assistant editor. It meant that, along with his regular beat, he was responsible for one weekly editorial and an op-ed piece about policing and crime in London.

Sean had kept his apartment on a six-month lease. A year-long commitment at this point in his life seemed like a major thing to do. It wasn't that he was planning on leaving London. He simply didn't want to make any decisions that were too far-reaching.

He always paid a month in advance and had recently opted for another six months. His landlord lived in one of the top floor apartments and appreciated that he never had to chase Sean for the rent.

Sean mostly kept to himself. He developed friends at the paper and occasionally went out drinking with a few of them. Sometimes there was lunch with one of his contacts. However, that was the only socializing he did. Most evenings he worked late, following up on leads and expanding his list of contacts.

He took his meals at a local pub, the Rose & Crown, where he was known as someone who ate alone and tipped generously.

The city's cosmopolitan ambiance wasn't lost on Sean. With its museums, theatres, restaurants, and historical sites, London begged to be explored. When he'd first arrived, Sean had completed several walking tours that included a number of museums, the Tower of London, and Piccadilly Circus. However, he was alone. Not having someone to share the sights with had left the experience barren and joyless. Since then, he'd focused on his work. Just the same, having another person in his life at this time wasn't part of his agenda.

He was content with his relatively solitary existence. London was giving him a chance to reflect on what he wanted to do with his life. Although he enjoyed working at *The Advocate*, he knew the paper wasn't his final stop.

For now, he was taking everything one day at a time. The two years had gone quickly. He realized with startling clarity how engrossing his work had become. He'd fallen into journalism. To his surprise, he found that not only was it a profession he enjoyed but that he also had an innate instinct for what made a good story.

His writing skills were improving. At the beginning, he'd been heavily edited by Pitt. Sean had been forced to do a number of total rewrites during the first six months. However, he was a quick study, and since his promotion, the red lines marking his computer copy had continued to decrease with each month.

# CHAPTER 21

Larry returned his cell phone to the coffee table. He walked to the front window of his well-appointed brownstone. Deep in thought, he stared out at January's wintry weather with sightless eyes.

He'd just had a conversation with Elijah. The Prophet had said it was time for Sean to visit Janus and asked for Larry's assistance in getting him there. Larry hoped he was up to the mission. The island was a special place and this task was different than offering a job with the UN or at *The Advocate*. As always, the request had been made in such a way that Larry knew he was under no obligation. But if having Sean on the island was what the Prophet wanted then Larry would do everything in his power to make it happen.

Janus was an unchartered island in the North Atlantic. Located north of the Shetland Islands, it was known to no government and its citizens existed in complete isolation. Despite the advances in modern cartography, the island remained unmapped and had yet to be discovered. The islanders were adamant in their desire to remain apart from the world.

Elijah had already contacted Elder, and the publisher was in the process of arranging for Sean to have the necessary time away from *The Advocate*. As had been the case in Afghanistan, Sean hadn't taken any holidays since he'd been at the paper and was owed the time. Elijah would work with Larry in convincing Sean to spend his sabbatical on Janus.

The plan was to have Sean visit the island beginning in April.

Larry's role was to get in touch with Sean and let him know that he'd be receiving an e-mail from Elijah. The Prophet didn't explain what the correspondence would contain. More importantly, Larry was to lay the groundwork with Sean by convincing him to read the e-mail and letting him know that Elijah was offering a unique opportunity.

Once that was completed, Larry was to contact Elijah in Inverness and the Prophet would handle the rest.

Larry, knowing of the Prophet's interest in Sean, had maintained a regular connection. The two spoke once every couple of months, under the guise that Larry hoped Sean would reconsider a career with the United Nations. So his touching base wouldn't come as a surprise to Sean. The task was to convince Sean that reading an e-mail from someone recommended by Larry would be to his benefit.

After several more minutes of thought, Larry picked up the phone. First, he'd speak to Elder and get some advice. Sean had to be reeled in slowly, like a fish on the end of a line. He had to believe that visiting Janus was his idea.

#########

Sean had just arrived home from a long day at *The Advocate*.

He picked up the TV remote and was about to switch the television on when his cell phone buzzed. Sean flipped the instrument open and put it to his ear. He was surprised to hear Larry's voice. The man usually phoned him at the paper.

As usual, Larry wasn't one to spend time on idle chat. After a few words about the new year, he got straight to the point and explained that a friend of his would shortly be sending Sean an e-mail.

"The man's name is Elijah. I'd like you to read what he's written and give the words a lot of thought," said Larry.

Sean was perplexed. "Listen Larry," he said, "you're catching me off guard. Who is this Elijah and what does he want? Is it about a story he hopes I'll write?"

"It has nothing to do with *The Advocate*," responded Larry. "Elijah has a proposal that I think you'll find interesting. And you know I'd never steer you wrong."

Sean's curiosity was piqued. Larry was right. Whether it was Afghanistan or *The Advocate*, Larry had been instrumental in Sean's life for almost six years. And so far, things had worked out. What harm would there be in reading an e-mail? "Fine, I'll give it a read," Sean responded. "What happens then?"

"The e-mail will be self-explanatory. After that, whatever decisions you make are up to you. But if you want to talk it through, give me a call."

"I'll do that," said Sean. "Is there anything I should know before I'm contacted?"

"Not really. All I ask is that you approach what's written with an open mind and accept that life is best lived as an adventure."

Sean frowned. It wasn't like Larry to be so free-wheeling with his words. He was a button-down guy who carefully measured what he said. Still, it was one e-mail. Their friendship was worth at least that much.

"Let Elijah know I'm interested."

"That's great," responded Larry. "Elijah's a special person, and I'm sure you'll find what he has to say quite interesting."

With both wishing each other a good year, the two men ended the conversation. As he closed the phone, Sean couldn't help but wonder what Larry was up to. It was an unusual request, but he'd wait and read the e-mail before coming to any conclusions.

# Chapter 22

It was late February and a piercing rain was falling as Sean left the Rose & Crown and turned toward home. He didn't have an umbrella and could feel the cold rain dripping down the back of his neck.

Arriving at his apartment, he changed into a T-shirt and sweatpants. He put on the TV and began a show that was part of BBC's *Masterpiece Theatre*. It didn't hold his interest. The adrenalin was still racing from the day's intensity of writing and filing copy against deadline. Putting the TV off, he picked up the computer and punched in his password for e-mails. An envelope had arrived from Elijah.

He'd almost forgotten about his talk with Larry. It had been a month since their conversation, and the day-to-day rhythm of producing stories for *The Advocate*'s pages had pushed to the back of his mind any thought about an e-mail from someone he didn't know.

But here it was. He opened the file:

As Larry told you, my name is Elijah. If you are reading these words, it means you've opened my e-mail, and I thank you for doing so.

We live in difficult times, and trust for one's fellow traveler is in short supply. That's a sad truth of today's globe. It seems the more the world has been brought together by technology, the greater we have distanced ourselves from human contact with those who are different from us. We mistrust others for the color of their skin, their religion, their culture, or their ethnicity.

We all come into and leave this world through birth and death. It's what happens between those extraordinary events that shape our contribution to the human race. Regardless of who we are, all human beings have a necessity for fulfillment—a feeling that our lives must mean something. Irrespective of the culture, people struggle for recognition. Yet, within this striving for an acknowledgement of one's contribution, people often lose sight of the most valuable lesson offered by life.

Is it so hard to accept the joy of living each day to the fullest? I believe the key to doing so lies in capturing the moments and acknowledging that longing for the past or wishing for the future is to waste the precious gift of today.

Then again, that's the essence of life, isn't it? Many people lead such predictable lives. They get on the road well-traveled, looking neither to the left nor to the right. Unfortunately, it's because of this very routine existence that they are caught by surprise when incidents of significance overtake them. We are all subject to the unforeseen. You have overcome a number of such events because you've chosen to take risks and readily embrace change. It's this desire to venture into the unknown that makes you such a person of interest.

I've been following your articles for *The Advocate*. I admire the passion you bring to your work. While your writing was not what first brought you to my attention, it helped show that my opinions about you were sound.

You're undoubtedly asking yourself a lot of questions. The answers, should you want them, will soon be made clear for you. For now, I'm gratified that you've accepted to open this note.

However, I have no wish to interfere with your life. If I receive no response, I'll assume you have either left this e-mail unopened or have decided not to answer. In that case, you'll not hear from me again. If you'd like to know more, simply reply using whatever words you care to choose.

I anxiously await your decision.

Sean read the message several times. His birthmark was throbbing. Who was this Elijah? Was the man a philosopher, a defrocked priest, or perhaps simply a radical seeking someone to share his views? Unfortunately, his e-mail didn't yield any clues.

Although wary, Sean was curious. He wasn't sure what to write back or even if he wanted to. Yet the man was somehow connected to Larry. That alone necessitated a response. He hit reply and began to type:

I'm not sure what to make of your thought-provoking e-mail. While I appreciate your philosophy about life, I don't understand why you're sharing it with me. In fact, I'm wondering why you've contacted me.

He hit send and went back to the TV. The throbbing in his leg had gradually lessened as he'd typed, until it no longer bothered him.

A tape of a football match between Manchester United and Aston Villa was on TV. United had just taken a one-goal lead when his computer issued a yawning sound, announcing he'd received an e-mail. He checked and saw the envelope was from Elijah. *That was quick*, thought Sean. He opened the file:

I hope my previous message didn't create a concern. That obviously was not the intent. More than anything, I wanted to establish a rapport with you that extends beyond the trivial nature of so many relationships. It's important to me that you regard my entry into your life as an effort at friendship.

The reason for revealing my philosophy is because I think it's something to which you can relate. Your life to date has left you with many questions. Like most people, you are probably seeking a fulfillment that goes beyond what passes for happiness in so many parts of today's world. Can I provide that for you? My belief is I can.

I live in a place that is unique for its peace and abiding belief in the goodness of our neighbors. It is somewhere I know you'd enjoy. Perhaps one day you'll visit us.

For Sean, the response was intriguing. What was meant by referring to his life having left him with many questions? And the last sentence about visiting? He pondered the implications for a few minutes. While he knew nothing would probably come of it, he found the possibility interesting. He'd been working flat out for more than two years. He hadn't taken any time off. Even his weekends were mostly devoted to the paper.

He'd purposely created an existence in London where only his work mattered. All of his emotional commitment was based on a day-to-day passion for digging out leads; using his sources to gather information; and, finally, producing finished copy. *The Advocate* had become his life.

One of the reasons he worked so hard was because he didn't want to spend too much time alone with thoughts of Hilary. Sean realized that, at some point, he'd have to get on with his life.

He knew there was more to life than being emotionally fulfilled by work. Yet here he was, sitting alone in one of the world's most exciting cities. He'd made no effort to discover what London had to offer. What did that say about his future?

A few days away might be just what he needed. Spring would be coming soon. It would be the perfect time to get away from the city. There were many places he could visit. Sean again realized how much he missed Hilary. He went into the bedroom and picked up her picture. He'd placed it on the bureau. It was the last thing he looked at before switching off the light and the first thing he saw in the morning.

He laughed to himself. What would he do with a few days off? After more than two years, he still hadn't visited any of part of London, other than where his job took him.

He vaguely noted that Aston Villa had tied the score. He thought of going to the pub, but it was late and he planned to be at the paper early in the morning. He decided to send Elijah a quick e-mail. Sean wanted to put any thoughts of visiting to rest, at least for the time being.

He wrote quickly:

Don't believe I'll be visiting anytime soon. However, let's stay in touch. One never knows what the future may hold.

# Chapter 23

The evening's cold darkness had again impaled London. A month had passed since Sean had sent his e-mail to Elijah. There hadn't been a reply. It had been a busy time at the paper, and he'd given little thought to time away or to Elijah.

He was at his regular table in the Rose & Crown, enjoying an evening meal of Shepherd's pie along with a pint. Sean's cell rang. It was Larry. As usual, his former classmate got straight to the point.

"I've spoken to Elijah, and he thinks it would be a good idea for you to visit."

Sean was taken aback. "If Elijah's that interested in seeing me, why isn't he making the call?"

"He thought that, since you and I are friends, it would be easier for me to make the arrangements.

Sean let the air slowly escape his lungs in a prolonged sigh. "Look, Larry," he began, "you've helped me out in the past. And that's something I really appreciate. But it's really busy at work. I just don't have any time to go wandering off on holiday."

"You should accept Elijah's invitation."

Sean noted Larry's insistence and was curious. "Why does this mean so much to you?"

A few moments of silence followed before Larry responded. It seemed to Sean he chose he words carefully. "I want you to do this because it will probably change your life."

"Isn't changing my life a bit melodramatic?"

"Not at all. The island is one of the world's most unique places. It's unlike anywhere you've ever been."

"Is that where Elijah lives—on an island? Does this island have a name?"

Larry's voice became guarded. "Those are things you'll find out if you decide to visit."

Sean began to rub his forehead in exasperation. The conversation was going nowhere. It was time to bring it to an end. But he didn't want to hurt Larry's feelings.

""Why don't we leave it that, if I take some time away from the paper, I'll give you a call and we can make arrangements for me to visit this island? How does that sound?"

"It's a fair compromise." Larry laughed.

The call ended with both men promising to stay in touch.

Closing the phone, Sean sat back and pondered what could be behind Larry's desire for him to meet Elijah. And why was this Elijah person, a man who Sean had never met, so interested in having him come to some island? All they'd done was exchange a couple of e-mails. It was all a bit strange but intriguing in a way that had piqued Sean's interest.

Anyway he wasn't planning on taking any time away from *The Advocate* so the whole idea was a nonstarter.

# Chapter 24

It had been a rainy and a chilly March, but as the calendar had turned, so had the weather. April's sun bathed the city in its benevolent and warm glow. Flowers were starting to bloom. Buds had appeared on the trees. Coats were giving way to sweaters and light jackets.

Sean was at his desk editing some copy when Elder came over and asked if he'd join him in his office. The publisher went behind his desk and sat down. Sean took a seat on the comfortable leather sofa.

"I want you to take some time off. I've checked and you haven't had a day of holiday since you joined us."

Sean was about to object when Elder raised his hand. "Listen, Sean, you're an excellent writer. You're a valuable part of the paper, and I don't want to see you burning out. No one is indispensable. We owe you the time. The paper will still be here when you get back. There are people who can fill in while you're gone. Take a couple of days to tie up any loose ends. After that, I don't want to see you around here for at least a month."

"A month?"

"That's right. At least a month. Everyone needs a break. It'll be good for you."

"What about Pitt? How does he feel about my leaving for that long?"

"He's not happy to be losing his top reporter. He complained about not having you for such a long time but realizes it's for the best. The break will do you good."

Sean was at a loss. He'd been going full tilt for more than two and a half years. Suddenly, a month was staring at him with nothing to fill it. His well-ordered life had hit a speed bump. He thought of what he'd do and wondered if it made sense to approach Elijah.

The two men stood. Elder reached his right hand across the desk. As Sean shook it, the publisher said cryptically, "If there's something you've been thinking about doing, now's the time. Perhaps a trip away from the city might be in order."

For the next three days, Sean followed Elder's instructions and made preparations for being away from *The Advocate*. He put six stories, along with three op-ed pieces to bed.

To celebrate his last day, the reporters, along with Pitt, took him out to a pub for a few drinks. It turned into a fun-filled evening of darts, drinks, good food, and newsroom stories. By the time Sean fell into bed, the clock had moved well past midnight.

The next morning, Sean was awake at his usual time. It took a few moments to realize a full day stretched in front of him with nothing that had to be done. He lay in bed for close to an hour debating whether he should take Elijah up on his offer of a visit. He certainly had the time.

There was also the knowledge that many of the issues that had plagued him through his life about a purpose and finding a place to belong were still waiting to be resolved. Could Elijah represent an opportunity to find some answers? It was a remote possibility, but even if nothing came from meeting Elijah, it could prove to be an interesting adventure. He reached for the phone and put in a call to Larry.

Sean closed the phone. It had been a curious call. Larry hadn't seemed surprised that Sean had been given time away from *The Advocate*. It was as if he had been expecting the call. Once Sean explained that he wanted to visit Elijah, Larry said he'd handle the arrangements.

"It'll take me a couple of days to set things up," Larry had said. "Once all the details are finalized, I'll telephone. I'm glad you're going. It's a decision you won't regret. It'll change your perspective on the way people can live together."

"You're making this sound like a life-changing event," said Sean with a chuckle. "I'm just looking for a place to relax and perhaps have some interesting experiences."

Larry hadn't commented on Sean's observation, ending the conversation by saying only that he'd soon be in touch.

# Chapter 25

The call came just before midnight. Rain was performing a steady drumbeat against the living room window. The early-April weather had turned damp and chilly. It had been two days since Sean had spoken with Larry. He'd fallen asleep on the couch, while watching the *BBC News at Ten*. The cell awakened him. Groaning inwardly and still half asleep, he opened the phone. It was Larry.

He began by explaining that arrangements had been made for Sean to be on a flight to Inverness, Scotland, departing from Gatwick the next evening. A ticket and a boarding pass were waiting for him at the airport's British Airways counter.

Sean was suddenly wide awake. "What happens when I get to Inverness?" he asked.

"You'll be met by Andrew. He's what we call a Guardian."

"Guardian," said Sean, surprised by the term. "What's that supposed to mean?"

"It'll become clear once you meet Elijah and travel to the island."

"Where will I be staying?"

"That's been taken care of," responded Larry. "Elijah will have the details."

And then Larry dropped a bombshell.

"It would be good if you could arrange to be away for a couple of months."

"A couple of months." Sean was stunned. "Elder only gave me a month. I can't just phone him and ask for more time away."

"Why not give him a call and see what can be worked out?" suggested Larry. "I gathered from what you told me during our last talk that you haven't taken any time off since starting at the paper. I'm sure Elder will give you the extra month."

"What makes you so sure?" asked Sean.

Silence descended on the line and Sean wondered if the connection had been broken.

"Just get in touch with Elder and see what he says," Larry finally answered.

This was all too sudden for Sean. What was going on? Who were these people? Fifteen minutes ago, he'd been asleep on his couch. The most exciting thing the next day was supposed to hold was a couple of meals at the Rose & Crown. Now he was being asked to pack everything and get ready for a two-month jaunt to some island, the location of which no one had told him.

"Where's the island?" he thought to ask.

"It's off the northern coast of Scotland."

"North of Scotland is where I'm expected to spend two months. You can't be serious. There's nothing up there but a lot of uninhabited islands, some farmers, and a whole bunch of sheep. What am I supposed to do once I get there?"

"All that will be made clear when you meet Elijah," said Larry.

"I've got to give this some thought," said Sean. "Before speaking with Elder I want to be sure disappearing for two months on an island is what I want to do. When will you be in your office tomorrow? I'll give you a call."

"Call me any time after eight," came the reply. "This is a great opportunity. Don't let it pass you by. It's an experience you'll never forget."

The phone went dead. Sean flipped his cell closed.

He sat back on the couch. Sean needed time to think everything through. He hadn't planned any of what was being suggested. Suddenly the exchange of e-mails had moved to Larry telling him he had to be at the airport in less than twenty-four hours for a two-month trip.

Still, he was the one who'd phoned Larry. What was he going to do if he didn't get on the plane to Inverness? This sounded far more interesting than touring around London, or visiting some tropical destination.

Sean knew it was late, but he put a call into his publisher. The phone was answered on the first ring. He told Elder about his conversation with Larry and ended by asking if it was feasible for him to take that much time away.

"You should take advantage of the opportunity," responded Elder. "It sounds like quite an adventure. And you're owed the time."

The two men spoke for several more minutes about how Sean's crime beat would be handled while he was away. Elder ended the conversation by wishing Sean an excellent vacation and telling him to enjoy the experience.

Sean's mind was so preoccupied with the thought of spending two months away from London that it wasn't until much later he recognized how neatly everything had fallen into place.

Closing his cell phone, he went over what he'd be leaving behind in London and realized with startling clarity that it was nothing more than the security of the familiar. He'd left a number of places to live in London. What was to be gained by staying except the safety of doing what he'd done for a couple of years?

There wouldn't be any problems with his rent. He was already paid up a month in advance. Sean would see the landlord early in the morning, give him a check for the extra time he'd be away and ask to have his mail collected.

With his mind made up, Sean went into the bedroom and pulled down his duffel bag, along with an overnight case. It didn't take long to complete his packing. When he'd finished, the closet was empty, as was his clothes chest. He looked around the room and realized that, after more than two years, the only personal item he'd added was the framed photograph of Hilary. He stared at it for a few minutes, remembering what it had felt like to be in love, when the future had seemed limitless, and there was nothing the two of them couldn't accomplish.

He took the photograph and carefully tucked it between his clothes. He placed the bags by the front door. The only things left to pack were his alarm clock, toiletries, and shaving gear. He'd take care of that in the morning.

After that, he'd telephone Larry, see his landlord, and make sure he was at Gatwick in plenty of time to pick up his ticket.

# Chapter 26

Heaving his duffel bag over his shoulder, Sean left the baggage carousel and walked into the Inverness Airport arrivals' area. He'd been told by Larry that Andrew, the man he was meeting, would be waiting for him in front of the WH Smith newsstand.

It took Sean a moment to get his bearings, but he was soon headed in the right direction. He noticed with some irritation that his birthmark was throbbing. As he approached the store a tall, well-built man put a magazine back on the rack and came toward him. Putting out a large, rawboned hand, he said in a soft Scottish lilt, "Hello, Sean, I'm Andrew."

Taking his hand, Sean noted the short, coal black hair; heavily bearded face; and dark brown eyes that stared back at him. The handshake was firm.

"Why don't I take your duffel bag and we can go to the parking lot," said Andrew.

Sean handed over the bag and followed his newfound companion out of the terminal. Banks of lights lit the parking lot, pushing back the night's darkness. A cold mist greeted the men. His birthmark continued to ache.

Andrew stopped at a blue Ford van. He put the duffel bag in the back and climbed in the driver's side while Sean got into the passenger seat. It was chilly inside the vehicle. Andrew started the engine, got the wipers going, and put on the heat. He eased the van out of the parking lot.

"Can we stop by a bank machine?" asked Sean. "I haven't got much cash with me."

"That won't be necessary," replied Andrew. "Cash isn't needed on the island."

"Is it an all-inclusive resort where everything's covered then?"

"It's not, but then you'll find that out when we get there."

*As usual*, thought Sean; he was left with more questions than answers. Just the same, he reminded himself, no one had forced him on this trip. He noticed his birthmark was no longer hammering. *Must just have been nerves*, he thought.

"The Prophet will be glad to see you," said Andrew as they crossed Beauly Firth on the Kessock Bridge.

"Do you mean Elijah?" asked Sean.

"That's right."

"Why do you call him the Prophet?"

"Because Elijah is our mentor. He's a guide and counselor for the relationship everyone on the island has with the Spirit," responded Andrew.

"The Spirit?" questioned Sean.

"It's the universal force that many people refer to as God," answered Andrew.

"Why do you call him the Spirit? And what sort of a relationship do Elijah and your island people have with God?"

"That will all become clear once you meet the Prophet and travel with us to Janus," responded Andrew.

"Is that the name of your island?"

"It is. You won't find it on any map, because it's an unusual and extraordinary place."

Uneasiness gripped Sean. Neither Larry nor Elijah had ever referred to God. And there certainly had never been the mention of Elijah and the rest of those living on the island believing they had a unique connection to the Almighty.

He began to wonder if he was on his way to meet some cult leader.

"What's Elijah like?"

"You'll find him to be kind, humble, patient, and understanding."

"Is he fanatical about this relationship with God?"

Andrew took his eyes off the road long enough to turn his head and stare at Sean. "If you're wondering whether you've stumbled into some sort of religious sect, I can assure you that we're nothing of the kind. And Elijah is the farthest thing from a zealot that you'll find."

The reverence in Andrew's voice was impossible to miss.

"When will I meet him?"

"Soon," responded Andrew, returning his attention to the road.

# Chapter 27

Approaching the Inverness outskirts, Andrew pulled into the driveway of a large, sprawling, and secluded house. A spotlight illuminated the driveway.

"We're here," he said.

The front door opened, and a tall, thin man emerged. As he ambled down the stairs and got near the van, Sean saw close-cropped, red hair; pale gray eyes; pronounced cheekbones that created a channel for a prominent nose; and thin, almost bloodless lips.

Sean opened his door, and the night's cool mist immediately invaded the vehicle's interior. Shivering slightly, he stepped out of the van. He heard, rather than saw, Andrew's door opening.

Looking over the vehicle's hood, he saw the men hug and then walk around the front of the Ford toward him.

"Sean, this is Leyland," stated Andrew. "Like me, he's a Guardian and will be joining us on our trip to Janus."

"Welcome to Inverness," offered Leyland, a large smile creasing his face.

"Let's get inside," said Andrew. "There's someone I'd like you to meet. Don't bother with your bags. We'll be spending the night aboard our ship."

*Aboard a ship*, thought Sean. That would be something new. Already, the trip was proving to be interesting.

Following the men into the house, Sean was glad to feel the home's warmth. He was wearing only a light jacket, and the chilly night air had left him feeling cold.

The trio walked down a narrow hallway before stepping inside a large kitchen. Seated at the table were two men, who stood as the group entered. Introduced by Andrew as Malcolm and Joseph, the two, Sean saw, were identical twins. Slightly shorter than Sean, the twins had wavy, blond hair parted in the middle; pale blue eyes; and strong, prominent jaws. What drew Sean's attention was their bodybuilder physiques. Wide shoulders, heavy chests, and thin waists showed the men regularly worked out.

Obviously used to having the twins confused with each other, Andrew offered, "The way you can tell them apart is that Malcolm has a cleft in his chin."

A noise behind Sean caught his attention. He turned and saw a small, thin man enter the room. He was no more than a few inches over five feet.

"I'm Elijah," he said, shaking Sean's hand. The grip was firm and deliberate.

"It's a pleasure to finally meet you," Elijah offered in a quiet voice that carried a soft lilt.

"The pleasure is mine," responded Sean.

So this was the man who garnered everyone's respect. The only description Sean could think of was that Elijah was too ordinary. He'd imagined a tall, younger, more dominating figure.

Elijah looked to be in his late sixties or early seventies. His thinning gray hair was cut short.

Liquid brown eyes were surrounded by a pair of frameless, round glasses, perched delicately on a prominent nose. Hollowed-out cheeks gave way to full, rich lips that, when parted, revealed a complete set of slightly yellowed teeth. His skin was the color of dried leather.

A green, heavy cotton shirt, buttoned to the throat, was tucked into a pair of brown corduroy pants. On his feet were heavy work boots. Although thin, he appeared fit, with no sign of a paunch or the stooped shoulders that often mark men of his age.

Elijah projected a sense of peace and tranquility that immediately put Sean at ease. He was surprised at the feeling. Throughout his travels, he'd met many people. However, no one had had the immediate impact on him that this unique individual was having.

"We're leaving for the harbor," said Elijah, speaking directly to Sean. "That way we can get an early start in the morning."

As they followed the four Guardians out of the house, Elijah told Sean, "The name of our ship is *Journey*. The trip should take us about twenty-four hours, and we like to arrive at first light."

Getting into the van, it was obvious to Sean that everyone expected Elijah to sit next to him.

"This is the Guardians' main house in Inverness," explained the Prophet as Andrew skillfully guided the vehicle into traffic.

"Nine Guardians live there and work in various businesses throughout the city. Besides living quarters, there are offices with all the conveniences of the modern world, including computers, telephones, and satellite communications."

"Is that where Andrew and Leyland live?" asked Sean.

"No, they live in a small house several miles out of town.

"We also have several other community houses in the city occupied by Guardians who perform a variety of functions for the island," continued Elijah.

"And, there's a large computer center in the middle of Inverness that's the Guardians' headquarters. It's our central tech hub. It was from there that I sent you my e-mails."

"Why didn't you e-mail me from Janus?" wondered Sean. "It would have been much easier than coming all the way into Inverness."

Elijah smiled.

"Once you get to the island, you'll understand why any form of external communication has to be handled through our computer center."

Sean nodded, wondering what sort of Internet facilities existed on Janus.

"How many live on the island?"

"We have slightly more than two thousand people," responded Elijah.

Arriving at the wharf, the six climbed out of the van. Large overhead spotlights illuminated the dock, pushing the darkness into the area's farthest corners. Sean had his first view of *Journey*.

The ship was large. Sean later learned from Leyland that she was one hundred and twenty-eight feet long. She looked to be in superb condition. Her hull was painted a startling white, while her bridge and cabin stood in contrast, colored a deep, rich blue. The pine planking on her deck was a dark brown lacquer. All her ropes and pulleys looked as though they'd just been bought at the outfitter's shop.

On the dock was a large flatbed truck loaded with pallets containing crates of fruit, vegetables, and meat along with other large cases. Andrew climbed aboard a forklift truck and, with the guidance of the three Guardians, leveraged the pallets onto the dock.

"Whenever *Journey* travels to Janus, it arrives with a full load of supplies," explained Elijah. "The Guardians provide the island with a number of items that we don't grow enough of or aren't found naturally."

Once the truck was unloaded, Andrew signed the driver's waybill form. Amid a funnel of black exhaust smoke, the truck pulled off the dock and into the night.

While the Guardians loaded the crates into *Journey*'s cargo hold, Sean and Elijah boarded the craft.

It had a spacious, enclosed cabin that was well laid out. There was a sleeping area for eight, a space that was set up similar to a living room with couches and armchairs, and a small galley where meals could be prepared and eaten. Everything was spotless.

The bunks were aligned from port to starboard against the ship's stern, two deep in four rows. Elijah told him to choose the one he wanted. Sean selected a bottom one on the outside closest to the starboard side. Throwing his luggage on the floor at the foot of the bunk, he joined Elijah in the kitchen. The Prophet was brewing a pot of coffee, and soon the two were seated opposite each other across the galley table.

"Now that you're here, I suppose you want to know why I've asked you to come and visit us on Janus," began Elijah.

"The thought crossed my mind a number of times," Sean admitted with a wry smile.

"You were curious enough to open my e-mails," offered Elijah. "I thought you'd like to see for yourself the society we've built. For a number of reasons, our island is different from any place in the world. I believe it will be valuable for you to experience all that we have to offer."

Although Sean was interested in what made Janus so unique, he had more pressing matters to discuss with Elijah. "Where am I staying?" he asked. "Will it be with you? Is there a bed-and-breakfast on the island? I don't have a lot of cash. So I hope credit cards are accepted. Is there a bank?"

Sean was rewarded with an impassive look from Elijah. "First you won't be staying with me. You'll be in the home of a woman called Mrs. Irene Kerr. We've put you there for a reason. Slightly more than a year ago, she lost her husband and two sons at sea. They were fishermen and got caught in a vicious North Sea storm. We never recovered the boat or the bodies, and the tragedy has affected Mrs. Kerr. She's been withdrawn since the accident. She accepts that her misfortune was not the fault of the Spirit, but has nevertheless chosen to live by herself in a house that is too big for just one person."

"The Spirit is the term everyone on Janus uses when they refer to God?" interjected Sean.

"Yes," responded Elijah. "We also don't give the Spirit a sex, instead using the term *it*. To us the Spirit is an amorphous entity that exists throughout the universe, and calling it he or she seems an arrogant use of a human term. But we'll talk more about that once you're on the island."

"Fine," said Sean. "What else should I know about Mrs. Kerr?"

"All of us on the island are hoping that having someone in the house will help her return to being an integral part of the community," explained Elijah.

*This doesn't sound very promising*, thought Sean. *Being looked upon to rescue a woman who's distressed about losing her husband and sons won't be the most relaxed way to spend time on an island.*

Reluctant to get off on the wrong foot, he decided that, instead of saying anything about Mrs. Kerr, he'd use the excuse that, "I'm used to living on my own. I value my privacy."

"It's not as bad as it sounds," responded the Prophet. "Mrs. Kerr is a lovely woman. She won't interfere with your privacy. You'll be free to come and go as you wish. Of course you'll share meals, but I don't think that's exactly a drawback for a bachelor."

Sean had to concede Elijah was right. One of the things he detested was cooking for himself. Having taken most of his meals at the Rose & Crown for more than two years, he was happy to have an arrangement where meals would be prepared for him.

"I don't suppose there are any restaurants on Janus," he asked hopefully.

Elijah smiled and shook his head. “I think you should prepare yourself for a place that you’ve never before experienced.”

“If I can survive three years in Afghanistan, I guess I can live for two months on Janus. But I’m wondering how much it will cost to stay with Mrs. Kerr?”

“All that’s been taken care of,” answered Elijah. “You’re considered a guest of the island. Also, we don’t have any banks. You won’t need cash or credit cards. Everything we do is by barter.”

Sean was stunned. “What do you mean I’m a guest of the island? I’m supposed to live rent free for two months and eat my meals without paying anything to Mrs. Kerr?”

“That’s right,” replied Elijah. “Once you’re on Janus, you’ll see how we live and, hopefully, it’s a lifestyle you’ll want to join.”

The implication that he might want to stay on the island far longer than the two months to which he’d committed surprised Sean. He was uncomfortable about Elijah’s inference. Yet the man had such a calm demeanor that Sean was hesitant to voice any concern.

However, there was a question he wanted to ask. “Where exactly is Janus?”

“We’re a small island in the North Sea located just north of the Shetland Islands and south of the Faroe Islands.”

“That’s a fairly distant location,” noted Sean. “Are you on any of the regular shipping lanes? Do you have ferry service to any of the islands in the Shetlands or the Orkneys?”

Elijah shook his head. “We’re independent from the world, though not as much as we used to be.

"For many centuries, we eked out a subsistence living on the island. The islanders had virtually no contact with the outside world. The occasional fishing boat would dock at our wharves needing a safe harbor during a particularly violent storm. We'd trade with them, offering wheat or barley for whatever fish they could supply, but generally we didn't need anything from them. Once the storm passed, they'd leave. No strangers would pass our way until the next storm, which could be several years.

"But the last century has brought change to Janus. Our population was expanding, and there's obviously a finite amount of land on an island. Unless there was evolution and progress, we would suffer the fate of all societies that don't recognize the need for change. We would soon face extinction. Our lands were becoming barren, because we had farmed them too heavily. Our sheep herds were suffering from disease because of too much inbreeding.

"We decided to establish a diaspora of our young people. Over the years, they've gradually spread throughout the globe. It has saved our island from internal destruction and allowed us to interact with the world without giving up our independence.

"It was a risky plan, though, fraught with unknown perils. The issue was how to send people into the world while preserving the island's independence. We have a secret that must, at all costs, be preserved. Every person who leaves the island swears to uphold this sacred trust."

Sean was curious. "What's this sacred trust and is it something that will affect me? I don't want to get involved in some ritual that will mean I can't leave the island unless I commit to not revealing what's happened."

A laugh that started deep within Elijah's chest spilled passed his lips and rippled across the room.

"I assure you it's nothing of the sort," said a still chuckling Prophet. "We are people dedicated to peace and would never impose our will on anyone. There are no rituals and you'll be able to leave whenever you want."

"That's good to hear," said Sean. "So tell me about this sacred trust."

"The answer will have to wait until you get to the island. For the moment, it must remain something that only the islanders know. But I can tell you that it relates to the relationship every islander has with the Spirit. What you must also understand is that we do not look at the Spirit as a superior entity. We view it as an equal. We are fully aware of its shortcomings, and it knows ours."

Sean thought of what he considered were the needless deaths of Ahmad and Hilary, along with the world's many inequities and silently agreed that the islanders' Spirit had a long list of faults.

"It seems as though the islanders have a close relationship with this Spirit," he noted. "How can you worship it, yet not believe it is a superior being?"

Sean had purposely slipped into the practice of referring to God as the Spirit. Like the islanders, he had also stripped the Supreme Being of any sexual connotation with the reference to *it*. Making the reference to God or the Spirit made little difference to him.

"We neither worship nor rely on it," began Elijah. "We never ask it to protect our crops, to keep our animals healthy, or to ensure the world doesn't intrude on our island. Rather, we have a mutual understanding that the Spirit is a force with which we have philosophical discussions. We seek to understand the planet, rather than just be a part of it. These conversations focus on our place in the world, why we are on Janus, and what is the purpose of our continuing existence, not only as individuals but as an island community."

"If you seek to be independent from the world, why the necessity of trying to comprehend what happens beyond your borders?" wondered Sean.

"The world is in a constant state of change," replied Elijah. "Our belief is that, if we can understand the transformations, we are better prepared to protect Janus from external influences."

"I understand what you're saying," said Sean, "but I still don't see how, after all these centuries, you could retain independence from every country that borders the North Sea."

"The island's independence is based on our relationship with the Spirit. Janus is the one place on earth where the Spirit knows it can be the being that it is. We have no religions or places of worship. Janus is the Spirit's earthly touchstone. Through our ability to communicate directly with it, the Spirit seeks to understand our world. We offer a refuge from the globe's problems—a place where the Spirit can come without fear of criticism or demands.

"In return, it ensures we remain unknown and uncharted."

Sean experienced the same sense of uneasiness that he'd felt during his earlier conversation with Andrew in the van. "I don't mean to disparage your beliefs, but this seems very much like a cult," he said.

"I assure you that's not the case, as you'll discover when you arrive on Janus," replied Elijah, seeming unperturbed by the observation.

Elijah's words didn't alleviate Sean's concern. "Well you have to admit that you sound like a single-minded fanatic when it comes to your views about this Spirit."

"Single-minded, yes, but not a fanatic," replied Elijah. "It's an important distinction."

"What's the difference?"

"Fanaticism is uncritical devotion to a person or a cause. As I said, we know the Spirit is not perfect. It willingly accepts our view of its failings. One only has to take a brief look around the world to realize that there is too much bloodshed, too much inequality, and too many injustices. This is not paradise. But at the same time, we are committed to working with the Spirit in making the world a better and more humane place."

"That's a fairly thin distinction." Sean laughed.

"Ah, but you have to admit the difference does exist," replied an equally cheerful Elijah.

"I'm curious about the origin of the island's name. Why Janus?"

"In Roman mythology," began Elijah, "Janus was the god of all endings, beginnings, and time, along with gates, doors, and doorways. Our ancestors named the island Janus to reflect their belief that all those who followed should always remember the past and use it to shape the present and the future. They also believed that time is comprised of gates and doorways that allowed them to directly converse with the Spirit, without the hindrance of any religious leaders or icons."

"What does it mean to converse with the Spirit?" asked Sean. "You mean worship it, don't you?"

"No, I use the word converse with purpose, and it reflects exactly what we do. Once you're on Janus for a time, you'll come to fully understand our relationship with the Spirit."

The conversation had so intrigued Sean that he was surprised when the cabin door opened and the four Guardians strode in. Sean looked at his watch and was startled to see that it was well past midnight. It had been a long day, and he was ready to turn in. Not so with the Guardians and Elijah. Andrew was in the process of pouring everyone coffee. Sean declined and said he was going to bed.

As Sean climbed into his bunk, Malcolm got up from the table and turned the cabin lights down low. The last thing Sean remembered was the steady, quiet drone of voices coming from the kitchen.

# Chapter 28

Sean awoke feeling refreshed and to the smell of frying eggs and ham, along with coffee. It took him several moments to realize where he was. When he did, a surge of anticipation swept over him at knowing he'd soon be on his way to the mysterious island known as Janus.

Breakfast was a relatively quiet affair. No one seemed inclined to say much. The Guardians talked briefly about the expected weather the ship would encounter, while Elijah's only words were to ask Sean if he'd had a good night. The Prophet seemed pleased that he'd slept well but, after that, lapsed into silence.

Following the meal, Leyland did the cleaning up while the other Guardians readied *Journey* for her voyage. Sean went on deck and was an interested observer as Malcolm and Joseph let go the lines while Andrew engaged the twin Rolls-Royce diesel engines, slowly powering the ship away from the dock and into the channel.

They were travelling through the Inner Moray Firth, where Sean could just make out a colony of bottlenose dolphins cavorting in the water. The harbor appeared to be busy and thriving. They passed tied-up cargo ships from countries in Scandinavia, the European Union, and the Baltics. There were also a couple of massive oil tankers unloading their crude.

Dressed warmly in a large seaman's sweater and heavy coat that Leyland had given him, Sean stood for a while on deck, enjoying the sea breeze and the ship's gentle motion. Andrew guided them toward open water and the voyage northward. Leyland joined him on the bridge. Elijah had explained that Andrew and Leyland would take the first four-hour watch, with Malcolm and Joseph handling the next four hours. They would alternate each watch until reaching Janus.

"We'll pass through the Orkney Islands before heading northward toward the Shetlands and the Faroe Islands," Elijah had said.

Sean wondered what awaited him on Janus.

After Toronto, Kabul, and London, would the answers he was seeking be found there? Sean knew that an island perched somewhere in the North Sea was an unlikely place to find the goal he was seeking.

And yet, here he was, a lifetime away from the quiet apartment he'd been living in only slightly more than a day before. If he hadn't been filled with the insatiable need to find his life's purpose, he'd never have accepted Elijah's invitation. However, Sean believed, more than he had at any other stop along the roadway of his life, that there was a purpose to visiting Janus. He couldn't grasp what the feeling meant but knew this stop was more than a random unfolding of his universe.

Beneath a sky that was pockmarked with dark and ominous clouds, *Journey* plunged and rolled, challenging a gray sea that was almost black in spots, with white caps bobbing like corks. The ship drove into troughs, with water cascading over the bow. A steady, cold wind soon drove Sean inside, where he met Joseph.

"The weather is calling for strong winds, and the sea promises to be turbulent," said the Guardian. "I hope you're not prone to seasickness."

"No," replied Sean. "I'm feeling fine. Is the North Sea usually this rough?"

Joseph laughed and said, "If you think this is rough, you should travel with us during December or January."

Elijah was on the bridge with Andrew and Leyland. Malcolm and Joseph were down below ensuring the cargo was well secured. Left on his own, Sean rummaged in his duffel bag and pulled out a murder-mystery book that he'd just started. He settled in one of the cabin's armchairs and lost himself in the novel's pages. As the morning wore on, Andrew and Leyland relinquished the bridge to Malcolm and Joseph, while Elijah used the time to read or have quiet conversations with each of the Guardians.

The cabin was warm and comfortable. *Journey* was riding out the turbulent seas relatively well, although the farther north they went, the more the ship rolled and pitched.

About midmorning, Elijah settled himself on a chair across from Sean.

"I suppose you'd like to know a little bit more about Janus," he offered.

Sean put down his book and said, "To begin with, I was wondering how long your island has been settled."

"Janus had been inhabited since the first century."

Sean was amazed. "There have been people on the island for two thousand years? That's remarkable. Is there anyone left on the island who can trace their genealogy back to the first ancestors?"

"There are several families. But over the last hundred years, especially, we have become a wonderfully diverse society. In many ways we are a reflection of the world. It came about as our diaspora spread throughout the globe. As our citizens got married and then returned to take up the land or fishing boats of their parents we became a multi-cultural society. We are an island of many peoples dedicated to living in harmony."

"Where did your ancestors come from?" wondered Sean. "And what led them to Janus?"

"They originated in the ancient land of Judea. Our ancestors were driven out by the Romans because of their Jewish beliefs. Guided by the Spirit, they made the great trek from Joppa and Jerusalem across northern Africa, through the Iberian Peninsula, into what is now known as upper Europe and finally by ship across to Janus.

"It was a journey of epic proportions and took several years to complete. During that time the island's settlers came to know that their survival depended on being able to understand and accept the needs of one another. It meant sharing and watching out for the group's welfare instead of seeking individual gain. The lessons learned by our ancestors have been passed from generation to generation and are an integral part of the Janus culture."

"That's quite a legacy," said Sean. "So this relationship with the Spirit has been a part of Janus since the very beginning."

"It's a partnership that has lasted through the centuries and is unique to our island," responded Elijah.

"But don't all religions claim a special understanding with their god?" wondered Sean.

"You're right," acknowledged the Prophet. "But two things are important to remember. Since no religion is present on Janus, we have a direct relationship with the Spirit. There are no rabbis, priests, ministers, or any other individuals who define our connection. And second, the essence of our bond is a fundamental commitment to nonviolence. It's how we've lived for centuries."

"I'm not going to dispute your first point because I haven't been on the island," said Sean. "But all primary religions have, as a core value, a dedication to peace."

"Unfortunately," answered Elijah, "so many wars have been fought in the name of a god that it has become a mockery to use religion as a foundation for peace. On Janus, though, we have never had one act of violence in the two centuries our people have been on the island."

Sean wasn't sure he'd heard correctly. "Are you saying that no one has ever harmed another person? I find that impossible to believe."

"The story of Janus has many chapters," said Elijah, his voice barely rising above the sound of the wind pummeling the ship. As I've said before, we are a place unlike any other in the world. You are about to meet a group of people who will open your eyes to what the world can be if we all lived by the principle of understanding, tolerance, equality, and peace."

"Those are interesting words," said Sean. "I'm looking forward to seeing how they apply on Janus."

Before Elijah could reply, Leyland called out that lunch was ready.

After a meal of grilled halibut with the ever present coffee, Sean returned to his book. It had only been a few days, but he realized that spending some time away from *The Advocate* was a good thing. It had been all-consuming since he'd arrived in London. Time away, especially on an island that sounded intriguing, would give him a fresh perspective for when he returned.

He was startled when Joseph announced they'd be having dinner in about an hour. The Guardians obviously believed in being well-fed for the task of bringing *Journey* to her destination.

Malcolm soon called everyone to the dinner table. He'd cooked up hearty helpings of Atlantic cod, along with boiled potatoes and peas.

Sean offered to wash up, but Malcolm and Joseph said it wasn't necessary. That task would fall to Andrew and Leyland when they descended from the bridge. Sean admired the symmetry that characterized the way the Guardians went about their tasks. It was obvious the four had been together for many voyages. Every action was coordinated, from cooking meals to ensuring the bilge pumps were in good working order to keeping the large cabin spotless and to the four-hour rotation on the bridge.

Shortly after the meal was completed and the table cleared, Malcolm and Joseph climbed the ladder to the wheelhouse. A few moments later, a weary-looking Andrew and Leyland were in the cabin.

After finishing their meal and cleaning up the kitchen, both men got into port side bunks and were quickly asleep.

"Time goes quickly when you're at sea and have to be on the bridge in four hours," explained Elijah.

"Is this one of the Guardians' main functions, running *Journey* between Inverness and Janus?" asked Sean.

"Not at all," responded Elijah. "The Guardians perform many tasks for the island and our diaspora. They provide a buffer between Janus and the world.

"When they were established in the late sixteenth century, the group comprised six young men and women whose primary responsibility was to help around the island, especially during the planting and harvesting seasons. And up until the early twentieth century, that's what the Guardians were—a group of six young people who lived in a house on the island. When one married or wanted to retire, a volunteer would take his or her place."

"What changed it all?"

"The island's population was growing, and many of the families were becoming more self-reliant. The Guardians weren't needed around Janus to the degree they had been. At the same time, it became apparent we were losing touch with our diaspora. It required an advanced form of communication that couldn't be provided by people who were committed to living apart from the world. This was further complicated because, by that time, our diaspora had spread throughout North America, Australia, Europe, and Asia.

"It was decided to locate the Guardians in Inverness where they could be close to Janus, while acting as a conduit between the islanders and their relatives who were living in other parts of the world."

"How many Guardians are there?"

"We have close to seventeen hundred. The unit comprises men and women of all ages with a range of skills that covers every aspect of modern society. About five hundred are located in Inverness. That's the center of our global computer and technology operations.

"Recently, as the group's number has grown, we reached out to our diaspora by having members located in various countries where the majority of our people are located, especially in North America and Europe. Each Guardian is committed to the preservation of Janus and our worldwide diaspora. This collective dedication makes for a close, tight-knit network.

"We have Guardians in several embassies, multinational corporations, international banks, and government agencies, including national technology operations. We've created a global web that not only offers a soft landing for anyone who has problems but can facilitate our diaspora's mission of spreading the Janus message of peace and sound ecological stewardship throughout the world.

"The Guardians are available to our diaspora on a round-the-clock basis. It depends on the situation and where the member of our diaspora is located, but once contacted, we can usually have one or two Guardians there within twenty-four to forty-eight hours."

"How large is your diaspora?" wondered Sean.

"Through the years, it has grown to about eighteen thousand people. It's become a challenge for everyone to stay in touch with their relatives on the island. But that's where modern computer technology has brought our people closer together. The computer center in Inverness serves as a clearing house for e-mails and letters between our worldwide community and the island."

Darkness had descended, capturing the ship along with its crew and passengers in its grip. Elijah dimmed the cabin lights.

"Andrew told me we're making good time and should reach Janus by early morning," the Prophet told Sean.

Sean experienced a slight feeling of apprehension, much like a brief breeze over a still lake. Although everything had so far gone well, he didn't know what to expect once they reached the island.

"I think I'll turn in now," he said. "Tomorrow promises to be a long day and I want to be well rested when we reach Janus."

Elijah nodded and replied that he was going up to the bridge to see how Malcolm and Joseph were coping with the weather and the rough seas. He walked into the galley, poured two large cups of coffee, and ascended the ladder.

Left on his own, Sean crawled into his bunk. Sleep was elusive. The frequent pitching of the ship as it fought off the onrushing waves, along with the relentless wind combined to keep him awake.

Turning on the night-light attached to the bulkhead, he read several chapters. Soon, however, even the ship's uneven motion couldn't keep Sean awake. He fell asleep, the book resting on his chest.

# CHAPTER 29

Sean came awake suddenly, struggling to orient himself. Someone had been gently shaking him. It was Elijah, standing by his bunk with a steaming mug of coffee in his outstretched hand.

He took the coffee gratefully and slowly looked around. His eyes found a porthole. Rays of light, announcing the coming dawn, were beginning to break through the darkly clouded sky. *Journey* was still rolling and pitching as wave after relentless wave struck her.

"We're about thirty minutes away from docking," said the Prophet. "Why don't you come on deck with me and see Janus in its early morning beauty."

He handed Sean a slicker along with rubber boots. Emerging on deck, the pair was met with a cold blast of wind and sea spray rising over the bow.

The wind had worsened since the previous morning and was blowing hard against the ship's starboard side. The water looked dark and foreboding, while above, heavy battleship gray clouds shrouded the horizon. Although Sean had the large seaman's sweater on that he'd worn the previous day, he still felt chilled.

Sean looked, and all he could see was the horizon meeting water. The rays of sunlight he'd seen earlier had vanished. It appeared as though they were sailing directly into the low cloud cover. The sea churned and boiled as *Journey* drove steadily through high and frothing waves.

"Where's Janus?" he asked. "I can't see anything."

Elijah pointed to the bow. "Look over there," he shouted. "You can just make out the island's outline."

As if on cue, the sea became calmer, and the heavy clouds began rolling westward, revealing patches of blue sky. The air had become suddenly still.

"We'll be docking on the island's southern side," said Elijah. "That's where the fishing wharves are. It's a secluded bay that's protected on the east and west sides by steep cliffs."

Sean looked and could just make out what appeared to be a rocky and forbidding landmass coming up hard on *Journey*'s bow. The whole coastline, not just the harbor, was bordered by cliffs. He could easily see the waves battering themselves against the rocky base in a fierce ballet of power versus silent strength that was as old as time.

Four mountainous peaks dominated Janus's interior. As they came up on the island's southeastern arc, he could just make out a series of houses grouped close together.

"That's our village," said Elijah excitedly. "Most of our fishermen live on the southern side of what we call the Ring Road. It gives them easy access to their boats."

Sean looked around the harbor, and there wasn't a boat in sight.

Elijah, following his gaze, said, "The boats go out as dawn breaks and don't come back until just before dark. It's a hard life, but our fishermen and fisherwomen wouldn't trade it for any other job in the world.

"The general store and some of our farms are on the Ring Road's northern side."

"Do you live in the village?"

"No. My house, along with Mrs. Kerr's and a group of farms, is located further west along the road."

"It's called the Ring Road because—?"

"It's the only road that encircles the island," Elijah finished Sean's question.

*Journey* drew closer to the harbor. Sean could see that the village houses' stone bases supported clapboard walls and peaked, tiled roofs. He was surprised.

"I thought in this part of the world, you'd have thatched roofs," he said. "Shingles seem quite modern."

"We used to have thatched roofs," replied Elijah. "Then, several years ago, an islander suggested we switch to shingles. Although unlike thatch, there's a cost involved with shingles, they're easier to maintain, last for years, and don't let the heat out in the winter the way thatch does.

"The Guardians purchase the supplies in Inverness, and gradually we've changed from thatch to shingles. We only have a few more houses to complete. As a matter of fact, part of the supplies we're carrying are shingles for two of the remaining homes."

As Elijah spoke, a group of seagulls was lining up in formation and following *Journey* into port. They swooped and spiraled downward to the boat's stern, only to turn at the last moment and pull themselves skyward on powerful wings.

"They think we're one of the fishing boats and will throw them scraps from our catch," explained Elijah.

For the first time since they'd left the safe harbor waters of Inverness, Sean could feel the twin Rolls-Royce engines gradually being slowed. The island was coming into a more sharpened focus.

Sean could see four concrete, reinforced wharves with wooden pylons to protect boats' hulls from scraping against the dock, and the tackle sheds with nets and fishing floats hung up on the outside walls. Elijah pointed out a hut, explaining it was where the catch was sorted during bad weather.

*Journey* slowly entered the bay's calm waters. Looking toward the bridge, Sean saw that it was Andrew at the wheel. He could feel the engines being thrust into reverse and then forward as Andrew expertly brought *Journey* alongside a wharf that looked just long enough to hold the vessel. Malcolm and Joseph threw the docking ropes over the ship's side where they were caught by a couple of young men. Both stern and bow ropes were attached to large bollards.

Andrew cut the engines, and Sean felt an immediate sense of stillness. A group of islanders who had begun gathering on the dock when *Journey* was in the bay had swelled into numbers that left the wharf crowded, with some people spilling over to the deeply rutted path that led from the Ring Road down to the harbor.

Malcolm and Joseph leveraged the gangplank into place. Soon they were off-loading the cargo into neat stacks on the dock. Andrew and Leyland quickly joined them.

Sean and Elijah had gone back inside the cabin to collect their gear. When Sean came on deck, he was surprised at the crowd. The wharf was buzzing with an obvious air of anticipation.

"Are they waiting for the cargo to be distributed?" he asked.

Elijah laughed. "That's part of it. The fruits, vegetables, meat and other supplies are divided equally among all the islanders. But the real reason they're here this morning is to meet you."

Taken aback, Sean asked, "What do you mean?"

"You're the first person who doesn't have a direct tie to the island that's visited us in a few years. Your impending arrival has generated excitement among everyone on Janus. They're anxious to meet and talk with someone who can bring us a different perspective. You should also be excited. This is a new experience.

"I've told you a bit about our history and the way we've lived with little outside contact. Our population has grown and diversified, but we've remained dedicated to the preservation of our culture. Think what you can learn from that in terms of resiliency and the courage to remain true to one's convictions.

"When you step ashore, do so with a free mind—one that is eager to share what we have, while imparting what you know. Open your heart and mind to us. It's something you'll never regret."

"But I'm a stranger," answered Sean. "I can't just walk up to people and start talking to them. They'll think I'm a fool."

"Don't look at this as New York or London or Toronto. People want to meet and talk with you. You're entering a new world, where ideas and thoughts triumph over violence and money. I know it may seem unnerving, but people will seek you out.

Once you meet them, you'll begin to enjoy the dialogue. We have many interesting people on Janus."

A long sigh escaped Sean's lips. "Well, I didn't travel all this way to be a hermit."

Elijah clapped him the back. "That's the idea."

# Chapter 30

The cargo had been off-loaded, and the four Guardians were standing at the bottom of the gangplank, waiting for Elijah and Sean to disembark.

"I suppose they're looking forward to spending time on the island," said Sean, nodding toward the men.

"They'll visit with their families and see friends," responded Elijah. "In a couple of days, *Journey* will begin the trip back to Inverness."

"When will she return?"

"In two months. We have a regular schedule. It allows everyone to plan for when supplies will be delivered."

Andrew suggested they give their bags to him and Leyland. "It's going to take you both a while to get through the crowd. Let me have your bag, Elijah, and I'll drop it off on your front porch. Leyland will take Sean's and do the same thing at Mrs. Kerr's."

Elijah led Sean through the islanders. For almost thirty minutes, it was a blur of shaking hands and being told names he knew he'd never remember. Everyone it seemed was glad to see him, and all expressed their happiness he'd joined them on Janus. He noticed that Elijah received an equally warm reception.

Sean couldn't help but notice the crowd's diverse ethnicity. He heard multiple accents and met people whose backgrounds originated from Africa to Europe and from Asia to North America. It reminded him of walking into the cafeteria at the United Nations.

Elijah and Sean made their way through the crowd and up the path to the Ring Road. The crowd was slowly dispersing as the two turned west along the road.

"We'll be at Mrs. Kerr's in a few minutes. I live just a short walk farther along."

The wind was brisk and Sean could feel its chill through the leather jacket he was wearing. Elijah seemed not to notice the cold. They soon arrived at a green clapboard house. An inlaid stone pathway led from the road to the front steps. A large gallery ran across the home's front.

"Here we are," said Elijah.

"The house looks well cared for," noted Sean.

"Since the death of her husband and sons, the islanders take turns doing the needed repairs and exterior painting," replied Elijah.

Arriving at the front door, Elijah knocked, while Sean picked up his bags.

The door opened, revealing a short, stout woman, with white, neatly coiffed hair and wearing a floral print housedress. Her face had lines that only deep emotional pain can cause, and her coal black eyes reflected a hurt that would never be fully resolved. She slowly smiled, showing yellowed teeth. Sean guessed that she was in her early sixties.

As Elijah introduced them, she held out a liver-spotted hand and beckoned them in. She had a soft, lilting voice that was pleasant to the ear. Sean followed the two of them into the house. He found himself in a long hallway. A hint of rosewater was in the air.

The one-story house was built north to south in an effort to protect the rooms from the winter wind sweeping in off the sea. There were three bedrooms, all located to the right of the hallway. Mrs. Kerr told Sean he would be in the one closest to the home's front.

He walked in, while she and Elijah continued to the kitchen. Sean knew instantly the room had belonged to one of her sons. The furniture was sparse. It comprised a single bed covered with a large sheepskin blanket, a night table with a small lamp, and a chest of drawers. On the wall were photographs of sailing ships. The cupboard was empty. He left his bags for unpacking later. Walking into the hallway, he turned toward the kitchen.

On the way he passed a living room to the hallway's left. He looked in and saw a sofa with a couple of easy chairs. In the center, a coffee table sat atop a small rug. Framed paintings of what he guessed were island scenes adorned the walls. The room was dominated by a large fireplace.

Walking farther up the hallway, he passed another bedroom, which he guessed had belonged to her other son. He then came to what he supposed was Mrs. Kerr's room. It had a large double bed, a bureau, and a chest of drawers. A large framed photograph of an older man and two men who looked to be in their early twenties dominated the wall over the bed.

Sean stopped and stared at it for several seconds. He knew how difficult Hilary's death had been for him and wondered how someone could ever recover from losing her family.

To the right of the hallway and just across from the main bedroom was the bathroom. He continued to the kitchen—the last room in the house. Elijah was seated at the table, while Mrs. Kerr was working over a hotplate.

"We're having ham for lunch," he told a surprised Sean, who hadn't given much thought to eating. He was still getting used to the fact that just a few days ago he'd been in London. Now he was about to sit down to a meal of ham on an unknown island in the North Sea.

Mrs. Kerr had mixed some potatoes and carrots in with the dish. The three ate in silence, with the only words spoken coming at the end of the meal when Mrs. Kerr said, "Elijah says you'll be staying for at least two months or maybe longer. Well, consider this your home for however long you choose to be with us. Elijah's arranged for everything."

Sean looked first at Mrs. Kerr and then at Elijah.

"I'm not sure what to say," he said, overwhelmed by the generosity. "Perhaps there are things I can do around the house that will help out."

"There's always something to do around a house," answered Mrs. Kerr. "But we'll wait until you've been here a while before planning any projects."

Sean offered to wash the dishes. However, Mrs. Kerr had another idea. "Why don't you go to your room and unpack. That way you can settle in. I'll take care of the dishes."

Elijah accompanied him along the hallway.

They'd made it midway down the corridor when a knock sounded at the front door. Mrs. Kerr called out, asking if one of them would answer it. Elijah opened the door, and on the gallery was a large crate of fruit, one of vegetables, and several plastic bags of meat—delivered that morning aboard *Journey*.

Sean marveled at the island's efficiency. It was just early afternoon, and he guessed that most of the deliveries had probably already been completed, since Mrs. Kerr's house was outside the village. He carried the crates, one at a time, into the kitchen, where she told him to leave them on the floor. Elijah brought in the meat.

"I'll unpack everything as soon as I finish the dishes. Now get to your room and settle in," she gently scolded Sean.

He hurried down the corridor. Elijah was already at the front door, ready to leave.

"When will we get together?" Sean asked.

"Probably in a couple of days," answered the Prophet. "I've got some things to do around the farm. You should use the time to tour the island. Get to know the place. Why not go into the village and meet some of the people?"

"That's a good idea. What do I tell them if they ask why I'm here?"

"No one will ask. That's not our way. Your privacy will be respected."

"Wouldn't it make sense if I knew the reason you've given everyone for my being on the island?"

"I've explained that you're important to our future."

Sean frowned, not understanding what Elijah meant.

"That's pretty vague. Is there an agenda here that I should know about?"

"There's plenty of time for that."

Elijah then slipped out the door, before Sean had a chance to continue the conversation.

Standing in the doorway, he watched as the Prophet walked quickly down the pathway and onto the Ring Road. Sean wondered at Elijah's cryptic response, but decided he'd let it go for now. He was on the island for a couple of months. There was plenty of time to find out what was behind Elijah's invitation.

Sean closed the door and went to his room. He finished unpacking. Placing Hilary's picture on top of the chest, he angled it so the photograph would be seen from the bed.

# Chapter 31

It was Sean's second day on the island. He and Mrs. Kerr had just finished cleaning up the breakfast dishes when there was a knock at the front door. Busy putting things away, Mrs. Kerr asked if he'd see who was there.

Opening the door, he was met by a young woman dressed in a large, wool sweater; baggy jeans; and heavy work boots. She was holding a small basket in the crook of her left arm. Thrusting out her right hand, she took his in a firm grasp and gave it a strong shake.

"Hi, I'm Diane Dunfield. And you're Sean. I dropped by with some eggs for Mrs. Kerr."

The first thing Sean noticed was her smile. Warm and welcoming, it was highlighted by two rows of perfect, ivory white teeth.

Behind him, Sean could hear Mrs. Kerr walking purposefully down the hallway. She moved in beside him. "Why, hello, Diane. It's always good to see you. To what do I owe this visit?"

"I just came by to drop off some eggs. Knowing you have a guest, I thought you could use an extra supply."

Diane handed the basket to Mrs. Kerr.

"That's very kind of you. I see you've met Sean. Why don't you come in? We've just finished breakfast, but I'll put the coffee on.

"Sean, would you take our guest into the living room."

Standing in the doorway with Mrs. Kerr, Sean couldn't help but notice that Diane was attractive.

He guessed she was about thirty years old. Her auburn hair was tied back with a red ribbon. She wore no makeup. Her angular face was tanned a light shade of brown. She looked at the world through deep brown eyes. High cheekbones framed a petite nose that ran straight to full, naturally red lips. Diane looked to be several inches above five feet. Although she was wearing clothes that did little to reveal her figure, Sean could make out the swell of her breasts beneath the sweater.

As Mrs. Kerr went to the kitchen, Diane shook off her boots. She followed Sean into the living room. Diane took one of the easy chairs, while Sean sat on the sofa.

Sean suspected he knew but still asked the question. "How did you know my name?"

Diane's laugh was light and breezy. "You'll find out soon enough. Janus is a small island. There isn't much that happens around here that everybody doesn't know about. You're the first true stranger we've had on the island since our engineer, Ted Adams arrived. And that was a few years ago. The newcomers we get are part of our diaspora who are returning to take up the land or fishing boats from their relatives. Everyone is versed in the Janus way. It will be interesting to have a new perspective around here. So, as you can see, it's only natural that news of your arrival traveled quickly.

"Then again, we all knew you were coming. Once it was agreed that you'd be with us, it was just a question of when you'd get here."

Before Sean could ask what Diane meant by agreed, she'd skipped along to asking how the trip on *Journey* had been. "It can be a rough crossing at this time of year," she noted.

He was going to tell her about the wind and the cold, when Mrs. Kerr arrived. She had a tray filled with two cups of coffee, sugar, cream, and some scones. The tray was placed on the center table.

"I won't be joining you," she announced. "There's some work to do in the kitchen. I'm sure the two of you can find enough to talk about without having me around."

With that, she bustled out and headed down the hallway.

"I guess we're on our own." Sean quietly chuckled.

"She's a fine lady," said Diane somberly. "After what she's been through, it'll be good to have you living with her while you're here."

"Elijah told me that her husband and sons were lost at sea. That's quite a tragedy to live through. I wonder how she's managed to keep going."

"Mrs. Kerr is a strong person. It's hard to imagine having the will to go on after something like that. She's an island woman, though. We're raised to be resilient."

Sean sensed a warmth and openness about Diane that immediately drew him in. He'd felt at ease with her a few minutes after they sat down. There wasn't any of the awkwardness that sometimes accompanied his first encounter with strangers.

He assumed Diane had always lived on Janus and wondered what she did.

"From what Elijah told me, everyone on Janus either farms, herds sheep, or has a fishing boat. What is it that you do?"

It turned out that, among other things, Diane was the island's nurse and midwife. Born on the island, she'd left at seventeen. Her travels had first taken her to New York, where she'd studied nursing. After that it was London and work in a hospital. From there, it had been off to Australia. She'd worked at a hospital in Sydney for two years before returning to the island shortly after her mother's death.

Her father had died when she was ten. She lived alone on the family farm where she'd been raised. Like her mother, she operated the small farm by herself, except for the spring planting and fall harvesting when several of the island's older teenagers assisted with the work.

"That's the sum total of my life to date," she said with a light laugh.

Diane took a deep drink of coffee.

"Now that I've told you about my life, I think it's only fair that I learn some of the things you've done."

Sean was surprised at how easy it was to talk to her.

He told her about his stint as a lawyer, the years with the United Nations in Afghanistan, and how he'd been working at *The Advocate*.

He didn't mention Hilary. That was a part of his life that he wanted to keep private, at least for now. Her death was still a raw wound. It was easier to avoid the details than get into a discussion about the separation, her cancer, and her eventual death.

Sean suddenly realized he'd been talking for a while. "Sorry, I've been rambling a bit."

"Quite the contrary. You've led a fascinating life."

The cups were empty, the scones eaten.

"I suppose it's time for me to be getting home. There are a number of chores still to be done. One thing about animals—you work on their timetable, not your own."

"Where do you live?"

"My house is just a few doors west of here."

"Why don't I walk you home?"

It had been several years since Sean had met a woman he wanted to know more about. Diane seemed special, and already he hoped to spend more time with her.

"It's not far. I don't want to trouble you."

"It wouldn't be a problem. The walk will do me good."

Diane put on her boots and waited at the door. Sean went in search of Mrs. Kerr to let her know he was going out. He found her still in the kitchen. She was knitting what appeared to be a shawl.

"I'm walking Diane home, so I'll just be gone a few minutes."

Glancing up from her work, Mrs. Kerr smiled. "I thought you might," she said. "Just remember, lunch is at midday."

"I won't be gone that long."

"Not this time. But who knows what the future may bring."

Sean could swear he heard a low chuckle escape Mrs. Kerr's lips. However, she had said her piece with a straight face and innocent eyes.

As they got to the end of the stone pathway and started walking along the Ring Road, Diane explained, "While there's paths that lead off it, if you want to get anywhere on Janus, you start by traveling the road."

Looking northward, Sean could see the four peaks he'd noticed from the ship rising up from beyond the shoreline. Farmland stretched along the southern side of the two peaks he could see clearly.

"What's in the center of those four peaks?'

Diane stopped and followed Sean's gaze. "There's a deep valley that contains farms and grazing land. There's also a small wood lot. When our ancestors arrived, they settled in that valley. Some of their descendants still live and work the land.

"Once the population started to increase, people moved outside the valley and began to build along the southern shore. That's where we are now. Over the years, the settlement spread east and west. Gradually we grew out to where about three-quarters of the island is inhabited and cultivated. The rest is used for sheep grazing."

Diane had stopped in front of a gate that opened onto a curved, crushed stone walkway, which led to a tidy, one-story clapboard house. What looked to be new shingles covered a peaked roof. Three windows looked out over the front yard. A large stone chimney hugged the home's east side.

A wooden gallery, painted a rich brown, ran along the entire front. Several wooden chairs were lined up neatly facing the road. In the back, Sean could see a large barn with a silo attached. A flock of sheep, heavy with fleece, was grazing in the field bordering the barn.

"Well, here we are," she said.

Sean was sorry the walk was over.

"What are your plans now that you've settled in at Mrs. Kerr's?"

"I don't really know. It's not as though I've given it a lot of thought. Things have happened quickly since I left London. Mostly, I'd planned on going for some walks and getting a feel for the island."

"Your first stop should be the Knob."

"What's the Knob?"

"It's our general store. It's on the other side of the village. Marcus Burne is the owner. It would be good to meet him. It's also where everyone goes for supplies, so you'll get to see a lot of people."

Sean decided to take a chance. "Why don't you come along and introduce me to Marcus?"

"Well"—there was a dramatic pause—"I do have to get some supplies."

"Good, how about tomorrow?"

Sean knew he was rushing things. He didn't want to appear pushy or needy. He would like to see her again, and there really wasn't any time like the present. "Why don't I come by around ten?"

"You probably haven't noticed, but we don't have any clocks on the island. Also, no one wears a watch. But there's a growing movement to change that. Meantime, we go by the sun."

"Oh, well when should I be here?"

"It makes more sense if I pick you up. I have to pass Mrs. Kerr's to go into the village. The animals have to be fed and their stalls mucked out. So, about midmorning is good for me."

"Sounds great," said Sean. "I'll see you then."

A feeling of awkwardness swept over him. Out of practice being with a woman who interested him, he wasn't sure how to end things. Should he shake hands? A kiss on the cheek seemed inappropriate since they'd just met.

Fortunately, Diane reached out and took his hand. "It was great to meet you. I'll be there tomorrow."

With that, she let his hand go and walked through the gate. Sean was still standing on the road when she reached the gallery. Diane turned, waved and then disappeared inside.

Feeling somewhat foolish at his ineptitude, Sean began the short jaunt back to Mrs. Kerr's.

Walking slowly, his thoughts were filled with Diane. It seemed strange after spending only a short time with her, but she'd stirred an interest he hadn't felt for a long time. Diane had told him a lot about herself but hadn't said anything about a man in her life.

Sean chided himself. He'd only just met her. And, as always, there was the memory of Hilary. Regardless of how hard he tried not to, he always found himself comparing any woman he met to her.

Unfortunately, none of them measured up to recollections of his former wife. He realized that he'd lived with Hilary's memory for so long that it had become like a comfortable coat. As is the case with most memories of loved ones, he'd long ago shed the bad moments and remembered only the good times.

Yet there was something about Diane that made him want to see more of her. He was looking forward to the morning.

# CHAPTER 32

As he awoke, it took Sean only a moment to remember that he and Diane were going to the Knob later that morning. Mrs. Kerr could be heard in the kitchen.

He got up slowly and wandered into the bathroom.

There was little talk over breakfast. Both had been used to living on their own for so long that meal conversations were not their strong point. Breakfast, as Sean was to discover, generally consisted of a large bowl of porridge, liberally sprinkled with brown sugar. It was accompanied by slabs of home-made bread. There was a choice of preserved strawberry jam, apple jelly, or honey. The meal was rounded out with coffee. Every Saturday, an omelet was substituted for the porridge.

It was a satisfying start to the day. After helping with the washing up, Sean waited in his room for Diane. He'd become so engrossed in the book he was reading that he was startled when Mrs. Kerr appeared in his doorway and announced that Diane was on the gallery waiting for him.

Quickly throwing on a sweater, he hurried outside. Diane was wearing a large, cotton work shirt; faded blue corduroys; and what seemed to be her usual footwear, heavy work boots. When they were on the Ring Road, Diane told Sean she wouldn't be able to stay long at the Knob.

"I'll introduce you to Marcus and quickly pick up some supplies. Then I'll get back to the farm. Two of my ewes are ready to drop their lambs, and I'm meeting our vet around midday."

Sean didn't let his disappointment show. He'd been looking forward to spending some time with Diane. Still, he couldn't expect she'd disrupt her life just because he'd arrived on Janus.

Sean had decided that, since he'd be on the island for a couple of months, he needed some supplies, including toothpaste, shaving cream, razor blades, a pair of boots, pants, and a heavy wool or cotton shirt.

The Knob was located at the far eastern end of the village. Facing directly onto the Ring Road, it was a one-story building. Large and rambling, the Knob was about four times as large in both width and length of any village structure Sean had seen so far. At the rear was what appeared to be a large, round-roofed warehouse. Farther back, and one field removed from the warehouse, was the barn.

Similar to most of the village's houses, the Knob was built from clapboard on a stone foundation. It looked from the way the wood had weathered that the store had been enlarged several times.

The welcome bell jangled as Sean and Diane walked through the front door. The wooden floors were well worn and had long ago given up whatever paint had originally been applied. Expecting it to be similar to other general stores he'd been in, where goods were stacked haphazardly on shelves and tucked in corners, he was pleasantly surprised at the organized neatness confronting him.

The shop and lending library portion occupied the building's front while the family quarters were at the rear. A tattered curtain for a door separated the two areas. Diane told Sean that the Knob had been operated by the Burne family for more than twelve generations.

Everything from boots to shirts, from dresses to winter jackets was either hung neatly on racks or stacked in orderly piles and rows on large counters that ran the store's length. On one wall hung small farm implements, such as pitchforks, shovels, and clipping shears, along with the usual hardware implements like hammers and screwdrivers.

There were bins of nails and screws and nuts and bolts that seemed to run the gamut of anything an islander would need. In one section were plumbing materials, and in another, kitchen and bathroom supplies, along with a large glass and china display. The aisles were wide and could easily handle people passing each other.

"Whatever's not in here can be found in the warehouse," explained Diane. "He's got everything out there, from bales of hay to ploughs and donkey harnesses."

Standing just inside the front door, she called out for Marcus. Sean was taking in the various supplies, including materials, such as books and pencils, which he assumed were for homeschooling, when he saw a person he supposed was the shop's owner walking rapidly toward them. His right arm was outstretched.

"Hello, Diane, and this must be Sean," he said in a deep bass voice.

As the man took his hand in a firm shake, he offered a hearty, "Welcome to the Knob. It's good to meet you. I'm Marcus, and this is my shop."

Marcus was a tall, lanky man, wearing a gray sweatshirt and jeans that bagged in the rear. Sean guessed his age to be somewhere in the midforties. A shock of black hair worn combed back was complemented by a full, dark beard that engulfed his face.

After chatting for a few minutes, Diane left the two men and went looking for the needed supplies.

“Is there anything I can help you with? Or would you like to take your time and look around?” asked Marcus.

“Since this is my first visit, I think I’ll just take a wander and become familiar with everything you have in here,” Sean responded.

Telling Sean not to forget the library, Marcus went in search of Diane.

In the front, off to the right side was an area that contained three tables and twelve chairs. A counter with a sink ran along part of the wall. Stacked neatly on the counter were mugs and plates. A large urn gave off a pleasing aroma of just brewed coffee.

On the way over, Diane had told him that cigarettes, alcohol, and recreational drugs weren’t part of the Janus culture. Sean could only shake his head and marvel at how much the world had bypassed the island.

“When you live with almost no outside contact and an island is your home, it’s easy to realize that those stimulants aren’t needed,” Diane explained. “We don’t criticize the world for having them. In fact, some of our diaspora use them. It’s simply that on Janus they’re not needed. However, we do have a vice. It’s caffeine. We probably drink more coffee per person than any country.”

To the left of the door and running along the front wall were burlap gunnysacks with their contents clearly labeled. Bags of sheep wool, barley, and oat seeds were piled two and three deep. Vegetable seeds for such items as tomatoes, cucumbers, and peppers were in smaller bags and placed one on top of the other. Sacks of flour, which Sean knew came from the island's mill, ran down the last part of the front wall and partially along the side.

It seemed as though the Knob had everything an islander could need. Sean knew from his trip on *Journey* that the store worked with the Guardians to meet some of the island's requirements. He wondered if the Guardians were the only external supplier or if the Knob had other methods for stocking its shelves and helping individual islanders with specific items.

Diane arrived with a bag full of nails and slung one of the smaller sacks of flour over her shoulder. Sean was impressed. No wonder she could work a farm on her own.

"Are all the women on Janus as capable as you?"

"We grow up working in the fields or on fishing boats. One thing you'll learn is that men and women are equal on the island."

Laughing, she said a quick good-bye and was out the door before Sean had a chance to respond. He'd planned on asking her to sit with him, but obviously that wasn't going to happen.

Moving through the shop, he'd picked up the required toiletries; a pair of brown corduroy pants; and a blue, heavy woolen shirt when he saw hanging against one of the side walls a collection of pea jackets. He hadn't worn one since the mideighties, but something made him decide to look them over. There were several sizes, and he picked out a large. The coat obviously wasn't new but was still in such good condition that he couldn't put it back.

Sean gathered everything up and placed them on a counter at the back of the store. There was no cash register, only an old-fashioned adding machine. A brass bell was beside the register. Sean pushed the bell's plunger.

About a minute later, Marcus strolled out from behind the curtain, wiping what appeared to be bread crumbs from around his mouth.

"You seem to have found what you were looking for," he said.

"Yes, but nothing has a price tag."

"Oh, I guess neither Mrs. Kerr nor Diane explained how our shop operates."

"No. Is there something special I should know?"

"We're a trading shop. Cash is very seldom used here. Most times when people come in, they bring things, such as parts of their crop or clothes they no longer need to build up a credit. Then when they need something, I take it off the credit they've accumulated.

"Other times, people may need something but don't have anything to trade. They build up a debit until such time as their crops come in or they get a really good catch of fish or have slaughtered one of their animals.

"Those large freezers on the far wall"—he pointed to the right side of the shop, where three old and battered Amana freezers stood side by side—"are where I keep meat, fish, and produce.

"I also have four larger freezers in the warehouse that I can use when those get full."

Sean was fascinated. "You seem to have a lot of stock. How do you maintain your supply?"

"Most of what I have in the store comes through trade with the families," said Marcus. "And in some cases, particularly with meat and fish, families will trade with each other. We try to be as self-sustaining as possible. Even so, there are some items that are impossible to get on Janus.

"We trade with the farmers on the Orkney's Mainland. They get many of their supplies through the ferries that dock there from northern Scotland. Several of our families have stalls at the farmers' market next to St. Magnus Cathedral in Kirkwall. The market operates the last Saturday of each month. The Knob has had a stall there for many years.

"Some shoppers at our stalls simply want to pay cash for our goods.

"I administer the cash we get from Kirkwall, and twice a year, once in June and the other in November, all the islanders put together another list. These contain items that we haven't been able to get by trading with others throughout the Orkney Islands or in Kirkwall.

"I give the money we've collected to the Guardians along with the list, and they shop for us either in Inverness or in Glasgow. Obviously not everything on the list can be obtained, but the Guardians do a good job of getting us things we need. And an item that isn't found the first time it goes on the list usually gets bought during the second or third visit by the Guardians."

Turning his attention to the practical matter of how he was going to pay for the goods he'd placed on the counter, Sean said, "I don't have any goods to trade, but I can give you cash. I've got some pounds with me, and I'd rather not start by building up a debit."

"It's not a problem either way," smiled Marcus. "I'll just add up the total of everything you have here. Since you'll be staying with us for a while, you can run a tab like the other islanders."

According to Marcus, everything that Sean had picked out came to seven pounds.

"Are you sure that's correct," he said in amazement. "The pea jacket alone should be worth about forty pounds."

"Since ours is a goods-based economy, where the bulk of what we purchase is in trade and the value is set by an annual meeting of the islanders, we don't have inflation. For example, your pea jacket has been equal to four pounds of potatoes or two pounds of fish for as long as I can remember."

Sean handed over the cash.

"I'll put this with the money we get from our stalls in Kirkwall," said Marcus.

Since he didn't have to be anywhere, Sean thought he'd have a coffee and look through the library. He asked how much a cup cost.

"It's free to everyone who visits the Knob," he was told. "We also have scones, and I've just taken a batch out of the oven. I'll put a few in a basket and bring them over to you."

"This is quite the shop. You and your family must put in a lot of hours keeping everything organized."

"Yes we do. I have two adopted sons. We brought them over from Taiwan when they were just babies. The Guardians helped us arrange the adoption. They're wonderful boys. Alex is ten, and George is eight.

"You haven't met Ted. He's my partner. We've lived together as a couple since about six months after he arrived on Janus.

"It's Ted who's responsible for designing and, along with everyone on Janus and a large group of Guardians, building the dam on the western part of the island that supplies us all with electricity. It took sixteen years to complete, including wiring the farms. But Ted is someone who won't let anything stop him. He started the project a year after he'd been on the island, and we've had electricity for three years. It has made an incredible difference in our lives.

"It's a fairly basic system but has meant we no longer rely on coal and peat. The drop in air pollution has been dramatic, and with coal, we're conserving a nonrenewable resource. It's all part of the conservation program Ted has established.

"The island practiced conservation before he arrived. But it was just something we did, recognizing that in order to survive we had to live as one with nature. Ted has become completely involved and has organized the island's conservation efforts. He's taught everyone the value of ensuring that we not only conserve but continue to examine new ways of improving our efforts."

"Where's Ted now?" asked Sean. "If he's around, it would be nice to meet him."

"He's out working our ten acres. The boys are with him. We have a few head of cattle, some sheep, and chickens. We also grow barley and wheat. I'm so proud of Ted. Before he came to Janus, he'd never been near a farm. The closest he got to beef was in a supermarket. Now he works the land as though his family had farmed for generations.

"You won't see him today. He won't be back until the sun sets, but I'm sure Elijah will arrange a meeting. I know Ted wants to meet you."

"How long have the two of you been together?"

Marcus smiled. "Ted and I lived together for several years and were married eleven years ago in the same way all couples on Janus are married. We said our vows and were officially pronounced a couple by Elijah. Everyone on the island attended.

"Janus is an open, tolerant, and understanding society. Homosexuality is viewed as a normal expression of one human being's love for another. It's been that way since the first settlers landed. Our culture accepts there is no distinction between same sex, heterosexual, or transgender couples."

Marcus laughed and said, "But that's enough about Ted and me. I'm sure there are other things you want to know about Janus."

One aspect of island life that had intrigued Sean since he'd learned Diane had taken over her family's farm and Marcus had been the one in his family to inherit the Knob was how the decision was made about who in a family got the property. By definition, an island had only so much land, and the islanders would have long ago run out of property to support everyone. That was why they'd established their diaspora. Fighting over land inheritance was a common occurrence. How was it resolved on Janus?

"I don't mean to be pushy," he began. "But how did you come to own the Knob and not one of your siblings?"

"You don't seem to be the pushy type," smiled Marcus. "You're talking about the Janus line of succession. The centuries-old custom on Janus is that, in a marriage, there's joint ownership of all property, regardless of which partner brought the property into the marriage. When one partner passes on, the property reverts to the surviving spouse. When that person dies, what they own, whether it's a farm, a fishing boat, or a store like the Knob, automatically goes to the eldest child. In our case it should have gone to my sister. However, she didn't want to come back to the island because of her career in London.

"Tradition states that the person, in this case my sister, is given two months to decide. After that, it goes to the second oldest, which was me.

"Your next question," said Marcus with a wide grin "is what happens if the couple's children don't want to return to the island or, as in rare cases, the children predecease their parents. There are three other stipulations, besides succession, to owning property on Janus.

"If no one is directly in line, the oldest niece or nephew has the right of first refusal. If he or she already owns property or declines, it is offered down the line to the next oldest niece or nephew. On the island, it is of major importance that a property, if at all possible, stay in the family.

"Now, in the rare instance—and it has only happened twice in the last hundred years—that a niece or nephew doesn't want the property, it is offered to the oldest Guardian. If the eldest declines, it is then offered to the next oldest right down to the youngest.

"On those two occasions, the oldest Guardian accepted the property. If, however, all the Guardians were to decline, it would be offered to anyone who was born on the island and wished to return. Should two or more want to return, it would be given to the oldest. If no one wanted to return, which I doubt would ever happen, it would then be given to someone who has come to the island and lived here for a minimum of fifteen years. That has never happened.

"In the case where both parties in a couple bring property to the marriage, they are permitted to keep the largest parcel of land. After that, the line of succession takes over for the family of the one giving up the property."

"What about available land?" asked Sean. "Is there any left?"

"After two thousand years, every piece of farmland, along with all the houses down by the dock, is occupied."

Sean was fascinated. The Janus society appeared to be well structured and able to deal with whatever contingency should arrive. However, he remained curious about a couple of aspects.

"What happens if a couple or a person gets too old to handle the farming or fishing. How is the line of succession applied?"

"In the same way as I've just explained. The next in line takes over the property. The former owners or owner has the choice of staying in the house or moving to a retirement home in Inverness that is maintained by the Guardians. The building has thirty rooms and they're not usually all filled."

"I don't want to be morbid," said Sean, "but how do you handle death? This is a relatively small island. Surely you haven't buried everybody who has died on the island since your ancestors first arrived. You'd run out of room."

"We have a cemetery near the western tip of the island. However, we stopped burying people in the early thirteen hundreds.

"The procedure for taking care of our dead was changed. Since we're a small island, it was decided at the time that we didn't have the room for an expanded cemetery. Now, when a person dies, there's a service which everyone attends and is presided over by Elijah.

"The body is then cremated. We have a small crematorium out near the dam. The ashes are collected and the family takes them out to sea where they're spread over the ocean.

"The rules are strict because it's the only way we can manage Janus' finite resources. We also believe in taking from the ground and the sea only what we can use."

The bell at the store's front door rang.

Marcus looked up.

"That's Mrs. McManus. She's come to settle her account with eggs and some strawberry preserves. It's been good to talk. I hope you haven't been bored."

"Not at all," replied Sean. "I found it extremely interesting."

He was rewarded with a large smile as Marcus walked out from behind the counter and down one of the aisles to see how he could assist Mrs. McManus.

# Chapter 33

The Knob's library was comprised of seven large, six-shelf bookcases set side by side. Ranged against the wall on the opposite side of the front door from the coffee area, they were filled with dog-eared hard and soft cover books. Sean was amazed to see the variety of titles, running the gamut from modern fiction to philosophy, from scientific and economic theories to biographies, and just about everything in between.

Three large oak tables were set in front of the shelves. Each was surrounded by a grouping of chairs. While two tables were clear, one was piled high with various newspapers ranging from *The London Times* to *The Inverness Scotsman* and from *The New York Times* to Canada's *Globe and Mail*. Magazines included *Time*; *The New Yorker*; and the British medical journal, *Lancet*. Looking at the dates, he saw that some of the journals were more than six months old, with none more recent than several weeks. Nevertheless, he was impressed at the diversity and assumed it was the Guardians who supplied the Knob with such a disparate selection.

Marcus had stopped talking with Mrs. McManus and was on his way over with a large basket of scones.

"How do I take out a book?" wondered Sean.

"There are no library cards or late fines," said Marcus. "A book can be kept out as long as needed. And we don't have a library cataloguing system. I keep the books grouped according to category."

"So everyone takes books out and returns them through the honor system," noted Sean.

Marcus seemed surprised. "I've never thought of it that way. It's just how things have always been done. The written word is a vital foundation block of our society. We believe that unfettered access to information opens the mind to new and exciting possibilities. Some of us may not always agree with what we read, but access to knowledge helps broaden everyone's horizon. It's hard to understand regimes that curtail and even stop the free flow of information. Societies can only progress if every person has the ability to access knowledge.

"Janus is a reclusive society, but it's important we understand what has shaped and what continues to shape the world beyond our border. Books, newspapers, and magazines serve as our window. They provide an insight into new ideas and ways of doing things. For example, everyone on the island benefits when new methods are introduced to improve our farming, fishing, and herding techniques.

"It's also fascinating to follow the way new concepts and beliefs take shape in the world. It allows us to not only place the development of our society in perspective but to also guard against complacency. Janus is a unique society, and we must always work at ensuring that it remains what our ancestors envisioned—committed to understanding, tolerance, equality, and peace."

"How do you keep your titles current? I saw books that can't be more than two or three years old. What happens to the older books? Your shelves are overflowing, and you obviously don't have space to expand the bookcases."

"It's really quite simple," explained Marcus. "Twice a year, the collection is enlarged when *Journey* drops off one or two crates of books. I immediately put the new titles out. The books I'm replacing are placed into the just arrived crates for storage. During the spring, I take the crated books to the farmers' market in Kirkwall. The money raised from selling them is put back into the island's library fund for the Guardians to purchase new books."

Sean was impressed. The system was practical, met the island's needs, and kept a steady flow of new information available to everyone.

"I assume the newspapers and magazines are brought in with *Journey*," he said.

"That's right," responded Marcus. "The Guardians bring over a large stack with every visit."

"Is that how everyone on Janus keeps up with world events?"

"It's one way," explained Marcus. "There's also a handful of islanders who have shortwave radios and pick up the BBC's *News of the World*. If anything major happens off the island, it gets around Janus in a hurry."

Sean offered his thanks and returned to the small library. Looking through the bookcases he found, what he thought were several unusual books for the Knob's collection. The titles claimed that the paperbacks explored and answered the question of the meaning to life. They looked to be well-used paperbacks, and Sean was intrigued that the islanders were so obviously interested in the subject.

Taking one of the books with him, he poured a cup of coffee and collected a scone. Making his way to a table, Sean settled into one of the chairs. After several sips of coffee, he began reading through the paperback.

He sensed the arrival of another person and looked up, expecting to see Marcus. It was Elijah.

"Do you mind if I join you?" asked the Prophet. "I came in to pick up some supplies, and since there's no reason to rush back to the house, perhaps I could answer some questions you might have about our island."

"That would be great."

Elijah took a seat opposite Sean.

"I see you've discovered one of our books on the meaning of life," said the Prophet. "It's a fairly broad subject. Are you looking for a scientific, religious, or philosophical answer?"

Sean paused, thinking for a moment. "I suppose at the moment I'm more fascinated with what the islanders view as the reason for their existence. Everyone leads a relatively simple life when compared to the rest of the world.

"Is that the answer? The islanders are content that they'll live and die on Janus. However, is contentment the definition of existence? Or does every person view his or her relationship with the Spirit as the answer to why they're here?"

Elijah nodded, his eyes sparkling with curiosity at where Sean would take the conversation.

"In order for the Janus community to have survived this long," Sean continued, "and to have expanded beyond the island's shores, there must be some well-developed tenets for how life should be lived. What are they?"

"When our ancestors first came to the island," the Prophet began, "they quickly learned that their survival depended upon living a life as defined by the Hellenistic period. During that time, the Cynic philosophers identified the purpose of life as living a life of purity that is at one with nature.

"It's an existence that depends on self-sufficiency and being in complete control of one's mind. In this way, it's possible to live without negative emotions, such as sadness, anger, and self-pity.

"We practice the same philosophy to this day. Like the Cynics, we reject the normal desires for the worldly aspirations of wealth, power, and fame. We do this by freeing ourselves from the need for acquiring possessions."

"But Marcus told me that all land and fishing vessels are owned by the island's families," interjected Sean. "That seems counter to what you just said."

"Not really. Ownership is merely a human convenience for ensuring that, whenever land or boats pass from one family member to another, the line of succession allows for an orderly transfer. It doesn't take away from the fact the current owner believes the property is on loan from the collective that comprises every islander.

"We've also borrowed from the Stoic philosophy that inner peace can be achieved through logic and reflection.

"Another part of our philosophy is based on the belief that we're each responsible for leading lives that benefit the group. We contend that every person's general well-being is dependent on every other person. It unites us in a common goal of ensuring that we're kind, patient, and understanding with each other. When assistance is required, it is given freely and without thought to personal gain.

"True, it's a simplistic existence, and we occasionally have some trappings from the world, such as electricity. But again, we view these things as borrowed, not owned. For example, we use water to generate electricity. Obviously, we do not own the water. We borrow it for the time it is being used to generate the electricity and then return the water to the ocean.

"As sentient beings, we believe that the world belongs to everyone and that, if people gave up their pursuit of material wealth, there would be no wars or the resulting famines and poverty that follow from these terrible disputes."

Elijah paused.

"That explains how the people of Janus live," said Sean. "But it doesn't answer the overriding question of what the islanders consider is the meaning of life."

"We believe," said Elijah, "that it's the responsibility of each person to establish his or her own meaning. On Janus every human is accountable for his or her actions.

"Our meaning is created through a common purpose of living with nature, assisting one another when needed, and ensuring our children are prepared to be the next generation. The foundation of our society is based on the four words that I've already mentioned—understanding, tolerance, equality, and peace.

"We fundamentally believe that those words form a philosophy in which there is no need for government or religion. Our emphasis is on living for today in harmony with all those on the island."

"Except, not everything is perfect," noted Sean. "There are people like Mrs. Kerr who lost her husband and sons. Now she never ventures from her house."

"That's true," conceded Elijah. "Life isn't ideal, even on Janus. We've had years when our harvest was poor and the fishing terrible. It produced difficult winters with food at a premium. But we've survived the bad years and enjoyed the good ones."

"Did anyone ever blame the Spirit during those difficult periods or ask it to provide better times for the future?"

Elijah paused a moment before answering.

"Our relationship with the Spirit is not based on asking for things that are material or related to nature and our crops. The Spirit is a confidant, a counsellor. We discuss things that are troubling us or for which we need advice. The Spirit offers its thoughts, but it is up to each individual whether or not its words are followed.

"We live a simple life and separate our day-to-day existence from our relationship with the Spirit. We strive to ensure that our land is not overburdened by crops and animals, that we don't take more than we need from the oceans, and that we are good to one another. Our belief in the Spirit is based on the knowledge that it exists.

"However, it would be wrong to say we live this way solely to please the Spirit. The society we've built is what gives meaning to our lives. It guarantees the survival of our culture, language, beliefs, and respect for the environment from one generation to the next. Living solely to please the Spirit would take away so much of the pleasures that we enjoy on Janus. We live independently of the Spirit."

"So what you're saying is that a person doesn't have to believe in the Spirit to lead a meaningful and caring life," said Sean. "To accomplish that, you have to live well. Living well means doing something that people respect, that contributes to the greater good, that protects and nurtures the lives of those around you, and that ensures your value system is passed on to the next generation."

Elijah pondered Sean's rationale for a few moments. "Whether or not a person believes in the Spirit, the fact is that it exists," the Prophet finally replied. "We're fully aware of that on Janus. But having said that, I would concede that any individual can lead a meaningful life based on the parameters you describe without having a belief in the Spirit."

A momentary and comfortable silence settled between the two men. Sean took a sip of coffee and bit into his scone.

Elijah asked, "Is there anything else on your mind that I can answer before I head back to the farm?"

Sean thought a moment. Putting down his cup, he finished chewing. "There is something you can help me understand. Is it the individual or the community that takes priority? And how are disputes settled?"

"We have a form of governance in which both are treated with equal importance," explained Elijah. "Our system has evolved over the centuries. We've matured as a society. During our time on the island, we've come to understand that individual rights can be balanced with the collective good.

"I would never tell you that our system of governance is better than what is beyond Janus. But I will tell you that what we have on Janus has allowed our island to not only survive but to grow and prosper."

"It only works because you're a small community and there's no need for such things as a judicial system or a legislative body," noted Sean.

"That's because each person on Janus, sixteen years and older, knows he or she has individual rights. At sixteen, one is considered an adult and has an inherent responsibility to the group. There's the awareness that the collective is only as strong as the contribution every person makes to ensuring it remains viable."

"What rights does someone under sixteen have?"

"They have the all privileges and freedoms associated with childhood. We place little responsibility on our children. Homeschooling plays a large part in their lives. It is here they are taught the required subjects necessary to get them into colleges and universities away from the island. They also learn about our society's tenets in preparation for when they turn sixteen. We believe a sound education is the basis for a strong and functioning society that respects the rights of all individuals, regardless of age.

"We have a participatory government in which there are two distinct bodies—the Assembly and the Council. Together they form the Congress.

"Every adult is a member of the Assembly that debates and votes on all matters of policy," continued Elijah. "The Assembly is where everyone comes together to plan whatever changes to the island's social and economic structure that may be needed.

"Additionally, every citizen can be expected at various points in his or her life to be chosen for a six-year term of service on the Council of nine that draws up the measures the Assembly votes on.

"Every two years, one-third of the council is replaced. Each adult islander's name, with the exception of the three that have just served and the six currently serving is written on paper and placed in the sacred urn that was brought to the island with the first settlers. I then randomly choose three names to replace the outgoing councilors. Citizen's names are placed back in the urn six years after they've served on the Council.

"The Assembly meets on the first Monday of every third month, starting in January. We've just had our April session, and the next one will happen in July. The Council gathers one week before that to draw up the agenda. It's then that anyone wishing to have something brought before the Assembly brings it to Council. The Council also meets one week after the Assembly to review what has been approved by the islanders. It's at this Council meeting where the agreed-to projects are set in motion.

"Every adult on Janus is a true citizen of the island. We have the ultimate in participatory government, and each person has a direct influence on all decisions that are made at the Assemblies.

"The Assembly is a forum of open discussion. For each session, a chairperson is chosen by placing the names of all those present in a container. I reach in, select a name, and that individual guides the discussion. If no consensus is reached, the subject and the interested parties go before the Council.

"We don't live in a fool's paradise. From time to time, there will be disagreements. That is also why we have the Council.

"The sides enunciate their positions before the Council members. It is never difficult because the focus is on the positive aspects of the sides being presented. There is no discussion about the negatives of the opposing position. We do not believe in attacking a contrasting view.

"Council's role is not to decide the merits of one proposition over the other. Its function is to seek a common ground between the proposals. It may take many hours, sometimes days, but the Council is a mediator, not a judge. The Council at all times seeks to have those involved in a disagreement reach a compromise, where the strengths of each proposal are recognized.

"In this way, all parties are involved in the project as it moves forward."

"What happens if common ground can't be reached?" wondered Sean.

"There's always a common ground. True, sometimes one person has to give up a bit more than the other to arrive at the middle. However, through patience and a desire for compromise, it's achieved. It all goes back to our belief that the strength of any individual is magnified when working in a group. There is also the realization that any form of discord would eventually create factions and possibly destroy what we have."

"Suppose there's a major disagreement between citizens outside of the Assembly?" asked Sean. "How is the dispute settled?"

"Disagreements are rare, but if one does occur, it's brought to the Assembly, which renders a judgment through discussion and a vote."

"And if one of the citizens involved in the dispute disagrees with the Assembly's decision?"

"That's even rarer. It has only happened once during my time. When that occurred, it was my responsibility to sit with the Council and arrive at a solution that was beneficial to both parties. It also needed to be one the Assembly could feel comfortable in accepting. At all times, there was and is a commitment to compromise. There was no need for a second vote by the Assembly."

"Our culture is based on a profound respect for the rights, thoughts, and beliefs of our fellow islanders. This is something that has been passed down from parent to child throughout the centuries. It's a part of our culture and one that we fervently treasure."

“Aren’t you asking each individual to subjugate their rights to the good of the collective? Isn’t that a form of socialism?”

“It may appear to be a socialist state to you, but that would be putting the incorrect definition on what we have on Janus. Every individual—whether the owner of a farm or a fishing boat or people, such as Marcus and Ted, along with our doctor, vet, and dentist— has the right to decide what he or she will contribute to the rest of the island. In return for a person’s goods or services, he or she is compensated at a rate equal to that of whatever is received for a similar effort by any other islander.

“What we have is nothing like socialism,” continued Elijah. “That’s an economic and political system in which the means of production are publicly or commonly owned and controlled through a cooperative. We do not, as socialism advocates, base our social equality and distribution of whatever is produced on one’s contribution to our society. On Janus, everyone owns his or her land or ship and is responsible for whatever is produced. There are no syndicates or worker cooperatives. Everyone is independent.

“Part of the fabric of this independent framework is the knowledge that each farmer or fisherman is accountable for contributing to the whole and will receive back what is needed to maintain his or her part of the equality that is Janus.

“We are a barter society. There is no acquisition of personal wealth. That alone reduces the danger of one person harming another. Also we have a strict moral code that is passed on from generation to generation. And with our small population, it is far easier to have it adhered to than, say, larger societies where opportunities for equality are not as prevalent.”

“But suppose you have a year where storms damage crops or those same storms don’t allow the fishing boats to go out and the catch for a season is worse than normal?”

"We have a tithe system for times like that. Each year, every farmer puts aside 10 percent of his or her crop and it is stored in granaries on the southwestern part of the island. Our fishermen, through the market at Kirkwall, put an equal amount of their catch up for sale. It is the only product we do not trade. We accept only cash for this fish. That is put into a fund, which is kept by the Council. We now have enough set aside that we could easily survive several years of barren fields or poor fishing by our fleet.

"The tithe also contributes to paying for the college and university education of our sons and daughters. Most of it, though, is handled through the Guardians."

"So is the tithe mandated?"

Elijah appeared confused. "The tithe is and has always been mandated by all the islanders. You must understand that it's agreed to by every individual because that's the way we're raised. From the time children are old enough to comprehend, they are taught that, without everyone contributing to all aspects of the island's economy and welfare, we will not survive."

Sean leaned back in his chair. He found the conversation fascinating. A new world was opening up for him.

"I'll have to be going soon," said Elijah. "There are many things I want you to learn about Janus, and as time goes by, I will explain everything to you."

"Before you go, I just have a couple more questions," said Sean. "How have you been able to maintain a society for close to two thousand years without anyone ever expressing the need for free will? Haven't you ever had people who rebelled against the thought of their individual achievements being subjugated and shared throughout the collective?

"It seems to me that you stifle any form of leadership within your community. Every family, every society has those people who are natural born leaders."

"I don't know how you can say that," responded Elijah. "We honor and cherish free will. For centuries, we didn't have electricity. When Ted came and joined our island, he proposed to the Assembly the building of dams on the western part of the island and the creation of a grid that would generate enough power to bring electricity to every home, barn, and dock.

"The island, as you can see, has been wired to facilitate Ted's dream. True, as Marcus has probably explained to you, it took many years for the last house to receive electricity. But Ted was able to innovate. Wouldn't you call that having him exercise his free will? He had an idea that we accepted, and he saw it through to reality."

"I believe you're missing the point of what I mean by free will," argued Sean. "Philosophically, free will means that individuals, regardless of external forces can and do choose some of their actions."

"And where do you see that not happening on Janus?" replied Elijah. "People are free to farm or fish as they want. What they do inside their homes is up to them. All that we ask—as do all societies—is that a person doesn't commit murder, doesn't perpetrate other crimes that would harm the general populace, and contributes to the general welfare of everyone on the island.

"We encourage everyone to leave the island and get a college or university education. We have the resources to make that possible. We don't mandate what institute should be attended or what courses must be studied. Once their education is completed, our diaspora assists them in getting jobs. When and if they return to Janus, all that experience, along with the island's core values comes with them.

"I don't believe your argument is applicable," continued the Prophet. "Rather than postulate that we don't allow free will or that the collective supersedes the rights of every person, I think you should accept that we have achieved a balance between the rights of the many and the rights of the individual.

"The concept may be foreign to the rest of the world. We have been able to sustain our culture based on the understanding that, as individuals, we are responsible for the well-being of everyone else on the island. If I was to put a name to our economic structure, I would call it a social contract that every individual has with the island's population."

The doorbell rang, and Sean looked up to see Diane walk in. He was surprised to see her at the Knob, believing that once she'd returned home, work on the farm would have kept her there for the day. Carrying an armful of plaid shirts and a basket of eggs and tomatoes, she charged into the shop calling out for Marcus. Glancing neither left nor right, she headed straight toward the farm implements' section.

Elijah looked across the table at Sean and said, "I believe this is as good a time as any for me to be getting back to the farm. It's almost midday, and there's work I should be doing before sundown."

The Prophet got up and made his way out of the Knob, leaving Sean to ponder an unusual and interesting conversation.

# Chapter 34

Marcus had appeared, and Diane was having an earnest conversation with him about needing a new pitchfork. The one she'd been working with had had two of its rusted tines finally break off that morning.

"My great-grandfather first brought the thing home. That's how long our family's been using it. I feel as though I've lost an old friend," she complained.

No one else was in the Knob, and Sean could clearly hear the voices as Diane and Marcus debated the merits of the various pitchforks the shop had available. He was fascinated by the amount of detail involved in purchasing the implement.

Never having lifted a pitchfork in his life, he was amazed to learn that Marcus carried four- and five-tine models. Some were good for digging earth, others for moving hay and manure, while some could do all jobs. All were secondhand, having been used in trade for some of the Knob's other merchandise. Diane chose one of the newer models with five stainless steel tines and a shock-absorbing grip. They retreated to the back of the store and the checkout counter to work out the sale details.

Sean sat wondering what to do next. He laughed to himself, remembering how in the past, it seemed that every minute of every day had to be filled with what appeared to be meaningful tasks. The island had no need for cell phones or Blackberries, and he realized how much he didn't miss the need to be in constant communication.

He decided to spend a few minutes reading *The New York Times* before returning to Mrs. Kerr's for lunch. As he crossed in front of the door to make his way over to the table containing the newspapers, he was run into by Diane who seemed intent on getting out of the Knob as quickly as possible.

She was carrying the newly acquired pitchfork in one hand and her empty basket in the other. Fortunately, while she was carrying the fork parallel to the ground, the tines were pointed backward. As it was, Sean was rammed in the stomach by the butt end of the implement's handle.

Letting out a large oomph, he doubled over as the pain seared its way toward his groin. A look of profound shock registered on Diane's face. She dropped the fork, and the clattering sound brought Marcus on the run. Feeling embarrassed and not wishing to create a scene, Sean stretched to his full height. Meanwhile Marcus picked up the fork and handed it to Diane, who stared forlornly at Sean.

Looking at his two customers and correctly reading the situation, Marcus wisely said, "Well, it looks as though I've done all I can. If there's anything else, just let me know."

"I'm fine," said Sean, hoping to erase the "I've just lost my favorite kitten" look from Diane's face. Not wanting to remain standing in front of the door, he suggested they move over to the tables. The pain was fading, and he was able to make the short distance without any sign of discomfort, to the apparent relief of Diane, who hadn't yet uttered a word.

"I didn't see you there," she finally said. "At least let me get us some coffee."

Sean was feeling the pressure on his bladder from the coffee he'd already had. However, he didn't want to pass up an opportunity to sit with Diane. He replied that, while she was getting everything, he'd be right back. Seeking out Marcus, who pointed him in the direction to the bathroom, Sean returned feeling somewhat lighter and much better. Taking a seat opposite Diane, he noticed that she'd placed the pitchfork and basket in a corner by the counter.

"How are you feeling?" she asked.

"No damage done, and I get to spend some time with you. I'd say it worked out well for me," he said, trying to sound casual.

"I'm glad there was no permanent damage," she said with a mischievous smile. "When I saw you bent over, I thought the worst."

"No, fortunately you missed all the vital parts," he replied, a smile also pulling at his lips.

Sean took a sip of his coffee. With thoughts of his conversation with Elijah still fresh in his mind, he wondered how Diane had adapted to the island's culture after her return following so much time spent away from Janus.

"Do you ever miss all that the rest of the world has to offer?" he asked.

"What do you mean?"

"Well, you've lived away from Janus and experienced things that don't exist here. Don't you ever want to go out to a fine restaurant, take in a movie, or even watch television?"

Diane stared at him, a look of curiosity on her face. "I made a conscious decision to come back here when my mother died.

During my time away, I enjoyed the life I had for the most part. But in the back of my mind, I always knew I'd return to Janus. What I didn't know was the twists and turns I'd have to go through before getting back here.

"My first stop was New York. For someone who'd never been off the island, the initial experience was mind altering. But I'd received a good grounding from my years on Janus, and I survived those first few weeks in the Big Apple. After that, I settled in and went about the business of living in the city.

"The Guardians had found me a small studio apartment. I got myself a job waitressing at night and enrolled at the Monroe School of Nursing. It was difficult, but I kept to myself and studied hard. After four years, I graduated with a bachelor of science degree in nursing.

"After graduation, I went to England and got a job in a London hospital. It was extremely satisfying to be working at something that I'd trained to do. I loved everything about nursing. It was a job I'd always wanted. I felt needed and knew I was contributing to the welfare of my patients."

Diane took a sip of coffee and paused, seemingly lost in thought about those early years way from Janus.

While Diane remained silent, Sean momentarily pondered what her reasons for telling him all this might be. The pause dragged on, and he wondered if she'd suddenly realized who she was talking to and decided that enough had been said. He was surprised when Diane began again.

"For three years, life went along pretty well as planned. I had a nice apartment just a couple of tube stops from the hospital. There were some men in my life but nothing serious. And I spent my holidays back on Janus with my mother. Then, like so often happens, things took a back seat to something I hadn't foreseen."

"What happened?"

"I fell in love. He's an Australian and was in his second to last year of residency to becoming a neurosurgeon. Bruce, that's his name, is eight years older than me.

"Two months after we met, I was living with him. Six months later, we were married. In the beginning, I truly believe we loved each other. But it's hard to make a marriage work when one of the partners is seldom around. All the stories you've heard about doctors' residencies are true. It was nothing for Bruce to be at the hospital for thirty-six straight hours. He'd come home, immediately fall into bed, sleep for a few hours, and then it was back on duty. It was a difficult time for us.

"I had my own shifts. There were some weeks where we wouldn't see each other for days. The only way I'd know he'd been home was his dirty clothes in the hamper. When you seldom spend time together, everything becomes rushed. There's no time to plan or to talk things over. It becomes easy to drift apart.

"We'd been married five years and both of us knew the marriage was in trouble. Unfortunately, like most failed marriages, we weren't prepared to give up on each other and spent the next several years trying to save something that was already broken.

"Bruce had finished his residency and written the necessary board exams. The next step was to practice as a neurosurgeon.

"I don't know how to explain it, but somehow during that time, Janus became an albatross around my neck. I thought of all the problems we were having. Every day seemed more difficult than the last.

"It seems unreal to me now, but there was a time I felt totally forsaken by the Spirit. There were just too many problems to handle. And the worst thing of all was that I was feeling increasingly sorry for myself. So when Bruce suggested we go to Australia to live, I leaped at the chance. He had a position waiting for him at a hospital in Sydney, and we knew I could get a job in any one of the city's several hospitals. But the most important thing to me was that it was about as far away from Janus as I could get."

Diane suddenly stopped and, for the first time, took a drink of her coffee. It had gone cold and she grimaced at the taste.

Sean, getting the message without having to be asked, picked up the two mugs. Emptying both out in the sink, he refilled them and headed back to the table.

Sitting, he put both mugs down. Diane sipped from her mug. Sean did the same from his, knowing he'd missed a lunch that Mrs. Kerr would undoubtedly have prepared. He felt a large sense of guilt because, upon leaving that morning, she'd asked him if he wanted lunch prepared and he'd responded that he'd be home in time.

She was a kind lady and had welcomed him into her home, treating him as though he was part of her extended family. Sean knew he was probably making too much over a missed meal, but his conscience was bothering him. He resolved to somehow make it up to Mrs. Kerr.

Diane put her mug down, and Sean wondered about the work that needed doing on her farm. He was about to ask but then stopped himself, afraid that if he reminded her, she might leave. He found himself intrigued not only with the story but with Diane. Selfishly, he thought if she was revealing all this, she might be interested in him. For the time being, he didn't want to let that go.

She looked into his eyes and smiled. For a fleeting moment, Sean had the admittedly ridiculous notion that she knew what he was thinking. Realizing it was impossible, he decided to keep the attention on her story.

"What happened in Australia?" he asked.

Diane uttered a self-mocking laugh. "It was a disaster from the start. We thought that, with a fresh start, our problems would be left behind. We were wrong. Bruce and I worked at different hospitals, and that meant we could never get our shifts to match. One of us was always coming home, while the other was leaving. When we were together, which was seldom, we spent most of the time blaming each other for not being able to spend more time together.

"It took us another year to realize the marriage wasn't going to work."

"That must have been difficult," said Sean softly. "You were in a strange country, a long way from home, and your life was falling apart."

"Have you ever been divorced?" asked Diane.

Sean was silent for a few moments. How much should he tell her? What importance did the separation and the firing hold for him anymore? It was Hilary's death that battered his heart and soul. "I was married," he said quietly. "But she died. It was cancer."

Silence overtook the table for a few moments, until Diane spoke. "I'm so sorry. That must have been heartbreaking. Were you deeply in love?"

"I loved her very much," Sean said simply, not wanting to awaken old and bitter memories.

"Do you have children?"

"No, we were both too interested in our careers. She was especially driven to succeed. There just wasn't any time in our lives for something that would distract from her road to the top.

"But that's enough about me," he said, desperately wanting to keep the conversation away from Hilary. "We were talking about you."

Diane looked at him, a shrewd expression hooding her eyes. "Elijah said you're a private person. I should warn you, though, that, on Janus, secrets don't stay hidden for long."

"I'll take that under advisement." Sean laughed. "Tell you what. Finish your story, and I promise, the next time we get together, I'll tell you about my life. But I warn you, it's not very interesting. You should prepare to be bored."

Sean was amazed at how relaxed he felt with Diane. Considering the short time they'd known each other, the two were kibitzing like old friends. The burgeoning relationship felt comfortable. While Sean had long ago learned to never take anything for granted, he wondered how deep their friendship could become.

"What comes next?" he asked. "How did you get from Australia to here?"

"There really isn't much more to tell," she said.

"While we both knew it had ended after our first year in Australia, the decision was made to give it more time. That was my idea. I desperately wanted it to work because I was afraid. It seems foolish now, but I felt completely cut off from Janus. Although I'd been alone in New York and London, the sense that Elijah and my mother were there for me was always present. I didn't feel that way in Sydney. My world was Bruce. The only people I knew were other nurses on the ward. Most of them were married with children. There wasn't any socializing after work. I'd go home to an empty house and wait for him to come through the door.

"Bruce, on the other hand, had his family, his old chums, and plenty of women who wanted to keep a potentially rich neurosurgeon company.

"I shouldn't have been, but I was surprised when he started phoning, telling me that he was so busy that he'd be sleeping at the hospital. His absences became more frequent as the months went by. It dawned on me that our marriage was over when I realized he'd only been home for three days out of two weeks. And even then, it was just to get a bunch of clothes that he threw in a suitcase.

"That was the low point in my life. My marriage was in ruins. I was in a strange country with no friends."

"How'd you get out of the mess?" asked an intrigued Sean.

"We had a computer at home. I took a few drinks for courage and wrote to Elijah through the Guardians' e-mail address. I must have written for two hours. I poured everything onto the keyboard. The words just kept trailing across the screen, while I kept drinking. The more I wrote, the more I wanted to write.

"When I hit send, I didn't know how long it would take for him to receive it and then answer me. I was desperate to get out of my marriage and the country. I just wanted to come home to Janus.

"A week later, two Guardians arrived at my house. They explained Elijah had sent them to bring me back to Inverness. I packed a couple of suitcases and left a letter for Bruce explaining that I'd left him. The Guardians took me to the bank where I emptied my account.

"Fortunately, Bruce and I kept separate accounts.

"Two days later I was living in a room at the Inverness house kept by the Guardians. I'd been told to wait for Elijah's arrival.

"I was in shock. One moment I'm in Sydney, living a life that I'd grown to hate. Before I realized what was happening, I'm sitting in a room in Inverness waiting for Elijah. It was nerve-racking.

"While I appreciated all that had been done, no one would tell me what was going on. Every question I asked was met with the same two responses, 'Get some sleep, and Elijah will be able to answer that for you.'

"Elijah arrived the next morning. It was then that I learned my mother had died two weeks earlier. I'd come home just in time to be too late. That was devastating. My e-mail arrived in Inverness just as Elijah was preparing to telephone. That's why everything moved so quickly.

"Thank goodness it was Elijah who told me and saw me through the difficult time I had handling it. We spent about a week living at the house. Every day, we'd talk for a few hours and then go out for dinner to a restaurant. Our favorite was a place on Ness Walk. Their pasta dishes were delicious.

"Elijah, as he always does, looked at the positive. He was the one who reminded me that the reason I'd left the island was to become a nurse. Well, I'd become one. Not only that, but while in Australia, I'd studied and practiced midwifery."

"What about your marriage? Did you ever get a divorce from Bruce?"

Diane explained that a divorce had been handled through Elijah and the Guardians. "All I had to do was sign some papers while in Inverness. A few months after I arrived back on Janus, I received several legal documents certifying that my marriage was ended. The Guardians had gone to Bruce with papers for a no-fault divorce, and he'd signed. Knowing him, he'd probably already found someone to share his bed. By then, I was long past caring. It was just wonderful to be on Janus and free of anything resembling my past life."

Diane looked down at the table. She was silent for such a long time that Sean thought she'd finished her story. He sat waiting, not sure if he should say anything. She seemed lost in thought, and he was loath to interrupt.

Sean waited. She gave him a long stare and then broke her silence. "And now I've been here for four years, working the farm and helping our doctor to deliver babies. It can be difficult at times, but I enjoy it."

"It must sometimes be a lonely life," noted Sean.

"The winters can be long," she conceded. "Once you've made the trip to the barn, checked on the animals, cleaned out their stalls, and fed them, there isn't really that much to do. It's a big house, and sometimes I feel like I'm rattling around in it. There are only so many days one can come to the Knob and chat with your neighbors.

"I read a lot, patch my old clothes, and sew or knit new ones." She laughed. "It's not exactly the life I had when I was away from Janus. But I wouldn't trade it for anything. This is where I belong. It took me a lot of years to realize that. Maybe it's what makes Janus so precious. I was out in the world. For me, this is the best place to be.

"And then there are days like this. The spring air feels fresh and clean, and there is just a hint that summer is coming. The animals are restless to get into the fields, and you can feel their excitement. Spring planting means long days in the fields, and the summer is filled with so many chores that the days seem to fly by. With the fall comes the time for harvesting and getting prepared for winter.

"It's the rhythm of the seasons and the fact we can sense every new day that I enjoy so much about my island.

"I didn't realize until I came back that I'd taken certain aspects of living on Janus for granted. Those opportunities weren't available out in the world, and I've happily decided this is where I'll spend the rest of my life. I know that because I don't have those days when I was away from the island of looking in the mirror and wondering who I really was."

"I think we all do that at times," said Sean. "Sometimes we get caught in situations that make us question what we really want out of life. The years pass by so quickly, and suddenly you start questioning some of the decisions you've made along the way. But by then it's too late.

"When I was younger, I believed that happiness was like a mountain," he continued. "It might take you half a lifetime to scale it and reach the peak, but once there, you'd find and keep happiness for the rest of your life."

"Do you still believe that?"

"No. I've learned differently. In my world anyway, true happiness is like a butterfly. If it touches you even once or twice a year, there's such a feeling of tranquility and joy that it makes up for the bad times."

"What happens if the butterfly never lands on your shoulder?"

"Oh it does. You just have to recognize and appreciate the moment. Maybe that's the lesson life teaches—learning to understand and enjoy the good times."

"Has this been a good time?" Diane asked shyly.

Caught off guard by the question, Sean took a moment to answer. "It's been a very good time," he said quietly.

"I've also enjoyed it," responded Diane. "But I should be getting back. It's late in the day, and there's work to do on the farm."

"I suppose we should be going," offered Sean reluctantly.

They got up from the table and washed their cups in the sink. Diane picked up the pitchfork and basket and waited, while Sean went in search of Marcus to tell him they were leaving.

Since he hadn't made it back to Mrs. Kerr's for lunch, Sean asked Marcus if there was anything that his landlady would like as a treat. Expecting to be told something like chocolates, he nevertheless wasn't surprised when Marcus said pickled eggs.

Sean picked up two large jars and placed a one pound note on the counter.

"That's way too much," said Marcus.

"Can I use whatever is left over as a credit for the next time I buy something?"

"You certainly can," responded the shopkeeper. "I'll post it in my ledger."

# Chapter 35

Walking out of the Knob, Diane turned to Sean. "I can't believe I've told you so much about my life. You're too darn easy to talk to," she said in a faux accusatory tone. "You have the ability to draw people out of themselves. I hardly know you, and yet I'm telling you things I've only shared with Elijah.

"You're similar to him, you know. You have an air of compassion and calmness that makes it easy to share things with you. You're a patient listener with the ability to ask the right questions, without appearing to be intrusive. And you always appear interested, even if you're not," Diane finished with a self-conscious laugh.

"But I am interested," Sean said with conviction.

"Are you?"

She stopped in the middle of the road to stare at him. "I'm flattered you think my life interesting enough that you're willing to give up so much time listening to what I have to say. I did go on a bit, and I'm thankful you didn't die of boredom. I promise you, though, the next time we meet, I'll be far less talkative about myself. It's quite unlike me to unload my life's mistakes on a complete stranger."

"I'm not really a stranger," Sean quietly said. "I thought we were getting to know each other."

They'd walked for several minutes without a word passing between them when Diane said, "I didn't mean that the way it sounded. We have the beginning of a friendship. But you've only been here a couple of days, and I really don't know that much about you. In fact, none of us know why you're here. It was Elijah who brought you to Janus, so the reason must be important."

"What has he told everybody about me?"

Now that Diane had brought up the subject, Sean was curious as to what people knew about him.

"Not that much. When Elijah spoke to the Assembly, he told us that it was important you be brought to Janus because you represented the next stage in the island's evolution.

"He also told us a bit about your background. No one was quite sure what you could possibly bring to Janus, but since it was Elijah and he seemed so positive that you would influence the island's future, we agreed to have you join us.

"Why are you here?" Puzzlement deepened the lines on her forehead and cast a shadow over her eyes. Sean found the effect somewhat distracting.

"I don't really know. I tried bringing up the matter with Elijah, but he put me off to another day."

"So why did you come?"

His birthmark was beginning to ache. "I'm not sure," Sean began hesitantly. It wasn't lost on him that he was now opening up to Diane in the same way she had revealed part of her past to him. He was surprised at how easy it felt. She seemed to be a warm and giving person. While he found her intensity disconcerting, it wasn't bothersome enough to make him want the talk to end.

Avoiding her gaze, he stared down the road. "I don't know why Elijah reached out to me. We exchanged a couple of e-mails, and a friend of mine from the UN recommended that I consider what Elijah had to say. At first I didn't give it much thought. But I was given an extensive leave by my publisher. Elijah's e-mails promised an interesting experience. I had the time, and so I'm here."

"So how long are you going to be on Janus?" Diane asked quietly.

"I'm here for a couple of months. It worked out that my visit is timed with *Journey*'s schedule. I'm looking at it as an extended holiday. Once it's over, I'll return to my job in London."

Diane slowly nodded, saying nothing. The two walked together in silence.

It was late afternoon. The sun's thin rays were no longer providing the heat they'd bestowed upon Janus earlier in the day. A wind had come up, blowing in from the west. Sean could feel the ocean's chill. He put on his newly purchased pea jacket. The changing temperature didn't seem to bother Diane.

They had passed Mrs. Kerr's. Sean noted, with pleasure, that it was now taken for granted he'd walk Diane home.

Arriving at her front gate, Diane said, "I'd invite you in, but there's lots of work waiting for me in the barn."

"Is there anything I can do?" asked Sean hopefully.

Diane's laugh was low and throaty. "Thanks for the offer, but I don't think a city boy like you is quite ready to muck out stalls and handle bringing sheep in from the fields. Perhaps when you've been on the island a bit longer and I've had time to teach you some things about taking care of animals, you'll be able to help. Today, though I'm running late and should get back to the barn."

With that, Diane leaned forward and gave him a sisterly kiss on the cheek. Before he had time to react, she was through the gate and walking along a well-worn path that led around the house's front and toward the barn in the rear. Just before disappearing from view, she turned, gave him a wide smile, and was gone.

He stood in the road for a few more moments and then started back toward Mrs. Kerr's. The birthmark was no longer throbbing.

Walking through the front door, he heard her call out from the kitchen. He continued through the hallway to the back of the house. She was setting the places for the evening meal. The smell of cooking chicken emanated from a Crock-Pot.

Before he could get out a hello and hand her the jars of pickled eggs, she asked, "So how was your day?"

There seemed to be no chagrin that he'd been absent for lunch.

"I spent it at the Knob talking with Marcus, Elijah, and Diane. I was having such a great time the day got away from me."

Mrs. Kerr took the jars from him, placing them on the counter. "I suppose this is for missing lunch," she said with mock severity.

"Yes," he replied. "Marcus told me they're one of your favorite treats."

"Well it's very nice of you. There isn't a woman alive who doesn't appreciate receiving a thoughtful gift. Now why don't you go and wash up. Dinner will be on the table in just a bit, and we don't want it going cold."

# Chapter 36

Covered in violent shades of red, along with spotty hues of yellow and orange, the evening sky had the color of a battered boxer's face who'd gone too many brutal and disappointing rounds with his opponent.

Waiting outside Mrs. Kerr's, Sean noticed that coming in from the east were dark and menacing clouds. They appeared heavily laden with rain. A slight chill was in the air. Just for a moment, he wondered if he should go inside to fetch his pea jacket.

He was saved from having to make the decision with the arrival of Elijah. The Prophet was wearing a light sweater over a white T-shirt on top of a pair of hiking shorts. On his feet were leather sandals. Sean, with his heavy sweater, jeans, and boots felt overdressed.

As they walked along the Ring Road to the Community Hall, Elijah explained they would be meeting two people—Richard, the island's veterinarian, and Eve, the Janus dentist.

"It's a good opportunity for you to learn more about our island."

"Will anyone else be there?" asked Sean.

"I've invited Diane to join us. I hope you're comfortable with that." Elijah was smiling.

Sean returned the smile but said nothing.

He was pleased Diane would be present. Spending time with her was becoming one of the major attractions to being on Janus.

Arriving at the hall, Sean was surprised to see that the discussion was to take place outside. A fire had been built. Elijah made the introductions.

Sean guessed Richard was in his late forties. Tall and heavily built, he had a receding hairline that exposed a prominent forehead. Dense, blond eyebrows sat atop light blue eyes. A large nose ran straight to a wide mouth that oversaw a strong chin.

Eve, of Chinese descent was small and slender with long, coal black hair that rested easily on her shoulders. Dark brown eyes were complemented by high cheekbones, a gently upturned nose; and delicate lips. Elijah had told Sean the dentist was in her mid-thirties.

Four benches surrounded the fire pit. Richard and Eve were seated on opposite sides, while Diane was on another bench. Elijah took a seat beside Richard. Sean chose to sit with Diane. Looking skyward, he noticed the dark clouds still bearing down on the island and wondered how long they would have for their discussion.

Following his gaze and seeming to read his mind, Elijah said, "I expect we have a couple of hours before the rain arrives. That should allow plenty of time for us to have an enjoyable talk."

He looked over at Richard and nodded.

“As you’ve already heard from Elijah,” began the vet, “our society is based on individual pluralism, rather than an adherence to a group. In most pluralistic societies, factions with the same value and thought systems are naturally formed. On Janus, it would seem normal for farmers to think one way, while those who fish would think another. However, that’s not the case.

“We believe ideas should coexist, not permanent groups. Political parties or other forms of governing, such as dictatorships, often become corrupted by power or fall victim to the dogma of their founding beliefs. They lose sight that a society is made up of individuals; most striving to live life as best they can.

“The island does not have political parties or societal units. It is individuals who support or disagree with an idea. During an Assembly they may naturally form into a group simply on the basis of where they stand during a particular discussion. It does not mean the same islanders will agree or disagree in similar fashion when another idea is raised.

“There are no wrong ideas. Every suggestion brought before the Assembly is considered valid, and we discuss it without parameters. The foundation of our life structure is that all individuals contribute to the needs of the many.”

“That’s why,” chimed in Eve, “we have separated ourselves from the world’s general society and are bound by our faith in each other, our commitment to our island’s independence, and a relationship with the Spirit. This is what allows for constant harmony between every islander.”

Sean was having difficulty believing that a group of people could live together in continuing accord. From what he’d seen in the world, it wasn’t possible.

"It doesn't seem natural that as human beings, there wouldn't be the occasional disagreement over an idea or a proposal to change something on the island," he said. "At some point, haven't neighbors become angry with each other over a real or perceived slight?"

Sean's four companions looked at each other.

Finally, Elijah spoke. "You've only just arrived on Janus. I realize, from your experience, the notion of a collective harmony may be difficult to accept. But it's possible for a group of people who share a common goal to live in peace.

"Beyond our shores, cynicism is rampant. People's motives, especially if they seek to do good works, are often questioned. That's not how we live. We believe in the worthy intentions of everyone on Janus. It isn't something we think about. This is just the way our island functions.

"Our independence has allowed us to form a society that is codependent and values what each individual contributes to the group's ongoing welfare. We have always realized that living peacefully with the others who share Janus is the only way to ensure our society's survival."

"So the harmony you're describing is more a result of necessity than it is attributable to the goodness that everyone hopes is an inherent quality in most humans," responded Sean.

"Ah the skepticism," said Richard with a chuckle, taking the edge off his comment. "It isn't a question of morality. We live the way we do because we have inherited from preceding generations the belief that this is the best way to live. There's no reason to change. We have found that living in peace with one another is the greatest gift that life has to offer."

The group sat silently for a couple of minutes.

Sean gazed skyward and saw the rain clouds coming close to the island. Facing the fire, he could feel a chill on his back as the wind's intensity began to strengthen.

Sean was the first to speak. "Over the past two weeks, I've heard a lot about the island's independence. A moment ago, Elijah talked about the same thing. How independent can you be? You must be part of some country. The Orkneys and the Shetland Islands belong to Britain. The governments in London and Edinburgh must know you're here. The Faroe Islands are part of Denmark. What about Copenhagen?

"You can't live here without some interaction with the rest of the Shetland, Orkney, or Faroe islands. What about taxes, health care, government programs, and your children's education?"

"We don't appear on any map," Diane responded.

"How can that be possible?" wondered Sean.

"The Spirit ensures our anonymity."

Sean looked at his companions. "You're telling me that, because of the Spirit, Janus has remained hidden all these years. What about weather satellites, aircraft and fishing boats? Surely someone must know you're here."

"It's not as dramatic as it sounds," said Elijah. "It's true the Spirit has allowed us to remain invisible to the world, but we do have some interaction with outsiders.

"There are the markets on the mainland. We get the infrequent tourist or fishing boat that needs some repair. Occasionally a census taker will bravely try to determine how many of us live here. And while our children are homeschooled, they must travel to Inverness in order to write and pass school board exams that allow them to attend college and university.

"But it doesn't matter because nobody wants this island. Governments and bureaucrats come and go. Why pay attention to us, when there are so many other distractions to keep them occupied?

"And most importantly, we don't need the world. For health care, we have our own doctor, midwife, and dentist. For the very ill, the Guardians have contacts throughout hospitals in Glasgow and Edinburgh.

"Richard is here to take care of our animals.

"And as you know, the Guardians provide whatever supplies and services are needed."

"But I don't understand why you don't appear on any map or haven't been tracked. To say that the Spirit enables this doesn't seem logical or possible to me."

"Well the reality is that we don't appear on a map," said Elijah. "Once you're here a bit longer, you'll understand the Spirit's power."

Sean leaned back. Who was he to argue with what these people believed? He was sure a rational explanation lay somewhere behind their beliefs, but wasn't prepared to argue the point. He decided instead to take the conversation in another direction.

"How have you been able to retain your independence and create such a strong and vibrant culture without needing to reach out to the world?" Sean asked.

"Our margin for error as to how we live is small," answered Eve. "Unless we fully cooperate with each other, work to preserve the ecological balance, and understand the other person's rationale for being here, we can destroy the island's entire ecosystem in just a few seasons.

"The most important commitment, next to each other, is to the island's ecology. Our people have survived on this island for two thousand years because we treat the island and its resources with respect. Everything we do, from land management to caring for our animals and governing the water supply takes into account that the island's ecology must be sustained in order for us to live as we do."

"That seems fine," began Sean, "but your population isn't static. I've seen several children. What happens when they get older?"

"We encourage them to leave," said Diane. "We tell our children to go and see the world. We encourage them to seek higher education and to get jobs.

"Some of our children choose to stay. Others, like me, return after acquiring an education and experience that will benefit the island. That is how we balance the population with those who die. Most, though, leave and only come back to visit. We hope that, both individually and collectively, they are a force of good and kindness."

"Aren't you creating a diaspora that promotes your views?" wondered Sean. "How are you different from any other culture that wants to spread its beliefs beyond its homeland?"

"Our diaspora is striving to convince people in developed countries that such initiatives as education and water and earth management, along with proper shelter and nourishing food must become the world's focus," interjected Richard. "What our people are striving for is the recognition on the part of global leaders that, only through peace, a commitment to the planet's ecological welfare, and the recognition that resources must be shared will earth survive.

"All of us would agree with you that our diaspora is promoting our views. But wouldn't you agree that, given the problems confronting the world, the diaspora's mission is valid?"

"There's so much strife in the world," agreed Sean. "How much influence can your diaspora have?"

"It's a slow process," conceded Elijah. "Our beliefs are not mirrored in numerous parts of the world. Many among our diaspora are lone voices raised against the growing tide of human warfare and ecological destruction. But we hope that may change one day.

"Let me ask you a question. Although you've only been here a couple of weeks, do you feel the world is ready for the message of Janus? Suppose our island had someone who was willing to lead the island, the Guardians, and our diaspora in showing the world what Janus has to offer?"

Sean ran a hand over his face. He massaged his temples and gently rubbed his eyes. Slowly collecting his thoughts, he began, "Janus is a tiny island with a small population. You've been able to live in peace because you've all agreed that it is the only way you can survive.

"The problem with what you're asking is that the type of world you describe is unattainable as long as humans fail to comprehend that peace is more than the absence of war. It is developed countries assisting poorer nations to break free from their chains of poverty and violence. There has to be the understanding that every individual, regardless of location in the world, is entitled to a fundamental level of food, housing, health care, education, and employment.

"Also, all individuals must have the right to believe, speak, write, and live in total freedom, without the fear of repression, as long as their decisions respect the rights of others to believe, speak, write, and live. And there has to be some form of global commitment to doing all this while finding ways to reverse the destruction that has been done to earth's ecosystem.

"The bedrock of everlasting peace is hope. It's what motivates and challenges humans. Hope in the future anchors almost everything we do. It is the essence of human emotion and the inspiration that creates medical innovations and solves the genetic codes of the most ravaging diseases. It is there when nations sign peace treaties and is the foundation for the belief that parents have in a better future for their children.

"Unfortunately, natural aggression trumps hope. Every living thing, including plants, insects, animals, and people fight for survival. Even human babies become aggressive when they don't get their own way. That is the reality of our world. The human body and mind continue to evolve with matching survival tools so that both can continue to exist and succeed in an increasingly complicated and dangerous globe."

"I understand what you're saying," responded Elijah. "So let me ask you another question. What if we took the Janus message to the world with the Spirit's assistance?"

Sean lapsed into silence, striving to get his thoughts in order so that he could make a rational reply to Elijah. "I assume you're talking hypothetically," said Sean.

"Why would you think that?" replied an obviously puzzled Elijah.

"Because, as the world stumbles from one tragedy to the next, many people are left to wonder if the Spirit really exists or whether we are alone on this journey through space and time."

"Of course the Spirit exists," responded the Prophet. "Let's accept that I'm not talking hypothetically."

“I know that every person on this island believes the Spirit exists,” responded Sean. “However, I’ve seen no evidence of the Spirit. Religions try to convince people that their god is real, but no one has been able to prove a deity’s existence.”

“What if it could be proven to you that the Spirit is real?” asked Elijah.

It was said so casually that Sean almost missed the inference. After several seconds, the suggestion hit home and he wondered if, as he’d originally suspected, he’d actually been drawn into some form of cult.

The birthmark was aching, the pain becoming more agonizing as he sat and wondered what Elijah was driving at.

“What exactly are you telling me?” he said.

Elijah looked at the other three. Each gave an imperceptible nod.

Finally he spoke. “We commune with the Spirit on a one-to-one basis.”

“And does the Spirit ever respond?” asked Sean, intensely curious at what the reply would be.

“Yes,” the four of them chorused, answering his question with such intensity that Sean was startled.

“In fact,” said Elijah, “we converse with the Spirit directly and in our own time.”

Sean took a deep breath. Was he really having this conversation?

“I know it’s hard to believe,” said Elijah, his voice quiet. “But don’t dismiss what we’re saying as some strange fantasy. You were curious enough to come here. Let that interest be your guide on what could be a fascinating journey. Open your mind to our reality."

The fire was burning low. Most of the flames had gone out. The coals, though, were radiating a strong heat. Sean felt warm. He was sweating, and his birthmark was beating a steady rhythm.

Darkness was beginning to descend on the group. The evening stars were gradually being forced out of sight by the encroaching band of heavy, black clouds.

Something about the discussion was bothering Sean. The more he thought about it, the more elusive it seemed. Then, as if a door had opened in his mind, he realized what it was he wanted to ask. "The only force I've heard about this evening is the Spirit," he slowly said. "What about the devil? Does he exist on this island? In your minds, does he exist in the world?"

"We don't call that force the devil," responded Elijah. "Our ancestors referred to it as Abaddon, the Hebrew term for destruction. We don't dignify Abaddon with any other reference, but always use Abaddon. And if one believes in the Spirit, then it is within the normal boundaries of earth that you must also believe in Abaddon."

"What does that mean?"

"In its purest form, the world exists in a state of balance. There is light and darkness, wind and calm, fire and water, summer and winter, hard and soft, and so on. All of these things exist as a counterbalance to the other and are codependent. Therefore, if there is good in the world represented by the Spirit, there must be evil, represented by Abaddon."

"But what if someone doesn't believe in the Spirit?" asked Sean. "Suppose this person is an agnostic or an atheist."

"It doesn't really matter does it," responded Elijah. "Whatever name anyone chooses to put to it, good and evil exist in the world. The Chinese refer to the world's balance as the yin and the yang. Just as there is dark, cold, contracting, and weak, which is yin, there is yang, which is bright, hot, active, expanding, and strong. They cannot exist without each other. Together, they express the interdependence of opposites.

"In its most basic form, yang stands for peace and serenity, while yin encompasses confusion and turmoil. The balance is not static. It's constantly evolving, and sometimes one is stronger than the other. The continuing movement of these two energies, yin to yang and yang to yin, causes everything to occur—just as things expand and contract and temperature changes from hot to cold.

"Abaddon exists in the world, as surely as evil is real, just as the Spirit and goodness exist," said a somber Elijah.

"The question then becomes," continued Sean, "why does the Spirit allow evil in the world? Couldn't one argue that the Spirit should be stronger than Abaddon?"

"It's not a question of the Spirit allowing evil or that one is stronger than the other," responded Elijah.

"What is it then?" Sean probed.

"We're talking about the classic human dilemma," said Elijah. "Every individual has been given a free will. With that, comes the ability to decide whether to live a life in which you will not cause suffering through committing evil acts or whether you will make those around you endure emotional, mental, and physical strife.

"It's the coexistence of good and evil in the world. On the island, we believe that evil is present in the world as a counter to the good that exists, not the other way around. We believe that the vast majority of the world's population is inherently good. However, one evil act can offset a myriad of good causes and people. And thus we have the balance."

"But there are many natural examples of suffering that aren't caused by evil people," argued Sean. "I can think of such things as disease, earthquakes, floods, and famine, to name only a few."

"And the counter to that," answered Elijah, "would be the bountiful farmlands of many countries. Yes, there are floods, but there is also rain that allows plants and crops to grow throughout the world. The oceans, lakes, and rivers supply a diverse range of sea and freshwater life. Forests take carbon from the air and turn it into oxygen. And there are farm animals that provide sustenance for all manner of people."

"What about individuals?" asked Sean. "Why do some people do evil things? Where is the balance within these people?"

"That's a difficult question to answer," noted Elijah. "Since the two forces are never static, there are occasions within some people and possibly always in others, where the yin is sometimes or always stronger than the yang. We believe that, regardless of one's disposition, it is a person's responsibility to understand the forces that are present within his or her body, mind, heart, and soul. Only by studying oneself and understanding the powers that are present can a person achieve true harmony.

"I know this doesn't totally answer your question, but from what I've learned, any guiding philosophy, regardless of the culture, goes back to the fact that every individual has free will. Within any society, it is ultimately an individual's choice whether to commit evil."

"There's something I'm not clear on," said Sean. "If the Spirit is not perfect in the eyes of the islanders, then is it possible that Abaddon is not entirely evil?"

"We believe there can be shades of goodness," argued Elijah, "but how can you have shades of evil? If any act is based on an immoral foundation, then the end result must be some form of evil. I can only speak for the islanders but we are fixed in our view that Abaddon has no redeeming qualities."

Sean sat back, trying to fully grasp all that he'd just heard. His thoughts were quickly interrupted because the heavy, black clouds were now directly overhead and the rain had started. Falling drops hit the few remaining coals. The once bright fire pit hissed and popped. The five ran for cover into the community building, signaling the meeting's end.

Eve lived to the west of the Community Hall. Leaving first, she shook Sean's hand. "It was a pleasure meeting you. I enjoyed our discussion. Hopefully we'll have more in the future."

Sean replied in kind.

Eve ducked out the door and began running toward home.

Elijah explained that he wanted to speak with Richard for a few minutes about an ailing ewe. He said there were umbrellas in one corner of the building. They were there for just such an occurrence as the evening's downpour.

"It's an honor system," Elijah explained. "You borrow one. When you have the time, it can be returned."

Sean, seeing Diane eyeing the umbrellas, asked if she'd like to share one since they lived so close together. She accepted with a smile. Sean took the biggest one he could find, and soon the two were walking east along the Ring Road as the rain pelted around them. Everything was wet except underneath the umbrella's cocoon.

She was a head shorter than Sean. They walked side by side, their bodies close but not touching. A sublime intimacy that he hadn't felt with any woman since Hilary embraced him. He admitted to himself that Diane walking close to him under an umbrella didn't necessarily mean anything. It was simply two people going home together in the rain.

However, he realized the physical closeness of a woman was a feeling that he'd missed.

The rain was a drumbeat tattoo on the umbrella, while the wind was blowing cold and steady. Sean was glad he'd worn his sweater and heavy boots. Diane, dressed in a large fisherman's sweater, jeans, and Wellington boots, seemed impervious to the weather.

"So what do you think of our island now?" she asked.

"I admire the way you islanders live. You all have a reverence for life that's special. I'm beginning to understand what brought you back."

"I realized after getting home from the Knob the other day that I'd shared a large part of my life's story with you," said Diane. "I'm not usually that talkative with someone I've just met. I hope you weren't scared off."

"That couldn't possibly happen," Sean's voice was somber.

Diane turned her head to look at him. "Be careful what you wish for." Her tone matched Sean's.

Suddenly, she dashed out into the rain. Laughing, she raised her head, spread her arms, and spun like a top.

A few moments later, she joined him under the umbrella. "How's Mrs. Kerr?"

Sean didn't need a crystal ball to know that Diane didn't want to continue their previous discussion.

"She's seems to be doing fine. I'm well taken care of. Elijah couldn't have picked a better place for me to stay."

The rain was coming harder, biting into the road's surface. The wind was making it difficult to keep from getting wet, and conversation was impractical as the two struggled to stay dry under the umbrella. Their boots made loud splashing noises as the water started to gather in puddles.

After several minutes, they stopped in front of Diane's house.

She kissed him lightly on the cheek.

With that, Diane turned abruptly and ran lightly up the path, stopping on the porch. She turned, waved, yelled thank you, and was gone through the front door.

Left alone with his thoughts, Sean turned and walked slowly to Mrs. Kerr's. He was dimly aware that his birthmark had stopped aching.

Rather than go straight in, he stood outside for a few minutes, letting the wind, rain, and cold batter him. For the first time in years, his thoughts were captured by a woman other than Hilary. He thought of Diane's auburn, windswept hair. Her face that bore no makeup or lipstick was etched in his mind. He fantasized about holding her in his arms.

He knew he wanted to see more of Diane. The question was, did she want to see him?

# CHAPTER 37

Built in the twelfth century, the chapel was dominated by the hand-hewn, wooden beams and stone foundation that instilled a comfortable feel of permanence. With its cross, the altar was a shining beacon of hope for all those who believed in the majesty of the holy triumvirate—God, Jesus Christ, and the Holy Ghost. An air of solitude within the building served as a refuge for all those who visited and sought understanding from their god.

It was warm inside the building on this April morning. Dante Sabatini could feel the sweat running down his chest and back. It glistened on his forehead and coated his hands. He sat alone in the chapel, his thoughts focused on Janus, Elijah, and Sean Brennan. The file he'd brought lay beside him on the pew.

Of average height, Dante had thick, gray, close-cropped hair. Deep-set, luminous, brown eyes were cratered behind high cheekbones and sat alongside a pencil thin nose that flared at the end. A strong jawline exuded power. In his midsixties, he carried himself with the grace and bearing of man fifteen years his junior, the result of a strictly controlled diet and regular exercise.

He wielded immense but virtually unseen power. Dante was the prelate, or head, of the Praetorian Order. Established in 957 by Pope John XII, the order is a clandestine organization within the Roman Catholic Church. When founded, its mandate was to defend the Church against all external and internal attacks, whether philosophical, intellectual, financial, or physical.

To this end, the order developed an all-encompassing range of covert activities that ranged from spying and bribery to theft and sanctioned killings. While the order was effective in all its endeavors, a notable expertise had been developed in the art of secret assassinations when deemed necessary by the Vatican. Throughout the centuries, an unbroken line of lethal assassins had been produced within its headquarters at the Chateau Valencia in Spain. It was a point of pride that, through the years, the secrets, methods, and training regimens were passed down and improved upon from assassin to assassin.

Only the Pope and those in the College of Cardinals were aware of the order's existence. It was also known within the Vatican by the code name Fraternity.

Throughout most of its existence, the order's finances were handled through the College of Cardinals. This ensured the impossibility of independent action. And any notion that the Fraternity would act without the Vatican's approval was beyond the thinking of those heading the order.

That had dramatically changed with Dante.

In the almost four decades he'd been prelate, Dante had radically altered the order and its relationship with Rome. Under his rule, the order had gone from an instrument of Church policy to an independent organization that answered only to the prelate. While it theoretically still reported to the Vatican, the order was a powerful, self-financing body that paid little attention to the dictates of the Pope. Dante had bolstered its financial strength with the introduction of self-financing corporations, leading-edge technology, state-of-the-art marketing, and an upgraded system of clandestine operations.

The order still fulfilled its mandate of protecting the Church, but its actions no longer solely reflected the needs of Rome. Any activity undertaken by Dante ensured the order benefited both financially and politically. His control over the order was absolute, and he'd created an organization that wielded immense, though virtually invisible global power.

The prelate took great pride in what he'd accomplished. He had built the Praetorian Order into a clandestine financial empire that rivalled any international corporation. At the same time, he'd ensured the Church received whatever Fraternity resource was required.

Not a man open to compromise, Dante fundamentally believed that Christianity was the only true form of worship and Roman Catholicism the only genuine church. He viewed all other faiths, regardless of their commitment to God, as blasphemous.

On this day, he was deeply troubled. His vast, state-of-the-art technology bureau had intercepted the e-mails between Elijah and Sean Brennan. Dante was aware that Elijah had invited Brennan to visit Janus. The prelate had dispatched a team of watchers to Inverness. Its function was to relay back whether Brennan arrived in the city and boarded *Journey*.

When the news came through that Brennan was on his way to Janus, Dante realized Elijah was planning something that could pose a major threat for the Roman Catholic Church and, therefore, for the order.

If what he thought was correct, then Elijah's actions represented a new era on Janus. It would destroy the compromise that had existed for centuries between Janus and the Church.

Dante leaned back in the pew. He opened the file. While he was well-versed in the cojoined history of the Church, the order, and Janus, the prelate had pulled up the data-encrypted pages from the Fraternity's central drive and had them printed. The prelate was a thorough tactician. He believed that, in a sea of change, it was best to have a boat built of solid information. The chapel, with its natural tranquility, was the perfect place to begin solving the problem of Janus. He began to read.

Although the Orkney and Shetland islands had been Christianized in the late tenth century by then Norwegian king Olav Tryggvasson, it wasn't until 1157 that the Roman Catholic Church became aware of Janus. In 1118, a young French priest, Jean Louis Pannier, traveling between the northernmost island in the Shetland group and the Faroe Islands, encountered Janus. The lone island appeared on no map and had missed the attention of both Danish and Norwegian fishing vessels. As he brought his boat closer to the island, Pannier saw houses and people.

The priest believed he had been guided by God to bring Christianity to the unknown islanders. He landed on the island's southern coast and was surprised to see well-built docks with moored fishing boats. He traveled throughout the island and found a reclusive, self-sufficient, and Hebrew-speaking society.

Pannier spent more than five years on Janus. He learned Hebrew so that he was able to converse with the islanders. Despite his efforts, though, none of them was prepared to accept his Christian teachings.

Pannier knew the island contained a secret because he heard people speaking about the Spirit, yet they professed to have no religion. He was determined to discover the answer, believing it would help him in his efforts, guided by God, to Christianize the island. Pannier was a resourceful man. He ingratiated himself with an island family called Kirsch.

The priest helped with the farming and sheep herding. He became well known on Janus as a caring, hardworking, and understanding man. Pannier stopped speaking about Christianity. The priest professed to have no faith, although he secretly prayed for forgiveness at the falsehood.

Much of his time was spent with the family's oldest son, Solomon. He steadily gained the man's confidence. From the young man, he learned about the triangle-shaped birthmark that was imprinted on his left thigh. It was the sign of the Spirit and referred to by the islanders as the Mark of Janus.

The priest also learned of a cave where the islanders supposedly conversed with the Spirit. Pannier, not understanding the implications of the birthmark or the cave, believed he had stumbled upon a society that worshipped a false god. He was determined to see the cave for himself and asked God in prayer how he could bring these people to Christianity.

Pannier told everyone he wanted to visit the cave. However, the islanders met several times and decided he had not been among them long enough to share their secret. The frustrated priest decided to take matters into his own hands.

One day, knowing Solomon was traveling to the cave, Pannier followed him. As the man entered the cavern, the priest, not wishing to be discovered, stood just inside the entrance. He watched as Solomon sat on a bench and began speaking to the Spirit.

The priest heard a voice responding. Believing it must be a trick or the devil at work, Pannier rushed into the cave, intent on exposing the deceit. He grabbed the young man by the shoulders and implored him to accept Christ and God as the true saviors. The Spirit spoke, this time directly to Pannier, admonishing him for his treachery in betraying the young man's trust. The Spirit banished him from the island.

Pannier was terrified and ran from the cave. Stopping briefly at the house, he took some food, hurried to the dock, and launched his small boat out to sea. Once on the water, he hoisted his sail. Frightened at again angering the Spirit, he let the wind guide the boat. The priest assumed that, if he made land, he'd escaped God's wrath. If he died at sea, it was God's will. Fortunately, a strong east wind was blowing, and three days later, his boat pushed up against the Danish coast.

Pannier decided his next destination had to be Rome. He needed to warn the Pope of what he'd experienced. It took him four years to make his way to the holy city. The priest traveled through many countries. At times, during harsh winter weather, he was forced to stop for months in monasteries. There were periods when he endured severe hardships, including prolonged hunger and sickness. More than once, he almost relinquished his quest to warn the Church's hierarchy of what he'd seen and heard.

During those bleak times, Pannier took strength from believing that it was God's way of testing him. He understood that, if the islanders' ability to speak directly with the Supreme Being was ever exposed, it would destroy the Roman Catholic Church. While Pannier knew the islanders were committed to a cloistered lifestyle and maintaining their secret about the Spirit, he didn't believe they could be trusted. Without the Roman Catholic faith to guide their lives and offer salvation it would only be a matter of time before the islanders would try to poison the world with their beliefs.

Since they couldn't be converted to Catholicism, the only answer was their destruction.

Finally arriving in Rome, he begged for an audience with Pope Honorius II. The request was rejected. Pannier knew what he'd seen and heard. He was not to be denied. He stubbornly stayed in Rome and, over the next twenty-eight years, gradually, through diligence and devotion, rose through the Church's hierarchy. Pannier told no one his story, believing it should only be for the ears of the Pope. In 1154, he was transferred to Valencia and assigned to the Praetorian Order. Three years later, he became the order's prelate and was summoned to Rome to meet with Pope Adrian IV.

During his session with the Pope, Pannier told his story about Janus. At first, the Pope questioned whether Pannier was mentally stable or had grown senile. For a time, Adrian IV wondered at the wisdom of keeping Pannier as the Praetorian Order's prelate.

However, Pannier could not be swayed from his story. He continually drove home the threat the Church would face if the island's way of worshipping the Spirit became known outside Janus. Pannier offered to lead a group of his Praetorian Order soldiers to the island. He pledged to have everyone on Janus killed, the buildings razed, and the cave walled up.

The Pope declined the plan. Adrian IV believed that, if what Pannier said was true and the Spirit did speak to the islanders, he'd incur God's everlasting wrath by having Janus destroyed without first offering a peaceful resolution to the threat. Adrian IV didn't want his self-proclaimed throne in heaven jeopardized by an overly zealous prelate.

After much thought and prayer, he instructed Pannier and the dean of the College of Cardinals, Alfonso Benedetti, to travel to the island. Pannier's inclusion was necessary because he was the only one who knew the island's location. The men were instructed by the Pope to achieve a settlement that would protect the Church while leaving the islanders in peace—as long as one overriding condition was met:

Janus would be free to follow its isolated course if the islanders agreed to never disclose to the world that a cave existed where their Spirit conversed with them. In a major concession to Pannier, the Pope allowed the men to also carry the message that, if the islanders didn't agree or at any time began to export their secret, the Roman Catholic Church would unleash the full force of the Praetorian Order's soldiers on Janus and destroy the community, while denouncing the island's settlers as heretics.

Adrian IV had reversed his earlier position of not attacking Janus because he believed the islanders were being offered a fair and just settlement that would protect the Roman Catholic Church. If they declined or at some time in the future broke the agreement, the Church had every right to defend itself as the only true voice of God on earth.

The men arrived on Janus during the summer of 1158.

It had been thirty-five years since Pannier had left the island. He wasn't sure what to expect. The prelate was fully aware of the islanders' strongly held commitment to peace and understanding among all peoples. However, he had lied about his intentions and angered the Spirit. And now he was back to demand an agreement.

Pannier had no need to be concerned. Solomon, who had taken over the family farm on his father's death, welcomed both men into his home. Pannier and Benedetti were treated as friends throughout the island. Several days after their arrival, the men met with the island's Council. Pannier, as the only one who spoke Hebrew, explained the Church's position. He was told any request for an agreement would have to go before an Assembly.

Two weeks later, the proposal was brought to the Assembly. The island's small population was more than willing to abide by the arrangement. The islanders had no aspirations of sharing their secret with anyone. They were united and strong in their conviction to keep the world away from Janus.

Before leaving Rome, Pannier had written the agreement on four identical scrolls. Written in Latin and Hebrew, each had been signed with the seal of Pope Adrian IV. The nine-member

Janus Council added their names. One copy was left on the island. Another was for Pannier as the Praetorian Order's prelate. The third was for Benedetti in his capacity as dean of the College of Cardinals. And the final document was for the Pope's private library.

When Pannier and Benedetti arrived back in Rome, they were sworn to secrecy by the Pope. The secret had remained to this day, with only Dante, the Pope, and the dean of the College of Cardinals knowing about Janus.

Dante came to a copy of the agreement. He studied the Hebrew and Latin texts and traced the signatures with his finger. He wondered if there actually was a cave where his god spoke to the islanders. Or was it some Middle Ages fallacy? The appearance of God in some remote cave seemed impossible. And yet, he knew the island existed. Somehow, throughout the centuries, the secret had never been revealed by those who were born on Janus.

Only one event impacting the agreement had occurred during that time. Before his death in 1168, Pannier had written about his experience on the island, including the Mark of Janus being the sign of the Spirit. He had also drawn a detailed map of the island's location. Just two copies of each document existed. One set was with the Pope, the other with the Fraternity.

Dante leaned against the back of the pew and focused on what else he knew.

Ever since Pannier's return from the island, the Praetorian Order had kept a watch on Janus. Doing so was difficult at first. Mostly, the order had dispatched men claiming to be fishermen whose vessels needed repair. What they found was a community that continued as an isolated society and showed no inclination of sharing its secret with the world.

The island surveillance had changed with Dante and the growing advances in technology. Through the use of spy cams and electronic monitoring equipment, the prelate learned about the Guardians and the computer center in Inverness. For its global Internet network, the Guardians had established myriad levels of security, including sophisticated firewalls and a forest of revolving codes. However, the order's hackers were among the best. Even so, only occasionally and limited to mere minutes could they break through. But it was enough for Dante to learn of the island's worldwide diaspora. Most importantly, he had discovered Elijah.

During the past twenty years, through scattered bits of briefly intercepted conversations, the occasionally hacked e-mail, what appeared to be chance encounters with *Journey*'s crew or other Guardians in Inverness, and visits to the islanders' market stall at Kirkwall, a profile of the man known as the Prophet had been painstakingly built.

What worried Dante were scattered remnants of a cell phone conversation the order's listening devices had picked up between Elijah and one of his senior Guardians. It had taken place about a year ago. The Prophet was discussing the Spirit's desire to take the Janus message global. The transmission had broken apart for several minutes, and then Elijah's voice could be heard saying that could only be accomplished if they brought to the island the one who bore the Mark of Janus.

If that happened, the Roman Catholic Church, and every other organized religion for that matter, would be destroyed.

The prelate had not shared the information with the Pope. Having established the Praetorian Order as a global force, he had little time for the petty politics, assignations, and false piety that characterized the Vatican. Mostly, though, he didn't trust the advisors, including members of the College of Cardinals that surrounded the Holy Father. Dante believed in the adage that knowledge is power, and he wasn't about to share what he knew of Janus.

The question uppermost in Dante's mind was what sort of a threat Brennan represented. Closing the file, he knew what his next step would be. It was time to find out all he could about the man Elijah had brought to Janus. Was he who the Prophet had been searching for?

Dante got up from the pew. The prelate stepped into the aisle, made the sign of the cross, and bowed to the altar. He needed to speak with Anna, his head of technology. Through her, every field operative would be contacted. The mission, regardless of the country or the expense, would be focused on finding whatever information there was about Brennan. Nothing was to be spared. No fact, regardless of how inconsequential, was to be ignored.

The prelate hurried to his office. Upon his arrival, he walked straight over to the shredder. Slowly, he dropped each piece of paper into the machine's serrated teeth. A thorough man, Dante included the file folder. He used the intercom to contact Anna.

# CHAPTER 38

The early afternoon sun hung above the island like a golden orb, radiating heat and light. It was the final week of April, and this was the warmest and brightest day Sean had experienced since arriving. Diane had met him at Mrs. Kerr's. They were on their way to meet Ian McKenzie, the island's doctor. Elijah had asked him to brief Sean on some aspects of the Janus social structure.

Diane had been there when Elijah had suggested the visit. To Elijah's obvious surprise and Sean's pleasure, she'd invited herself along.

Seeing the look on Elijah's face, Diane had laughed and said, "Don't be so surprised, Elijah. I usually see the doctor once every couple of weeks to ask if my services are needed anywhere on the island. Look at this as one of my regular visits."

Elijah had responded with a wry smile but said nothing.

The doctor's office was in his home, about a mile east along the Ring Road from Mrs. Kerr's. As they walked to the house, Diane linked arms with Sean. He wasn't sure if it was meant as a gradual acceptance that their relationship was moving beyond the convenient companion stage or whether it was just an act of friendship. Then again, he thought sardonically, he could be reading too much into something as simple as Diane taking his arm while they walked.

It had been a long time since a woman had taken his arm, and he was amazed at how much it lightened his mood.

She was wearing a short-sleeve, cotton dress that buttoned up the front. Sean couldn't help but notice that it showed off her well-shaped legs and nicely defined arms, fit snuggly over her hips, and emphasized the outline of her breasts. Her hair was tied back in a ponytail, and as usual, she wore no makeup.

This was the first time he'd seen Diane in anything but baggy jeans and a heavy, wool shirt or long fisherman's sweater. She looked lithe and attractive.

Soon, the couple came to a small collection of houses with farm fields stretching behind them. As they neared the last house, Diane pointed out that they were at the doctor's home.

Walking up the crushed stone path toward the house, Sean caught his first glimpse of the doctor, who was waiting in the doorway, ready to greet them. He was a giant of a man with the girth to match. Standing well over six feet, he had a mane of white hair that was worn combed back off his forehead and reached to his shoulders. His face was covered by a neatly clipped white beard, topped off by a pair of eyes that were the same ice blue as those of a Siberian husky.

What could be seen of his face and neck were weathered a deep brown. He was wearing a blue, woolen shirt, with jeans held up by black suspenders. His stomach protruded like a battering ram, and Sean guessed his weight at close to three hundred pounds. Sean extended his hand. It was enveloped in a handshake characterized by a soft palm and huge, pudgy fingers.

As Diane and Sean entered the house, Ian brought them in with a jovial, "Welcome to my home. I wasn't expecting Diane to be with you, but I'm more than pleased to invite both of you in. Elijah has asked me to spend some time with you, and I'm happy to oblige."

Leading them into his sitting room, he turned and said that his wife, Edith, along with their teenage sons, was helping at a neighboring farm. The farmer had fallen and broken a leg that Ian had set. The boys were working the fields with his wife, while Edith was helping care for the patient.

Ian asked if they wanted lemonade, which Sean and Diane accepted with enthusiasm. The walk, while pleasant, had been hot, and both were thirsty. While the doctor was busy in the kitchen, Sean asked Diane if the lemons had been delivered during *Journey*'s last run.

"Yes, we all got some," she replied. "The Guardians keep us well stocked with fruits and vegetables that we can't grow."

With that, Diane loosened the tie around her ponytail. Her hair parted naturally in the middle and fell in soft waves, framing her face and resting gently on her shoulders.

The doctor arrived with the lemonade and three glasses. As Sean expected, the drink was thin on lemons but heavy on sugar and cold water. It was, nevertheless, thirst-quenching, and he was glad of the liquid. Ian had also brought in some bread and cheese.

Sipping on the lemonade, Ian began. "As both individuals and as a group," he explained, "we're a society in which there is total equality. It's not something we consciously practice. It's the way we live and has been passed on from one generation to the next. Our children are taught from an early age that all people are equal.

"The island's concept of parity encompasses everyone on Janus. It governs the way we distribute our resources and respect each other on a continuing basis and the decisions made at the Assembly.

"Every man and woman is viewed as equal in terms of opportunity, contribution, responsibility, and accountability."

"I'm willing to accept that all islanders practice equality in terms of your social, political, and economic structure," said Sean. "But it seems to me that Elijah is more equal than the rest of you.

"From what I saw of the deference paid by the Guardians and the way he seems to be treated on the island, it appears that Elijah garners more respect than others."

"That's not true," said Ian softly. "Whether it's in the production and allocation of food, the use of electricity, or his influence in the Assembly and Council, Elijah is treated no differently than the rest of us. Everyone, including Elijah, has the identical rights and privileges that come with being a part of the Janus community. That includes the Guardians and our diaspora."

"But isn't Elijah your de facto leader?" questioned Sean.

"No," replied Ian. "Just as I'm the island's doctor, Eve is our dentist, Richard is the vet, and Marcus operates the Knob, Elijah is our spiritual mentor. That's his function. It has nothing to do with leadership. We have no leaders on Janus. All decisions are made by the collective through our participation in the Assembly. As a mentor, Elijah is there to guide, but his advice can be followed or ignored.

"Elijah's role, similar to those who have gone before and those who will come after him, is simply to serve as a counselor in our relationship with the Spirit. He does not profess to have a unique bond with the Spirit that brings him closer to it than the rest of us. And the Spirit has never claimed to have a special relationship with Elijah."

"Then why does he seem to be treated with such reverence?" Sean wondered.

"That isn't the case," said Diane. "It's just that, in his role, he deals with people in times of stress and crisis, such as with Mrs. Kerr during the time immediately following her loss. A special bond is formed. But it's no different from the connection Ian develops with his patients or Richard has with farmers.

"We're not robots. Janus may be separate from the world, but we all share the same emotions that every human possesses. It's only natural that some relationships are deeper than others. But that doesn't mean Elijah or anyone else is more equal than the rest of us."

"When you put it in those terms, it makes sense," responded Sean.

Ian and Diane both looked relieved the subject had been brought to a close.

Something, though, was puzzling Sean, and it had nothing to do with the Spirit or Elijah. Instead it was a more practical question about the doctor's practice. "How do you get your medicines and equipment?" he asked. "You can't very well trade for them at a market. You must have a supplier, and I'm sure the company would want money for whatever materials you need."

"The Guardians handle all that for me," answered Ian. "I put together a list of supplies and equipment that I need. They deal with a number of companies and take care of everything, including payment."

The doctor rose slowly from his chair, and Sean was once again reminded what an imposing figure he presented.

"Can I get some more lemonade?' he asked.

However, it was already late afternoon, and Sean could sense Diane's restlessness. He wasn't surprised when she said, "Thanks, but we should be going. I've got my animals to care for, and I don't want to be working in the dark."

"Perfectly understandable," he answered.

Walking Diane and Sean toward the door, Ian offered, "I hope my explanation has provided you with a greater understanding of how our society functions. Elijah was specific as to my part of the story. It's extremely important to him that you learn as much as possible about us during your stay, however long that may be."

The doctor's words again reminded Sean that his visit seemed to have a purpose more complex than what he'd been told. It was all part of the mystery that surrounded this secluded society. He was looking forward to the time when the Prophet would reveal some of the island's closely held secrets. Perhaps, thought Sean, that would help explain his presence on Janus.

As they strolled back along the Ring Road, Diane took his arm. A comfortable silence rested between them. Diane's dress was ruffled by a light breeze that also danced playfully through her hair. She quickly tied it back.

When they arrived at Diane's front gate, she surprised Sean by saying, "I enjoy our time together. Hopefully we can see each other more often."

Sean was momentarily caught off guard. He wasn't used to such directness and thought how inured he'd become to such friendly gestures in the world so far away from Janus.

"I'd like that very much," he said. "Perhaps we can get together for dinner one evening."

Diane smiled, and said, "That would be nice. Let's see what can be arranged."

With that, she turned, gave him a kiss on the cheek, thanked him for an interesting afternoon, and ran lightly up the path to her front door. It was over so quickly that Sean was momentarily caught standing alone in the street. Seeing he was still there, she waved and blew him a kiss before disappearing inside.

Turning, he walked back to Mrs. Kerr's. Entering the front door, he heard her call out that dinner would soon be ready. As Sean washed up, he caught himself thinking of Diane. Somehow, the afternoon's conversation with Ian had taken a backseat to his thoughts about her.

At the same time, he felt foolish in assuming that a relationship could develop with Diane. He'd known her for slightly more than a month and seen her just a few times. All they'd done was set up a tentative dinner date. In a few short weeks, he'd be gone. He finished drying his hands and face, looked in the mirror, and smiled at his reflection, admitting that he was allowing his emotions to get tangled up in a quagmire of his own making. Sighing at the thought, he made his way to the kitchen.

As he took his place at the table, Mrs. Kerr placed a plate of chicken, turnips, and potatoes in front of him. It smelled and looked delicious.

Sitting across from Sean, she asked what he'd learned at the doctor's house. Before answering, he picked up a thick slice of hot, homemade bread and slathered it with butter. He began eating, first telling her how much he was enjoying the meal. She acknowledged his compliment with a smile. Sean then told her what he'd learned from Ian.

As she cleared the table, cut two large pieces of cake, and prepared a pot of coffee, Mrs. Kerr asked, "What do you think of our island now that you've discovered some things about us?"

"It's a unique place," noted Sean. "I have a feeling there's a lot more to Janus than appears on the surface. I suppose being cut off from the world has its advantages. But would I want to spend the rest of my life without learning about or seeing what is happening in the world? It would be difficult."

"Are you enjoying your time here?"

"Very much. It's a wonderful holiday, and I couldn't think of a better place to be at this point in my life."

"You should keep those thoughts close and not worry about what's happening in the world. You'll find, as we all do on the island, that it can get along without you. And when you return, it'll still be there.

"In the meantime, enjoy your stay. With Elijah as your guide, you'll continue to discover many aspects of a peaceful way of life that, from what I'm told, most people can only imagine."

It was rare for Mrs. Kerr to be so forthright, and the words seemed to have displayed a depth of feeling that surprised her. She responded with a shy smile and immediately retreated into her customary role by suggesting they clear the dishes from the table.

After doing his share of the washing up, Sean read for a while in the living room. Afterward, undressed and lying in bed, his thoughts seemed to naturally turn toward Diane. He drifted off to sleep with thoughts of her running through the mists of his mind.

# Chapter 39

Anna had wasted no time after being briefed by Dante. Every resource at the Praetorian Order's disposal was put on alert. In a matter of hours, one of the world's most effective and efficient clandestine organizations had swung into action. Dante's lieutenants, after having been contacted through Anna's e-mail, set the process in motion. Anna assumed control of compiling, sorting, and inputting the information they garnered about Sean Brennan.

Dante had specified twelve days for the project's completion. Three hours before deadline, Anna telephoned and said the information was ready. Having worked with Dante for twenty-five years, Anna understood his mind. She placed all the data, including the material about Pannier, on a memory stick. Before delivering it to his office, she wiped everything from the order's central files. Dante, obsessively committed to secrecy, wanted to be the only one with the information.

After Anna dropped off the stick, Dante placed it in his computer's USB port. He clicked the mouse, opening the file, and scrolled slowly through the information.

The order's representatives had pulled every piece of material, regardless of how insignificant, they could find about Brennan. The data included everything from his high school graduation marks to articles from the university law review to

Hilary's newspaper death notice. Dante's first surprise came when he read of the accident that had killed Brennan's parents, Lucas and Nora Kilgore, and his subsequent adoption by Tom and Margaret Brennan. *So he was born Sean Jason Kilgore*, thought Dante.

Notes from the birthing room doctor detailed Brennan's unusual birthmark. A faded photograph of the baby's leg showed it in stark detail. Although given to little emotion regardless of the circumstance, Dante's breathing nevertheless increased slightly.

Still it was just an unusual birthmark. The triangle didn't mean it was the Mark of Janus.

He then combed through the file until he found what he was looking for. It was the photos of Lucas and Margaret taken at the hospital where they'd been pronounced dead before being transported to a funeral home in Toronto. Dante searched the photos of Lucas. It wasn't easy to spot. But it was there. The man bore the same birthmark as Brennan.

The prelate dug deeper into the file. He found where Brennan had hired a private investigator to unearth information about the Kilgore family. The investigator's report was contained in the electronic dossier. He read the letter from Brennan's grandfather asking if Lucas had the birthmark.

Dante saw with interest that the detective had only been able to trace the family back as far as Brennan's great-great-grandfather, Joseph Kilgore. He read how the detective had found no information on the Kilgore family prior to Joseph's arrival in Canada.

But there was more. An electronic envelope with a note from Anna described how the contents had been obtained by hacking into the Guardians' mainframe in Inverness. The Guardians, like the order, were one of the world's most secretive organizations. Although the current Praetorian Order was largely his creation, Dante took a moment to savor and be impressed at the resourcefulness of the global technological spy network he'd built. Anna deserved to be congratulated.

He opened the file and discovered that Joseph Kilgore had been born on Janus. And then Dante came to a page that set his mind and his pulse racing. Two pieces of information rocketed off the computer screen. First, according to the Guardians' information, Joseph Kilgore had borne the same birthmark as Brennan. But the most devastating detail was that Kilgore had changed his name from Kirsch when he left Janus.

Dante hurriedly clicked through the files until he found the one containing the material on Pannier. He'd already read the man's notes, and knew what he'd find. But something made him need to double-check the facts. There it was. The islander who'd befriended Pannier, the one named Solomon Kirsch, had carried the Mark of Janus—a triangle on his left thigh.

So that's why Sean Brennan had been brought to Janus. He carried the Mark of Janus. And he would be expected to take the Janus message worldwide.

Dante's worst fears would be realized.

The Pannier agreement would be destroyed. More importantly, if the island's message went global, it would call into question the Church's foundation. And once that began to crumble, everything else would falter. Eventually, the Church and all other religions would cease to exist. That made Brennan a grave threat.

And yet, the islanders were committed to living apart from the world. This would change everything about Janus. Were the islanders aware of Elijah's plans?

Dante was puzzled. He wondered if what Elijah wanted to accomplish was even possible. Global peace seemed an unrealistic goal. And yet if the Supreme Being was involved, it had to be taken seriously.

The prelate knew he couldn't wait to have events unfold before initiating his own preventative strategy. It had been almost a year since Dante had seen Angelica. He pulled the computer keyboard closer. The prelate typed the one word code, Avenger, that would bring her to Spain. He allowed himself a brief smile. She would soon be joining him at the chateau.

# CHAPTER 40

The bed was warm and comfortable. Sean rolled over and felt the soft mattress give way as he shifted his weight. Diane was still sleeping. Lying on her back, her tousled hair was splayed randomly across her pillow. The covers had pulled back sometime during the night, exposing her breasts and hardened nipples. Sitting up slowly and resting his back against the plain, wooden headboard, he looked over and marveled at the serenity that marked her face.

Her breathing was rhythmic, her breasts rising and falling in a slow symphony of motion. Suddenly feeling modest, which he knew was ridiculous after the night they'd shared, he gently pulled the sheet and sheepskin blanket up over her breasts. She made a soft purring sound and turned her back to him, pulling the sheets up under her chin.

Lacing his hands behind his head, he thought back over the previous day and marveled how relationships could change in such a short time. His morning had started as it usually did with a quiet breakfast. He'd stayed around the house during the morning helping Mrs. Kerr with the housework and doing some reading.

After lunch he'd set out for the western part of the island. Fascinated by the story Marcus had told him about building the dam, Sean wanted to see the area for himself. The shopkeeper had arranged for Ted to meet him at the site.

Mrs. Kerr had packed him a snack of bread, pickled eggs, cheese, and water. She'd also given him explicit written instructions because, as he'd discovered shortly after arriving on Janus, no road or pathway was signed.

"It's a small island, and we all know our way around, so why put up signs to tell people what they already know," explained Elijah.

When Sean noted that it made it difficult for a visitor, Elijah had chuckled saying, "And how many visitors do you think we get? We're not exactly a tourist destination."

So with instructions in hand, Sean turned west from Mrs. Kerr's and walked several miles along the Ring Road. The sun was trying its best to heat the land, but it was often obscured by gray clouds. A chilly wind was blowing in off the water, and he was glad he'd worn his pea jacket.

It was obvious that spring planting and sheep shearing were now the island's main focus, for he passed no one. Following Mrs. Kerr's directions, he turned off the road after first passing several paths that he assumed led to farms and headed north along a well-worn trail that climbed steadily for about a mile. He decided to stop for a few minutes.

Sitting down on an exposed rock, he ate the light meal Mrs. Kerr had put together.

In the distance, he could hear the sound of rushing water. He set off again; the noise grew louder as he prepared to crest the hill. He could also see and feel a fine salt spray that was kicked skyward as the ocean water pounded the shoreline's rocks. It was a steep walk, and Sean had to stop several times to catch his breath.

Glancing toward the ground, he saw two power lines rising up from below the crest and heading eastward toward the village. They weren't on wooden or steel poles but were partially buried alongside the path he'd just walked.

The wind was strong and seemed unrelenting. It was blowing in from the ocean, tugging at Sean's clothes and whistling past his ears.

Moving on, he crested the hill and was greeted with a sight at once so awesome and a complete dichotomy to what he'd experienced on Janus. He saw that the crest he was standing on was part of a much larger rock formation stretching about a half mile around a U-shaped bay. Below him, built into the cliffs were three concrete and wooden barriers or dams. The area behind the dams had been carved out of the sand and rock, creating reservoirs into which flowed water from three rivers that plunged down the rock face.

Sean later learned from Ted that the dams, which were constructed across and partway into the bay, linking the bay's walls, stretched about eighteen hundred feet from side to side.

Metal steps built on a trestle-like frame and clinging to the cliff face led to what he knew was a generating station.

Walking up the hill toward him was a short, powerfully built black man, taking the stairs two at a time. Sean guessed his age at somewhere in his midfifties. He had thinning hair and, like most islanders, appeared to be in good shape. As the man got closer, Sean could see a heavily lined forehead, bushy black eyebrows, and possibly the blackest eyes he'd ever seen. A well-trimmed greying beard framed a face that was open and friendly.

The man neared where Sean was standing and reached out his hand. He took Sean's in a grip that radiated strength and firmness.

"Hello, Sean. It's great to finally meet you," he said. "I'm Ted. Marcus has told me quite a bit about the discussions the two of you've had. He enjoys them and hopes you'll have more. What do you think of our little project?"

"I'm impressed," replied Sean. "To see something like this on Janus is like stumbling across an airplane in the bowels of a pyramid. I know you have things to do on your farm. Thanks for taking the time to show me around and explain how it operates."

"I'm glad to," was the cheerful response. "Follow me down the stairs, but be careful. They're steep, and since this is your first time, it would be better to go slowly."

Ted again took the stairs two at a time, while Sean cautiously navigated his way down the steep decline. Reaching the bottom platform, he noticed the tremendous noise that was coming from inside the power station and from the water pouring down the hillside. Ted led him along a well-worn path into the station. The noise was almost deafening.

Standing on a metal platform that encircled the power station's interior, Ted, in a loud voice, explained, "We hold the water behind the dams, creating an artificial lake or reservoir. This raises the water level. We release it through gates in the dam. The water, already creating energy because it has been forced through the gates, is fed into pipes, creating more energy. We use the pipes to carry the water to this turbine in the powerhouse," he said, pointing to a large machine that looked to Sean like a turbine in an airplane's jet engine.

"The turbine is a type of water wheel that spins and converts the water's energy into mechanical power. It's connected to a generator, and the turbine's spinning causes the generator to rotate, producing electricity.

"Two things then happen. First, the electricity is channeled along these cables." Ted pointed to the power lines that Sean had seen. "And second, once the water has passed through the power station, it's fed back into the reservoir, lessening our need for water from the rivers that flow into the basin."

"This is quite an achievement," shouted Sean.

"Our system is rudimentary. It requires a great deal of maintenance and my attention. However, it has taken the island out of the Middle Ages. We now have electricity for light, heat, water pumps, stoves, and refrigerators."

"I notice that Mrs. Kerr uses a hot plate or a Crock-Pot to do much of her cooking," said Sean. "Is there a shortage of electricity?"

"Not really, but we do have to be careful. It's the way everyone cooks. Crock-Pots and hot plates use less electricity than stoves, which are only used on rare occasions. The less stress we put on the system, the less likely we'll have a failure. No one takes what we have for granted. It's the same with everything we do on Janus. Conservation isn't just a word. It's the way everyone lives."

Sean looked around the site and marveled at the accomplishment.

"How was the project completed?"

"We built everything by hand," began Ted. "We couldn't have started it without the Guardians and every islander. We built it like an old-fashioned barn raising. When it wasn't planting or harvesting season, we'd gather here for three or four days a week. Every family would bring food, and we'd build one section at a time. The Guardians brought in some gas generators, and that provided electricity for many of the tools and equipment we used."

"What about the winter months?" wondered Sean.

"That's part of why the project took so long. We cut it back to one week a month, and only those who were directly involved in the project came out. We also had to deal with the cold and shortness of daylight. But we kept the project going, and once the warmer months came, construction went back to a full schedule.

"We had portable mixers for the cement, and the men used wheelbarrows to dump the cement in the wooden structural frames for the dams. Fortunately, with the bay a natural U-shape, we were able to get away with a minimum of drilling into the rock. Even so, it was long, sometimes tedious, and always dangerous work.

"I believe Marcus has already told you it took us sixteen years to build. The Guardians even purchased a large barge so that we could move equipment like the turbine. If we'd used our fishing boats or *Journey* to transport everything, it would have meant taking apart a lot of equipment and then reassembling it here. The task would have been monumental, and I'm not sure if it could have been accomplished.

"Most of the materials and equipment were purchased in Inverness and Edinburgh. In some cases, like the turbine, we had to order it from manufacturers in Europe and have it shipped to Inverness."

A thought suddenly struck Sean. "What about the port authorities in Inverness? Wouldn't they need documents like bills of lading for equipment and machinery coming into and leaving the port?"

"There isn't one part of the city, including the port, in which the Guardians don't have connections or direct access," replied Ted. "I just told them what I needed and didn't ask any questions. The material arrived, and we built an electrical system for the island."

"How did you know what had to be done?" said a still astonished Sean.

"I have an advanced degree in structural engineering from Michigan State University. Along with a couple of the Guardians who also have engineering experience, we put together the plans and supervised the work."

Sean could only marvel at the drive and the determination of the man. He seemed to be in constant motion, bouncing around the station, offering explanations while ensuring that every dial and meter was performing as it should.

For the first time since arriving on Janus, Sean felt a rush of enthusiasm to get started on whatever project Elijah had brought him here to complete. Just being with Ted and his boundless energy was enough to get him excited.

Switching from engineer to farmer, Ted said, "I'd love to stay longer and show you some more, especially how we constructed the dams. But it's planting season, and I should be getting back to the farm. I've still got some things to take care of before nightfall."

Leaving the power station, Ted charged up the stairs, again taking two at a time. It was a steep climb, and Sean, who planted a foot carefully on each step, found Ted waiting for him at the hill's crest. Reaching the Ring Road, they turned eastward and headed toward the village.

"I'm surprised you didn't meet any resistance from some of the residents," said Sean. "Weren't there a few who would've preferred things staying as they were?"

"Oh there was some opposition. Every society has that small minority that never wants to experience change. If they'd had their way, we'd still have ships with sails and be sleeping in lean-to huts.

"Elijah can be a very persuasive speaker. It took a couple of meetings at the Assembly, but soon everyone was on board. Once the project got the go-ahead, it took on a life of its own. In fact, some of the original detractors were those who put in the most amount of work."

The village was in sight, and the men walked the rest of the way in silence. As they entered the Knob, Ted shook Sean's hand, thanked him again for coming out to the dam, and disappeared behind the curtain.

It wasn't that late. Sean knew he had some time before he had to get home for the evening meal. He decided to stay for a few minutes and pick out a book. He soon discovered a dog-eared copy of Ayn Rand's *Atlas Shrugged.* He'd read the book years before and thought rereading it would be like visiting an old friend.

The doorbell rang, but Sean paid no attention, preoccupied with seeing if there was another book he wanted to read. He heard a familiar voice calling for Marcus. It was Diane.

A week had passed since they'd last spoken. Walking around the corner of the bookcase, he saw her standing by the counter talking with Marcus. Her back was to him. As Sean walked toward Diane, he could see that her hair was pulled back in its usual tight ponytail. She was wearing a blue denim shirt hanging over dirty jeans that were tucked into mud-encrusted Wellingtons. From her basket, she was handing over several cartons of eggs. It seemed to be for either building up a credit or getting her debt in order, for Marcus was busily scribbling figures on a piece of paper.

Having finished her business with Marcus, she turned and saw Sean coming toward her down the aisle. A smile with enough warmth to melt the northern polar ice cap lit up her face. It split her lips wide, revealing her teeth. Surprised by her obvious happiness at seeing him, Sean was momentarily dumbfounded.

"Well I didn't expect to see you here," she said, grabbing him by the shoulders and kissing him on both cheeks. Looking over her shoulder, Sean could see that Marcus was taking all this in with barely contained amusement.

"It's been a while," he said, finally finding his voice.

"A week, but who's counting?" she said, letting him go. "You knew where I was. It wouldn't have hurt to drop by," she continued with feigned severity.

Suddenly feeling defensive, he retorted, "Elijah told me the spring was one of the busiest times on the farm. Until the planting is done and the sheep brought back from shearing, the only time people leave their homes is to pick up supplies at the Knob."

"I'm only joking," she said, her voice ringing with laughter. Turning and waving good-bye to Marcus, she took his arm, and together they walked out of the store.

"Listen," she said, "I've been doing nothing but working these last few weeks. The only company I've had is the neighbor's kids, who came and helped with the planting. Why don't you come for dinner tonight? It won't be anything special. I haven't had time to prepare, but I've got some cooked chicken and rice that we could heat up. We can have cheese and fruit for dessert. How's that sound?"

Thrilled with the invitation, Sean took a moment to remember that he should stop at Mrs. Kerr's and explain he wouldn't be there for her evening meal. "It sounds perfect. But I've got to stop and tell Mrs. Kerr not to prepare dinner for me."

"Fine, you stop and I'll go on ahead to start getting things ready. I've also got to change." She laughed self-consciously.

Reaching Mrs. Kerr's, Diane said, "Give me until sunset to get things ready and then come on over."

Sean was excited. This was his first date in years. It had been so long, he wasn't sure if he'd remember how to act. Pushing the concern aside, he went through the door and headed toward the kitchen, where he knew he'd find his landlady.

She was cutting up carrots and tomatoes, preparing them for a pot with boiling water on the hotplate.

"So how was the dam?" she asked, without turning around.

"It's a fantastic achievement for the island," enthused Sean.

"Did Ted tell you that some islanders were originally against the project? I was one of them. But now that I see the advantages, I know he and Elijah were right."

Sean was eager to wash up. He didn't want to be late for getting over to Diane's and wasn't interested in chatting about his day. He moved to cut off the conversation. "Mrs. Kerr I won't be staying for supper tonight. So please don't go to any extra trouble on my account," he added lamely, looking at the vegetables she was chopping.

"I'm having dinner with Diane."

"Why that's grand," she said. "I was a bit worried you'd been spending too much time alone, sitting in your room reading until all hours. This is a good thing. Both you and Diane need somebody special in your lives."

"But it's only dinner," Sean protested, suddenly concerned that Mrs. Kerr was reading more into the invitation than just two friends having a meal together.

"Ah, that's right. And when should you be there?"

"At sundown."

"Well, you'd better get ready. It wouldn't be nice to keep the lady waiting," said Mrs. Kerr, her brogue as thick as the fog that sometimes rolled in over Janus.

Coming out of his room, Sean was surprised to see Mrs. Kerr waiting for him at the front door. She had a large earthenware jar in her hand, overflowing with oatmeal cookies and wrapped in red ribbon.

"What's that for," asked an unsure Sean.

"It's tradition on the island that, when a person is asked to dinner, they bring a small gift. I knew you hadn't thought of anything, so I packed these for you."

Sean was so overcome with her thoughtfulness that, without thinking, he planted a kiss on her lined cheek. He was rewarded with a motherly pat on his back and a, "Now you go and have a good evening. And don't mind what time you come home."

# Chapter 41

Sean had chosen to wear his gray dress pants, a white shirt open at the neck, and a black suit jacket. Black loafers completed the ensemble. Walking up the broken stone pathway to Diane's front door with the jar in his hand, Sean felt a sense of nervousness that he hadn't experienced in a long while. He tried to remember the last time he'd been on an actual date. It would have been with Hilary just before they were married. It was a movie and dinner.

His thoughts lingered on Hilary for a few moments. It was time, he thought, to start living in the present with respect to Hilary, not the past. He knew he would always treasure the life they'd shared, but he was ready to move on. Sean didn't know if he was building too much expectation into a dinner invitation, but he was anxious to see what the future might hold with Diane.

He was halfway across the porch when the door opened, revealing a sight that even in his dreams he couldn't have imagined. Diane was wearing a formfitting black dress with a low-cut neckline and a hem that ended just above the knee. The shoes were black leather pumps. Her freshly washed hair was flowing to her shoulders in loose ringlets. She was wearing smoky eye shadow and pink lipstick. Matching earrings and necklace completed the vision standing before him. Sean was speechless. He suddenly realized he was staring and had the presence of mind to hand over the cookie jar.

After a few seconds, Sean found his voice. "You look ravishing. I didn't know people dressed like this on Janus. I don't suppose you found it hanging on a rack at the Knob."

He was rewarded with a light lilting laugh. "No, it's not from the Knob. I brought it with me when I came back to the island. It's the first chance I've had to wear it, and I'd almost forgotten how nice it is to dress up for the evening."

Once they were inside and the door was closed, an uncomfortable silence descended as they both stood in the hallway.

"Is this where I tell you that I feel a bit awkward?" said Sean. "It's been a long time since I've been alone with a woman, except of course for Mrs. Kerr. I'm a bit out of practice."

"Not to worry," said Diane, taking his hand and leading him through to the kitchen, where two places had been set. Four candles, two at each end of the table, were lit. From one of the kitchen cupboards, she pulled out a bottle of Merlot.

"I didn't realize wine was available on Janus," remarked Sean.

"It's not," Diane replied. "Like the dress, it came back to the island with me. I've been saving it for a special occasion."

Sean was touched. "And this is a special occasion? I hope it meets your expectations."

"It already has," she said with a smile.

The wine proved a nice accompaniment with the meal. The conversation, although both were trying hard, started and stalled several times as they each tried to find something common to both.

Mostly they talked about the planting and the islanders' hope for a good growing season. Dinner over, Sean complimented Diane on the meal and helped clear the dinner plates. He volunteered to dry while she washed. The offer was accepted with a smile that turned into an easy laugh as she handed him a towel.

There was still some wine left, so with the dishes washed and dried, the couple went to the living room. Placing the wine and the glasses on the coffee table, Diane took a seat on the couch. Sean, still playing by his rules of a first date and assuming that conversation was the order of the evening, sat in a Queen Anne chair directly across from Diane. The coffee table offered a safe buffer zone between them.

He noted it was a room to feel comfortable in. The wooden floor was covered with a variety of colorful rugs. All of them looked as though they'd been hooked by hand. Sean assumed the work had been done by Diane's mother.

A large, stone-faced fireplace dominated one wall. The couch was against the wall that faced a large window, which looked out over the barn and yard where Diane kept her pigs and chickens. Three Queen Anne chairs and a bookcase on the wall facing the fireplace made up the room's other pieces of furniture. Four large paintings that looked to be copies of the works by John Constable added to the room's peaceful atmosphere.

She saw him looking around the room and said, "All of this belonged to my mother. The only thing I brought with me when I left Bruce was two suitcases full of clothes. Not knowing how long I wanted to stay, I decided to travel light, in case it didn't work out."

"You're still here, so I suppose you're happy living and working on a farm."

"I am. As time has passed I've come to enjoy living here. It obviously isn't London or New York, but it has a unique charm. There's an innocence about the people that you don't find out in the world. It's not that we're naive or simple. When your life exists by farming or fishing, you have a healthy respect and knowledge of nature's vagaries and what they can do to your livelihood."

"You sound as though you're talking from experience."

"In many ways I am. It took me a couple of years to learn, but life's pleasures can be found in simple things like going to the farmers' market in Kirkwall and finding a real bargain. There's a comfort in knowing everyone on Janus by their first names and having grown up here. No one's judgmental. You're the person you are, and everyone accepts you for that.

"It's also watching your crops take root in the fields and seeing them become ready for harvest. We don't have televisions, and only a few have a radio, so it's getting a book from the Knob and spending time reading for the sheer pleasure of enjoying a good story.

"The absence of violence, the kindness we show our neighbors, and the way everyone pulls together to ensure the island is ecologically responsible are other parts of the life that I treasure.

"What I've found is that so much of what happens here comes down to our simple belief of understanding, tolerance, equality, and peace. It isn't merely a useful slogan with no real meaning for the people of Janus. We live it every day and have done so for more than two thousand years.

"And of course, there's the accessibility to the Spirit that you can't find anywhere else in the world. That's an incredible gift and one that I lost sight of when I was away."

Suddenly Diane stopped. Looking sheepish, she said, "I've been going on a bit, haven't I?"

"Not at all," Sean said quietly. "It's good to talk and get to know more about one another. It seems as though, when you returned to Janus, you were looking for something special. From what you're telling me, you've taken time to find it, and you do seem at peace with the life you have."

"That's true," Diane replied. "There's no place I'd rather be."

"Is the Spirit the reason the islanders have endured and even prospered all these years?" asked Sean.

"I don't believe so," said Diane, slowly and thoughtfully.

"The Spirit didn't tell our ancestors that, in order to survive on Janus, we'd have to live together in peace; educate our young; practice equality in all phases of our society; renew and protect our resources; care for the environment; and understand that, in improving our lives as individuals, we collectively preserve the island's future."

Sean noticed that his birthmark was aching; the pain was arching up toward his groin. It was uncomfortable but not distracting.

"What happens on our island is up to each person," continued Diane. "The Spirit is a friend and companion to all those who wish to speak with it. But it doesn't get involved. And the Spirit certainly doesn't give us life lessons. Those are learned through experience, observation and knowledge of the past."

Diane stopped and chuckled.

"I've gone and done it again," she said after a few moments. "I seem to be the one who's always doing the talking. So now it's your turn. Why don't you tell me something about yourself?"

Diane picked up her wine glass, took a long sip, and stared expectantly at Sean.

"I took a long and winding road to get here," said Sean. "I was fourteen when my parents told me I was adopted. It was a shock that I'm not sure I've ever recovered from. It's left me with the feeling that I need to find someplace where I truly belong. I suppose that's why I've tried a number of different things in my life.

"I have a hunger to feel comfortable in my own skin. Most days I can push it aside. But every now and then, that sense of suddenly discovering your adopted, of realizing that everything you took for granted wasn't what it seemed, takes hold and I wonder what can be trusted.

"My parents are wonderful people, don't get me wrong. They raised me with love and kindness. The problem lies within me. I'm always wondering when the next bad surprise will come to change everything."

Sean stopped, embarrassed that he'd revealed so much of himself, hoping that it didn't sound as though he was whining about his life.

"What are you searching for?" asked Diane.

"Probably the same things most people seek in their life—some form of inner peace, a belief that my life is worthwhile and means something and that I'm not just making footprints in the sand to be washed away by the surf when I die. I find that, as I get older, I worry more about death. I've become fearful that life is nothing more than a transitory phase of some cosmic form that we pass through on the way to something else.

“The problem with life is that one gets so caught up in living the day-to-day experience that you forget what’s important. We lose sight of what makes us happy while chasing the things we mistakenly believe will satisfy our desire for a meaningful existence.

“The world’s libraries are overrun with self-help books about living each day as if it were your last and experiencing everything as though for the first time. The Internet is filled with articles saying the same thing. But what about all those people with kids, a mortgage, and jobs they hate? When do they take time out to smell the roses?”

Sean suddenly realized he’d gone off on a tangent. What was it about Diane that was making him open up like this? She was easy to talk to, and he felt so damn comfortable with her.

“I was rambling a bit,” he said. “Sorry about that.”

“You need to visit the cave and have a good, long conversation with the Spirit,” said Diane with emphasis.

“Elijah mentioned a cave. What happens there?”

“It’s where the Spirit comes to earth and talks with us.”

“Why don’t you take me there one day? I’d like to see it.”

“That’s up to Elijah and the Spirit. They decide when it’s time. Our first session in the cave is very special and only comes after Elijah and the Spirit believe we’re ready. After that, we can visit anytime.”

“What if I decide to go on my own?”

"Then all you'll find will be a simple cave with a fire pit, some sleeping bags, and tools for cooking a meal."

"So if I want to visit with the Spirit, I have to wait for Elijah to arrange the session. That's assuming I'm here to meet with it."

"Only Elijah would know what the Spirit has planned."

Sean sat back in his chair. The birthmark was throbbing dully. He hadn't given any thought to meeting with the Spirit, and besides, he was curious to hear Diane's view on something he'd been thinking about since arriving on Janus.

"What does the Spirit do besides counsel the islanders? You said that it doesn't get involved. So, what's its relationship with the rest of earth? If it does exist, why is there so much pain and suffering in the world? How do the people on Janus reconcile these terrible events in their discussions with the Spirit?

"When we were with Richard and Eve at the Community Hall, Elijah spoke about good and evil as the yin and yang of life. But it still doesn't explain how the Spirit can sit back and watch all the evil and destruction that happens in the world."

"Sean, I can't provide all the answers," Diane responded with some dismay. "But I believe the world has more good people than bad. There are more people living their lives as best they can. They don't hurt others and are trying to leave earth a better place for their children and all those who will follow."

"But we're talking about two different things," claimed Sean. "One is the Spirit's role in the world, and the other is how people are living their lives."

"That's true to a point," acknowledged Diane. "I was just trying to make the argument that, while the world has many problems, most people simply try, in their own small way, to do good."

"But if there is a Spirit, why is earth in such bad shape and getting worse by the day?"

"Are you an atheist?" asked a surprised Diane.

"I'm neither an atheist nor an agnostic," responded Sean. "But it does seem as though the forces of darkness are expanding slowly and surely."

"So what are you then?"

"I'm simply a person who gives no thought to the question of a higher power because whether or not one exists has no impact on my life."

Diane eyed him over her glass. "You won't think that way once you meet the Spirit," she said, breaking the silence that had overtaken the room. "Spending time with the Spirit is beyond anything you'll experience. Life takes on a more intense meaning."

"Elijah hasn't said anything about having a conversation with the Spirit. And even if I do, what's really changed? I'm only one person. What's been accomplished?"

"I think you were brought here to meet with the Spirit. Elijah wouldn't have gone to all the trouble of finding and then bringing you here, just to add one more person to our population for a couple of months. Perhaps there's more to your visit than the Prophet has told you. Many of the islanders feel that way, especially since Elijah told us at the Assembly that you'd influence our future.

"How else can you do that, except by meeting with the Spirit? You're not an engineer like Ted or even a farmer with new ideas. Yet you're on Janus."

It took Sean a moment to digest what Diane was saying.

"I don't think anyone should read too much into why I'm here," he finally responded. "For me it's a holiday and a chance to experience something new. When it's over, I'll be aboard *Journey*, headed back to London."

Diane put her empty glass on the table.

""Is that what I am?" she asked. "Something new?"

"That's not what I meant," replied Sean, fully contrite. "I wasn't talking about us. I'm sorry if I've upset you. What you and I have has nothing to do with Elijah or the Spirit."

"What exactly do we have?" questioned Diane.

"Something that I haven't had for a very long time," said Sean.

"And that means?"

"There's something I should tell you," Sean said.

"What's that?" Concern gripped Diane's voice. "Are you married? Is there someone waiting for you in London?"

"There isn't anyone."

He moved over to the couch and took Diane's hand. For the next fifteen minutes, he told her everything about Hilary and the impact she'd had on his life. He talked about their life together, the reason he'd gone to Afghanistan, and finally her death. He also explained how there hadn't been anyone since their separation.

When he was finished, neither spoke. They stared at each other, both unsure what the next move should be. The silence cloaked them in a blanket of confusion. Sean felt he should say something.

"Like I told you, it's been a while," he said quietly.

"For both of us," she replied.

Diane stood up, surprising Sean. "Now I think we've done enough serious talking for one evening," she said with a smile, effectively ending the conversation. "It's time to move on to other things."

The birthmark had stopped throbbing. Sean wondered briefly what it meant but didn't give it much thought.

The wine had long since been finished. Diane suggested they have coffee and some of the cookies he'd brought over.

She'd put cinnamon in the coffee while it was brewing. Sean noticed it gave the drink an aromatic flavor that was enjoyable. The two talked sporadically about the books they were reading and some of the articles Sean had written for *The Advocate* as they sipped their coffees and put a sizeable dent in Mrs. Kerr's cookies.

It was getting late and, knowing that Diane had to work her fields in the morning, Sean took a last sip of the coffee. He offered to help clean up the remaining dishes before leaving. She gave him a brief smile, picked up the cups, and went into the kitchen.

She was reaching over, placing the cups in the sink. Without thinking, Sean came up beside her and slipped the plates into the sink. He assumed that, as before, she'd wash while he dried.

He was reaching for the towel when she turned toward him. "So it's been a long time since you kissed a woman," she said.

Caught off guard, Sean could only stammer that she was right.

"Well don't you think it's about time you got back in practice," she offered, a mischievous glint in her eyes.

Reaching out, he put both hands on her shoulders and gently pulled her closer. Her body was rigid, but still she came, although several inches still separated them. Slowly she rested her head against his shoulder. Cupping her chin in his right hand, he raised her head, until her mouth was mere inches away from his.

He circled his arms around her back and pulled her into his body. He felt her breasts pushing against his chest. His hands moved downward, pulling her hips into his. For a few moments they stood there, saying nothing, luxuriating in the feeling of having another person close after such a long time.

His mouth found hers, and her lips parted willingly, letting his tongue inside. The kiss was long and deep. She could feel his hardness and ground herself into him. He pulled back slightly. He knew his face was as flushed as hers.

"Are you sure this is what you want?" he asked softly.

"I could ask you the same thing," her voice husky, her breath coming in short gasps. "I don't want to open any doors to the past about Hilary."

"This isn't about her. And those doors are now firmly shut." He was surprised at how much weight had been removed from his shoulders with just those few words. It was true. With Diane in front of him, Hilary was no longer a factor. She was a strong memory, he realized, but just that, a memory. For too long, he'd let her have an almost unbreakable grip on him. It was time to let go. She would always be important to him. But she was part of his past, and that's where she should stay.

"This is about us," he said. "There isn't any ex-husband or former wife standing between us. I've thought about this since the first time I saw you," he said, pulling her hips closer so that they were welded together.

"Well we should do something about that," she said with laughter in her voice.

She pulled away from him, and for a moment he was surprised.

"Take my hand," she said softly.

Sean did as he was asked. Together they walked out of the kitchen and down to the end of a small hallway, which opened into a neatly decorated bedroom, dominated by a large bed, a chest of drawers, and a nightstand with a soft light. A large window showed a crescent moon surrounded by a myriad of stars. The faint scent of honeysuckle hung in the air.

The low, soft light cast their shadows about the room, making the moment intimate and sexually charged.

The top bedsheet and comforter had been pulled back. Four large pillows stood guard against the bed's headboard.

Standing beside the bed, she turned and pulled him close. They both kicked off their shoes and kissed in a passionate embrace. Somehow, they managed to fall onto the bed, still coupled. They made love, gently and with a slow–to-build passion.

The end came for Sean in a loud groan of ecstasy and pinpoint lights that flashed across his eyes. A moment later, Diane crashed down on his chest. They lay together, silent, both gasping for air.

Diane's head was resting on his chest. Her hair had the scent of fresh strawberries, and he couldn't remember when he'd smelled something as beautiful.

They made love twice more that night, each more satisfying and mutually pleasing than the last. Talk came easily as they shared thoughts and hopes about the future. They occasionally slept, comfortable in each other's arms, their bodies entwined.

It was deep into the night. Sunrise was only a few hours away. They lay curled up against each other, their bodies and their sweat mingling. For the moment, nothing else mattered but the memory of their lovemaking and the intimacy of their bodies.

After several minutes, Diane raised her head from where it had been resting on Sean's chest.

"Can I ask you something?" she whispered.

"You can ask anything you want."

"When we were talking about Hilary, you said how much she'd been a part of your life. Do you still feel the same way? Is there room in your heart for someone else?"

Sean raised himself up, his head resting in the palm of his hand, his elbow on the bed. He looked straight into her brown eyes. He paused before answering. "It's not so much whether I have room in my heart to love someone else. I've passed the stage of loving her. Hilary will always be a part of my life, but it's my past life. The question should be, am I ready to love someone."

“And are you?”

“I could ask you the same thing.”

“I’m willing to assume that we have a relationship and that we’re slowly working toward love. It’s not that I doubt you, but we’ve spent one night together and a few hours talking. And it’s not as though I’m seeing anyone else. I really believe Elijah brought you here for a reason, and it certainly wasn’t to fall in love with me. So, let’s give it some time before we get serious about each other.”

“That sounds partially fair,” replied Sean. “I’m comfortable with the idea of moving slowly. But tonight is important to me, and I don’t want to lose the feelings we have for each other. I respect Elijah, but I’m not sure what he has to do with whatever decisions you and I decide to make.”

Diane uttered a long and lingering sigh.

“I shouldn’t have mentioned anything about Elijah,” she continued. “Why don’t we just be two people who are starting a very special relationship and see where it takes us?”

Sean smiled. “That’s a wonderful way to enjoy what we have. Now don’t you think it’s time you got some sleep? I understand the morning comes early for farmers.”

He lay down with his back on the bed. Diane kissed him gently and rested her head against his shoulder. She was soon asleep, her breathing slow and regular.

Sean couldn’t find sleep. He relived everything about the evening and savored the tranquility that encompassed his mind. For the first time in many years, he felt at complete peace. Hilary was the past, Diane the present. What the future held, he didn’t know. But for tonight at least, he was content to live, as the islanders did, in the here and now.

# Chapter 42

Mid-May and the weather was pleasantly mild in Valencia, Spain. It was a time for residents and tourists alike to casually stroll the avenues, enjoy the outdoor cafes, and wander through the city sites, including the Plaza del Mercado and Le Catedral de la Virgen.

And while the city lay only a short drive from the chateau, Dante was never seen on its streets. He was not a man who took weekends or holidays. The order was his life, and he made few concessions to the passion that drove him. When he wasn't on one of his business trips, Dante was a virtual recluse, living and working in the climate-controlled chateau.

On this morning, he was preparing for Angelica's visit.

Dante printed all the pages he thought would help in briefing her. Sliding them into a file folder, he reached for a memory stick and copied onto it the material he'd just printed. He popped the stick into the folder. Finally, Dante took another memory stick and copied everything from his hard drive relating to Brennan and Janus. He wiped the material from his hard drive. Taking the stick from the computer, he got up and walked over to a wall safe located behind an unknown Sandro Botticelli fifteenth century painting of Jesus feeding the multitude. After undergoing a retina scan, which opened the door, he placed the stick inside.

Closing the safe, Dante looked at his watch. It was 7:00 a.m. Angelica would be arriving in thirty minutes. As was always the case, she would have flown in the night before and checked into one of the city's hotels so she could be at the chateau for 7:30. Dante knew she used a different hotel each time she visited and never thought to ask where she was staying. It was extra information and wasn't required in their relationship.

He telephoned Anna to see what new intelligence concerning Brennan had been delivered. She told him Brennan was still on Janus and relayed information about Larry Blaine, Ahmad's death, and the fact Brennan had paid a two month advance on his apartment lease. None of the material was necessary for his session with Angelica, so Dante asked that it be delivered to his office following the same procedure used earlier. He would review it after his meeting.

Of major interest to Dante was the news about Brennan's apartment lease. While he was still on Janus, it was obvious a commitment to the island had not been made. Dante viewed that as a positive sign. However, he wasn't prepared to alter the instructions he was about to give Angelica. The normal pace of change on Janus might be exceedingly slow, but Dante didn't believe this was a normal situation. He wanted to be prepared for any eventuality.

Dante looked at his watch. Angelica would be at the chateau in twenty minutes. He picked up the file; left his office; and, for the first time that day, prepared to commune with his god.

He slipped into the chapel. It was empty, as he'd requested. The prelate walked slowly up the center aisle. He chose a pew to the altar's left and several rows from the front. He made the sign of the cross, bowed, took a seat, and knelt down.

The irony was not lost on Dante. He was alone in the chapel praying to his god for guidance in resolving a problem that implicated the same god, who supposedly spoke to the islanders on Janus.

In Dante's mind, the Roman Catholic Church gave God, Jesus, and the Holy Ghost the respect and veneration that no other religion could hope to provide. The communion, in which Christ's body, blood, soul, and divinity were represented by bread and wine, was an act of reverence that always instilled within Dante a feeling that he was as close to heaven as he would ever get until his death.

And yet, the people of Janus had no respect for Jesus or the Holy Ghost. They claimed their Spirit talked to them and shared their thoughts. Although Dante had never been on Janus, he had always harbored an intense dislike of the islanders. What right did they have to claim this falsehood? And now Elijah wanted that lie spread throughout the world. Not as long as he was prelate of the Praetorian Order.

The door at the back of the chapel opened slowly. As he knelt, head down in supplication, Dante heard the slow, padded steps, like those of a panther make their way up the aisle. He didn't need to glance up to know who it was. His eyes were closed as he waited in anticipation. The footsteps drew closer. They stopped beside his pew.

There was a momentary silence.

"Hello, Dante," the voice was soft and silky, enveloping him like a warm embrace.

He looked up. Her coal black hair was longer than he remembered. It wasn't below her shoulders the last time they'd met. She'd changed the color of her lipstick to a more subtle red. She was wearing less eye shadow than he was used to seeing. As usual, she was dressed all in black. A silk blouse tucked into tight black pants emphasized her slim figure. A small black handbag hung from her shoulder. The only jewelry was a petite, gold cross on a gold chain around her neck and worn just below her collarbone. It had been a gift from Dante when she'd left the chateau for the last time to take up the calling for which she'd been trained.

"Hello, Angelica," he softly said. "It's been a while since we last met. I'm glad to see you looking so well."

# Chapter 43

It had been a couple of days since he'd seen Diane. She was busy with her farm's planting. For Sean, it had been a period of wandering the island and meeting and talking with the farmers and herdsmen. It had been an enjoyable and relaxing experience, as he got to know more of the islanders. But Sean knew he was just filling time until he could again be with Diane.

When she'd dropped by Mrs. Kerr's early that afternoon to announce the planting was going well and inviting him to dinner, Sean had eagerly accepted.

Mrs. Kerr had sent him off with a blueberry pie and the wish that he'd have an enjoyable evening.

When he arrived at the house, Diane seemed to be in a contemplative mood. She took the pie without saying anything and gave him an absentminded kiss.

"Is there a problem?" Sean asked. "This isn't like you. If there's something bothering you, we should talk about it."

"It's nothing," she said, but Sean could tell Diane was holding something back.

Was this where their relationship came crashing down? Was she trying to find a way to tell him it was over? If that was the case, he'd make it easy. There'd be no angry words or recriminations.

"Why won't you tell me what's going on?" he asked.

Diane's eyes filled with tears. Sean went to hold her, but she backed away.

Taking a deep breath, she blurted out, "I lost a lamb this afternoon. It died at birth. There was nothing Richard could do. It was terrible and so very sad."

Sean was taken aback. He didn't want to appear unfeeling but thought that Diane should be used to animals dying or being put down.

"Why is this lamb so important to you?" he said as gently as possible.

"I don't really know," Diane answered. "It was such a difficult birth, and I suppose I got caught up in the struggle. The lamb lived for about two hours, and I could tell it was fighting to stay alive. Its death seemed so senseless, and for a while, I was reminded of how pointless all our lives are."

Sean was momentarily nonplussed. This was a side of Diane he'd never seen. Anytime he'd been with her, she'd been cheerful, thoughtful, and excited by the opportunities each day held for new adventures. He'd always believed her to be someone who was in complete control of her emotions and had a clear understanding of who she was and what she wanted from life.

If anything, her vulnerability made her even more appealing.

"No one's life is pointless as long as he or she takes control of their own beliefs, thoughts, aspirations, and actions," argued Sean. "Life is only pointless if you allow two things to happen—you give up on yourself or you allow someone to control your life."

"I understand what you're saying," she answered. "And you're right, of course. It's just that sometimes I wonder what the purpose is for all of us living on this island. This is one of those times, and somehow my lamb's death sent me over the edge."

"How do you feel now?"

"Better since we're talking about it."

They moved over to the couch and sat down. Diane continued. "Janus is such an anomaly to the way so many people live. When I talk to the Spirit, I speak about what I've seen and what's happening beyond the island. I'd like to believe my words are making a difference, and that I'm possibly pushing it toward becoming more involved in human affairs. But I don't know. I want us to share what we have on the island, but it's as though the Spirit is waiting for some kind of savior."

He knew it was selfish, but he had to ask. "What about us? Doesn't that bring you happiness and give you a purpose?"

Without warning, she threw her arms around him and brought him close. Her chin was resting on his shoulder. "Of course it does," she whispered. "You're the best thing that's ever happened to me."

Lifting her head, she kissed him with a passion that demonstrated emphatically the feelings behind her words.

Sean knew that a line had been crossed in their relationship. It wasn't too late for either of them to turn back, without hurting the other. However, they were definitely moving to a point where serious thought would have to be made about some form of commitment.

"I feel the same way," he said quietly, gently wiping away her tears. Her mascara had run, and black lines stained her face.

"Look at me," she said. "I must be quite the mess. Why don't you wait here while I clean up and check how our dinner is coming along. I'll be back in a few minutes."

She gave him a quick kiss and was out of the room before he had a chance to say anything.

Sean became lost in thought as he contemplated what had passed between them.

He realized with startling clarity that he wanted Diane to be a permanent part of his life. This was his new reality. It had nothing to do with Janus, the Spirit, Elijah or anything else. He wanted to build a solid, lasting, and loving relationship.

Diane was all the things he wanted in a woman. Kind, generous, gentle, patient, and a wonderful and caring lover, she made him happy. Together they laughed at many of life's inane happenings. He knew that Diane created within him intense feelings. She made him want to be a better person than he believed he was.

He and Diane were forging a bond of understanding and commitment. They trusted each other. Their feelings reached a depth that he knew could only exist because of the complexities, failures, and victories they'd experienced before meeting.

He couldn't help but marvel at how Diane's grief over death had brought about the emotional intensity he was now feeling.

He felt Diane's touch on his arm.

"Dinner's just about ready. You can wash up and meet me in the kitchen."

Diane had prepared a meal of Atlantic salmon, boiled potatoes, and peas. For dessert, there was Mrs. Kerr's blueberry pie. Sean enjoyed every mouthful.

As dinner came to a close, Diane suggested they go for a walk. It sounded like a good idea to Sean. They decided to head toward the western edge of the island, which would bring them past the Prophet's house.

# Chapter 44

Elijah was on the balcony as they walked by and invited them in for coffee. This was Sean's first visit to Elijah's home, and the Prophet showed him around while Diane waited in the living room.

The house was constructed similar to Mrs. Kerr's, with a hallway running down the center. On one side were three rooms, which faced onto a large living room and a bathroom. The kitchen was large and at the home's rear. One of the rooms served as Elijah's office, another as a guest room, and then his bedroom, next to the kitchen.

In both the living room and Elijah's office, three walls were covered by floor-to-ceiling bookshelves. The Prophet's book collection was almost as extensive as the Knob's. Elijah saw Sean looking at the shelves and told him that he was welcome to examine the collection and borrow whatever books he wanted.

The home was decorated in what Sean thought was typical of Elijah's pragmatic character. The wood furniture looked old, solid, and hand carved. There were no knickknacks or personal items scattered about. The walls were bare of photographs and paintings. No carpets adorned the floors. Elijah's only concession to any form of comfort was the books adorning his shelves.

Once Elijah had prepared the coffee, he joined Sean and Diane in the living room, sitting opposite the couple, who were on a wooden backed couch. Elijah had taken a rocking chair.

Sean had noticed a preponderance of books on Elijah's shelves that dealt with global peace. It sparked his interest because of the island's commitment to remaining apart from the world.

Taking a sip from his mug, Sean pointed to the bookshelves and asked why Elijah would be interested in peace beyond the shores of Janus.

"A couple of years ago, the Spirit asked me if the Janus model of peace could be extended throughout the world," responded the Prophet. "The query surprised me. I'd never given the matter any thought, but the Spirit kept asking, and I decided to study the subject to determine if what it had asked was possible.

"I asked the Guardians to find me whatever books they could that explored both the philosophical and the practical aspects of nations coexisting in harmony."

"And what did you find?" wondered a fascinated Sean.

"That taking what we have here and extending it beyond our shores would be difficult.

"What can't be ignored is that the foundation of our peace is isolationism. We have lived it since coming to this island. It's based on the model of being self-sustaining. We trade sporadically with the mainland, and our children are sent into the world with the message of peace and preserving the planet. Our peace, though, was borne of a collective need to stay alive on this island, and we, therefore, became dependent on each other for that survival.

"We have prospered because of our awareness that survival depends upon a collective dependency. Whatever we do as individuals is based on the knowledge that it directly or indirectly impacts the island and everyone who lives here."

"What you have here though is a something that seems beyond the grasp of the rest of the world," said Sean. "Regardless of how it's been achieved, you have collective and individual peace. There is no crime and, therefore, no need for punishment. Why is it impossible for humans on a global scale to achieve what you have here?"

"I believe one of the primary reasons," began Elijah, "is that too many people are weighted down by the belief in the inevitability of violence. Whether it's the requirement to overthrow a violent, dictatorial regime with corresponding force; the needs of nations to defend their sovereignty through the use of highly technical weapons; or the simple case of neighbors arguing over some form of perceived wrong, the world has become inured to force being the ultimate resolution.

"And until that can be solved, any real hope of unraveling the other problems confronting the world, including the ongoing destruction of the planet, poverty, and disease, as well as the lack of an educational infrastructure in many countries, remain but a faint possibility."

"How did the Spirit react when you brought this information back to it?" asked Sean.

"It was strangely adamant that Janus could provide an example to the world," responded Elijah. "It even suggested what we needed was a messenger to carry the island's story beyond our borders."

Sean could feel his birthmark beginning to ache. *Why's this happening now?* he wondered. The pain was bothersome, but it didn't prevent him from asking what he felt was an important question. "If the Spirit is so interested in what happens to the world, why hasn't it become directly involved? If it truly cares about the human race, shouldn't there have already been an intervention that speaks unequivocally to the fact the Spirit can at least give humanity the assistance to begin solving the problems that confront the earth?"

"I don't know," admitted the Prophet.

"Have you ever asked it?"

Elijah appeared uncomfortable. For several moments, silence hung heavily over the room.

"The Spirit doesn't believe it should interfere," said Elijah, breaking the quiet.

"And why's that?"

"The Spirit is convinced it's still not too late for humans to rescue themselves and this planet. As I said before, it believes a messenger from Janus, carrying our story worldwide, is what's needed to bring about global peace."

"That's an incredibly idealistic thought," countered Sean. "Unfortunately, the world is too complex, too divided, and too ideological for one person to make a difference."

"The Spirit seems to think it's possible," countered Elijah.

A sudden thought crossed Sean's mind. "Are you that messenger?" he asked, staring intently at the Prophet.

A look of shock, like lightning on a summer evening, flashed across Elijah's face. "This isn't anything to do with me," he stammered. "My life and my world is Janus. I've not been asked by the Spirit, nor would I ever be. The messenger must be someone who is comfortable here on Janus and has experienced the world."

The birthmark's ache was growing more intense. Sean shifted on the couch, hoping to lessen the pain. It was agonizing and irritating. He pressed down on it with his palm. It eased the throbbing.

"That probably means someone from among the Guardians or the diaspora," noted Sean. "I suppose it could even be somebody like Ted. You'll just have to wait and see who the Spirit chooses."

"The decision won't rest with the Spirit," countered Diane. "It will be up to whoever it asks. As Elijah said, the Spirit never interferes. It only suggests and then let's each of us decide."

"That would be quite the discussion," said Sean. "Still, I think it's an impossible task unless the Spirit intends to be directly involved."

"We'll just have to wait and see what the Spirit decides," concluded Elijah.

It was getting late, and since the end to his stay on Janus was nearing, Sean wanted to spend as much time as possible alone with Diane. It had been a good talk with Elijah, but now he wanted to be on the Ring Road headed for Diane's home and her bed.

"Thanks for the coffee and the discussion," he told the Prophet. "But we should be going."

"You're right," said Elijah. "I've enjoyed your visit, but the morning will soon be here and there's some work to do in the barn."

After saying their good-byes the couple walked, hand in hand, along the Ring Road until they arrived at Diane's house. Janus was quiet, with the only sound being the breaking of waves against the island's rocky base.

They wordlessly walked through the front door and down the hallway to Diane's bedroom. It was only after they'd made love and Diane was asleep in his arms that Sean noticed the birthmark was no longer aching.

With the coming of dawn's light, they had a breakfast of pancakes and coffee. Diane would be busy for the next few days finishing the planting. It would be a long and tiring time. Both agreed they'd hold off seeing each other until the majority of the planting was done. A lingering good-bye was said on the home's front steps.

# Chapter 45

It had been a week since Sean had seen Diane. He'd spent most of his time at the Knob, reading, and having meals with Mrs. Kerr.

It was a leisurely life, and while he enjoyed the experience, he missed Diane. She filled most of his thoughts. It was something he hadn't had for many years and left him with the deepening knowledge that Diane was becoming an important part of his life.

One night after dinner with Mrs. Kerr he went, as usual, to the living room. Sean began to read. The book was a mystery detective novel that completely captured his attention. He was surprised when Mrs. Kerr came down the hallway and said she was going to bed. He hadn't realized it was that late.

Sean read through to the last page and had the ambivalent feeling that all readers have when finishing an excellent novel—satisfied at concluding a good read but disappointed at having to say farewell to the characters.

He washed up in the bathroom and crossed the hallway to his bedroom. After changing into a T-shirt and boxers, he was about to climb into bed when Hilary's picture caught his attention. He knew it was time to place that part of his life firmly in the past. His love for Diane continued to grow. Sean didn't know what the future held, but he desperately wanted Diane to be a part of it.

Sean no longer felt the overburdening weight of Hilary's memory. He'd never forget her, but it was time to move on.

A change had overtaken his life. For the past few years he'd used Hilary's rejection of their marriage and her death as a shield. He'd always viewed the marriage's breakdown as his fault. Afraid to fail again, he'd clung to her memory as a form of protection.

But Diane had changed all that. Sean knew it was too soon to assume anything about their relationship. Yet, just knowing he could have someone in his life after such a long time of being alone, made him realize that retreating behind a memory was a lonely way to live. The people of Janus were right. While the past should always play a role in one's present, it shouldn't control it.

He stared at the picture for a few more minutes before deciding what to do. It wasn't easy saying good-bye to a past that had been so much a part of his life. He took the photograph and walked over to the cupboard. Reaching deep inside, Sean found one of his duffel bags. Without another thought, he placed the picture in the bag and shoved the holdall into the cupboard's deepest recess.

It was done.

He knew he wasn't saying a final farewell to Hilary. She'd always be a part of his memories. It was simply that Diane was the woman he wanted to concentrate his feelings, hopes, and desires on.

He got into bed, reached for the lamp, turned the switch, and the room plummeted into darkness. Sleep came easily.

# Chapter 46

Sean awoke to bright sunlight streaming through his bedroom window. His landlady was already up and moving around. It was time to begin a new day. Sean got slowly out of bed.

Mrs. Kerr had opened the side windows along with the front and back doors. A pleasant morning breeze was blowing through the house. The rooms smelled fresh, and an invigorating feeling gave the home a vibrant charge.

Entering the kitchen, Sean saw that Mrs. Kerr had fixed them a breakfast of the usual porridge, thick slices of bread, and coffee. As always, the meal was eaten mostly in silence. Partway through, Mrs. Kerr asked him if he was going to the Knob.

"I am," he said. "It's always a pleasant way to spend a morning. Is there anything we need that I can bring back?"

Mrs. Kerr appeared lost in thought and didn't answer.

Sean was about to ask again if anything was needed when she quietly said, "Don't tell anyone, but I'm planning on visiting the Knob tomorrow."

The words were so unexpected Sean wasn't sure how to respond. He knew what a big step this was for her. After several seconds, he responded with a simple, "I won't say a word."

She placed her spoon in the bowl.

"Having you here has helped me a lot," she said. "Grief is insidious. It gets inside your mind and affects your body. I didn't realize how much I'd changed until you moved in. When my family was lost, I instantly went from being a wife and mother to an old woman. Anger and sadness had overtaken my life. I wanted to be left alone. I thought it was the best way to grieve. Having you here helped show me I was wrong."

"But I haven't done anything," responded Sean. "You're the one who accepted me into your home and gave me a place to live. If it hadn't been for you and Elijah, I wouldn't even be on Janus."

Mrs. Kerr put up her hand. "I'm only going to talk about this once, and I want you to pay attention."

The tone was motherly, the implication clear. Mrs. Kerr had something to say. Sean leaned back, ready to listen.

"When Elijah approached me about your staying, I wasn't sure. I'd been alone for almost a year and wasn't prepared for someone being in my house and using a room that once belonged to one of my sons. It would mean sharing meals, a loss of privacy, and having to make conversation. All this with a complete stranger. It seemed terrifying.

"I'd hardly been out of the house since my family was lost. Most days the longest walk I had was going up and down the hallway. To this day, I still haven't visited with the Spirit or gone to an Assembly. People were very kind. They left food and supplies for me. Then again, I wasn't eating much. Cooking and baking seemed like such a chore that most days I just ate bread and cheese. Even making coffee seemed like too much work."

"What changed your mind about having me stay?"

"When Elijah first asked, I said no. He'd arrived here after an Assembly meeting, where everyone had agreed to your coming to the island. I'm ashamed to admit it now, but I didn't even invite him in. We spoke at the front door.

"Elijah explained how the islanders had talked to him about me at the Assembly. They thought I'd grieved alone long enough and wanted something done. Everyone was concerned. Elijah explained that there'd been a long discussion about helping me. But no one wanted to intrude. Finally, Ian had suggested that having you stay here would be a way of helping me begin to get back on my feet. It was decided that Elijah should be the one who'd talk to me.

"That first discussion was difficult for both of us. I hadn't had anybody in my house since my family was lost. It had been months since I'd spoken with anyone. And I was adamant that I didn't want you staying with me. But Elijah was patient. He didn't try and convince me. We just talked about how your coming to Janus would provide everyone with a fresh perspective on what was happening in the world.

"Elijah gave me a week to think it over. It was entirely my decision. If I'd decided no, there were other places you could have lived.

"During the week, I really didn't give it much thought. My resolve was firm. I needed to be left alone, and having a stranger in my house was the last thing I wanted.

"When Elijah knocked on my door, I was ready to say no. But in the few moments it took me to walk from the kitchen to meet Elijah, I realized how lonely my life had become. I'd shut myself off from friends and neighbors who were kind and understanding. This was an opportunity to change things. Still, I wasn't sure if it was what I wanted. I opened the door and invited him in.

"We talked for a long time. He filled me in on all that had happened on the island. We laughed a lot. I realized that just having him in the house lifted my spirits. It had been so long since I'd had something to think about besides my grief. That's when I decided to say yes. After telling him, I think we both knew I'd turned a corner."

Mrs. Kerr stopped for a moment. She was lost in thought. Sean waited. He realized with a too infrequent flash of self-awareness, that he'd become more patient since being on Janus. He was adopting the island mind-set. The headlong rush into the future and having to do everything immediately that characterized so much of his life away from the island seemed, for the moment, a distant memory.

"When you lose someone close," she began, "there's an emptiness inside that you think will never be filled. Suddenly the purpose is lost from your life. It's hard not to think of all the things you would have done differently if you'd had another chance. But it's more than that. Simple things like getting out of bed become incredibly difficult. You ask yourself what's the point, and suddenly a week has gone by and all you've done is stayed in bed.

"People knocked on the door, and I didn't have the strength, nor did I even care to answer. They left food on the gallery, and much of it went rotten because I couldn't be bothered to always open the door. Every basket of food contained a note letting me know that my neighbors and friends were there for me. No one ever lost faith. They'd come and take away what food I hadn't brought in and leave a fresh supply. They left me alone to work through my grief, but every islander let me know I wasn't alone.

"Everyone knew, though, that I couldn't live the rest of my life as a hermit. So when Elijah had the Assembly vote on you coming to the island, Ian's idea of having you stay here seemed the perfect Janus solution. I could be approached by Elijah about something new that was happening on the island without it seeming as though people were trying to interfere with my life."

"What would've happened if I hadn't been coming to Janus?" wondered Sean.

"But you did come." Mrs. Kerr seemed perplexed by the question. "What's the point of trying to determine what might have been when you're sitting across the table in my kitchen?"

Sean smiled. Her reply was typical of the islanders' mind-set that he'd come to expect. They lived in the moment's reality. There was no point in wondering what might have been or wishing that things were different. Every islander faced each new day with the certainty that life was to be lived as it unfolded. There was nothing ambiguous in their approach. They confronted events head-on and dealt with everything as it happened.

A comfortable silence settled over the table. He was about to get up and head off to the Knob when Mrs. Kerr took a deep breath.

"My sons were good boys and gave me a great deal of pride," she said quietly. "Tom and I were married for almost forty years. When the boys joined him, it was one of the happiest days of our lives. Fishing is a tough way to make a living. It's hard, backbreaking work to lay out the nets and then to reel them back in, separating the fish and putting them in the container holds. But Tom was born to be on the ocean.

"That's the reason we named our ship *Shiran*. It's Hebrew for "happy song." She was called that because Tom loved the sound of the wind while he was at sea. He said it always made him realize how lucky he was to be doing exactly what he wanted with his life.

"Every day, I'd go with the other crews' husbands and wives to meet the fleet when it came in. Just as they do now, we'd help prepare the catch for distribution throughout the island. The day they didn't come back had started like this one—warm with a nice breeze blowing in from the south. By midafternoon though, storm clouds had gathered. The wind had turned. It was coming from the west and growing stronger. The waves were building, and everyone knew the fleet was going to have a difficult time heading back.

"The storm caught them about fifteen miles from the island. We hadn't had a blow like that in several years. By nightfall, only two of the vessels had made port. Their decks, hull, and nets were heavily damaged. The storm had scattered the fleet, and the returning crews didn't know what had happened to the other boats.

"Gradually as the night wore on, more ships straggled in. Every one of them was severely battered. We waited in the shed where the fish are sorted.

"By dawn the *Shiran* was the only ship still missing.

"The North Atlantic is a cold and rough sea," she continued slowly. "There are treacherous undertows and waves that can dwarf a fishing trawler. It seldom shows mercy for a crippled vessel. The fleet searched for five days. *Journey* had been contacted, and her crew looked day and night. When the fleet returned with no news after the fifth day, we all knew it was hopeless. There'd been no sign of the *Shiran*, her lifeboat, or even a piece of wreckage.

"I hadn't left the hut in a week. Going home when Tom and the boys were out there, seemed like a form of desertion. Every day, a new group of islanders would come and stay with me. Elijah was always there.

"I don't recall too much after Elijah told me they were calling off the search. He took care of all the arrangements. There's a vague memory of a service in the Community Hall.

"After that, Elijah must have brought me home. It's hard to remember, but I did notice that, for some reason, the house smelled different. It must have been my imagination, but the rooms seemed musty, as though they hadn't been lived in for a long time. My house didn't feel like home. Wherever I walked, it felt as though I was a stranger intruding on someone else's life. Even this kitchen seemed unfamiliar.

"At first, I couldn't believe they weren't coming home. For days, whenever I heard a sound on the gallery or around the house, I was sure it was them. I'd rush to the front door or to one of the boys' rooms, expecting to find Tom or my sons.

"When you lose the people you love, it's hard not to wonder why you're alive and they're not. I went through an intense period of remorse. Although there wasn't any reason I should have been on *Shiran*, I would have gladly traded my life for those of my sons. They had their lives in front of them. I've lived close to seventy years and felt that it should have been me, not them who died. The feeling was so intense it felt as though there was a huge weight on my chest.

"After lying beside someone for most of your life, the feeling of despair when getting into bed alone is mind-numbing. For weeks, I avoided the bed and slept on the couch. The living room became my world. I avoided the kitchen as much as I could because it was where we used to gather as a family. The bedrooms were filled with too many memories. We seldom used the living room, so that's where I retreated to."

Sean felt the depth of Mrs. Kerr's emotions and the intensity of her words. It was as though a tap had been opened and her feelings were pouring out.

"Did you ever think of talking to the Spirit or Elijah?" wondered Sean. "I'm sure they would have helped you through your grief if you'd asked."

"I haven't spoken to the Spirit, Elijah, or any of my friends about the things I've just told you. For a long time, I wanted to be alone with my grief. It wasn't something I felt like sharing. I knew that everyone, including the Spirit, was there for me if I needed them. We're not just a community of like-minded people. We genuinely care for each other. And we'll do everything in our power to support one another during a crisis.

"Knowing that helped me cope with my grief. But losing my family was also something I had to work through on my own. Times, though, change. While everyone was prepared to let me grieve alone for a while, they also knew it couldn't be allowed to continue forever. Ian and Elijah were right to have you come live with me.

"Since you moved in, we've talked about many things. What I've just shared with you was a part of that. I can't tell you why it happened today. Getting up this morning, I had no intention of telling you about my year. But now that I've done it, I feel so much better. My mind has been freed of all the negative thoughts I was carrying with me.

"If I've learned anything during the time apart from my friends, it's that a person has to move on. We only get one chance at life. What I'd lost sight of is that everyone on Janus appreciates and lives for the moment. We try to seize each day and take as much enjoyment as we can out of it.

"Everyone has to grieve a loss, but there comes a time when you've got to realize that moving forward is not being unfaithful to those you loved. You can hold a person's memory close and treasure it. But it's wrong to love what's no longer there, at the expense of having happiness in your life. No one should be a hostage to the past.

"When you told me you were going to the Knob, I suddenly realized how much I missed the island's routine. I'm ready to be a part of life again."

Mrs. Kerr got up from the table and began clearing the dishes. The conversation was over.

"Are you going to be here for lunch? Or will you have some of Marcus' scones to hold you over until dinner?"

"I'll have something at the Knob and see you for dinner."

Leaving the house and walking to the store, Sean thought that, of all the people Mrs. Kerr could have shared her story with, he felt the most unlikely and, he had to admit, the most unworthy. The woman had laid all her emotions in front of him—a stranger just a few weeks ago. The more Sean thought about it, the more incongruous it seemed. And yet, perhaps it was simply because she wanted to share with someone who she knew had suffered a loss.

Sean couldn't help but relate her story to the life he and Hilary had built. Strolling through the village with only the sound of the wind breaking the silence, he thought back to the times they'd shared. But there was no longer any pain. Now the future, hopefully, belonged to a life with Diane. Just the thought of her brought a smile to his face.

# Chapter 47

Entering the Knob, Sean saw the store was crowded.

Marcus was busy behind the counter, helping people with merchandise or ensuring there was enough coffee and scones to satisfy those who stopped to sit and read or chat. A quiet hum of activity permeated the store. Farm implements were being selected, clothes chosen, and in several places among the aisles, people had gathered to catch up on the latest news since they'd last met.

By now, he'd come to know all of the islanders by name. No longer did he feel like a stranger. Striding throughout the store he felt a sense of comfort, joining in conversations, being asked for advice about books to read, and assisting Marcus with replenishing the coffee and scones.

Nothing was being done in a hurry. Sean had come to realize there was a gentle pace to the Janus way of life. The islanders achieved all they wanted in a day, without the necessity of filled in-boxes, streams of e-mails, conference calls, countless meetings, or harried commutes to and from work. Was it a life he wanted, at least for a little while longer?

It was something he would think long and hard about before making a decision. And of course, nothing would be decided without talking it over with Diane.

Sean picked up a three-month old copy of *Newsweek*, took a seat, and lost himself in the magazine's pages.

He only partially heard the ringing doorbell as islanders streamed in and out of the Knob. He'd become so engrossed in an article about nuclear energy that it took him a few moments to realize everyone had gone quiet. He looked up and was taken aback to see Mrs. Kerr heading his way.

For Sean, there was a momentary disconnect. He'd never seen his landlady anyplace but in her home and wearing a housedress. To see her in the Knob, dressed in a floral blouse and tailored slacks, with her hair done in stylish, tight curls was so at odds with his perception of Mrs. Kerr that he was momentarily speechless.

As she arrived at his table, he found his voice enough to say, "I thought you weren't coming until tomorrow."

"That's what I intended. But once you left the house, I thought there was no point in putting it off. After our talk, I felt ready to meet my neighbors."

That was as far as Mrs. Kerr got before she was surrounded by a flock of islanders. There was a joyous atmosphere to the Knob that Sean found contagious. Marcus rushed over and gave her a gigantic hug. Sean knew the news would soon spread throughout the island. Mrs. Kerr would be spending the afternoon at the Knob greeting friends and being welcomed back into the Janus family.

Once his table was overrun by eager islanders anxious to speak with Mrs. Kerr, Sean retreated to the bookshelves. He selected a biography of John Lennon and quietly slipped out of the Knob.

Walking along the Ring Road, he encountered a number of people, including entire families on their way to the Knob.

Everyone either waved or stopped to chat. They were all happy for Mrs. Kerr. A few short weeks ago, he'd have been surprised beyond words that one lady emerging from her house after a year of relative solitude could create such excitement. At the time, he didn't know Janus existed. So many things had changed in his life since leaving London. He'd come to the island a stranger and now felt like he was part of a large family.

Arriving at Mrs. Kerr's, he decided to sit on the gallery and wait for her return. Sean opened the book he'd borrowed and began to read.

# CHAPTER 48

Mrs. Kerr had been unusually animated over dinner. Her lined face was freed from the scars of sadness. Eyes that once held a listless and weary look were now alive with anticipation, no longer filled only with the stark reality of tragedy. She laughed and told him what her neighbors were doing. Mrs. Kerr was a different woman from the one he'd first met.

As they sat eating, he listened to stories about her early days on Janus and how much the island had changed with the dam and electricity. She talked about her knitting, walking about the island, the book she'd borrowed from the Knob, and how the planting was progressing. Sean marveled at the simplicity of the pleasures she enjoyed. He knew there would be the occasional dark day ahead, but those would be fewer and farther apart as time passed.

Partway through the meal, she asked if he'd decided to stay or if he'd be returning to London.

"I haven't made up mind," he responded. "While getting to know the islanders has been nice, I feel there's more to my being on the island than Elijah has told me."

Mrs. Kerr nodded.

"Diane tells me that a lot of islanders also think that's the case," Sean continued.

"I know," responded his landlady. "A few of them mentioned that to me when I was at the Knob. But if there's another reason besides introducing some new ideas to the island and Elijah hasn't told you, then it has everything to do with the Spirit. That would be the only reason he'd be keeping something from you."

"What do you mean? I thought the Spirit didn't get involved in the island's affairs."

"It doesn't. If the Spirit has anything to do with you being on Janus, it would have to be for a reason that goes beyond anything we've ever experienced."

"Is that possible?" wondered Sean.

"I don't know," Mrs. Kerr mused. "The only way you'll find out is to ask Elijah."

"I'll think about it," said Sean. "*Journey* will be here at the end of the week. So, if he's got something in mind that no one knows about, it has to happen before then."

"If you decide to stay, and I hope you do, you're welcome to live here for as long as you wish."

Momentarily overcome by her kindness, Sean realized that, if he did leave Janus, he'd miss her. Mrs. Kerr was a strong woman who'd borne the loss of her family with a quiet dignity. She'd welcomed him into her house. Although he'd only lived here for a short time, her warmth and generosity had made it feel like a home.

"Thank you," he quietly said. "I'd like that."

# Chapter 49

Elijah had asked Sean to drop by that evening. With thoughts of the dinner conversation he'd had with Mrs. Kerr on his mind, he made the short walk to the Prophet's house. The sun's fading warmth caressed his face and chest. A light wind ruffled his hair.

When he arrived, Elijah was sitting in one of the chairs that stood watch on his gallery. The oncoming twilight was not yet dark enough to rub out the surrounding barns and houses.

"We don't get enough of these fine evenings," said the Prophet as Sean came up the path toward the house. "Instead of staying around here, why don't we go for walk?"

"Sounds like a good idea," responded Sean.

Leaving the house, the men strolled toward the setting sun.

"It's all over the island that Mrs. Kerr visited the Knob," said Elijah. "Everyone is incredibly happy for her and believes you had a lot to do with it."

"People keep saying that. I didn't do anything except move in and be there. I'm being given far more credit than I deserve."

"You did more than that, and the islanders are grateful for how you've helped her."

As they continued walking, Elijah said, "There's a reason I asked you to stop by this evening."

"And what would that be?" replied Sean.

"I was wondering if you've made a decision about staying longer with us."

"Mrs. Kerr asked me that while we were having dinner," responded Sean.

"What was your answer?" wondered the Prophet.

"I told her that I haven't made up my mind."

Sean paused for a few seconds before saying. "And we also discussed whether the Spirit has anything to do with my being here. Many of the islanders seem to believe it does."

It was Elijah's turn to be silent for several moments.

"The Spirit has never interfered with anything that happens on the island," he quietly said. "But it has shown an interest in meeting you."

The words took a moment to register with Sean. When they did, the shock forced his eyes wide, while his mouth moved spasmodically for several seconds. A sensation, like a slow-moving freight train rumbled through his stomach.

He stopped and stared at Elijah. "Why would the Spirit want to see me?" he was finally able to ask.

"I don't know," responded the Prophet.

"You don't know or you won't tell me," offered Sean.

A look of dismay swept across Elijah's face. "That's not the way we do things on Janus," he said. "I'd tell you if I knew."

The men had resumed walking, their footstep kicking up little eddies of dirt as they trod the road.

"Diane, Mrs. Kerr, and everyone else are right, aren't they?" said Sean. "There's more to my being on Janus than what you originally told me. The Spirit wouldn't be showing an interest in me if there wasn't."

"That's true," admitted Elijah.

"Why am I just now finding out about this? What was the point of keeping it from me?"

"Think back to your time in London," responded Elijah. "Suppose I'd written that the Spirit wanted to speak with you. What would you have thought? You'd have dismissed me as some type of cultist. You'd never have come to Janus."

"You're right." Sean shrugged. "But I've been here for almost two months. There was plenty of time to tell me."

Suddenly Sean had a thought. "Does this have anything to do with Brian Elder at *The Advocate*? Did you or one of your Guardians talk to him about my taking two months away from the paper? I've always wondered why it was so convenient for me to get the time off when I did."

"Brian is part of our diaspora."

The words had been uttered so casually that it took a moment for Sean to register their impact.

"You're telling me that Brian Elder was born on Janus," said Sean, gradually getting over his second shock of the evening.

Elijah nodded in silent agreement.

"Is there anyone else at *The Advocate* who has ties to the island?"

The Prophet shook his head. "No, Brian is the only one."

"If Brian is part of your diaspora, what about my friend at the United Nations. He not only got me the job in Afghanistan and on *The Advocate* but convinced me to read your first e-mail. Is Larry Blaine part of your network?"

"Yes."

Sean wasn't sure how to feel. Should he be angry or flattered that so much effort had been made to get him on Janus? This was like a mystery novel. Only it was life, and somehow he'd become a central character. Questions tore through his mind. How long had he been under Elijah's watchful eye? Had he been manipulated into coming to Janus? Why had he been chosen? And what was the purpose of it all?

"I know there must be a hundred thoughts rushing through your mind," said Elijah. "I'll answer as many of your questions as I can."

"Then let's start at the beginning. How long have you been watching me?"

Elijah walked a few steps in silence. "We've known about you since your birth," he finally said. "The Guardians have always known what you were doing."

"So you've kept tabs on me from the day I was born," said Sean, his voice resonating shock and confusion. "What right do you have to interfere with my life?"

He felt a surge of anger.

"Not only have you and the Guardians been watching me, you've basically engineered my life ever since I left my father's law firm. Did you have anything to do with my firing?"

"We weren't interfering, and your departure from BDK had nothing to do with us," Elijah replied. "We only became involved once you left. And on all three occasions, Larry offered you an opportunity you were free to decline. No one forced you to work for the UN or at *The Advocate* or to come here."

Elijah's words did little to lessen Sean's feeling that he'd been living his life under a microscope.

"Why were you so interested in what I was doing with my life? You were spying on me and I don't feel comfortable with that. In fact, you're giving me a good reason to leave Janus and, for the future, to never have anything to do with this island."

"I understand you're upset, but at least give me a few minutes to explain our interest in you."

The men had stopped walking and were standing in the middle of the road. Sean debated whether he wanted to hear the Prophet's rationale. It took several seconds, but his innate curiosity drove him to seek answers. "Fine, I'll listen. But I want to know everything."

Elijah nodded his agreement. "I'll do the best I can. Several years, before you began working full-time at BDK, you hired a private detective to investigate the Kilgore family. Lucas Kilgore was your birth father. The investigator could find no ancestors past your great-great-grandfather, Joshua Kilgore."

"That's right," said Sean, no longer surprised at what Elijah knew about his life. "But why would that interest you and the Guardians?"

"There was a time," said Elijah, "when the Kilgore family played an important role on Janus."

The surprise registered on Sean's face, pulling his eyes into slits as he tried to comprehend what Elijah was saying. It was turning into quite the evening of revelations. "Go on," he said, wondering where the story would lead.

"Joshua Kilgore was born here. He left after an argument with his younger brother, Kaleb, and his father, Samuel. Joshua was the eldest son. He couldn't accept that his father had broken with tradition and decided that, upon his death, the family land would be divided equally between the two sons. As you know, our custom holds that the land is always left to the eldest son or daughter.

"The unfortunate truth is that the land wasn't large enough to be successfully farmed by two families. Knowing this, Joshua asked Samuel to reverse his decision. The father wouldn't relent. Joshua went to Kaleb, who refused to give up his right to the land."

"Why did the father make such a choice, knowing it would cause dissension within the family?" asked Sean.

"No one knows," responded Elijah. "Looking back, it was probably some form of dementia, but those things weren't known at the time. It was merely thought of as a strange, unworkable decision. Unfortunately, it made Joshua so angry he left and wanted nothing to do with the island.

"It's a dark period in our history. We don't argue on Janus. As you know, we settle everything through compromise and understanding. To have dissension, particularly within a family, has always been viewed as a terrible tragedy. You were never told about it because your great-great-grandfather was so bitter that, when he married a woman who was not part of our diaspora, the story was not told to his wife or children.

"He effectively erased his background. As part of that process, he changed his surname from the Jewish *Kirsch* to the more anglicized *Kilgore*. In fact, Joshua was so successful that no records exist about his life before arriving in Canada."

"My family background is Jewish?" said a surprised Sean.

"It is," replied Elijah. "Most of our original settlers were Jewish. Many of the surnames have changed over time as members of our diaspora married and returned to the island. But some of the early names still survive."

"So my ancestor left Janus, changed his name, cut off all ties with the island, and disappeared into a new life in Canada."

"That's correct. And since your family was not part of our diaspora, there was no contact between it and the islanders. With each new generation, only the memory of the brother's feud has been kept alive on Janus. The story of what happened to his family is not part of our history.

"But the Guardians never lose sight of anyone born on Janus, and that includes their families. We knew about you and your adoption."

"Yet, there was more than just watching over me," said Sean. "You became involved in my life. I'm sure you don't do that with everyone."

"That's true," admitted Elijah.

"Why was that?"

Elijah hesitated before saying, “That’s a question only the Spirit can answer. All I can tell you is that I was asked by the Spirit to take a personal interest in your life. No reason was given. And there was no thought of having you come to Janus until it became apparent the Spirit wanted you here.”

“How long ago was that?”

“We’ve been talking about it since you were at BDK.”

“For that long?”

Rather than providing clarity, it seemed that every answer Elijah supplied only led to more questions. Sean took a deep breath. “And I suppose you can’t tell me why the Spirit is so interested in my welfare.”

Elijah shook his head slowly and held his hands out, palms facing upward.

“I’m answering your questions as best I can,” responded the Prophet. “But there’s a lot the Spirit hasn’t told me.”

Sean pursed his lips. “I have a raised birthmark in the shape of a triangle that my father and grandfather had. Does it have anything to do with Janus and the Kirsch family?”

Elijah again paused for several seconds. “The birthmark has been in the Kirsch family since before our ancestors landed on the island. They were in the group of first settlers. It’s been passed from one eldest son to the next. Your great-great-grandfather also had the birthmark.”

“What does it mean?”

This time Elijah didn’t hesitate. “You’ll have to stay on Janus for a while longer to find the answer to that question. Everything will become clear if you stay long enough to talk with the Spirit.”

"There's nothing else you can tell me about my birthmark."

Elijah shook his head. "If you stay, you'll understand its importance."

Again an answer that raised more questions. Sean decided to go in a different direction. "Do I have any relatives on Janus? Are some of them part of the diaspora?"

"You're the only remaining descendent," replied the Prophet. "There are no Kirsch family members on the island or living away from here."

"How many people know about my ties to Janus?"

"No one on the island or in our diaspora. Several of the Guardians know small parts of your background, but I'm the only one, along with you, who has the whole story."

"I'd prefer it remained that way," said Sean.

"Your past has been and will continue to be kept secret by me."

"Why are you just telling me all this now? Is it part of a ploy to keep me on the island?" Sean smiled, showing that no malice was meant by his questions.

"There's no scheme to keep you here. As to why I'm telling you now, I thought it would help in whatever decision you make."

"It seems that my being here is part of a much larger plan. Suddenly a simple holiday visit to your island has taken on implications that I never considered. I feel a like a puppet and someone is pulling my strings."

Elijah's eyes reflected his distress. "That's not the case. Both the Spirit and I hope you'll remain on the island, but only if it's what you want to do. Remember, you weren't forced into coming here."

"That's true," Sean admitted. "But suppose I want nothing to do with Janus?"

"You're free to go. I assure you, no one will stand in your way. If that's what you decide, your job and apartment are waiting for you."

Both men were silent. Darkness was slowly reaching out and drawing the men into her bosom. The Prophet suggested they head for home. They retraced their steps in silence.

A light mist began to move in from the ocean as they arrived at Elijah's house.

"I have a decision to make," said Sean.

"Yes you do. My hope is you'll choose to stay at least for another couple of months. I know I'm also speaking for the Spirit. Why not take some time and talk it over with Diane?"

"Whatever decision I make will only be made after talking to her."

"That's good," said Elijah. "Perhaps she'll convince you that Janus is a wonderful place to spend some time."

"When do you want me to let you know whether I'm staying?" responded Sean, ignoring Elijah's comment.

"Why not take until *Journey* arrives. You can tell me what you've decided then."

An idea was forming in Sean's mind. He needed time to think but wasn't prepared to let his life hang in limbo.

"Why don't we get together in a couple of days? I've got a few things to consider."

Elijah gave him a steady look for several seconds. "That sounds fine. There's work to do in the barn. That's where you'll probably find me. Come over when it's good for you."

"I'll see you then," said Sean.

Elijah turned and walked up the pathway without looking back. Sean watched the Prophet open the door and disappear into his house.

As he walked home, Sean began to realize that Janus was more than just a small island with a group of uncomplicated people somewhere in the North Sea. And Elijah was not the simple farmer and guide to every islander that he wanted Sean to believe. Through the Guardians and the diaspora, the Prophet had built an impressive global network with contacts and influence that extended far beyond the island and Inverness.

# Chapter 50

Following his conversation with Elijah, Sean had spent a restless and confused night. Brian Elder, Larry, the Spirit wanting to meet him, and his family ties to Janus jumbled through his mind like balls at a bingo game. And there was Diane. He needed to talk to her and put some order to what he'd learned.

More than anything, he needed to rationalize that the Spirit wanted to meet with him. It was an incredible prospect, if the Spirit was really the Supreme Being and not some weird apparition that was part of the island's collective conscience.

During breakfast with Mrs. Kerr, she'd asked how his conversation with Elijah had gone. He'd said little, other than the Prophet had given him a lot to think about. Mrs. Kerr had wisely stayed silent, letting Sean ponder his thoughts.

After helping Mrs. Kerr with the dishes, he walked over to Diane's. A feeling of disappointment flowed over him when he read the note attached to her door. She was working for the day with Ian, seeing patients, and wouldn't be back until later that evening.

Leaving the house he'd wandered down to the wharf. It was deserted, with the ships out on the North Atlantic as the crews searched for fish to fill their nets. He sat on one of the larger bollocks used to tie up *Journey*.

Sean went over everything Elijah had told him. He thought about Diane and how important she'd become in his life. He wasn't sure how long he'd sat there, but in the end, his mind was clear. Sean felt comfortable with his decision.

He spent the rest of the day at Mrs. Kerr's. His landlady was out, so he had the house to himself. He spent the time reading and reviewing his decision. The more he thought about it, the more comfortable he became.

When Mrs. Kerr arrived, she immediately set about making dinner and scolding him for skipping lunch. He only realized that he was hungry when he saw her frying up some pieces of cod.

As they finished dinner, Sean told Mrs. Kerr he was going to see Diane. After ensuring she didn't need help with the dishes, Sean slipped into his bulky sweater and ventured out into the evening. Although the sun had just begun its nightly descent, a breeze blowing in off the sea had cooled the temperature.

Arriving at Diane's, Sean noticed the door was open. A feeling of elation swept over him. He ran up the stairs and knocked. As she walked down the hallway from the kitchen, he saw her look of curiosity turn into a large smile.

"I was hoping it was you," she said.

"I'm glad you're home. I missed you," Sean replied.

"I wasn't gone that long," she laughed, before giving him a light kiss.

Diane brought him into the kitchen.

"I was just washing my dinner dishes. Why don't you make us some coffee while I finish?"

Sean set about brewing up a pot.

The coffee was ready for pouring as Diane finished putting the last of the dishes away. They took their cups into the living room, where Sean sat opposite Diane. She didn't attempt to hide the look of surprise that Sean had chosen not to sit beside her on the couch.

Taking a sip of the hot liquid, he said "We have a lot to talk about."

"With *Journey* arriving in a few days, I suppose we do."

Sean explained about his conversation with Elijah, including that he planned on seeing the Prophet in the morning.

"I was hoping we could discuss the future and whether there's room for me in your life," he concluded, somewhat awkwardly.

"There's more to this decision than just you and me. Is it really fair to make it all about us?" wondered Diane.

"I know it's about more than our relationship," he said defensively. "But you've become an important part of my world. I wanted to see if you agree with me that we have the beginning of something that could be very special."

"We have a relationship that is less than two months old," replied Diane. "Is that enough to keep you on Janus? You should be looking at other things in your life before making a final decision."

"I am, but your opinion counts for a lot," said Sean. "Talking it over with you seems the right thing to do."

Diane took a long drink from her cup. "I don't want to influence you either way. Both of us have had marriages that didn't succeed. We know that things don't always turn out as planned when reality comes knocking at the door."

Diane took a deep breath. "I have strong feelings for you. But you've known since you got here that this day would come. From my view, it's an easy thing to decide. It's either go back to a life you know and a job that you're good at. Or you can stay here and find out why the Spirit wants to meet with you. At the same time, it'll give us a chance to see about our future. You're making this more complicated than it needs to be."

Sean realized Diane was right.

Knowing that his job and apartment would still be there was something to consider. He also wanted to explore his bond with Diane. Although their relationship had only just begun, he wanted to see if it could be built into something permanent.

But there was still the pull of a world that seemed more meaningful than what the islanders were living. And what if he didn't get to visit with the Spirit over the next couple of months? He'd face the same decision again. Sean realized that, while Diane was integral to his future happiness, knowing why he was on the island was also a key factor in whatever decision about the future he was going to make.

And that began with visiting the Spirit before *Journey* arrived. It was a request he was going to make of the Prophet. And it was nonnegotiable.

"What have you told Elijah about us?" asked Diane, breaking into his thoughts.

"That you're a major part of whatever I decide."

Diane nodded and said, "So why don't we leave whatever decisions have to be made for the morning. In the meantime and on behalf of every islander, let's assume that for tonight it's my responsibility to convince you that staying on Janus is the right thing to do."

Her smile was wide, matched only by the laughter dancing in her eyes.

"Well, I'm always open to being persuaded," Sean said, joining in the moment's lighthearted mood.

Getting up from his chair, Sean slowly guided Diane to her feet. She came willingly into his arms. They kissed, gently at first and then with a rising passion. Without a word, they turned and walked toward Diane's bedroom.

Their lovemaking was filled with tender passion and discovery. After they'd fulfilled each other's desires and lain together for a long while, Sean lifted himself up, resting on his elbows. He looked into her eyes. She returned his gaze.

They shared words of love and both spoke about a future spent together. It was a time where their bodies and their emotions were as one. They were alone in a world they'd created, and it was beyond special. The morning would come with its decisions, but for now there was nothing but the two of them and the knowledge that love had truly entered their lives.

# CHAPTER 51

With the coming of dawn, Sean and Diane awoke to a new awareness. Their words reflected the beginning of love and commitment discovered during the deepest hours of darkness.

Sometime later that morning, after breakfast had been eaten and the dishes cleared, they sat across from each other at the kitchen table.

"What are you going to tell Elijah?" Diane asked.

"That I need to know why the Spirit wants me on Janus," said Sean. "Before I can make a decision, I have to talk with the Spirit. And I need to speak with it before *Journey* arrives. I don't want to be in limbo for another two months while Elijah and the Spirit take their time in letting me know why I'm here."

"You're going to give Elijah and the Spirit an ultimatum?" Diane's voice revealed her amazement.

Sean could see the tension reflected in her face, pulling her eyes and forehead together in a deep frown.

"I'm not sure I'd look at it that way," explained Sean. "It's simply that, before I can decide whether to stay on Janus, I have to know what the Spirit has planned for me."

"But to demand a meeting with the Spirit is something that's never been done. What if the Spirit refuses? You'll leave Janus having accomplished nothing."

"You're wrong," Sean said, reaching across the table and taking her hands. "I've met you, and that means everything to me. It's been a wonderful holiday, and I'm in love with someone special. That's a lot for two months."

"I meant what I said last night," said Sean, his voice charged with emotion. "I love you."

"And I love you too. But you're still not sure if you want to stay on Janus."

Sean understood where this was coming from. In her mind, he was showing some of the selfishness that was present in the world but not a part of Janus. But he was powerless to do anything about it until he'd talked with the Spirit. The last thing he wanted was to hurt Diane. He tried to make her understand what he was feeling. "I'm not a farmer, a sheepherder or a fisherman. Unless there's a solid reason for my being here, what am I going to do?"

"You can live with me. I'll teach you about farming."

"That's not really the issue"

"Well, what is the issue?"

"It isn't a question of not wanting to stay. There's a job waiting for me in London. It's one that I enjoy and gives me a lot of satisfaction. I don't want to give that up for something I'm not remotely qualified for or interested in doing."

Sean knew the talk could go on for hours and nothing would be resolved. He needed to see Elijah.

"It's time I was going," he said. "I'm not sure how long I'll be at Elijah's or if I'll have to wait for him. Why don't I stop by when we're finished and I'll let you know how it went?"

"I'd love that," she replied. "But I've got work to do in the barn and that could take most of the day. How about dinner?"

Sean was at first taken aback but then realized that was the island way. There was work to do on the farm and whatever agreement was reached with Elijah would still be there at the end of the day.

"That would be perfect."

They kissed before Sean walked out the door.

He stopped at the end of her pathway and turned. Standing in the doorway, she blew him a kiss. He waved one back and turned toward Elijah's.

# CHAPTER 52

Sean found the Prophet in his barn, mucking out one of the stalls.

"I'm glad you're here," Elijah said by way of a greeting. "Why don't I get some coffee and we can talk on the porch."

Sean took a seat on one of the chairs. It wasn't long before Elijah joined him with coffees and a plate of brownies. Sean took a couple of long sips from his mug and finished one of the brownies. The coffee was hot, the brownie chewy. Putting his mug down, he looked over at the Prophet. No words had passed between them since Sean's arrival in the barn.

"Before you begin," said Elijah, "let me just say that I've tried to have the Spirit explain why it wanted you here. I almost didn't carry out its wishes because I felt uncomfortable bringing you here without a clear reasoning."

"Why did you do it then?"

"Because the Spirit convinced me that having you here was part of a plan it had that involved not only Janus but the world."

Sean sat back in his chair. Once again, he felt trapped in the abys between the world's reality that he knew and understood and what seemed to pass for certainty on Janus.

"You were asked to bring me here by this being you all claim never interferes with the world yet suddenly has a plan that involves me. Do you realize how bizarre that sounds," said Sean, amazement tinging his voice. "And because of that, I'm spending two months on this island."

Elijah nodded but remained silent.

"And before we meet, the Spirit wants me to spend more time on Janus."

"That's right."

"Well, that's not good enough to keep me here."

"We haven't known each other that long," said Elijah. "But you trusted me when I asked you to come from London and spend some time with us.

"I can't provide all the answers you want. But I'm asking you to trust me again and give me a bit more time. Stay another couple of months and let's see what happens with the Spirit. You have to understand. The Spirit doesn't measure time the same way humans do. It exists on a plane of consciousness where the past and future within our context have no relevance.

"Don't leave until you find out the role it wants you to play. You must realize how incredible it is that the Spirit is calling upon you. This has never happened in our history. And it's no charlatan's trickery. This is real and beyond the world's imagination. Aren't you at least a bit curious as to why the Spirit has asked for you to be here?"

Sean waited a moment before answering. "It's hard for me to answer that question when I've only heard about your Spirit since arriving on Janus. I'm not part of the Janus culture. I look at things differently. Here, no one questions his or her destiny. People live the life of their ancestors and work to ensure the island's ongoing separation from the world. Even members of your diaspora, although some have been away for many years, are fully committed to moving the island's message of peace through whatever society they live in.

"While I admire the life everyone lives, I don't believe it's for me."

"But you don't know that," argued Elijah. "I'm asking for you to hold off making a final decision until you've spoken with the Spirit. All we're talking about now is extending your visit until that happens."

Sean thought hard. He realized the words he was about to say could forever change his life. "I'm leaving when *Journey* sails unless the Spirit talks to me and says something that convinces me staying is worthwhile."

"Are you demanding an immediate meeting with the Spirit?" Elijah said, his voice rising slightly.

"I wouldn't call it a demand," said Sean. "I don't have that right. But, if the Spirit hasn't spoken to me by the end of two months, I don't see what waiting another couple of months will achieve. I could be here for a year, even two and never understand the reason it had you bring me to Janus. I know what I have waiting for me in London. That's more than I can say for here. I don't farm or fish and can't live with Mrs. Kerr forever."

"But the Spirit always decides when we're ready for our first visit," explained Elijah. "That initial session has always been a rite of passage for every islander. And because the Spirit decides the timing, it forms an important part of our history's fabric."

"Well I'm not an islander," noted Sean. "I don't have to stand on tradition."

"Do you realize what you're asking for? This is the Spirit, and you're stipulating it meet on your terms."

"From my point of view, it's no more audacious then everyone claiming they have conversations with the Spirit."

"You're not leaving me much choice," responded Elijah. "I'll talk to the Spirit and see if a meeting can be arranged for some time over the next couple of days."

"That's all I want," said Sean.

"Have you talked this over with Diane?"

Sean paused for a few seconds before answering. "We've discussed the future, but a lot of what happens between us will depend on whether I get to meet the Spirit."

"Is there's a chance you'd stay for her?"

Sean thought about what they'd talked about in the night's dark hours. "I don't think we should make Diane part of this discussion," he said quietly. "The only thing that matters is whether I meet with the Spirit. What happens between Diane and me is a decision the two of us will make when the time is right."

Elijah heaved a large sigh. "I'm planning on visiting the cave this afternoon. I'll see what can be arranged. But I wouldn't count on anything."

"Remember, I'm not demanding a meeting," emphasized Sean. "I just want the Spirit to know that my plans are to leave unless it meets with me."

"I understand and will convey the difference," said Elijah.

# Chapter 53

Late afternoon and Sean was sitting in the Knob, a dated copy of *Time* spread out on the table in front of him. He'd poured himself a cup of coffee, but rather than reading, he was lost in thought.

A lot had happened during his time on Janus, and he marveled at the experience. He thought of what he'd learned about the islanders and his history, along with Elijah's role in his life. However, he saved most of his contemplation for Diane. She'd become an important part of his world. He realized their relationship was only in the beginning stages and the future was littered with many obstacles, not the least of which was his commitment to stay on Janus for only two months.

Still, he was hopeful the bonds they were building would lead to something strong and lasting.

The door swung wide, and in walked Mrs. Kerr. About to head farther into the store, she noticed Sean and came over. Following the exchange of greetings, he asked if she'd like to join him. After lowering herself into a chair, she looked around the Knob and noted that Elijah wasn't with him.

"He's at the cave," explained Sean.

Mrs. Kerr responded to the news with a nod. "*Journey* will be coming in sometime over the next few days and everyone will get their supplies topped up. It's surprising to think that the last time the Guardians were here was when you arrived at my house.

"So much has changed in my life over the past couple of months. Looking back, it's hard to believe I spent a year locked away in my home."

"I've changed too," noted Sean. "I never thought I'd meet someone like Diane, who would turn everything around for me. And finding that someplace like Janus, along with the Guardians and the diaspora exist in today's world is almost beyond comprehension.

"Just the same it amazes me that everyone is content to let the world pass them by. Haven't you ever once been curious about what's beyond Janus and the market at Kirkwall?"

Mrs. Kerr sat silently contemplating the question. "I have neither the inclination nor the desire to venture beyond our shores. It's not so much that I view the world in a negative light, but when I read the newspapers and magazines, I can't help but believe that most people are looking for what we have on Janus. We are an understanding and tolerant society that practices equality and peace.

"We can concentrate on the freedom that comes with knowing everyone has an equal part to play in the island's ongoing existence.

"And while our way of life has been passed down by our ancestors, we don't take what we have for granted. It's a life we continually affirm through our day-to-day interactions with each other and at the Assembly meetings. Every islander realizes what we have is unique and works hard at preserving our lifestyle. It takes a personal and collective commitment to live as we do on Janus. That's something none of us ever forget."

Mrs. Kerr folded her arms on the table and asked Sean if he wouldn't mind getting her a coffee, signaling that she'd come to the end of her explanation.

Sean got up and walked over to the counter. He'd finished filling a mug for Mrs. Kerr and was just about to pour a refill for himself when Elijah entered the Knob. He stopped in the doorway and looked around. His gaze came to rest on Sean. The Prophet hurried over to the counter, creating a moment Sean knew he'd always remember.

"The Spirit wants to meet you tomorrow afternoon," he said.

Sean felt a small measure of gratification. It was not a sense of victory. Rather, it seemed more like the natural flow of events that had begun long before he knew about Janus was now culminating in an experience that might prove to be beyond anything he could have ever imagined.

He was humbled and looked at the coming visit with nervous anticipation. If what the islanders said was true, he was going to have a conversation with the universe's Supreme Being.

The situation's reality played across his mind. More importantly, he was about to discover whether the islanders' Spirit was real and what it wanted from him.

"I'm all set," responded Sean. "What happens now?"

"I have a couple of things to do around the farm," said Elijah. "Why don't we get together tomorrow about midmorning at the house? You probably have some questions, and there are a couple of things you should know before going to the cave."

Elijah waved good-bye and was quickly out the door. Bringing over his mug, Sean deposited himself in a chair and looked at Mrs. Kerr. "I'm actually going to meet the Spirit. This is unbelievable. Suddenly I feel nervous and not too sure of myself."

Mrs. Kerr patted his arm. "Why don't you go over to Diane's? She's probably finished her work in the barn. The two of you can have dinner and a good talk. I think spending time together would be the best way to prepare for your first meeting with the Spirit."

*The always practical Mrs. Kerr,* thought Sean. And just what he needed before an experience that he knew would forever stay with him—regardless of what happened.

Together they washed their mugs, said good-bye to Marcus, and headed out into the day's fading sunlight.

# Chapter 54

Walking to Diane's, Sean couldn't help but contemplate the occasion's absurdity and the concept of talking with what Elijah and the islanders believed was their Spirit. However, there were certain realities he couldn't ignore. It was difficult to comprehend, yet Janus existed. It was unknown to the world. And its people genuinely cared for one another. He had seen the way they looked out for Mrs. Kerr and helped Diane with her farm.

But it didn't seem real. He knew he was still hampered by the complexities and doubts that were so much a part of what he'd experienced before coming to Janus. Those were realities that belonged to a world far away from the island. Was he jaded by his knowledge of what existed beyond the Janus shores? Perhaps he was seeking something sinister when there was nothing to look for.

He found Diane in the barn, repairing a halter for one of her donkeys.

"I'm seeing the Spirit tomorrow afternoon," he blurted as she put her tools down and wiped a stray hair from her face.

Shaking her head, Diane said, "I didn't believe it was possible. You must mean a great deal to the Spirit for it to agree to see you. Hopefully you'll find out why you're on the island."

"That's something I'm looking forward to learning," said Sean. "I'm still finding it hard to believe that tomorrow I'll be meeting with the Spirit. What's it going to be like?"

"We should talk about it over dinner," suggested Diane. "I need to get cleaned up. We can relax and I'll tell you whatever it is that you want to know."

"Sounds good to me," said Sean.

While Diane took a bath, Sean prepared a meal of sliced ham with potatoes and peas. He'd brought some scones from the Knob, and those were added to the fare.

After sitting down, he eagerly listened as she began to explain about meeting with the Spirit.

"Everyone experiences it differently," began Diane. "In my case, it's a regular conversation. For a few of the islanders, it takes place inside their head. They're conscious, but they tell me it's as if they go into a trance. And then there are others who lose consciousness and only remember the conversation a few minutes after awakening as though from a deep sleep."

"How do I start the conversation? Is there anything special I should say?"

"I wouldn't worry about that. The Spirit puts first timers at ease pretty quickly. After that, the conversation generally flows like any other talk. It ends when there isn't anything more to say."

"When was the last time you were at the cave?"

"Just before you arrived."

"And you haven't been back since? I'd have thought visiting with the Spirit is something everyone would do as much as possible."

Diane's throaty laugh cascaded throughout the room. "You might think that. But remember, the Spirit is a friend who's there whenever we visit the cave. We're raised with it as part of our lives. There really isn't any novelty to having a conversation with the Spirit. Some of us visit more than others. Farming and fishing take up a lot of time and it's not as though we take weekends off. Elijah is the one who's at the cave more than anyone, and he probably goes three or four times a month."

Sean could only shake his head.

"Well for all of you, it might seem routine, but I'm finding the expectation unnerving," he said. "This is the universe's creator. I'll be having a conversation with God, Allah, and whatever name every other religion calls their Supreme Being. To all of you it seems natural. But this will be an incredible experience. Philosophers, scholars, and just about every person throughout history have wondered what it would be like to have a conversation with the Spirit.

"But now that it's a reality, I feel as though I'm not prepared. There's so much I don't know about this world."

"The Spirit doesn't judge," she said slowly. "You don't have to prove anything. It doesn't need to be impressed. My advice would be to listen first and then talk. Meeting the Spirit for the first time can be intimidating. But remember, there are no expectations."

"What should I do when I first get there?"

"Elijah will explain everything to you. That's his role. Don't worry. He'll prepare you just as he readies everyone before their first encounter."

"It all seems so ordinary," said Sean.

"In many ways, it's one of the most normal things you'll ever experience. Put aside all your thoughts about God from the outside world and approach this as if you were truly an islander. Let Elijah be your guide and allow your mind to go places you never thought were possible."

"Do you realize the cave and the Spirit are probably the world's best kept secrets?" said Sean. "I can understand the islanders never speaking to an outsider about it. How is it possible, though, that no one in your diaspora has ever talked about it? Do you realize the wealth, not to mention the fame someone would acquire by selling your secret?"

"There's more to life than wealth and fame," replied Diane quietly.

"But in the world, people have financial problems. They're motivated by greed, love, jealousy, a need to share, and a desire to impress. There are so many factors that would drive a person to reveal not only the existence of Janus but the cave and the Spirit. It would change everything in the world."

"And yet it has never happened," countered Diane. "That's because we share what is called the sacred trust."

"Elijah mentioned that when we were on *Journey*. He said I'd find out what it meant when I got here."

"It means," began Diane, "that we all make a pledge with the Spirit not to destroy what we have by revealing it to the world. It's a fundamental part of who we are as islanders. The trust is a bond between us and the Spirit. Just as the cave is the crucible that forms every islander, our conversations with the Spirit are what guide our lives."

"I still don't understand why your secret hasn't been exposed. You were part of the diaspora. Weren't you ever tempted to tell your husband about Janus and the cave?"

Slowly shaking her head, Diane said, "You'll know the answer after your conversation with the Spirit."

"Is the experience that powerful?" wondered Sean.

"It's not a question of power," responded Diane. "The experience puts you in touch with the essence that forms your life. It's a living and breathing entity that you realize should be protected at all costs. You'll find out for yourself. Most of all, accept that it will change you in ways you can't begin to imagine."

"That sounds very deep and mysterious."

"Why don't we wait until you've visited the Spirit and then we can talk about what you've learned?"

They sat silent for a few minutes, before getting up from the table

"Is Mrs. Kerr expecting you back?" Diane asked.

"I've got permission to stay out all night."

"Good."

Without another word, he took her hand, and together they walked toward the softly lit bedroom.

Their lovemaking was slow and filled with many gentle moments. Sometime during the night, while lying in each other's arms and when early passion had turned to quiet reflection, both knew they were no longer two separate people wandering around the far reaches of love. They'd crossed over into that special place where being one with each other replaces being alone.

With the morning came the knowledge that they'd forged a bond neither wanted to break. Over breakfast, they laughed and reveled in their newfound happiness at being together. However, they carefully stayed away from any mention of the future.

After helping with clearing the dishes, Sean said, "It's time I was going. Why don't I stop by this evening and we can have dinner?"

"I'd love that," she replied. "But it won't happen."

"What do you mean?"

"Because this is your first meeting with the Spirit, you won't return from the cave until tomorrow morning," said Diane. "Elijah always meets with those who have their initial visit with the Spirit. It will be late by the time you're finished."

"What if I don't like what the Spirit has to say? Do I still have to meet with Elijah?"

"Elijah will stay the night with you. It's been a custom on our island since the early settlers that the counsellor stays with those who experience the Spirit for the first time. Nothing will change that."

The extraordinary implications of what might happen to him suddenly made Sean realize that this would be a day he'd remember for the rest of his life.

"I'm actually going to speak with the Spirit," he said, his voice hushed. "Do you realize how incredible that will be for me?"

Diane wrapped her arms around his waist and pulled him into her. “Whatever happens, remember to enjoy the experience. You’ll share in something that only a handful of people on this earth have done.”

They kissed before Sean walked toward the road and a future he still found difficult to comprehend.

# Chapter 55

As usual, they spoke in English. It was a language Angelica had become increasingly comfortable with while living in Lunenburg, Nova Scotia. For Dante, it was the language of business. And this visit certainly qualified.

"You're troubled old friend," she said, making the sign of the cross and bowing toward the altar before sliding in beside him. She wore no perfume. He drank in her freshness and felt comforted by her closeness. Only a file folder separated them.

"We live in difficult times," responded Dante. "Let us pray together for guidance."

Kneeling with him, Angelica was reminded of all the occasions when she was growing up at the chateau and they had used this chapel to pray. It brought her back to a simpler time. All that was important were her studies and the drills overseen by the chateau's specially trained instructors.

Dante had overseen every aspect of her life in Valencia. He had a nutritionist plan her meals, a doctor to plan her sleeping hours; he'd selected the exercise trainers, decided what subjects she would study, and handpicked her teachers. He had advised the assassin whose role she would fill what secrets to teach her. Finally he'd chosen the instructors and psychologists that would turn her into a lethal killer.

Somewhere deep in the small part of her mind that she still called her own, Angelica knew that her youth, and by extension her life, had been taken from her. Yet she harbored no ill-feelings toward Dante. If it hadn't been for him, she would have grown up in the Pakistan refugee camp. Angelica had no memory of the camp. She only knew that's where she came from because Dante had told her. The psychologists had done an excellent job of programming her to believe that her life had only truly begun when she was brought by Dante to Valencia.

Although known throughout the chateau as Angelica, Dante had often called her by his pet name, Azrael, known in some Christian writings as the Angel of Death. It was something special that only the two of them shared and made her feel that much closer to him. Angelica knew he was proud of her. Yet she was also aware that he'd had her create a life away from the chateau for a specific reason. If ever one of the assassinations that he sanctioned went bad and she was caught or killed, nothing could be traced back to the Praetorian Order.

While she understood and accepted the rationale, it had taken several years for her to recognize that nothing would ever come between Dante and his commitment to the Fraternity. He was a man with many sides, but in the end, they all faced the order.

When they met, he was always alone.

Little had changed in their relationship. He used to summon her by telephone; now his request was by coded e-mail. She still followed a circuitous route to the chateau, often taking two days and overnighting in one of several cities in either the United States or Europe. She generally traveled on a Canadian passport because of its easy acceptance throughout most of the world.

She was trained to follow his orders without question.

The prelate opened his eyes and sat back in the pew. Angelica felt him move and rose up from the kneeling pad to join him.

Dante reached out and squeezed her hand. It was an unusual gesture of affection, and Angelica was more surprised than pleased. Before she'd time to adjust, her mentor again startled her.

"I'm glad you're here," he said thoughtfully.

Angelica looked at him carefully. The two gestures of warmth were entirely out of character for the man and their relationship. What was bothering him, she wondered.

For several minutes, no words passed between them. Angelica waited patiently, something that came easily, given her training and experience. The prelate gathered his thoughts.

He turned toward Angelica. Speaking softly, Dante explained about Janus, Elijah, the Guardians, and Brennan. Angelica listened intently, focused on every word. Gone was everything from her world, except Dante's voice. Once again she was the devoted student, he the demanding mentor.

Dante opened the dossier. There was a photograph of Elijah taken in Inverness. Brennan's picture was an enlargement of the photo that headed his column from *The Advocate*. There were information sheets on both men that contained every physical attribute, including eye color, height, and weight.

The satellite images of Janus had been obtained through an order member who worked in the secretive National Reconnaissance Office, located in Chantilly, Virginia. The organization designed, built, and operated the United States spy satellites, along with coordinating the analysis of aerial surveillance and satellite imagery from several military and intelligence agencies, including the Central Intelligence Agency.

Angelica studied the photos, marveling at the resolution. These were high-grade satellite images that showed everything down to the finest detail. Angelica could see the expression on people's faces and determine what clothes they were wearing.

"Who's the designate?"

Dante and Angelica, along with her crew, never referred to the person planned for assassination as the target. It was something Dante had taught her as a means of depersonalizing the person she was to eliminate. From her first kill, Angelica had never seen the need for the deceptive word. This was her vocation. She was doing God's work. Dante had told her that so many times it was ingrained within her thought process. However, the prelate wanted the word used, and Angelica would never disappoint him.

Dante pointed to *The Advocate* photo of Brennan and then pulled out one of the satellite photos.

"That's the designate," the prelate said, pointing to Brennan in a photo that captured him and Diane leaving her house.

"Is the woman important?"

"She has nothing to do with our discussion. It must be someone the designate met on the island."

Angelica leaned back. She again studied the images. "It's an island. I've never carried out an assignment where there's so little ground cover. Does the designate ever leave the island and visit a city?"

Dante pursed his lips. Angelica knew the look. He wasn't looking for problems, only answers. However, there were certain realities she had to contend with. And although she wanted to please Dante, he'd never been in the field. If the prelate wanted her to succeed, he'd have to accept that this was going to be a job like no other she'd ever done.

"I know that's what you'd prefer," he responded. "But the only one who regularly leaves the island is Elijah. He's the man in the other photograph I gave you."

"Where's the island? I've never heard of Janus."

"That's because it's unknown to the world. It's in the North Sea between the Shetland and Faroe Islands."

He handed her detailed maps, secretly prepared by his agent at the National Reconnaissance Office. They showed Janus's proximity to the islands and to the Danish coast. He then gave her a map that showed the entire region, including northern Scotland and the Hebrides.

"What's the project's timetable? How soon does this have to be completed?"

"We have some time. I want you to get together with your team and plan how you can carry out the action. However, there are several complications."

"What are they?"

"It must appear to be an accident."

"That will be difficult. I don't see any cars, trucks, or farm machinery that we could use. But it's not impossible. There are cliffs and an ocean. Perhaps a fall could be arranged. What are the other problems?"

"No one is a stranger on Janus. If you land in daylight, people will immediately know you're an outsider. The assignment will have to be carried out at night."

"That should work in our favor. With these high resolution photographs we can find out where he lives. Possibly an accident at home could be the answer."

"There is something else."

"And that is?"

"The Guardians." Dante emptied the file of several pages, detailing everything the Fraternity knew about the organization.

Angelica slowly read the information, drinking in every fact. She turned the last page and looked up. Her brow was creased in a frown.

"This isn't good. The Guardians are like a small army. What do they know about the order?"

"Probably the same amount as we know about them."

"So they're aware of you and our chateau."

Dante nodded. "Yes," he said with a resigned air. "If we eliminate the designate without it looking like an accident, there will be open warfare between us and the Guardians."

"Why would they suspect us?"

"Elijah is an extremely intelligent man who plans for every eventuality. The Prophet, as he is known, may not often venture far from Janus, but he knows his history and of the enmity that exists between us and his island. And the Guardians have a long reach. It's important the job be completed with no possibility of a trail leading back to the order."

"That's the way I've handled every assignment," Angelica said quietly.

"I know," Dante responded quickly, belatedly realizing that she might be offended he'd called into question her professionalism. He hadn't meant to and felt badly it had sounded that way. It wasn't something that normally concerned him in his dealings with people. However, Angelica was different. She was his unique creation. He cared for her, although the prelate would have been hard-pressed to describe his emotion.

For her part, Angelica wasn't upset by Dante's words. Nothing he could ever say would lead her to be angry with him. Instead, the assassin was worried he might have doubts about her capability.

They sat silently for a few minutes—both, through temperament and training, unable to adequately express their feelings. The only thing that tied them together, and had always bound them, was their belief they were doing God's work in killing fellow human beings.

"How do you want to proceed?" she finally asked.

He handed Angelica the memory stick he'd prepared. She dropped it into her purse.

"All the material you've looked at is on the stick. Pull your team together. Study what I've given you. Come back to me with a plan and what you'll need to make it work. If you require more material or funds, contact me and I'll get it to you through the usual courier channels.

"We're watching the island and the Guardians' house in Inverness. If anything happens, I'll let you know."

Angelica slowly nodded. This was a tough assignment. It would take time to plan and to implement.

"Right now I have more questions than answers," she said.

"That's to be expected. But you've been successful with difficult assignments before. You've never failed me. You'll require a solid strategy, with at least a couple of backups. Take what time you and your crew need to bring me something that I know will work."

Dante picked up the file and stood. Angelica followed.

"Go with God, my Azrael," he said.

She smiled. "I will do as you command."

It was a good-bye ritual they'd had since the first time Angelica had left the chateau. There were no hugs, brief kisses on the cheek, or even a handshake.

The prelate turned and walked out of the chapel. Angelica stared after him until he left the building. Only then did she walk outside toward the parking lot, deep in thought.

Dante arrived at his office. He immediately shredded the material in the file, along with the folder. His mind was clear. The problem rested, for the moment, with Angelica. Information on Brennan would continue to be relayed to the chateau from the order's vast network. If it was important, he'd hold it for the next time they met. She had enough material to begin planning the eventual solution.

Angelica was staying at the Hotel Vincci Lys in Valencia and had rented a car. She was booked to fly out the following afternoon from Valencia Airport. The thought of taking time to visit one of the city's famed landmarks didn't occur to her. She was already deeply involved in trying to unravel the puzzle that was her assignment. Angelica planned on going back to her room, pulling out her laptop, and spending the rest of her stay studying the information on the stick.

# Chapter 56

Although they'd talked, there wasn't much Elijah could add to what Diane had already told him. Never having lived away from the island, the Prophet couldn't relate to the implausibility of the experience Sean was about to encounter.

Sean left Elijah's house and set out along the Ring Road heading through the village toward the eastern shoreline. The rising sun had burned off the early-morning clouds. It was a magnificent sight, with the sky turning into various shades of red and yellow as the orb climbed over the island. The breeze coming off the ocean gently tousled Sean's hair.

The road gradually wound its way northward along the coastline. The land was rugged and windswept. It was barren of trees. To the west lay large expanses of grassland that featured patches of colorful wildflowers, heather, moss, and lichen. The breeze had stiffened, and Sean could taste the sea salt in the air.

Passing the island's most northeasterly point, the road drew him westward. Soon he came to a clearly marked fork. Following Elijah's instructions, Sean took the path that bordered the sea and was heavily rutted.

He could feel a gradual downhill grade the further he traveled.

Iceland gulls circled overhead, looking for a careless fish lured close to the sea's surface by the sun's warmth. The inshore wind was getting stronger. Dark clouds were forming. Sean knew that, in this region, where the North Sea and the Atlantic Ocean meet, the weather was changeable. Within a few hours, clouds could cover the island, bringing with them heavy rains.

As the path narrowed, the ground changed from earth to a rocky bed. Formed by a natural crack between two rock formations, the path weaved and undulated its way closer to the water. Although many rocks jutted out along the corridor, Sean noticed that some of the flatter ones were worn smooth.

He couldn't help but wonder at the generations of islanders who had walked the path before him. His thoughts began to focus on the meaning of time's passage. What did it mean, he asked himself, and what was the purpose of these people? What were they accomplishing? They lived good lives without harming anyone. But was that the reason for their existence?

What was achieved in living apart from the world? True, there was the diaspora. Was that the goal, he wondered—to send people out into the world to gradually influence decisions made throughout national social, economic, and political institutions? Could a force for good ever overcome the overriding drive for individual, corporate, and national self-interest?

These people were living the life they wanted. No one wished for a better job, a bigger house, or a more expensive car. Money wasn't an issue. No hierarchy existed. Peace wasn't just a word or a concept. It was how the islanders lived—not through an imposed system but through a fundamental belief that infused every action and relationship.

Was that life's meaning? To live free from strife, at peace with your neighbor and be satisfied with the cards that were dealt? Or was life about a desire to accomplish more than was expected, to reach higher than anyone else, and to overcome obstacles on the road to a type of success the islanders would never experience? He lived the game of striving to achieve, and now he was briefly experiencing the coin's other side.

Two extremes—one a constant battle for recognition in a world of challenge, with success and failure a measurement of a person's worth; the other, acquiescing to the belief that happiness lay not in viewing the day's toil as a struggle, but in the acceptance that a life well lived depended upon how you treated those around you.

Or, and here his thoughts paused for a moment, was it a combination of the two? Was it possible to succeed in the world outside Janus by adhering to the island's philosophy? Why not? Couldn't one practice those four cornerstones of understanding, tolerance, equality, and peace while still being able to succeed in a world that admired and rewarded a ruthless drive to the top?

The wind was biting into his face and brought him back to the moment's reality. An answer would have to wait until he had time to ponder the issue's complexity. The trail continued its drop toward the water. The walls along each side of the path loomed higher. Soon the sky was just a slit above his head. He looked up and saw the clouds were dark and foreboding.

He came to a sharp decline that brought the path close to the water. Spray from the crashing waves made the descent slippery and difficult. Sean gradually slowed, aware that the only thing between him and the water was about a yard of rocky path.

The path divided into two trails. One veered left, sharply into the rock face, while the other continued downward to what looked like a large patch of sand. Arriving at the junction, Sean saw an overhang extending out from the rock and over the path. The trail went straight into the rock for about ten feet before curving to the right.

He stepped quickly into the cave's entrance and was mesmerized. The opening was about seven feet high and five feet wide at the base, tapering to four feet as it approached the ceiling. It appeared to have been naturally carved out of the stone. Water dripped from the roof, along the walls, and onto the path. It was damp, and Sean wondered how many centuries it had taken the water to create the opening and the trail.

Sean stopped for a few minutes to contemplate what he was about to do. He could feel his birthmark throbbing.

It was almost too much to comprehend. He was on the cusp of what billions the world over had long craved—a chance to talk with their God. History was littered with the bones of those who'd claimed to have done just that. But time and events had proved all claims to be false. This, though, could be real. The Spirit existed in the minds of every islander as surely as the cave was a part of this moment's reality.

He walked several feet and followed the right curve. Sean saw that this part of the path went for about eight feet before turning left. Taking the corner, he walked several yards and found himself in a cavern.

The cave was a stunning and massive structure in length and height. Formed by retreating glaciers during the last ice age, it had been created from the shifting mountains of rock and earth that had produced the outcropping ridge that now dominated the island's northern edge.

The cave's roof, naturally shaped, was rounded. Sean saw that stone along with a thin layer of sand formed the floor. The walls, for the most part, were smooth, but here and there, large rocks protruded, forming natural shelves.

Light streamed into the cave from several shafts in the cave's roof. Elijah later explained they also served as vents for the fire. Air currents pulled smoke up through the naturally formed shafts that opened out on the side opposite the ocean.

A large gash-like hole dominated the top of the cave's back wall, providing a view of the cloud-filled sky.

From the cave's rear, a small spring-fed stream, about two feet wide, gurgled up. It ran along the cavern's western side for about thirty feet until it disappeared under a low outcropping.

Several fluorescent lamps, attached to rudimentary wooden tripods, were located around the cave.

Situated close to the center was a fire pit. Surrounding it were three log benches. About one-quarter of each log had been hacked off along its length to provide a flat seating surface. The benches looked to Sean as though they could each hold two or three people.

A collection of sheepskin blankets was laid out against a side wall. Running along the other side wall were several mounds of dried peat. Buckets of coal piled five deep and four high were stacked along the back wall. Several stacks of driftwood were piled close to the fire pit. A wooden box contained cooking and eating utensils, while another held fire tools, such as tongs, a poker, and matches.

Looking somewhat incongruous was a green Coleman stove for cooking, a large canister of butane fuel for the stove, a two-gallon orange jug filled with water, and several large flashlights.

On one of the natural shelves rested four sleeping bags.

It had been a cold walk, with the wind whipping in from the ocean. Even here, inside the cavern, the wind's howl and screeching could be heard as it tried to force its way through the entranceway.

The cave felt cold and damp.

Shivering, he lit one of the spotlights and collected several buckets of coal, along with some peat. He began constructing the base for a fire. He lit the tinder and slowly built the fire up so that it was warming the area around the benches. Sean moved one of the benches over to where the heat from the fire was at its warmest and sat down.

Not sure what to do next, he closed his eyes and waited, listening as the flames devoured the very coal that gave the fire life. *A fitting analogy to the way humans are treating the planet*, he thought.

# Chapter 57

A gentle voice, as soft as butterfly wings, broke quietly across his mind.

"It's good to see you."

The voice was one with his thoughts. Although he couldn't hear it, Sean sensed every word. Hunching forward, he placed his hands on his knees, elbows resting on his thighs.

"And so we finally meet," said the Spirit. "I've been looking forward to your arrival. I'm sure there is much you want to know. That's not uncommon. I'm used to questions from those who visit the cave to speak with me. But this is your first time. For that reason, I believe our discussion will go well beyond my usual talks with the islanders."

Sean wasn't sure what he was experiencing. He'd expected something more dramatic, possibly a more ethereal occurrence. He wanted a separation of mind and body. He'd thought that a conversation with the Spirit would take place on another plane and that a new level of consciousness would be achieved. Where was the wisdom of a divine being? And then he understood.

The truth struck him like a sledgehammer between the eyes. He was having a conversation with the essence of the universe.

Whatever name other believers wanted to give it, he was communing directly with the islanders' Spirit. The conversation was within the boundary of his ability to comprehend.

This wasn't a hackneyed and trumped up séance. He hadn't passed over into another world. It was reality, and his encounter was all the more real because he was experiencing it with a mind that was conscious of all that was happening.

Sean could feel the blood flowing through his veins. He sensed every bone and sinew within his body. Every organ, from his brain to his heart, was linked and performing a ballet of incredible proportions that kept him living.

At the same time, he was acutely aware of everything that was happening around him. His senses were heightened. He could feel the heat from the flames, hear the ocean's waves battering themselves against the rocks, smell the cave's dampness, and sense the stone's hardness. Yet it was all on his mind's periphery. He'd never been more focused.

He was in a netherworld where reality and the Spirit were one. The feeling was unlike any he'd ever experienced. Nothing was physically stable. He felt the universe's ebb and flow as though it was expanding and contracting. It matched his breathing. He felt vibrantly alive but, at the same time, recognized the fragility of his existence.

He was experiencing neither fear nor courage. It was an awareness that he controlled his future, just as he'd chosen his past. There was no fate, nor destiny. His actions were his own, and how he moved through life was based on decisions he made. There was no one to blame, no one to thank. Being one with the universe meant success along with failure. It was the rhythm of life.

Somehow within the confines of the cave he felt closer to humanity than he'd ever experienced. There was the joy of parents with a newborn, the pain of losing someone close. The emotions moved through him like the wispy entrails of a morning mist. He felt a strong need to reach out and somehow connect with the mass of humanity inhabiting his deepest consciousness. There was a desire to tell everyone they should be gentle with each other—that there was too much anger in the world.

Were these his thoughts or did they belong to the Spirit? He'd become immersed in the liquidity of a tangential thought process with it. No longer was he sure where his thoughts ended and those of the Spirit began.

The birthmark continued to throb, bringing all his senses into one overwhelming and unifying force that locked him into the universal rhythm of existence. He felt truly connected with the Spirit.

Sean was suddenly possessed by a stark and blinding insight. The birthmark was his earthly link to the Spirit.

"What's the meaning of the birthmark on my leg?"

"It's a symbol."

"A symbol of what?" asked Sean.

"I took the signature of a triangle because it represents my message through Jesus that there are three elements necessary for humans to live in harmony with one another. The points represent understanding, tolerance, and equality. These three have to be present and linked in order to create the center which is peace.

"I ensured the birthmark was passed from generation to generation in order to serve as a constant reminder of how I hoped the islanders would live. My thought was that all those who were marked with the triangle would forever serve as a guide to what I believed could be possible.

"And I've been proven right. The islanders have lived my wish since arriving on Janus. Not only that, they could become a beacon of hope in a world that appears incapable of living peacefully and is squandering the many resources I've created for human use. And that's the reason I've been waiting for you."

"What do you mean?"

"I knew the day would come when the world would need someone to lead it back from the edge of the void—the abyss of destruction. That person is you."

Sean couldn't accept what he was hearing. "What makes you think anyone will listen to me? I have neither the power nor the platform to make one scrap of difference in the world. There are many who want peace, but there are just as many who believe violence is the only way to achieve their goals. It has been that way throughout history.

"Why do you believe I can change that?"

"You're a direct descendant of my son. You carry the Mark of Janus. It has been worn throughout the centuries by those who have followed in Jesus's footsteps. The world is rapidly moving toward a point of no return. Government, industrial, and religious leaders are incapable of reversing the tide. It must come from the people."

Sean was confused. "How can I be a direct descendant of Jesus? He died without any children to follow him."

"Jesus had two children, Daniel and Rachel, with the woman you know as Mary Magdalene. The eldest was Daniel. When he was born, I gave him the sign of the triangle because I knew what was going to happen to his father. Someone was needed to carry my message forward."

"Jesus had children?" asked a stunned Sean. "It has been written in the Bible and always believed that he died childless."

"That is a myth spread by men who wanted to be the only ones to benefit from being associated with Jesus. What chance did a wife with two small children have against the lies of so many men?

"But the people of Janus know differently. Their ancestors were driven out of Judea by the Romans because of their association with Jesus. Along with Mary, Daniel and Rachel, they made the great trek from Joppa and Jerusalem across northern Africa, through the Iberian Peninsula, into what is now known as upper Europe, and finally by ship across to Janus."

As Sean listened to the Spirit's words, tension filled his body and the pain in his leg was almost unbearable. "And you want me to believe that I'm a direct descendant of Jesus?"

"Whether you believe it or not, it's the truth," responded the Spirit. "That's why I had Elijah bring you to Janus. The mark went from Daniel to his eldest son and then the one after that and through the centuries. Throughout the Janus history, there has always been a direct descendent of Jesus who bore the mark. Your great-great-grandfather had it, and so did your biological father. The birthmark will validate your right to lead, just as my son led his movement in a search for everlasting peace."

"But the birthmark is only a physical manifestation of what has been passed on through the generations," said Sean. "I have no link with my birth father, let alone any ties to Janus. You've chosen the wrong person. The blood of Jesus certainly doesn't flow through my veins, just as a desire to lead the world to a more peaceful place has never been a personal aspiration."

"You wouldn't be alone," responded the Spirit. "It will take time, but there are the islanders, the Guardians, and the diaspora who will help spread the message. It can be done, and you're the person to make it happen. It means your commitment to remain on Janus is needed, because the island would serve as the movement's focal point.

"The islanders would show how they've lived in harmony with one another for more than two thousand years—and that the bedrock of this ongoing unity has been a willingness to understand other points of view, along with a commitment to seek compromise in the place of personal victory. Just as important is the belief that success is not the ability to have one's views or actions be paramount but is, instead, where all parties can walk away knowing they've achieved some of what they want."

"The person you should be talking to is Elijah," said Sean. "He is the island's moral leader. Everyone will listen to him. I have no standing on Janus."

"I have spoken to Elijah about this," responded the Spirit. "He realizes this is a process that will take many years. It will not be completed in his lifetime. That's why I'm looking to you. And for as long as he is with you, Elijah will help with the work needed to lead everyone associated with Janus."

A rushing sound filled Sean's ears. He felt as though his world had tilted off its axis.

"Who else knows about this?"

"I have discussed it with only Elijah."

Sean got up and began to walk. He couldn't believe what he'd just heard. So that's what the birthmark meant. The thought of being related to Jesus was staggering. And yet it didn't matter. What was being asked of him was impossible.

He was a simple man in a complex world. All he wanted was to live a life with a realistic amount of meaning. What he'd just experienced bordered on the bizarre.

He sat back down on the bench. The whole thing was surreal. It was beyond comprehension.

"I suppose you have many questions," the Spirit said.

Sean was still fighting to regain his composure. He stayed quiet for several minutes, trying to find some form of equilibrium. He was confused and felt as though he was in the midst of a giant fog that had descended on his life.

"Just because I have this mark doesn't necessarily mean the islanders will agree to what you're proposing. What do they have to gain by opening themselves to the world? If the ultimate goal is peace between all peoples, they've achieved that throughout Janus.

"Is it necessary to involve them in whatever plan you have for earth? And, why are you asking me to lead a movement that will disrupt their lives and has little chance of success?"

"I have no plan for you," the Spirit responded. "It's not for me to decide what you should do. The only one who can determine that is you. It is the same with earth. I'm merely an interested but benign observer; that's all.

"Why are you so sure my wish will fail?" continued the Spirit. "If everyone associated with Janus is given enough time to learn and understand what is expected of them, they would form a powerful force for good in the world."

"So my first task would be to prepare everyone for the mission of becoming messengers for peace," said Sean.

"Exactly."

"You realize that something as improbable as world peace would need everyone to accept that only through the absence of personal, national, and international violence would every human have the ability to pursue a meaningful life. And before any nation can claim to be at peace, all citizens must first put down their weapons."

"Do you believe that's possible?" asked the Spirit.

"I don't think so," Sean said slowly. "It would require every person to live like the islanders. On a global scale, it's personal greed and ambition that fuel the regional, political, and religious rivalries that cost so many people their lives. That doesn't even begin to take into account the violence between individuals. And then there are the disparities, such as extreme poverty, lack of education, and gender discrimination that render a nonviolent world almost impossible to comprehend."

"And yet it has been accomplished on Janus," noted the Spirit.

"That's true. But Janus is small, and its people long ago realized that only through cooperation could they survive. In a world where ultimate power is within the realm of the most ruthless, how can those who rule and defend with increasingly deadly weapons be convinced that global peace is more beneficial than a collection of warring nations?

"And even those who lay claim to being at peace are forced into maintaining it by the use of force against both internal and external enemies. Your world seems to grow progressively troubled with each passing day."

"It's not my world."

The response was so sharp and said with such passion that Sean was left momentarily speechless.

"What do you mean, it's not your world?" he finally asked. "There's a belief among many that you're bound to every person's life. Not only that; people believe you watch over earth and that it's your creation. Are you saying that's not true? Don't you have influence over everyone's life, including the timing of a person's death?

"What about Hilary and Ahmad? Are you claiming to have no role in their deaths? Why did they have to die so young, with so much of their lives in front of them?"

"Who?"

"You don't know who they were?"

A silence so profound that it seemed to Sean the world had lost the capability of sound filled the cave.

Finally the Spirit spoke. "I had nothing to do with their deaths," said the Spirit, ignoring whether it knew who Hilary and Ahmad were. "I do not interfere with what people choose to do with their lives. It is wrong to infer that I somehow control who lives and who dies. I do not ask people to worship me or even acknowledge my presence. It is enough for me to know that I exist within the paradigms of my universe."

"Doesn't that make you arrogant?"

"I'm neither egotistical nor humble. I am my own reality."

"What does that mean?"

"My power is absolute. Therefore, nothing can threaten or alter my existence. I am the universe. We are one. I came into being when the universe was formed. The essence of what I am is everything you see and all that you don't. Don't try and put human boundaries around me. I neither act nor react. I am the essence of existence.

"Earth is unique because there is an individual and collective level of consciousness that continually challenges what is perceived as axiomatic. A good example is the quest for global peace that we've been discussing. For you it seems impossible. Yet there are many who strive for some sort of understanding between all humans, in the belief that only once it is achieved can humanity reach its true potential."

"So why don't you become involved?" wondered Sean. "You've asked me to lead a concerted movement for peace. But you choose not to participate. Is it possible that you're powerless to influence what happens with earth and even throughout the universe?"

"I have power beyond your comprehension," said the Spirit. "But war and peace, like birth and death, are human realities. They are not mine. Do not place a human context against my reality. The extent of my humanity is the same as it is for every atom within my universe. We are one and the same."

Sean was becoming exasperated. Buried deep within his subconscious was a growing frustration that the Spirit was absolving itself of any responsibility for the cumulative and all-encompassing tragedy that was produced through earthly violence.

"Why are you so committed to noninterference in human affairs?" he asked.

"I sense and understand your frustration," the Spirit began. "But it's not for me to become involved in the day-to-day lives of every individual. Humans are part of the cosmos. They exist to the same degree as everything else within my universe. Humanity is neither more special nor less important than every other entity."

"If that's the case, why have you chosen to talk to the people of Janus within this cave?"

Again there was silence.

Sean felt a chill deep within his body. It was a blackness that defied description. He sensed a feeling of profound loneliness.

"I believe you've understood why I chose Janus."

"You're lonely?" Sean was incredulous.

"I'm alone but not lonely. There's a difference."

What Sean had felt was loneliness, but he wasn't going to argue.

"Is it because you're alone that you speak with the islanders?"

More silence. And then a stirring within Sean's subconscious.

"It all began with one man, Jesus. I broke my primary law with him and got involved in human affairs. I hoped this man, along with a dedicated group of followers, could bring peace to the world. But my mistake soon became apparent. Humanity had evolved but not in the way I'd hoped. Violence was still rampant. So I decided to end the folly. I chose to let humans bring my mission to a close. As you know from what history has told you, it went badly. No mercy was shown my messenger. He was put on a cross and vilified. This for a man of peace.

"It was then I vowed to never again break my own laws. I wouldn't become involved in anything to do with earth, especially humanity."

"I find it confusing," responded Sean, "that you want me to lead a movement for global peace, yet you claim there is no involvement on your part when it comes to earth."

"There's a difference," countered the Spirit. "I'm merely asking you to be a leader. Whether the world follows is entirely up to each individual, just as it is at your discretion whether you choose to be a messenger of peace.

"The right of every human, besides life, is free will. Unlike any other element or entity within my universe, humans should have the ability to choose the life they want. That isn't always the case, and it is wrong. Within the spectrum of his or her existence, each person must have the right to make his or her own choices. If that were the case, I believe peace would be attainable. But I will not interfere with individual decisions."

"Why is peace among humans so vital to you?"

"I want peace for the sake of humanity's future. Without it, the earth will gradually devolve into a mass of tribes with different ethnic, cultural, and religious beliefs fighting for continued survival. Weapons will become the currency of the strong. And once that happens, humanity will revert to an existence where brute power will replace knowledge. It will truly become a reality where only the fittest survive. And that is a law of diminishing returns."

"So what happens on earth does interest you."

The Spirit again retreated into momentary silence before responding. "I'm interested, but never mistake that for involvement," it said. "Earth will survive regardless of what happens to humanity. But if humans no longer inhabit the planet, the universe would lose a creative and curious species. It would be a loss for the cosmos, but nothing would change.

"Humanity is not the first thinking and supreme species to inhabit a planet throughout my universe. It is only the most recent. Throughout time, there have been several. The reasons for their passing are many, but the disappearance of these species has always resulted from varying forms of self-destruction.

“That is the choice for humanity. It can either seek peace and prosper or continue along a path that will lead to its demise.

“I will not determine whether humanity survives. That will be up to every individual. There have been men and women throughout history who have attempted to follow in the footsteps of my son. They were not guided by me, but possessed a singular desire and a profound realization that a full life is only possible through an individual and collective peace. I watched with interest, but did not interfere. Their efforts should be commended but the results have shown that humanity cannot achieve a world free from violence on its own.”

“Is that why you’ve chosen to become involved?”

“You’ve mistaken my interest for participation. Every movement needs a leader and that is what I’m asking of you.”

“What makes you think this time could be different?”

“I don’t know if it will be,” the Spirit said sadly. “But I have a cosmic duty to entrust a messenger with my concern. And humanity is owed the opportunity to seek a way that people can live together in peace. All human beings should have the right to find a path that allows them to meet whatever expectations they set for themselves. I’m asking you to lead a movement that will have the world’s people rise up and create a globe that is livable and sustainable. It’s time for each individual to remember and claim back his or her humanity.”

“People pray to you for peace. Why is it so impossible to grant what they seek?”

“Humans pray to me for many things. There are those who believe they can call upon divine intervention and their prayers will be answered. But, as I told you, I do not interfere.”

“So what decides if a prayer is answered?”

"I let the laws of the universe choose. Just as I will let those same laws decide the fate of humanity."

"But you created those laws."

"That's correct. I established them when the universe came into being to absolve me of the need to become involved throughout the cosmos."

"Well then what is it that you do?"

"Ah, the eternal question of humanity through the ages. The ego-driven humans who believe all answers must revolve around their questions. It's not that simple. And it's not what I *do* but what I *am*. The cosmos and I are one. My reality is the ebb and flow that happens within the universe."

"Who was it that first spoke about this cave? And why have you chosen the islanders as the only ones who can speak with you?"

"Another question but one I'm content to answer. Before his death, I spoke to Jesus about this cave, just as I am speaking with you. He told Mary, Daniel, and Rachel. They were the ones who guided the original settlers to Janus."

"So, why this cave and why Janus?"

"I was interested in the people who surrounded Jesus but were not his disciples. While the disciples collectively disowned Mary along with Daniel and Rachel after Jesus's time on the cross, there was a group that took the three of them in. These people had a commitment to peace I found intriguing. I'd failed so miserably at my first attempt to create peace on earth that I wanted to see if, with no guidance, those on Janus could succeed.

"I've never interfered with the islanders, but their dedication through the centuries has never wavered."

"So you have a selective involvement," reasoned Sean. "You communicate with the islanders in this cave but ignore the rest of the world."

"Don't mistake my conversations for something they're not," responded the Spirit, in a tone that was arrogant, almost dismissive. "We talk, but it goes no further."

"But you're conversations with the islanders are an integral part of what makes Janus unique," said Sean. "The talks are a tangible reminder of what it means to live in peace. I'm quite sure if everyone began to fight and argue amongst themselves you would no longer speak with them."

"That's true, but I don't understand your point."

"Well, if you want peace throughout earth, shouldn't the same opportunity be available to everyone? Don't you believe it would make a difference if people throughout the world could speak with their supreme being and know you exist?"

"I've already told you that I don't interfere. I became involved with the original settlers because they already practiced peace. If the message of Janus could be spread throughout your world, I might consider some form of benign association. But I'm not a savior. Don't look for me to lead. Earth's inhabitants must begin and end the journey to peace on their own. That is the only way it will be meaningful and will last."

Sean experienced a change within his subconscious. He sensed the Spirit had discussed what it wanted and the time had come to close the session.

"Our talk is coming to an end," said the Spirit, confirming Sean's feeling. "I've enjoyed our time together. It was stimulating and gave me the opportunity to explore your mind. Just as important was that you hear my request within the context of why I'm interested but will not be involved. I ask only that you think deeply before making your decision."

"When will we speak again?" asked Sean.

"As is the case with every islander, I'm available whenever you want to meet. But something tells me you'll not be a frequent visitor. Unlike the islanders, you've made your own way in the world. Your independence is to be admired. Just remember that I'm always here."

# Chapter 58

And then it was over. Where his mind had been filled with a presence, there was emptiness. His birthmark still pulsated. Mentally, Sean felt as though he'd been leaning against a wall and someone had removed it. His mind stumbled. Everyone had told him meeting with the Spirit would be an uplifting experience. Yet he felt intellectually and physically drained. An unexpected weariness sapped the strength from his body.

The fire had burned out, and he felt chilled. But to rebuild it would involve more effort than he could muster. Instead, he sat on the bench and gradually recovered. Getting up slowly, he walked out of the cave and stood on the path. Nothing had changed. The cave's rock face still felt cold to the touch. Seagulls were patrolling the water's edge. The clouds had rolled in, and the path back was bathed in a shadowy light. Waves attacked and retreated along the shoreline. The wind blew chilly across his face.

And yet, he was different. He had ventured into the realm of the universe's overriding mystery and discovered reality. No longer could he dismiss the presence of a force that existed within the cosmos. He had learned, though, that it wasn't a god or even a Supreme Being. It neither wanted nor acted on prayers. Instead, the Spirit was a benign observer of all that transpired throughout the universe. It wanted peace for earth, not for the individual suffering it would alleviate but because constant war would endanger humanity's survival. The rationale seemed more calculating than kind.

The experience had left Sean's mind in a heightened state of awareness. He'd spoken with the universe's life force, and that would forever shape his life. The Spirit existed. Perhaps that was all he needed to know. But the compassion and sense of purpose he'd expected wasn't there. And that left him with the knowledge that every human was individually responsible for discovering and using the life force within him or her. It meant challenging one's aspirations and acting upon the possibilities presented.

Perhaps that's what a conversation with the Spirit did for the islanders. It empowered them to understand that every day was filled with individual decisions that governed their lives. They alone were responsible for the outcome of those decisions.

Sean stared sightlessly out to the turbulent sea. His mind was a tumult of emotion, but there was one thought that remained grounded. Nothing could convince him to take on the task asked by the Spirit. He would talk to the Prophet but knew it was time to leave Janus.

He had but one life, and the deaths of Ahmad and Hilary had convinced him that he wanted to spend it doing something he believed in. He had no faith in the Spirit's plan. It was beyond reason to suppose that one man could change the world. The quest was futile and only demonstrated the Spirit's failure to grasp earth's reality.

Sean desperately needed to have an extensive conversation with Diane. They hadn't known each other that long, but a commitment of love had been made. He wanted her to leave with him. Would she go? It would mean giving up all that she'd grown comfortable with. But Sean knew he had no choice. Turning down the Spirit's request was only a small part of why he didn't want to stay.

The talk had merely brought the other reasons into focus. He wanted to get back to a life that he knew and understood. Already he was thinking of how he could translate what he'd experienced on Janus into *The Advocate*'s pages.

He had no intention of revealing the island's secret or anything else about Janus. He understood what Elijah and Diane meant about the sacred trust. Sean was filled with an almost supernatural desire to keep the cave and the Spirit a secret. But the idea of writing about the ideals of understanding, tolerance equality and peace had captivated his imagination.

Just as important, he couldn't envision staying and living his life as a farmer working the land with Diane.

He enjoyed the island and its people. But he was anxious to get back to *The Advocate*. The work was fulfilling, and Sean didn't believe that was possible on Janus.

# CHAPTER 59

Sean turned and saw Elijah walking toward him. He waved and the Prophet returned the greeting.

"You look thoughtful," Elijah said as he came up beside Sean. "It must have been an interesting talk."

"It was. Why don't we go inside, start a fire, and I'll tell you what happened."

After entering, Sean got the peat and several buckets of coal while Elijah built a fire.

The men stood silent as the flames moved up from the peat and began to lick at the coals. It wasn't long before a strong blaze was warming the area around the benches.

Elijah got the coffee pot, filled it with water from the stream, and placed it on the grate. Soon the men were sitting opposite each other on the benches and sipping warm sweetened coffee from metal mugs.

Sean told Elijah about his conversation. He left nothing out. When he came to the end, Sean could see that his recounting had affected the Prophet. Elijah was leaning forward as if afraid to miss a word. His face was flushed, and his eyes were burning bright with intensity.

"So you spoke about the birthmark," Elijah said after several moments. "How do you feel about being a direct descendant of Jesus?"

"I really haven't had time to take it all in," responded Sean. "It seems so implausible. And yet it must be true. But as I said to the Spirit, it doesn't have an impact on me. There's absolutely no documented proof. It's not as though I can go into the world and claim that I'm related to Jesus. And even if I could, what would be the purpose?"

"The islanders would believe you," noted Elijah. "The story of the birthmark and its importance is something that has been passed through the centuries."

"Throughout my life the birthmark has throbbed, and it has become more prominent as I got older," said Sean. "It always seemed to happen at stressful times in my life, and I put it down to a release from anxiety. But after today, I suppose I'll have to accept that it means so much more."

"I don't believe you realize how special the mark makes you," said Elijah.

"What do you mean? Being a direct descendent of Jesus is about as special as it can get."

"There's more. Stories from our ancestors tell us that Daniel's birthmark throbbed and grew more prominent as he aged. And there's no record of that happening to anyone else. Throughout the centuries, it has simply been the mark that connected the eldest in your family to Jesus. Until now, the Spirit has never called on anyone to carry out a mission, not even the men who bore the birthmark.

"That's why it had me bring you to Janus. Since the Spirit doesn't interfere in the lives of humans, I believe the fact your birthmark is so similar to Daniel's is a sign the Spirit was waiting for. But why it happened to you and why at this moment in the world's history the Spirit has decided to call upon you, I don't know."

"It doesn't matter," said Sean. "I've already decided that I'm not doing it. I'll be leaving Janus when *Journey* sails."

Elijah was clearly taken aback. It was obvious he hadn't expected such a swift decision. "You haven't given yourself much time to think about it," he responded. "*Journey* will be back in a couple of months. Why not wait and have some more talks with the Spirit. In the meantime, you and Diane could get to know each other. You might find that staying on Janus and farming is a good life. If you're still adamant about leaving, then you'll know that you've fully explored all your options."

"You don't understand," offered Sean. "I've been thinking about what it would be like to stay from the moment I got to Janus. It's very tempting. There are no pressures here. It isn't like the outside world. But I have a life that is beyond the island. That's what I want. The thought of being a messenger of peace and working with the islanders along with the Guardians and your diaspora doesn't interest me."

"Don't you realize it's the Spirit that has chosen you?" argued Elijah. "It has asked you to take on this mission. How can you refuse?"

Sean was quiet for a few moments. He could see through the vent in the cave's roof that night was approaching. The fire's warmth was comforting. Thinking of a response that would make Elijah appreciate his position, Sean realized being told why he was on Janus hadn't created a reason for him to stay. Instead, the knowledge had served only to convince him that he wanted a return to his old life.

Speaking with the Spirit had been an experience he'd never be able to duplicate unless he stayed on the island. But in those few moments of thinking what to tell Elijah, Sean realized that, while the talk had been beyond unique, he hadn't enjoyed his time with the Spirit. He'd expected to find a being that had warmth and was understanding. Instead the Spirit had seemed cold, calculating, and arrogant.

"It's not for me," Sean began haltingly. "I have no interest in starting a campaign for the world to be a more peaceful place.

"You can't possibly understand what it means to be told that you're a direct descendent of Jesus. The implication is beyond staggering. Yet it won't mean anything once I step off this island. Many people throughout history have claimed to be a reincarnation of Jesus or directly related to him. Apart from some deranged followers, nobody ever took them seriously.

"Can you for one moment understand what the reaction would be if I went into the world claiming that, because of a birthmark, I'm directly related to Jesus?"

"But the birthmark will give you credibility," said the Prophet

Sean was astounded at Elijah's lack of knowledge about the world beyond the Janus shores. "It will mean nothing outside this island," he responded. "What possible proof can I give that I'm directly descended from Jesus. All I have is this birthmark. I'll be looked upon as a fool at best and a con man at worst."

"Is the world so jaded that the truth no longer matters?"

Sean heaved an exasperated sigh. "What is truth?" he asked. "Truth is based on sustainable facts. The Spirit has already told me it will not interfere with the lives of humans. Therefore, I'm to go into the world preaching about the island's philosophy without a shred of evidence that I'm any different than anyone else who cries out for peace."

"What moral authority do I have?"

"You'll have the islanders, our diaspora, and the Guardians. Once we tell everyone of your mission, you'll have many supporters throughout the world. They'll be your disciples and help spread your message."

"That puzzles me," said Sean.

"What do you mean?"

"For more than two centuries, this island and its people have existed apart from the world. I don't understand why the islanders would want to give up the life they've been leading to become a part of the world. I don't think the Guardians or your diaspora would want to see that happen. This is a refuge from the rest of the globe. It's a place of tranquility. That would all change if we did what the Spirit is asking."

"It would be up to you and me to convince them that it's the right thing to do," said Elijah.

"Perhaps the Spirit could ask each person associated with the island to work with us."

"You know it doesn't interfere."

"So we'd be on our own. All the more reason why I don't want to be involved."

"But if you don't do it, who will?" wondered Elijah.

"Why not you?"

"I wasn't asked. For whatever reason, the Spirit believes you're the right person, and I agree. The Spirit isn't asking you to create peace. All it wants you to be is a messenger."

"Well you and the Spirit will have to find someone else."

A strained silence tented the men. It was broken by Elijah.

"Look, it's late," he offered. "We'll spend the night here and head back in the morning. There's some dried mutton in one of the lockers we can heat up."

Sean, deep in thought about how he was going to tell Diane of his plans, nodded his agreement. Elijah got up and began moving through the cave. He put more coal on the fire and prepared the meal. Sean remained almost immobile on the bench.

The meal was eaten in virtual silence, with only the odd sentence about the quality of the mutton passing between the two men. Sean roused himself enough to help clean up, put coal on the fire, and spread the sleeping bags.

Later, as Sean lay close to the fire, he remained awake long after Elijah's rhythmic breathing told him the Prophet was asleep. The throbbing in his leg had long since stopped. He wondered what it meant, now that he knew of his connection to Jesus.

He looked through the cave's vent at the night sky. The clouds had cleared. Somehow he managed to lose himself in the stars that met his gaze. For the first time in several weeks, he no longer felt the island's calming influence. His last thought before falling asleep was centered on what Diane's reaction would be when he told her he'd be leaving Janus.

# Chapter 60

It had been a fitful sleep. Several times during the night, Sean had awakened to thoughts of his talk with the Spirit. He'd lain, staring at the sky, playing the conversation over in his mind. The magnitude of what he'd experienced was staggering. He'd not only spoken with the Spirit but had learned of his direct relationship to Jesus. Both were so far beyond the realm of possibility that Sean wondered if it had been a dream.

But then he'd turn and see Elijah sleeping on the other side of the fire and knew it was now his reality.

He wondered how Diane would react to what he'd learned. Sean wanted to depart early so he could see Diane before she began work on the farm.

Sean realized it was impractical for him to expect that Diane would leave the island when *Journey* sailed. But he hoped to convince her that she should join him in London the next time the ship was making a return trip to Janus. That would give her a couple of months to settle everything about the farm with the Council.

Had they been together long enough to make that type of commitment? He'd known Hilary most of his life, and look what had happened with that relationship. All Sean knew was that he'd found someone who made him happy and he hoped would want to spend the rest of her life with him. This was a different love than with Hilary. The pressure to become lawyers and be groomed to take over their fathers' firm had buried the marriage under the weight of expectations. With Diane, he shared a free and unfettered love.

Elijah was moving in his sleeping bag. That was good. It meant an early start back to the village and to Diane.

He saw that Elijah was on his feet and rolling up his sleeping bag. Sean quickly did the same. The cave's early morning cold pierced his shirt, and he began to shiver.

Seeing the involuntarily movement, Elijah noted that what they both needed was some coffee.

"We'll use the Coleman stove," he said. "We won't be here long enough to have any use for a fire."

Nodding his head in agreement, Sean went over and took the stove down from the shelf. While Elijah got water in a pot, Sean lit the burners. Soon the two of them were sitting on their benches sipping from their mugs.

"Have you given any more thought to your conversation with the Spirit?" asked Elijah.

"I spent a large part of the night thinking about it," replied Sean. "And before you ask, I haven't changed my mind. I'm still planning on leaving when *Journey* sails."

"There'll be a lot of disappointed people," noted the Prophet. "You've made quite an impression around the island, and you'll be missed."

"I'd like to stay, but there isn't anything here for me."

"How can you say that?" wondered Elijah. "You can have a good life. You're well-liked and respected. Our lives are rich and full. We may not have much in a material sense, but we more than make up for it with the freedoms we enjoy. And I know you have a home with Mrs. Kerr for as long as you want."

"This may be hard to understand, but I'd miss the challenge of fighting for what I want and winning," Sean explained. "It's tough out there in the world. Very few people have success handed to them. You have to be willing to take chances, to make life-altering decisions, and to battle against incredible odds in order to succeed.

"It means setting goals, dreaming big, and then doing what it takes to achieve what you've set out to accomplish. And when you do, there's a tremendous sense of satisfaction. That would be missing from my life if I stayed on Janus."

"You seem to think that farming and fishing are without their challenges," said Elijah. "It's physical and difficult work that demands we set targets for how much our land produces or the quantity of fish brought in by our nets. Just because we have no suicides or murders doesn't mean our lives are free of stress and anxiety. The difference is that we do not compete on an individual basis. We work together to achieve collective goals. We share in the good and the bad times.

"I would argue that our way of life, in which a person's accomplishments are viewed with satisfaction by every islander, is better than a society in which personal achievement is rewarded by individual riches but viewed with envy and displeasure by many."

"I understand and agree with what you're saying," said Sean. "And I never meant to cast doubt on the validity of what the islanders do for a living. But you've missed my point. Each of us has a calling. Quite simply, mine isn't to farm or to fish. I have no skills that can be used on Janus. You have no need of lawyers, negotiators, or journalists. I need to get back to where I'm tested in the arena of individual competition. Working for *The Advocate* gives me a satisfaction that I don't believe I can find here."

"But you've been asked to do something special for the world by the Spirit," said Elijah. "Isn't that enough of a challenge for you?"

Sean paused a moment before answering. The Prophet, either by accident or design, had posed the one question Sean had hoped wouldn't be asked.

"It's too much of a challenge," he said slowly. "Everyone has to realize and accept his or her limitations or risk failure. I've reached that point in my life where I know what I'm capable of accomplishing. What the Spirit wants me to do doesn't fall into that category."

Elijah slowly nodded his head.

"I think it's time we headed back," said Sean, breaking the silence. "I want to see Diane. And I've got to tell Mrs. Kerr I'm leaving."

"Perhaps talking to Diane will change your view," offered the Prophet.

"It won't. My mind's made up. I'm leaving when *Journey* sails."

Together the men cleaned up the cave and headed out into the cool morning air. There was little conversation as they walked towards the village.

As they neared the harbor, *Journey* was being tied up by Malcolm and Joseph. Already a group of islanders had gathered, and more were coming along the Ring Road.

"She's here," said Elijah, excitement rippling through his voice. "I'll go down and meet them. Why don't you come along?"

Sean declined, explaining that he wanted to see Diane before news of *Journey*'s arrival reached her and she headed for the harbor.

Before they parted, Elijah took hold of his arm. "You have a couple of days before *Journey* leaves. Talk things over with Diane and think your decision through. I realize that London looks good right now, but give Janus and our people a fair hearing."

Sean promised he would. But both knew he'd already decided.

# CHAPTER 61

They were sitting in Diane's kitchen at opposite ends of the table, a mug of coffee in front of each of them. Sean had told her everything about his conversation with the Spirit.

"That was some talk," noted Diane when Sean had finished his narrative.

"It was. A day later it's still almost impossible to believe that I spoke directly with the being that so many people call God. It's an experience I'll never forget. And then to find out I'm directly related to Jesus is something I can't get my mind around."

"I don't know why it should be that difficult," responded Diane. "Once you discovered your ancestors were originally from the island, it must have given you some clue that being brought here was something more than just a visit."

Sean paused. Diane's response seemed unnatural. In it was a calm acceptance, as though she'd expected what he'd told her.

"You don't seem surprised that my ancestry goes back to Jesus."

"That's true," explained Diane. "Naturally, I was stunned it's you, but the Mark of Janus is an integral part of our history. And we learn that, even though Joseph Kirsch, your great-great-grandfather left the island and changed his name to Kilgore the Mark of Janus would always stay with the family. It was also believed that one of Joseph's descendants would one day return. When we met at Mrs. Kerr's, I didn't even think of the mark because your last name is Brennan.

"Then when we made love the first time and I saw the mark on your leg, I knew who you were."

"Why didn't you tell me any of this?"

Diane took a sip of her coffee. The silence hung in the air. "I didn't know what to make of it," she finally confessed. "I mean, it's true that the mark is part of our history. But I've been out in the world enough to know what Jesus means to every Christian. And to find out that the man in my bed was his direct descendant was overwhelming."

"Who else knows about me?"

A dagger of hurt pierced Diane's eyes, and Sean immediately felt terrible he'd asked the question. "I'm sorry," he said quickly. "It was stupid of me to ask. I know you'd never tell anyone."

Diane's response was a tentative smile. "The only other person who knows is Elijah and that's because you and the Spirit told him," she said quietly. "But the important thing is what it means to you. Are you going to do what the Spirit asks?"

This time, it was Sean's turn to hesitate. He took a drink of the by now lukewarm coffee. When he spoke, his voice was low and carried conviction. "I can't stay on Janus. This isn't for me. As I told Elijah, I need to be out in the world."

"And what about us?" wondered Diane.

"I want you to come and live with me in London. I'd like us to get married and share our lives," answered Sean.

"We've known each other for two months," said Diane. "That's the amount of time I knew Bruce before I was living with him. And then six months later, we were married. I won't make that mistake again."

"You wouldn't be making a mistake," countered Sean. "We can live together for a few months. If you're not happy, you can always come back to Janus. London isn't that far away. All I'm asking is that you give us a chance to be happy together."

"But it means giving up everything I have here. What would I do in London? Where would we live?"

"I still have my apartment. It's small, but it would do until we found something larger. And you're a trained nurse with experience. It shouldn't be any trouble for you to land a job. And you wouldn't have to give up your farm. I'm sure you could find someone to look after it until you're certain we could make it together."

"That's not the point. This is my home. I've lived in the world away from Janus and decided it wasn't for me. You're a good man, Sean, and I'm in love with you. But I'm not ready to leave what I have."

Sean realized he was losing the battle. Still, he had to keep trying. He'd already told her that *Journey* was docked at the harbor. They both knew it gave them two days to resolve their future.

"*Journey* will be back in a couple of months," he said. "Why not take that time to think it over? And maybe once you've given it some thought, you'll decide that living with me in London can make you happy. I know it would be everything I could hope for."

"I could say the same thing to you," she replied. "Why do you have to leave right away? Let's spend a couple more months really getting to know each other. We could live together. It makes more sense than you dashing off to London and me being alone for the next two months. If it doesn't work out between us, you can leave when *Journey* returns."

Taking a deep breath and knowing he was chancing the loss of future love, Sean said, "I can't stay. There are just too many reasons for returning to London."

Diane nodded her understanding before asking, "Have you told Mrs. Kerr?"

"No. I came straight here from the cave. I'll tell her later this morning."

"She's going to miss having you around the house. It's only been two months, but you've really helped her. She's back to the old Mrs. Kerr."

"I'm glad. I wasn't sure what it would be like when Elijah first told me that's where I'd be staying. But it worked well for both of us. She's a special lady, and I'll miss her when I'm gone."

Sean stood up, pushing his chair back. "I should be going," he said. "I want to tell Mrs. Kerr and spend the afternoon with her while I pack my stuff. Can we have dinner together?"

Standing up, Diane didn't hesitate in saying, "Of course we can. But let's promise each other that there'll be no more talk of leaving. I want to enjoy the time we have left."

"I feel the same way," said Sean.

Diane walked him down the hallway to the front door. They embraced.

"I'm going to miss you," Sean whispered.

Diane didn't say anything, but as he pulled away, the slightest trail of tears was beginning a sad journey down her cheeks.

# CHAPTER 62

When Sean entered the house, Mrs. Kerr could be heard in the kitchen. Taking off his boots, he walked down the hallway and entered the room. He wasn't looking forward to the conversation. His hands were clammy, and he felt a pain deep in his gut. He'd grown extremely fond of his landlady and knew that her comforting wisdom would be one of things he'd miss most on returning to London.

She was preparing a salad for lunch. The vegetables, including carrots, tomatoes, lettuce, and green pepper had come in with *Journey*. Turning from the counter, she told him to sit and immediately began adding to the salad.

Mrs. Kerr asked how things had gone at the cave. Although he answered that it was different from what he'd expected, she merely nodded and didn't question him further. To do so would have been impolite for an islander.

Once the salad was large enough for two, she cut some thick slices of bread and placed everything on the table. Sean didn't want to delay in telling her his news. His nerves were playing hopscotch with his mind, and he just wanted it over with.

"I'll be leaving with *Journey* when it sails," he told Mrs. Kerr the moment she sat down.

"I'm sorry to hear that," she slowly responded. "I know that your stay was supposed to be for only a couple of months, but we all hoped you'd decide to remain longer. You'll be missed, but everyone will understand. Janus isn't your home. Perhaps in the future it might be, but you can only know that once you get back to London and see what effect we've had on your life. You may find what happens in the world is no longer to your liking. The simple life we enjoy may call you back. If that happens, you'll be welcomed with open arms."

The words were said with such sincerity that Sean was momentarily speechless. When he did finally speak, it was to thank Mrs. Kerr for taking a stranger into her house and making him feel completely at home.

"I suppose Diane and Elijah know," she said.

Sean nodded but didn't say anything more as he slathered butter over a slice of bread. The meal was finished in relative silence except for a brief observation from Mrs. Kerr that she hoped the weather would be fine for *Journey*'s voyage back to Inverness.

Now that he'd told Mrs. Kerr, Sean was looking forward to staying at the house for the afternoon. He felt a strong sense of loyalty to his landlady and thought the best way of repaying her kindness was to share each other's company. Dinner and the night would be spent with Diane.

The afternoon passed quickly. Sean packed his few belongings. About midafternoon, he and Mrs. Kerr shared a pot of coffee and a plate of ginger cookies in the living room. Sean spoke of the work he planned to do once he got back to London, while Mrs. Kerr talked about the summer growing season and how the farmers were expecting a good crop. It was a comfortable time between the two, and Sean was surprised when Mrs. Kerr reminded him that he was expected at Diane's for dinner.

# Chapter 63

When Sean arrived at Diane's, he was taken aback to see the house was dark. But the barn was drenched with light. He walked around the house and along the path leading to the outbuilding. Entering the barn, he saw Diane in a stall with one of her ewes. The smell of dried hay and the heavy musk scent of animals filled his nostrils. A flock of chickens scattered at his approach.

"This is Molly," said Diane, before Sean could say hello. "She's going to be dropping a lamb tonight, and I need to be with her. It's not exactly the way I planned to have us spend the night. But I don't have a choice. Molly has had trouble delivering in the past, and I don't want her to be alone."

At the sight of Sean the ewe had become extremely agitated. Molly wouldn't stay still and several times collided with Diane while moving restlessly around her stall.

"Why don't you wait in the house?" suggested Diane. "There's some cold ham and bread in the fridge. Fix yourself something to eat. It'll be a while before I can leave Molly."

After giving Diane a quick kiss and telling her to take whatever time was needed, Sean left the barn. Once inside the house, he fixed himself a sandwich, along with a mug of coffee, and settled down in the living room.

He'd found his conversations with the Spirit and then later with Elijah stressful and tiring. Following those had been his talks with Diane and Mrs. Kerr. It had been a turbulent time, and Sean felt weariness in his shoulders and back. The coffee was hot and it was relaxing him. He was having trouble keeping his eyes open.

Finishing the sandwich and coffee, he washed out the dishes. Back in the living room, he looked at the couch and thought he'd lie down until Diane came in. His eyelids felt heavy, and he closed them, promising himself that he'd open them in a few minutes. He just needed a bit of time to rest.

Someone was calling his name from far away. He struggled through a foggy haze to see who was disturbing him. A crowing rooster brought him fully awake. He looked up and saw Diane. She was a mess. Her hair and clothes were covered in blood and muck. It took a moment for Sean to realize where he was and why Diane looked the way she did.

"Is everything good with Molly?" he asked.

"It was a challenging night and an even tougher birth, but she's fine," replied Diane, her voice saturated with exhaustion. "I'm going to get a bath and then crawl into bed. You're welcome to join me, but be warned that I won't be much fun. I need some sleep."

Sean offered to fix breakfast, but Diane declined, saying she was too tired to eat. Instead Sean fixed himself a plate of scrambled eggs and toast while Diane took a long bath. As he put her to bed, they agreed to meet for dinner that night. Before he was out of the room, she was asleep.

Throughout Sean's final day, he walked the island, saying good-bye to everyone he met. It was difficult and made him realize how much he was going to miss Janus and its people.

On his way back to Mrs. Kerr's, he stopped by the Knob. Marcus had already heard the news. The man clasped Sean's hand and said how much he'd be missed. There was little else to say, and the men parted as friends. When he arrived at Mrs. Kerr's, the house was empty. A note on the kitchen table said she was at a friend's and would see him in the morning. He picked up his gear, took one last walk around the house that had been his home for two months, and headed over to Diane's.

She'd slept most of the day and was embarrassed to tell him that nothing had been fixed for dinner. Sean laughed and said they could work together on preparing a meal. It wasn't fancy, but it didn't have to be. They used the last of the ham, boiled some potatoes, and added fresh peas. For dessert, there was coffee along with chocolate cookies.

With the dishes washed, Sean and Diane made their way to the bedroom. Getting into bed, they undressed each other, scattering clothes on the floor. The love they made was slow and lingering. It was filled with a loving passion that was both gentle and caring. When it was over, they held each other for a long time. They made love again and then spent the rest of the night talking. None of it touched on his leaving. He told her more about his time in Afghanistan, and she shared some of her Australian experiences. They agreed to correspond via e-mails through the Guardians in Inverness and Diane promised to visit him in London.

The dawn came far too quickly. Before Sean knew it, breakfast had been eaten and Elijah, along with Mrs. Kerr, was at the front door. The foursome walked slowly down to the dock. Elijah and Mrs. Kerr hung back while Sean and Diane hugged, kissed, and said their good-byes. After that, it was a hug from Mrs. Kerr and a firm handshake from Elijah. Nothing was said about his returning. Those words had already been spoken, and all that remained was for him to board the ship.

As *Journey* pulled away from the quay Sean stood on deck until Mrs. Kerr, Elijah, and Diane were no more than specks on the horizon. As they disappeared from view, Sean felt a deep sense of loss.

For most of the trip, Sean lay on his bunk and read or helped Joseph with getting the meals ready. No one asked why he was leaving the island, and he didn't offer an explanation. The seas remained relatively calm and *Journey* made good time.

As Sean was preparing to turn in for the night, Andrew came down the stairs from the bridge and sat on the bunk across from Sean's.

"We should be arriving shortly after dawn breaks," began the Guardian. "I've radioed ahead, and there'll be someone to meet you when we dock. She'll take you to the airport where you're booked on a flight that will get you into Gatwick close to seven o'clock.

"We've arranged for your ticket, and it can be picked up at the BA departure counter. It's in your name, and you'll notice it's a two-way ticket with the return date left open."

Sean was puzzled. He pulled out the return ticket from when they'd first flown into Inverness.

"I already have this," he said, showing it to Andrew.

"Why not give that to me," said Andrew, casually taking the ticket from Sean's hand.

Still confused, Sean let the document go without giving it much thought.

"I don't need a return ticket," he said. "I've got no plans to come back for a visit."

"Those were Elijah's instructions," said Andrew.

The Guardian held Sean's eyes for a few moments. "Never underestimate the Prophet," said Andrew. "He's a man of infinite wisdom and understanding about the future. He never does anything without a reason."

With that, the Guardian abruptly got up and returned to the bridge, leaving Sean to ponder what Elijah had in mind. His only tie to Janus was Diane, and he had every intention of persuading her to live with him in London. The Prophet may be plotting something with the Spirit, but as far as Sean was concerned, he'd left the island for good. With that settled in his mind, he climbed into the bunk. The boat's steady rocking motion as it plied the calm North Sea had him soon asleep.

Sean awoke to the enticing smell of scrambled eggs along with toast and coffee being prepared by Malcolm and Joseph. He got up, visited the head, and joined the two Guardians, telling them that in return for breakfast he'd wash the pans and dishes.

"Seems like a fair trade," laughed Malcolm, as the three sat down to eat. Andrew and Leyland had been served their meal on the bridge. As Sean was finishing the washing up, Leyland descended the stairs and announced they'd soon be entering the Moray Firth. He poured two mugs of coffee before going back up to join Andrew.

Sean donned his pea jacket and went on deck. Dark storm clouds were rolling in over the port, and a chill was in the air. However, the seas were still calm and the ship plowed ahead.

As Andrew skillfully guided *Journey* through the firth and into her berth, the ship was met by a group of four men who Sean assumed were Guardians. Together, with Malcolm and Joseph working the lines from the ship, *Journey* was secured against the dock.

Once the gangplank was let out, Sean went into the cabin. Gathering his bags, he said his farewells to the crew and descended to the firm ground of Inverness harbor. A late model Chevy Captiva pulled up, and out stepped a young woman who introduced herself as Andrea.

"I'm here to drive you to the airport," she said, as Sean put his gear on the back seat.

The Guardian was a focused, albeit furiously fast driver. There was little conversation as she hurtled past slower-moving traffic, braked late at stoplights, peeled rubber on several occasions, and hit the horn with startling frequency. After the slow pace of the last couple of months, it was a reality check for Sean. *Welcome back to city life*, he thought.

Their arrival at the airport terminal was marked by a lengthy screech of tires as Andrea braked hard and wrestled the Captiva in front of the departure area. As they stepped out of the car, the storm clouds that had been hovering since early morning unleashed rain in torrents. Sean quickly gathered his gear, shook hands with Andrea, and dashed into the terminal. He heard rather than saw Andrea gun the Captiva's engine as the vehicle skidded its way back into airport traffic.

Sean had several hours to wait before a boarding announcement would be made. He navigated his way to the BA counter, picked up his ticket, checked his bags, and then immediately headed to the WH Smith outlet. He bought copies of every newspaper and current affairs magazine the store carried. It had been two months since he'd heard or read any current news, and Sean was anxious to catch up.

Like a starving man in front of a well-stocked buffet, he devoured page after page. By midafternoon he'd become satiated on newspapers and magazines. Sean visited the airport restaurant, where he enjoyed a meat pie and a chilled glass of white wine.

The flight into the north terminal at London's Gatwick was uneventful. Sean waited until most of the passengers had left the aircraft before deplaning. He gathered his bags at the luggage carousel, walked out into the cool evening air, and got in line for a taxi. His ears were assaulted by the noise, he was jostled by people walking by, and the rancid smell of jet fuel filled his nostrils.

None of it mattered. He'd soon be back in central London and at his apartment.

# CHAPTER 64

Although what had happened was unusual, Angelica did not question her newest instructions. She had been summoned to the chateau, where Dante had told her to cancel the Janus assignment. Only once in the past had she been told to halt a project. And just as she had required no reason then, Angelica didn't expect one now.

That the directive could have been conveyed by an e-mail or a coded telephone call meant nothing to Angelica. As always, her life was lived for the prelate.

Dante had looked well, although a bit weary. Angelica worried about him. His age was unknown to her, but it was obvious he was not a young man. And yet the thought never occurred to her that a time must come when he'd no longer head the Praetorian Order. Death was a reality for everyone, but Dante had been a constant since Angelica could remember. It was beyond her comprehension that anything would happen to change that fact.

The session in the chapel had lasted all of ten minutes.

The journey from her home in Nova Scotia had taken more than fourteen hours. Her return trip would be the same again. But there was no hardship. She'd been in the presence of Dante. Nothing else mattered.

Most of her flights on this trip were uneventful. She existed in a cocoon of self-absorption that rarely extended beyond her assignments.

The only minor distraction was her seatmate on the London to New York flight. A young man had attempted to engage her in a conversation about the book she was reading. Unaware of her beauty or the attraction she held for the male of the species, Angelica was continually baffled by men who wanted to make conversation with her.

Although he was persistent it soon became apparent that Angelica was more committed to the pages of her novel than to talking. He soon lost interest, and she was left alone to live in her world of anonymity.

She would tell her team to stand down. Like her, none of them would question the instructions. Neither Angelica nor her team considered it ironic that, in a world where they controlled the lives of their targets, they were powerless when it came to deciding when or where their assignments took place.

# Chapter 65

It had been two years since he'd left Janus.

Sean clicked the mouse over the send icon on his screen. The editorial he'd been laboring over would appear in the queue for editing by Pitt. After that, it was on to Elder for a final review before being placed on the editorial page in the coming edition.

Leaning back in his chair, his thoughts naturally focused on Janus. He hadn't grasped it when he was on the island, but his stay had been a life-altering experience. He realized that, just as his time spent at the law firm and with Hilary, along with his stay in Afghanistan had, the months with Elijah and everyone else on Janus had profoundly affected him.

He'd noticed it the first time he'd walked back into the newsroom and met Elder. Knowing the man was part of the Janus diaspora and that both knew of the cave's secret had created a strong, albeit unspoken bond between the two men.

Sean had spent the first couple of months back working his old crime beat. It was a struggle. Before leaving for the island, he'd reveled in covering criminal gang activity and using his sources inside the police forces to break stories. However, Sean could no longer generate the enthusiasm he'd once had. After Janus and his talk with the Spirit, he felt the need to do more with his life.

Elder would often drop by his desk and ask how Sean was enjoying the work. When he first returned, Sean would offer the old bromide that it was good to be back and leave it at that. Elder, though, was a man whose life had been shaped through his association with Janus. He knew Sean had changed.

He took Sean off the crime beat and put him in charge of the paper's editorial and op-ed pages. While the front-page headlines sold papers and advertising paid the bills, Sean's section was *The Advocate*'s conscience.

Previously, the pages had been confined to issues that affected only London and had never strayed into opinions or thoughts about the wider world. Sean had changed that. He'd developed a collection of freelance writers who examined issues that went well beyond the day-to-day and broadened *The Advocate*'s opinion pages to comment on subjects that took a global view of events. His editorials were thought-provoking and sometimes controversial. But they were well-read. The paper's readers were being offered a view that explained how world issues had a bearing on what was happening in their lives.

The change was popular with readers, and *The Advocate*'s circulation was showing a steady increase.

At first, the move satisfied Sean. It gave him a platform to express views, and he enjoyed the public recognition that came with his writings. Yet there was something missing. Sean wanted a bigger audience. He took the concept of an online paper to Elder. The project was immediately approved. It took almost a year to get everything in place, but *The Advocate* was now competing against the big city dailies with its online edition. Sean's editorials and his op-ed pages had found a new and expanding readership.

However, Sean still wasn't happy. He wanted a larger reach. Something was continually stirring within him. His birthmark often ached. He yearned to do more, to reach out and tell people that things could be different if they'd only learn to understand and forgive each other. It was a constant companion, driving him during the day and causing sleepless nights. He was continually caught up with thoughts about the island and his conversation with the Spirit.

Although he'd received several e-mails from Elijah, none of them had mentioned the Spirit or asked him to return. They were newsy letters filled with the island happenings and mentioned how everyone wanted him to come for a visit.

The e-mails served to remind Sean that he had something waiting for him that was inherently much more profound than the day-to-day task of filling newspaper pages. He was grappling with the concept of committing to an idea and a project that went far beyond anything he'd ever imagined. He had thought that, with time and distance, the dilemma would settle itself on the side of staying at *The Advocate*. On his return to London, he'd been relieved to be back and believed he'd made the right decision. Yet, the longer he was away from Janus, making a decision that would forever close the door on his vacillation became more difficult.

In one way, he was doing something he truly enjoyed. In their own small way, the columns and editorials were conveying the Janus message of understanding, tolerance, equality, and peace. *The Advocate* was a poor substitute for the Spirit's desire to have the message spread throughout the world. But as Sean reasoned, every revolution begins with the first thrown rock.

However, as he walked to his apartment at the close of each day, his mind continually focused on the thought that he'd been given the opportunity to do much more than he was accomplishing at *The Advocate*.

Added to this were thoughts of Diane. He deeply missed her. Although they'd regularly communicated via e-mail and she'd visited him twice, Sean had found the separation increasingly difficult. The expectation leading up to her arrival was exciting, but the time she spent in London soon quickly disappeared. Before both knew it, they were on the road to Gatwick for her return flight to Inverness.

Her visits had been marked by intense discussion about their future together, often lasting long into the night. They were struggling to arrive at an arrangement that would let a long-term relationship work.

Sean knew a decision would soon have to be made. Either they were a full-time part of each other's lives, or the relationship would have to end. The current arrangement was proving too difficult for both of them. In all of their e-mails and talks, Diane had been steadfast in her refusal to leave Janus. Sean knew she wasn't being selfish. During her visits to London, Diane had repeatedly told him how much she loved and missed him.

She fully believed they could build a life on Janus, regardless of whether Sean heeded the Spirit's message. But if that wasn't what Sean wanted, Diane had indicated a willingness to visit London more often if that's what would keep the relationship alive. Left unspoken was the fact Sean hadn't once indicated a desire to spend time on Janus.

Although he had a simple rationale—*Journey's* sailing schedule wouldn't allow him to spend that much time away from *The Advocate*—pangs of guilt played across his mind whenever he received an e-mail from Diane.

Faced with these thoughts and the gnawing belief that he should be doing something more with his life, Sean was tormented with a restless stirring of how to arrive at a balance that would allow him to satisfy these conflicting needs.

After a particularly bad night, where sleep was as elusive as ever, Sean was sitting at his desk attempting without success to put words on the computer screen. As he sat and stared, trying to make sense of what he was going to write, Elder's assistant arrived and said the publisher wanted to see him.

With a feeling of relief, Sean escaped from the desk and headed down the hallway to Elder's office. As he got near, Sean heard two voices in deep conversation. The shock of who was speaking with the publisher made him stop in confusion. He knew what he was hearing, but his mind couldn't register the fact. The other voice belonged to Elijah. But that was impossible. The farthest the Prophet had ever been away from Janus was Inverness. What was he doing in London? More importantly, why was he in Elder's office?

Sean stepped warily through the doorway. Elder was sitting behind his desk. Elijah was on the couch against the side wall. The men stopped talking, their eyes swiveling to look at Sean as he walked into the room.

Without waiting for either man to say anything, Sean blurted in Elijah's direction, "What are you doing here?"

"Perhaps you should first sit down and we'll explain everything," countered Elder.

As he took one of the chairs in front of Elder's desk, Sean noticed that Elijah appeared tired and drawn. Bloodshot eyes were sunk deep in his head. The Prophet's usually tanned facial features were yellowed like old newspaper, and deep lines crisscrossed his face. He didn't seem anything like the wise and serene man who Sean had come to know.

Sean looked across at Elder, whose expression was stern, his lips pursed. Sean didn't need anyone to tell him that something was wrong on Janus.

"There are a couple of things we have to discuss," began Elder. "I'm going to let Elijah fill you in, but before that happens, I want you to know he has my full support. Sometimes people are called upon to do things that are necessary for the greater good, although they may not want to. Everyone desires to live a comfortable life, free of distractions. But that's not always possible."

Sean was beginning to have an inkling of why Elijah was in London. If it was about returning to Janus, he was prepared to listen; he owed Elder and the Prophet that much. But he believed his answer would be the same as when he'd left the island.

"This has been troubling me for a while," began Elijah. "I've tried not to involve you, but that has become impossible.

"The Spirit is threatening to stop talking with the Islanders unless you return. That's why I'm here. Since you left, the Spirit has been telling me that, if you weren't prepared to work with it, there would be consequences. We have spoken often but that's about all it wanted to discuss. It kept asking me to bring you back, and I always refused. The whole thing has been an ordeal. The strain on our relationship has been tremendous."

"Has this ever happened before?" asked Sean.

"Our history has no record of anything like this ever taking place. The Spirit has always been available to anyone who ventured into the cave and wanted to speak with it. For it to disappear from our lives would be an immense tragedy.

"I know how you feel about the Spirit's request. And as I said when you left Janus, it was your decision to make. But I now have to think of every islander, every Guardian, and every member of our diaspora. The problem has become bigger than just you and the Spirit. I need you to come back with me."

"But I thought the Spirit didn't interfere in the lives of humans," said Sean. "It told me that when we spoke."

"That's always been true, but obviously things have changed," responded Elijah.

"So why is the Spirit getting involved?" asked Sean. "And why is it being vindictive toward everyone associated with Janus? If it has a problem with me, the Spirit should deal with me directly. None of this makes any sense. A lot of what we talked about focused on how it was an emotionless entity. Yet here the Spirit is showing anger because I won't do what it has planned for me."

"The Spirit doesn't view it as anger," said Elijah. "Instead it looks at the move as a way of getting your attention."

Sean thought back to how he'd felt the Spirit was cold, calculating, and arrogant after they'd spoken. He wasn't sure if it was sadness or resentment he felt at seemingly being proved correct.

Elder cleared his throat and spoke. "You're a different person since you returned from Janus," the publisher said, staring intently at Sean. "I've noticed it in your writing. You're much more aware of the world's problems, and your editorials have continually taken on a more global view. You've written often of understanding and equality.

"It's as though you've been using *The Advocate*'s pages to test out theories about international tolerance and peace. I know these are ideals you took away from your stay on Janus and your visit with the Spirit.

"What harm would there be in going back and listening to what the Spirit has to say?"

"Nothing would be wrong if that's what I wanted to do," retorted Sean angrily. "But this is nothing more than bullying and blackmail. If I don't meet with the Spirit, the islanders will lose their connection. My first inclination is to test the Spirit's resolve and refuse to return."

"We both know you can't do that," responded Elijah. "You can certainly ignore my request, but you'll never be able to put aside that you once spoke with the Spirit and that it has asked something very special from you."

Sean knew the Prophet was right. And now that the Spirit was threatening to involve everyone associated with Janus, the likelihood he could continue as though nothing extraordinary had happened was impossible.

Yet there was something inherently wrong in returning because of a threat. Sean leaned back in his chair. He was beginning to feel cornered. He fought to think his way out of the box that was being built around him.

"Nothing has changed since I spoke with the Spirit," he said. "It's not that I don't believe in what the Spirit is trying to accomplish. But global peace is such a complex and elusive goal. I don't think it's possible unless the Spirit is willing to participate. And that didn't seem to be the case when we spoke."

"But the Spirit has told me it wants to be involved," replied Elijah.

The words lashed through the air like a giant meat cleaver. Sean's first reaction was disbelief, coupled with shock. After all the Spirit's talk about not interfering, it was now willing to work with humanity. The prospect was exciting, as well as daunting.

"That's a drastic change from what it told me," said Sean. "How would it participate?"

"I don't know," admitted Elijah. "It told me that's something the two of you would work out."

"So the Spirit is willing to work with me?" asked Sean, still incredulous and needing to hear confirmation.

"That's the message it asked me to pass along to you. The Spirit accepts it will be a long and difficult process and that before anything can be done, the islanders, along with the Guardians and our diaspora, have to be persuaded this is the right thing to do. That will take time, but the Spirit is willing to work with you in convincing them. And I'll be there to help you."

"What about when that's accomplished, if it is?" asked Sean. "Will it get involved in moving the quest for peace across the world?"

"That was the impression I was left with," answered Elijah. "For whatever reason, it believes you can succeed. I have to believe that the Spirit's commitment to become involved will go a long way toward turning things around. Don't forget, we're talking about the Supreme Being. There isn't a more powerful ally."

Sean ran a shaking hand over his face. The conversation was spiraling out of control. Elder and Elijah were talking about this as though it was the most normal thing in the world. But it wasn't.

"It can't be done," he said. "The issue isn't so much a global problem as it's an individual one. Each person has to be convinced that violence isn't the answer. And there are so many reasons—whether it's the emotion of the moment; the cold, calculated killing of a perceived enemy; or terrorists causing the deaths of civilians—that I don't see how the Spirit can achieve universal peace."

"Before you jump to conclusions, at least listen to what the Spirit has to say," urged Elijah. "Where's the harm in that? That's all it's asking. It's prepared to admit that it should have waited until you'd spoken a few more times before speaking about the plan it had for you. If it's willing to say it was wrong, the least you can do is give the Spirit a second chance."

The absurdity of Elijah's words didn't escape Sean. The Spirit was willing to apologize and compromise. What a bizarre situation he'd found himself in.

And yet, Sean was intrigued. If the Spirit was willing to be involved, that changed everything. What the Spirit had in mind he couldn't imagine. Was it worth a talk? The longer Sean pondered the question, the more he became convinced that it wasn't something he could easily dismiss. Still he was hesitant.

As Sean thought of what to say next, Elijah reached inside his jacket pocket and pulled out an envelope. He handed it to Sean with the words, "Diane asked me to give this to you."

Taking the envelope, Sean tore it open and began to read:

Dear Sean,
I've spoken with Elijah and asked that he deliver this letter when he meets with you in London. I want you to come back. My love for you has only deepened over the time you've been away. Visiting you in London and exchanging e-mails is no longer enough. I truly believe our futures belong together. You've often said you couldn't be happy on Janus, but I think that's wrong. Your visit only lasted a couple of months. And in the end, there was the pressure of what the Spirit asked you to do.

We can have a good life here. All I'm asking is that you give us a chance. I've tried to imagine what it would be like living away from the island. But I'm at home here in a way that I could never be out in the world. This is a special place, and I want the opportunity to share my experience with you.

Please don't take this as an ultimatum. I'm not saying if you don't return our relationship is ended. It's just that I believe we're both sacrificing much of our happiness if we don't try living together here on Janus.

From the little Elijah has told me, the Spirit wants you back on the island. If you won't return for the Spirit, then do it for me. I miss you and hope with all my being that you'll take this message to heart. We can make this work. I know we can.

The letter was signed, "All my Love, Diane."

Sean raised his eyes from the page to see both men looking at him. He folded the letter and placed it back in the envelope. Once again, the room's quiet was smothered in silence as they waited for him to speak. His gaze rested on Elijah.

"There's a lot I have to think about," Sean said. "How long are you in town?"

"For as long as it takes you to make up your mind. Andrew and Leyland are with me. We're staying with Brian," the Prophet said, nodding towards the publisher.

"Why don't you take the day off," offered Elder. "It's an important decision you're being asked to make."

"But I have an editorial to write," protested Sean.

"I'll handle that," responded Elder. "It's been awhile since I wrote a letter from the publisher."

Sean looked at Elder and then at Elijah. He nodded his acquiescence.

"I'm not going to drag this out," he said. "You'll have my answer tomorrow morning. I'll meet the two of you back here around ten. Is that convenient?"

Both men nodded. Sean got up, left the office, and retraced his steps down the hallway. Stopping by his desk just long enough to shut down the computer and pick up his jacket, he was soon out the door.

# CHAPTER 66

The early summer sun bathed everything in its warm glow as Sean walked the streets toward his apartment. London had been delivered from a cold winter and a wet spring. The promise of good weather to come was like an elixir. The city's mood was light, almost carefree. It was one of those rare days where people smiled at strangers and the gesture was happily returned.

But Sean was oblivious to everything around him.

Reaching his building, he pushed through the front door, climbed the stairs to his apartment, and let himself in. Kicking off his shoes, he padded his way into the bedroom, sat down on the bed, and pulled out Diane's letter. He began to reread the words. He read the letter several times. With each reading, he became more convinced. This had nothing to do with the Spirit. It was about love.

Did he want to lose this chance at happiness? He'd been alone for so long after Hilary's death. He didn't want to travel that road again. Perhaps the relationship with Diane could last under the current arrangement. Was that what he wanted? He knew it wasn't. He was in love with Diane. In that moment, he decided to go back.

Just the same, he couldn't ignore the Spirit. The opportunity to work together for global peace was almost beyond belief. Suddenly, Sean was gripped with excitement. His life had taken on a new meaning. *Global peace.* The words resonated in his mind.

From the moment he'd learned he was adopted throughout the period during which he worked as a lawyer and his life with Hilary, during the time he spent in Afghanistan, and even with his work at *The Advocate*, Sean had never felt as though he quite belonged. It's why he had initially journeyed to Janus. He was always looking past the next bend in the road, believing he'd find something to satisfy a desire he didn't quite understand. He knew only that he was searching for a challenge that would involve every aspect of his being.

Now, after so many years of feeling unfulfilled, Sean felt a passion that he'd never before experienced. At long last, he'd discovered his purpose. He felt a calmness that transcended every worry, anxiety, or fear he'd ever had.

He'd tell Elder and Elijah of his decision in the morning.

He was returning to Janus. It would take time to persuade everyone associated with the island to accept the proposal and become involved with the world. After that, there would be years of planning and convincing before beginning the long march toward global peace. Was it possible? History had shown that peace always dies on the rocks of greed, self-interest, and sustained violence. But history was not a linear equation. Just because something had always been, didn't mean it must forever be that way. The course of world events could be changed. It would be a long, arduous, and often disheartening struggle.

For Sean, there was no better way to spend his life.

# Chapter 67

There was little that surprised Dante. His world was one of continued calculation, planning, and execution. So the news delivered by Anna, his technology chief, only meant that his assumption was correct. However, it gave him little pleasure.

When his watchers in Inverness informed him that Elijah had boarded a plane bound for Gatwick Airport, Dante immediately notified a team in London to watch every movement made by the Prophet. This was the first time Elijah had been on an aircraft. Dante knew where Elijah was going. All he needed was confirmation. He also knew something incredible must have happened on the island to pull Elijah so far from home.

During the two years Brennan had been away from Janus, Dante had dramatically increased the Order's surveillance of the island and everything associated with the Guardians. Never one to be caught off guard, he'd also been curious about Brennan's associates at *The Advocate*. It had taken a great deal of time and money, but when he discovered the publisher was part of the Janus diaspora, Dante believed correctly that information about Brennan was being fed back to Elijah.

Dante also knew about Diane's visits to London. But being an emotional eunuch, the prelate viewed her as a minor distraction that had nothing to do with his almost pathological need to keep watch on Brennan.

When the Prophet, escorted by two Guardians, went straight from the airport to *The Advocate* offices, Dante knew Elijah was meeting with Brennan and that Elder was probably involved in the session. Once again, Dante surmised correctly that pressure was being exerted to have Brennan return to Janus. The only thing the prelate didn't know was whether Brennan would agree.

Thus, when Anna arrived with an intercepted e-mail from Elijah to the Guardians' Inverness computer center, it only confirmed what he suspected. After two years away, Brennan was going back to Janus. A problem Dante believed had been solved was now resurrected.

It was an issue that required a final solution. A man of few regrets and even less mistakes, Dante realized he should have had Brennan eliminated when he returned to London. The Mark of Janus he carried meant the man would always be a threat to the Church and to the Praetorian Order. But Dante was not one given to self-recrimination.

No damage had yet been done by Brennan or Elijah. Thus the situation's resolution remained well within his power. He shifted in his chair so that his hands rested comfortably on the computer keyboard. Dante pulled up a coded e-mail address, typed out the word *Avenger*, and waited for the response that would confirm Angelica's arrival time.

# Chapter 68

Angelica walked quietly and slowly up the chapel's center aisle. She could see her mentor, Dante, bent low in prayer. As was usual when the prelate met with her, the chapel was empty except for the two of them.

It had been six months since their last meeting. During that visit, he'd given her instructions to eliminate a New York banking executive. Along with her team, she'd spent two months planning and then executing the kill shot.

It had gone well and was just another homicide that would forever remain an unsolved case for the New York Police Department.

Angelica came alongside Dante's pew. She made the sign of the cross, bowed low toward the altar, and moved in alongside him. Kneeling in silent prayer, the assassin asked, as she always did, for the guidance and strength to carry out the mission Dante would be assigning her.

The prelate rose slowly and sat back in the pew. Angelica settled beside him, a lone file separating them.

"It's good to see you," said Dante, his words hushed. "Thank you for your work in New York. It's already paying dividends for the order."

"I'm here to serve you and God," replied Angelica.

The well-practiced reply hid the soaring joy she always felt when complimented by her mentor. He was the only person whose praise she coveted. And when it came, Angelica needed nothing else to make her life complete.

Dante opened the file and handed it to her. As she slowly reviewed the contents, Angelica noted that the designate was the same person she'd been assigned a little more than two years ago. She wasn't surprised that he was again a target. Angelica didn't need to know the reasons for what happened with her assignments. Her task was to carry out Dante's orders and eliminate the designate.

"Is he going to back to the island?" she asked, fully aware of the problems that would present.

"Yes, and once again, it must look like an accident," responded Dante.

"I would think nothing has changed," noted Angelica. "Since there are no strangers on Janus, it must be carried out at night. What time frame do I have?"

"This is complicated, so take however long you need," replied Dante. "Once you and your team have worked out the details, e-mail me the amount of funds you'll require. We'll use one of our banks in the Bahamas. I'll let you know which one when I send through the authorization."

Angelica knew there was no point in telling Dante it would be expensive. He already knew a ship, an amphibious craft for getting on and off the island, and the utilization of a spy satellite through the order member who worked in the National Reconnaissance Office would be needed. A helicopter would be too obvious. It would alert the Guardians, and once the designate was eliminated, regardless that the cause of death would appear accidental, suspicion would immediately lead back to the order.

This was the most difficult assignment she'd ever undertaken. But there was no doubt in Angelica's mind she'd complete the mission. She had been schooled by the instructors of the Praetorian Order. The training had prepared her for any eventuality.

The file, as usual, contained a memory stick. She took it and slipped it into her purse while handing the file back to Dante.

The session was over. They left the pew, bowed, and made the sign of the cross. There was no need for words as the assassin and her mentor walked toward the chapel's back door. Exchanging social pleasantries would have gone beyond the bounds of their relationship. Only one thing remained as they stepped out into the day's sunlight.

"Go with God, my Azrael," said Dante, as he turned and walked along the gravel path that led back to the chateau and the order's headquarters.

No response was expected, and none was given. Angelica continued on to the parking lot. She was booked on an afternoon flight to London. From there, it was on to New York. She'd check herself into the Hilton, contact her team and wait for them to arrive. After that, the planning would begin.

As Dante walked back to the chateau, he allowed himself a moment's reflection on what he'd just set in motion. Angelica had never failed to carry out a mission. Brennan would no longer be a problem. And with Brennan having no children, it would forever end the Mark of Janus being passed from generation to generation. The threat of taking the Janus message worldwide would be eliminated.

The Roman Catholic Church would remain strong and the world's central religion. The Praetorian Order would continue its growth and influence throughout the globe.

Before he reached the chateau's heavy wooden front doors, the Brennan issue had long been replaced by thoughts on how to consolidate the gains made by the New York banker's untimely death.

## *The Word of Janus* … An Excerpt

***The second book in the four-novel Janus Chronicles,* The Word of Janus*, is set for publication in spring 2016.***

Although focused on the computer screen, part of Dante's mind was restless. He had wanted to avoid a war with the Guardians, but events had conspired to the point where it was unavoidable. And if a battle with the Guardians was inevitable, Dante had ensured the Order was prepared. It would begin with the theft of the parchment, continue with Brennan's death, and end with the Guardians' destruction.

Dante still didn't know if he believed the parchment detailed that Christ hadn't died on the cross but had lived for many years as a carpenter in Judea. However, the intercepted message between the two Guardians had been explicit. The scroll, written two centuries previously, claimed that, not only had Jesus survived, but he'd married Mary Magdalene and together they'd had two children.

It seemed impossible. But if true, it would shatter the Roman Catholic Church's foundation. Dante couldn't afford to take that chance. The parchment had to be destroyed.

Elijah had made a tactical error in having the parchment brought to Inverness. The Guardians had established their own lab in the city for restoring the document. It was well guarded, but Dante had the advantage of surprise.

His team was fully prepared and easily outgunned and outnumbered the guards. Dante checked the large wall clock across from his desk. The men would be leaving the rented house in just under three hours. From there it was a forty-five minute drive to the lab. The operation would take no more than ten minutes. Once the parchment was secured, the team would head directly to the Inverness airport. The Order's executive jet was fuelled and ready for takeoff.

He'd be notified by coded message once the plane was in the air. It left more than four hours to wait. Dante turned his attention back to the computer. He had enough to keep him busy.

It was nearing 5:00 a.m., and the prelate was busy composing an e-mail based on his final review of the financial, legal, and operational documents for the order's Venezuelan partnership when his corporate e-mail account sounded that a message had come in. He opened the document, and the words blazed across the screen—*Holy Father.*

Leaning back in his chair, the Venezuelan deal put aside for the moment, Dante could only think that the long anticipated confrontation with the Guardians was underway. The scroll had been taken, and the crew was on its way to Valencia. At most, it would be only a few hours before the Guardians realized the document had been stolen by the order.

Once that happened, there would be no turning back for either side. The Guardians would have to retaliate. Elijah wouldn't know that everything had been planned for just this eventuality. The Guardians would be caught in a trap.

The prelate wondered how Elijah would justify using any form of violence to have the parchment returned. It would drive a wedge between the islanders, with their commitment to peace, and the Guardians, who would immediately want to hit back. Elijah would have to remain in Inverness. It was the only way he could keep control of the situation. And if Elijah remained in the city, that meant Brennan would also be staying.

Everyone would be focused on how the order should be confronted. No one would be thinking that Brennan was the next domino to fall.

CPSIA information can be obtained at www.ICGtesting.com
Printed in the USA
BVOW02*1422290915

420173BV00001B/7/P

9 781491 746950